What people are saying about …

The Project Restoration Series

"*The Renewal* is a sweet, gentle, authentic story that sneaks up on you and grabs hold of your heart. It's an unanticipated gift, a tender unfolding, a tale of two people who carry heavy emotional burdens and their struggle to finally shed those burdens and find new life. This is a very special story written by a very special author—a book of quiet peace, intense realism, and poignant God-inspired truth. I'll remember this book for a long time to come."

Kathleen Morgan, author of
As High as the Heavens and *One Perfect Gift*

"*The Renovation* is a beautifully crafted story about the broken relationship between a man and his son, and the joyful restoration of a mended heart and an old mansion. Engaging characters move the story along at a wonderful pace."

Lori Copeland, author of *Simple Gifts* and *Monday Morning Faith*

"In a captivating and evocative story, Terri Kraus skillfully weaves distance, longing, forgiveness, and redemption into a cast of unforgettable characters. [*The Renovation*] is a book to savor and ponder."

Nancy Ortberg, former teaching pastor at Willow Creek
Community Church and author of *Looking for God*

"Renovate your reading schedule to include this great new title by Terri Kraus! In *The Renovation*, Kraus crafts a tale that both tugs at the heart and tickles the funny bone."

Cyndy Salzmann, author of the highly acclaimed
Friday Afternoon Club Mystery series

"Terri Kraus has woven an absorbing and deeply felt story of forgiveness that touches both the magnificence of heaven and the tenderly drawn detail of human relationship. Subtly and with compassion she explores the struggle of ordinary people finding their way through the complex emotional legacies of past pain, to the simplicity and peace of experiencing God's forgiveness and love. This is a compelling, memorable, honest story, offering hope and deepening faith."

Penelope Wilcock, author of *The Clear Light of Day*

THE TRANSFORMATION

A PROJECT RESTORATION NOVEL

THE TRANSFORMATION

by
TERRI KRAUS

David C Cook®
transforming lives together

THE TRANSFORMATION
Published by David C. Cook
4050 Lee Vance View
Colorado Springs, CO 80918 U.S.A.

David C. Cook Distribution Canada
55 Woodslee Avenue, Paris, Ontario, Canada N3L 3E5

David C. Cook U.K., Kingsway Communications
Eastbourne, East Sussex BN23 6NT, England

David C. Cook and the graphic circle C logo
are registered trademarks of Cook Communications Ministries.

This story is a work of fiction. All characters and events are the product of the author's
imagination. Any resemblance to any person, living or dead, is coincidental.

LCCN 2009929671
ISBN 978-0-7814-4867-3
eISBN 978-0-7814-0346-7

© 2009 Terri Kraus
Published in association with the literary agency of Alive Communications,
Inc., 7680 Goddard St., Suite 200, Colorado Springs, CO 80920

The Team: Andrea Christian, Ramona Tucker, Sarah Schultz,
Jack Campbell, Caitlyn York, and Karen Athen
Cover Design: Amy Kiechlin
Cover Photos: iStockphoto; Corbis (woman)

Printed in the United States of America
First Edition 2009

1 2 3 4 5 6 7 8 9 10

061909

To Elliot—
My one and only:
I love you the whole wide world.

When all is said and done, you are part of me. That's the way it was meant to be. People are brought together for a reason, everything happens for a reason. I believe the reason that you and me were brought together was because we complete one another. We fill in each other's missing spots with love.

—Anonymous

Are we not like two volumes of one book?
—MARCELINE DESBORDES-VALMORE

PROLOGUE

Shadyside
Pittsburgh, Pennsylvania
1888

THE HOT IRON HISSED as it made contact with the solder, the silvery metal turning to liquid, rivulets running along the lead channel. Perrin Millet worked fast, not wanting the heat to shatter the shards of thickly tinted glass. He bent the lead frame easily, and with a deft touch, soldered the channel to the master frame.

Close to finishing, he stepped back. The large window was cradled at an angle in a large, supporting, adjustable wooden frame. A small coal stove held a dozen heating rods, all glowing bright orange, each ready to melt and bend the puzzle of glass and metal slowly growing into sharp definition.

The Presbyterians had indeed been generous with the budget for their new church. As an artist, Perrin liked Presbyterians. Not so much the Lutherans, whom he thought were somewhat dour, their church designs lacking ambition and creativity. The group of Presbyterian elders, seeking to make a statement with their fine new church on South Aiken Avenue in bucolic Shadyside, on the east side of Pittsburgh, far away from the belching sulfuric steel mills along the river, had presented him a commission to construct nine large storytelling windows. They even allowed him some latitude: He could select the scenes for his windows from more than a dozen approved Bible stories.

"We only ask that you make the windows big and impressive … and, of course, accurate," he was instructed.

Perrin, a master artisan who had created stained-glass windows all his life, was surprisingly not a religious man; he was also given to hard drink and coarse language. But this commission for the Presbyterians had done something to him. Exactly what it had done, Perrin wasn't certain, yet somehow he felt his completed subjects staring down on him—not in condemnation, but as witnesses to his genius, providing encouragement to his spirit as he labored, almost lost in the process of his handiwork.

His selections: Adam and Eve with the Serpent; Moses holding the Ten Commandments; Samson destroying the temple (it was Perrin's first time illustrating that wonderfully horrific story); Jesus holding a gentle lamb (an image Perrin could have done in his sleep); an anguished Jesus in the garden with the disciples, slumbering, in the background; the Last Supper, with Jesus standing off to one side (a novel approach, Perrin thought); Jesus being sentenced before Pilate and the crucifixion, with a wildly stormy background; and the day of Pentecost, complete with dancing flames and beatific expressions.

The last window, the great circular window to be hung above the high altar, would be a more nebulous subject.

"We want to see the power of God in that window," the elders had stated.

"Power of God?" Perrin had asked.

The elders were clear: the unbridled power of the almighty God.

And so Perrin labored for weeks and weeks—poring over pages of sketches, surrounded by wads of discarded papers, tossing and turning in the night with indecision. Then, finally, with his vision clearly before him, he built the large circular frame and meticulously selected the glass. Painstakingly he cut each intricate piece, carefully laying out the lead and solder and sensitively designing the placement of the colors from the center out in a shape that suggested an all-seeing eye. For what could express the power of God more accurately than the Almighty's ability to look inside the soul of man, casting His scathing light on its innermost parts in search of the truth?

As Perrin finished the darkness at the edge of the circle, the eye stared back at him. Colors melded from a near-black midnight blue at the edge to true blue, to purple, to burnt sienna, to umber, to a deep, thick, translucent gold in the very center. It was now midday. The work was complete at last.

Perrin called over two of his assistants, had them pull hard on the ropes, shouting that they must not loosen their holds, even for a moment, and then the window was upright.

"Turn it," Perrin commanded.

They slowly rotated the frame on its wheels, letting the light shine through the glass, allowing the full force of the sunlight to burst onto that all-seeing eye for the first time in all of creation.

As Perrin stared up at his work, the blues washed over his body and the gold spilled over his face and shoulders, making it necessary to squint; his eyes were filled with too much light and too much color. After a moment, he closed his eyes and let the golden light warm his face, the blue cool his body.

Finally, he opened them again.

The entire window erupted with color, filling and penetrating his soul and invading every inch of him. Blinking, he drew in deep breaths, spreading his arms to embrace the light.

"Let no man claim there is no God," Perrin said, maybe to himself, maybe to his assistants. "Whoever remains in this light will know the almighty God exists."

Then he knelt quietly, wondering why in the name of heaven those words had fallen from his lips … and if that great pellucid light had indeed transformed him.

———

Holy Trinity Church
Jeannette, Pennsylvania
Thirty years ago

Seated in the front row next to his mother, young Oliver Barnett was afraid to raise his head. The pastor had called for a time of silent prayer, so

Oliver prayed then was done. Yet every other head in the church remained bowed. He lifted his head a degree or two and opened his eyes a bit to see what might happen during a silent prayer, wanting to see if God really filled the room with something. Oliver looked for a magical presence, something that glowed perhaps, or hovered above them.

He did not see anything.

Above the pastor, over his left shoulder, stood Jesus in a thick, dark wooden frame, rendered in stained-glass in colors almost too vivid to be found in nature. Oliver never had sat this close to the front of the church before. From the back of the church, where he normally sat, Jesus appeared kinder, gentler, almost ambiguous in intent. But some twenty pews closer, Jesus' look became more distinct. There was an intensity in His expression, and His eyes—which Oliver once thought were closed in prayer—were open slightly, as if paying attention to those out in the pews who did not close their eyes during prayer.

Jesus sees me. Oh, God, Jesus sees me.

Oliver snapped his eyes shut and bowed his head deeper, scrunching his young body like a turtle at the sight of a fox or a badger. He hardly allowed himself to breathe. He prayed again that Jesus had not seen him, had not detected his disrespect.

The pastor rumbled and called for everyone to rise.

They sang a song that Oliver did not know. He tried to follow along, but the black squiggles on the page meant nothing to him. He heard his mother's voice, pitched sharp, knifelike, next to him.

They sat down again, and the pastor spoke for a few minutes, saying nice things about his father. Oliver heard his mother's name mentioned, his own name, then his brother's name. Tolliver was not in church because their mother said he was too young and so he was staying with a neighbor lady from across the street that morning.

A soloist stood up, an old lady with white hair, and began to sing. Oliver felt like crying, but he refused to cry where anyone could see him. Behind the soloist, in a large metal box, lay the body of his father. Oliver knew his father was dead. The pastor said he would be with Jesus. But that fact didn't make Oliver feel any better—not one bit.

As the old lady stopped singing, Rose, his mother, turned to Oliver and placed her hand on his knee, grabbing it with more force than neces-sary, almost hard, like when she wanted him to listen and listen good. She leaned down, her mouth near his ear.

"You're the man of the house now, Oliver. You know that, don't you?"

Oliver did not know what that meant exactly but nodded as if he did.

"You'll be a good boy, won't you, Oliver?" she asked, but it was more a demand than a request.

He nodded again.

"And, Oliver, you must remember about our secret. You must never tell anyone about our secret. Never. Do you understand?"

When she squeezed his knee harder still, he was afraid he would cry out in pain if he did not agree. He knew what the secret was. He knew how to keep secrets. He had kept lots and lots of secrets before.

He nodded.

"I need to hear you say it, Oliver," his mother said in almost a hiss. "Stop your nodding and shrugging and tell me with words."

Oliver fought the urge to nod again. "I'll keep the secret, Ma. I promise."

She relaxed the pressure on his knee, then smiled. But to Oliver, it looked like that sort of fake smile you give to teachers and big people when you really don't want to smile, but you have to.

"I promise, Ma. I promise."

———— ⋙⋘ ————

Taylor Allderdice High School
Squirrel Hill
Pittsburgh, Pennsylvania
Twenty years ago

Samantha Cohen stood at her locker in the long hallway of the west wing of Taylor Allderdice High School, all but oblivious to the maelstrom of students spinning past her, jostling her, shouting and crowing and laugh-ing. Most of them didn't know what had happened.

They couldn't know—could they?

Samantha was well known, with all her extracurricular activities, but close to only a few other students in the sophomore class. She stood a nickel under six feet tall, so most of the boys ignored her; and her classic good looks, with a touch of the exotic, made her an outsider to most of the girls.

She slipped her books onto the top shelf of the locker, took her notebook and math book, slammed the door, spun the lock, and headed to study hall. No one would care if she was a few minutes late. No one would dare say a word to her, not today of all days.

She was right. The room, filled with raucous laughter, swirling with students who didn't pay her one bit of unaccustomed attention, didn't settle down when she entered. A few noticed her, whispered to a friend, pointed, made gestures with their hands. Samantha paid none of them any mind. She took her seat, opened her math book, leafed through her notebook, took a pencil from her purse, and began trying to catch up on a week's worth of missed assignments.

Mr. Wansour entered the room, put a finger from each hand in his mouth, and attempted an ear-piercing whistle. The shrill sound was worse than the worst train whistle Samantha had ever heard. She hated him when he whistled like that.

"Settle down, people. Everyone. Quiet. Sit still, please. No hall passes for the first fifteen minutes."

The room stilled to a gentle undercurrent of whispers and passing notes and opening books. Mr. Wansour flapped a manila folder onto the desk and opened it, extracting a test sheet from two periods earlier. He took a pen from the pocket of his sport coat and began to click it methodically, obsessively.

Twenty minutes into the period, the classroom door opened and everyone looked up. An older woman, gray hair combed into a severe mannish style that caused most of the student body to wonder, entered the room, cradling a clipboard the way a fisherman would cradle a prize trout. "Samantha Cohen?"

The room erupted in a chorus of "Ooohhh," as if Samantha had already been indicted, tried, and convicted of some heinous student crime against authority.

Samantha hesitated, then raised her hand.

"Come with me," Miss Rosenberg, one of the school's four guidance counselors, said.

Another chorus of "Ooohhh" erupted, then snickers.

Samantha gathered her purse, book, and notebook to her chest and meekly got up from the desk. The soft soles of Miss Rosenberg's sensible shoes were hushed on the tile, her heels making a *squish, squish, squish* sound down the empty halls.

Samantha followed the counselor to a series of compact offices by the general administration office. To the right was the principal's secretary, presiding over his waiting room. To the left were the guidance offices.

"Come in. Sit down, Miss Cohen," Miss Rosenberg invited.

Over the counselor's right shoulder was a wire rack with neatly stacked college brochures lining the pockets. Samantha had never set foot in this office; she wasn't thinking about college yet, so she wondered why in the world she had been summoned.

"Miss Cohen, we are aware of what's happened. We know that losing your mother that way can be a shock. We just want you to know that if you need to talk to someone, you can always make an appointment with one of the guidance counselors. We're always available for appointments."

Samantha nodded.

"You understand?"

"I do," Samantha replied. "But I think I'll be fine."

Miss Rosenberg narrowed her eyes, obviously not believing a word Samantha said. "Look, Samantha, sometimes children think that this sort of behavior is hereditary or something equally as foolish. It isn't. I've done a lot of reading on the subject. You don't have anything to be worried about. You know, as I like to say, the sins of the father … or mother … don't always visit the children. Sometimes children think it's their fault. The school has a list of qualified therapists if you find that you are troubled. Or can't sleep. Or get weepy."

Samantha had no questions for this strange woman.

"You'll let us know if you run into problems? Help is only a phone call away. If you're having a hard time coping, there are a number of medications available, and I'll bet your family doctor would be happy to help you with that."

"No, Miss Rosenberg. I think I'm fine. Really."

The counselor allowed a long, long silence to fill the room. "Or a member of the clergy. We could call one for you."

"No. Thank you, though. I've … I've talked to our rabbi." Samantha, not skilled at lying, hoped keeping a solemn expression would help her made-up stories sound true.

"Okay then. Since it's almost time for your next class, why don't you stay here until the bell rings?"

Samantha had already stood up, smoothing her skirt. "No. If it's okay with you, I'll go back to study hall."

Miss Rosenberg shrugged. "Have it your way. Here's a pass to get back to class," she said. Then she began to write something in a notebook.

Samantha slowly gathered her books together. One of Samantha's talents was reading upside down—honed from reading her father's writing as he worked at his desk. As she unhurriedly collected her belongings, she watched Miss Rosenberg write.

Miss Cohen refused all efforts at outreach. Contact all teachers to keep watch. May be in denial. We want no repetition of what occurred last year.

Samantha knew what had happened last year. A fellow classmate had committed suicide after his older brother had been killed in a car accident. It was the talk of the school for weeks and weeks.

"Thank you, Miss Rosenberg," Samantha said as she slipped out the door.

It won't happen to me. It won't happen to me. I am nothing like her. Nothing like her at all.

She turned the corner and headed to the restroom, where she would wait until it was time for French class.

———

Pittsburgh, Pennsylvania
Five years ago

Tolliver Barnett let the crowds churn around him, a great wash of humanity all bent on celebrating. *Bent and twisted,* he thought. He grinned as faces passed before him—leering, joyful, drunk, some only semiconscious, desperate, hopeful, yearning. Tolliver could see it all in their faces, as if each were transparent, their souls and hearts and longings visible to him alone.

It's a gift, he thought as he smiled back at the ebb and flow of people.

It was New Year's Eve, and he was in downtown Pittsburgh. He had been invited to one of the more prestigious parties—a swank gala affair, hosted by the friend of a friend who happened to be some ranking officer in a national real-estate firm.

Tolliver had no connection to anyone here, but he enjoyed parties. He enjoyed seeking out the wounded

No ... not the wounded, really. But those women in need. You can tell who they are. The ones who laugh too loud. The ones who try too hard to please or impress. The ones who drink too much. You can see it in their eyes.

The party, held in the ornately decorated grand ballroom of the historic William Penn Hotel, overlooking downtown Pittsburgh, grew louder and more frenzied the closer the hour drew to midnight.

A woman he had never met latched onto his arm.

She's one of the wounded—one of the drinkers.

"Enjoying yourself?" she said, her words a bit too loud even for a boisterous party.

"I am," Tolliver responded.

The blonde, attractive in a sharp, angular way and on the brink of being labeled "mature," eyed Tolliver intently. "Are you a realtor?"

Tolliver laughed. "No. Just friends with someone who is friends with one of them. You folks have poor security, letting someone like me in."

The woman screeched out a laugh. "I could tell you weren't one of those realtors. You're much too cute."

Tolliver simply smiled in return.

The woman pointed to the large clock hung over the bar. It was clicking down—only minutes until the magic hour.

"You mind if I bring in the new year with you?" she asked, almost stroking his arm.

"I would be honored," Tolliver replied. He knew how to handle himself in these situations.

The clock struck twelve, and horns and shouts and squeals erupted. The woman grabbed his neck and pulled him down to herself, latching onto his lips like a lamprey. He kept his eyes open. In the corner he noticed an older couple, obviously married, quietly holding hands. They exchanged a nearly chaste kiss, looking into each other's eyes with reverence, love … and admiration.

In that moment, Tolliver hated the couple, hated their so-called happiness, hated the brazen flaunting of their blissful togetherness. They were taunting him, his past, and probably his future. He hated all they represented.

Tolliver angrily shut his eyes and returned the lamprey's kiss with one of his own, knowing exactly how this night would play itself out.

Caldwell, Ohio
Five years ago

Henry Pratt parked his car almost in the shadow of a great expanse of stone wall of the Noble Correctional Institute. He hated this place, had hated it every time he visited it. He despised the hard chiseled walls and the gate's echoed slam of metal on metal. He loathed the cold glister of razor wire that adorned the top of the wall.

But today was different. It would be the last visit. Never again would he be drawn to the darkness inside the massive walls.

He made his way to the entrance and waited. He looked at his watch: nearly noon. He could hear the rumbled announcements inside the walls, like a distant thunderstorm, and was just barely able to make out the words.

He waited longer. A few men with wide smiles passed him as he stood on one side of the walkway, each man trailing a mother, or a girlfriend, or a wife. There were no other men waiting with Henry. There were seldom men in the visiting area, either.

Men hold grudges more than women, I guess. And what father wants to see his son in this place?

Henry saw him as he exited the double doors—his youngest brother, Steven, walking slowly toward him, carrying only a paper sack. Henry did not move toward him but waited until his brother came within an arm's reach, then stuck out his hand. Steven did not accept the hand but embraced his brother with a ferocity that scared him.

When Steven dropped his arms, he drew a deep breath, then another, and another. "Air smells different out here. Cleaner, for sure."

Henry stood silently as his brother breathed fresh air for the first time in years, then asked, "You all set to head home?"

"I am, Henry. I am *so* ready."

Neither man moved.

"You're never coming back here, are you?" Henry asked, really more of a statement than a question. He had waited five years to say those words to his brother.

Steven shook his head. "With God as my witness, I'm never coming back here. That, I promise."

Henry waited. "Gene's at work. He wants us to hold off celebrating until he gets home."

"I've been waiting five years," Steven answered. "A few more hours won't kill me, I suppose."

And they walked, side by side, into the brilliant sunshine of an Ohio afternoon, in early summer, with only a hint of rain to come in the air.

Kane County, Pennsylvania
Five years ago

Bartholomew "Barth" Mills inspected each one of his tires, making sure all had the proper pressure and inflation, checking for nails and nicks in the rims. Everything looked good. He had checked the oil the night before, after loading the last of his belongings into the trailer. All he owned didn't amount to enough to hire a moving company; his possessions fit into his battered old Jeep and a rented U-Haul he'd hitched onto the back. On this morning, Rascal, his dog, sat in the front seat, his tongue lolling out. The window was open; a slight mountain breeze flittered down the valley.

Barth checked the trailer hitch once again, making sure the chains were secure and that the wires running to the taillights were well taped.

He stood in the gravel driveway of the parsonage, the place he and his wife, Ellen—God rest her soul—had called home for nearly two decades. The last two years had been less than pleasant, much less than pleasant, and Barth almost looked forward to leaving … to starting over again, to living once more in the neighborhood where he was born and raised.

Almost.

He had retired from the church two months prior and had received his first check from his retirement funds. It was not a large amount, but then again, he had simpler needs now—just him and the dog.

He walked slowly to the wooden front doors of the church. When he was pastor, the doors were never locked. Now they were only unlocked when the new pastor decided to grace the building with his presence—which didn't seem to be all that often. Barth tried his best not to feel bitter.

He peered through a pane of glass to the inside: just a dozen pews in depth, a small pulpit, and a wonderful, beveled window in the shape of a cross behind it. When he'd preached on certain days of the year, light had poured through that window and lit him up like he was some sort of Christmas tree—a tree standing up for Christ, he'd told himself. Even now, as he looked through the window once more, he could feel that warm light on his shoulder. He could feel the sunshine of better days.

I'll miss that, he thought. *I'll miss that window. I'll miss this sacred space.*

Today's weather promised to be overcast; maybe later there would be a thick mist or a rain shower. That sort of damp cold bothered his bones, and he wondered once again why he wasn't heading farther south than Pittsburgh as his final destination.

He touched the wood of the door with the tip of his finger, as if the building might say its good-byes. But he didn't feel anything other than the dry rasp of a door in need of fresh stain.

He climbed into the Jeep, slipped in the key, and the engine turned over. The little red man on the dash beeped and beeped until he fastened his seat belt—a practice he had never taken to and would never get accustomed to performing.

He pulled out of the driveway, carefully backing out onto Route 6, though traffic was seldom heavy at any time of day.

"Well, Rascal, say good-bye."

Rascal snuffled and wheezed in the brisk air as he leaned out the window.

"Now get inside, boy. Too cold to have an open window."

The dog obeyed and, within a few miles, was fast asleep, snoring as he napped, curled up tight against the seat.

Twenty miles down the road, Barth came to a stop sign. He stepped on the brake, looked, then continued. A troubling thought entered his consciousness—one that had been there for weeks and months ... one he kept pushing away and denying.

Good Lord, what am I going to do now?

The thought clamored about for another twenty miles of empty highway.

Lord, take me home ... or give me a reason to stay.

Rascal kicked his leg, evidently dreaming of rabbits or squirrels, two of his most hated animals.

Other than this blasted dog, that is. Give me a reason beyond Rascal. Please, Lord.

CHAPTER ONE

Shadyside
Pittsburgh, Pennsylvania
Early spring, present day

OLIVER CHECKED HIS WATCH. He squinted and positioned his wrist nearer to the glow of the truck's speedometer.

5:45 a.m. Too early.

Oliver knew it was much too early to be wandering around in a strange neighborhood, but heavy Pittsburgh traffic—even the threat of heavy traffic—gave him the willies. Leaving his home later in the morning meant heavy traffic, probably normal for everyone, but not normal for Oliver. Navigating his pickup through dense packs of automobiles was far removed from Oliver's comfort zone.

Too early.

He might risk the drive into Pittsburgh from Jeannette for a funeral or a wedding, or maybe a Steelers football game (if someone gave him free tickets), but not much else. Why risk life, limb, and sanity?

So today, Oliver had attempted to beat the traffic and the stress. He had gotten up at 4:30, not that much earlier than his normal wake-up time, had picked up a cup of Dunkin' Donuts coffee at the store a mile from his house, and had driven in the shimmery dark down Route 30. Traffic was light as he entered the flickering fluorescent-lit Squirrel

Hill tunnel. Then, following his GPS, which he'd begun to rely on but did not always trust, he'd crept along a baffling series of residential streets until he arrived at his destination. The voice from the GPS unit seemed more chipper than he remembered in announcing his success-ful journey.

"Destination ahead. You have reached your destination."

He pulled to the curb, scanning for street signs.

Cities have all sorts of laws about where you can and can't park and when, he remembered. *And I'm not about to get a ticket just giving someone a free estimate.*

He looked about again, turning sideways in the seat.

I can't just sit in the truck. That might look like I'm—what do they call it?—casing the place. I am, sort of—but not in that way.

He got out of the truck, jogged down the block, back to the front of his truck, then halfway up the block

"No signs," he said softly. "That's odd. Should be some sort of parking sign."

Oliver really disliked getting traffic tickets. He had received one speed-ing ticket in the last decade, but his parking violations occurred more frequently. Contractors sometimes had to double-park or park on side-walks. He hated seeing a fluttering yellow slip, lying in wait with a bad day written all over it, snuggled under his windshield wiper.

"It must be okay to park here then," he said out loud.

He walked slowly back toward his truck, tapped at the passenger-side window, and nearly pressed his face to the glass.

"Come on, Robert. Let's get started on the estimate."

Robert lifted his head and shook himself awake, blinking. He had slept through the entire trip. Not that the trip was that long, but he most often napped during any ride longer than ten minutes. He scrambled to his feet and stretched slowly and carefully.

Robert was Oliver's dog. Most often Oliver and a fair number of his friends and coworkers would say "Robert the Dog" when speaking about Robert the Dog, as opposed to just "Robert," because there were several other Roberts inhabiting Oliver's circle of friends. No one wanted to con-fuse man and dog—least of all, Oliver. Oliver actually liked the sound of that three-word name and began to use "Robert the Dog" almost exclusively, except when they were alone, like this morning.

Robert the Dog clambered down from the seat to the floor of the truck and jumped out to the curb, sniffing the air, the grass, the truck, and finally, Oliver's shoe. He might have been a pure-bred schnauzer but was the size of at least one and a half miniature schnauzers combined, though not as large as the giant variety, and his hair was mostly black. His head was almost the right schnauzer shape—not perfect to the breed, but close—so Oliver assumed a very small amount of some sort of nonschnauzer lineage had found its way into the good dog Robert.

Ever since Oliver had rescued Robert from the pound as a puppy, the two had gone everywhere and done everything together, including evaluating a new project ... a *possible* new project. In construction, Oliver found, nothing was certain until the contract was signed—and even then, things could happen.

Oliver did not have to worry about Robert the Dog taking off, running into traffic, or barking at the wrong time. Robert had never done any of those things and, more than likely, would not start demonstrating inappropriate behaviors this early on a still-sunless Monday in Shadyside, just on the outskirts of Pittsburgh.

Oliver looked at the address again. He had listened to the phone message carefully three times to get the return phone number, the exact name of the potential client, and the address of the potential job correct. Now he stood on South Aiken Street and looked east.

"But this is a church," he said to Robert the Dog.

Robert simply stared at the building, sniffing the cool morning air, as if he were not really interested.

"I mean ... it's a *real* church. I knew it was going to be a church, but not *this* kind of church."

When Samantha Cohen had left her message five days ago, she had said her new acquisition, her latest renovation project, was a church building. She planned on transforming it, doing "wonderful things" with it. Oliver had imagined a small frame building, a church-*like* building that might be easily changed into a gallery or antique shop—but not a heavy, old historic church-to-the-very-rafters sort of building.

This is a real church—and will always look like a real church.

"Can you meet me Monday morning?" Miss Cohen had said, her voice deep and raspy, in a memorable, alluring, black-and-white Lauren Bacall–movie kind of way. "I really need to talk this project through. Alice and Frank Adams, my friends in Butler, just raved about your work. Said you were brilliant with their displays and cabinets and all types of furnishings. I need brilliant. I'm willing to pay for brilliant. So Monday. Early. If you can make it. Leave me a return message. I'll get it, even if I don't call you back. I'm a little OC when it comes to checking messages."

Oliver had left a return message: "Early Monday. Sevenish? I might be there before seven just to look around the outside, if that's okay with you. I get up early."

What he was now staring at in the early light, and what Robert was sniffing, was an historically significant church. No one could lay eyes on this building, even in the dark on a foggy night, and see anything other than a rock-solid church. This was a church with a capital C. It had massive stone arches; huge stained-glass windows that traversed the sides of the church; a rotunda that certainly must hold the altar. There was a covered entranceway (the *port cochere*, Oliver knew it was called) done in huge stone blocks and a high tower with a cross and carillon.

Just standing there, thinking about remodeling the old structure into something other than a place of worship, gave Oliver a case of spiritual heebie-jeebies.

"This is a church," he repeated again.

He stood, wrapped in that early-morning silence that occurs even in big cities, like the soft, fragile, and short-in-duration crease in the day between the dark and its dark noises and the early-morning let's-get-the-commute-going sort of noises. Oliver wondered if he should just get back in his truck, pretend that he had never made the mistake of answering the phone message from Samantha Cohen, and move on to the next job.

I'll be tearing apart a church. God's house, where people have worshipped for what must be over a century.

He wanted to sigh but did not.

My mother will die if she finds out.

Oliver wondered, for just one split of a split second, if he could keep this job secret. Not that he liked keeping secrets from his mother, but sometimes parents could not be trusted to handle sensitive news.

Or I could walk away and wait for the next job. That actually might be easier ... safer ... less stressful.

Except he didn't have a next job. He could wait, wait for the next big *nonchurch* job, but there was no guarantee another one would come quickly, and in these sorts of wobbly economic times, Oliver knew he couldn't be picky.

And he was here; he'd already endured the traffic. He would stay. He'd do the estimate.

There's something about this place....

Now his words were softer, perhaps because of the silence. "A church ... but, well, she did say it *used* to be a church."

The holes in the stone facade were still visible where a sign had once hung.

"It's just a building now." He looked down at Robert the Dog. "Right, Robert? It's not a church anymore. Right?"

Robert looked up, as if considering Oliver's options, sniffed again, and then sneezed in a very uncanine-like manner.

CHAPTER TWO

THE EARLY SPRING MORNING warmed as the sun rose higher over the city. Oliver had walked around the building, the *church*, three times, each more slowly than before. It was Romanesque in design, massive in execution. The cornerstone of the building bore the chiseled date *1888*. The property it stood on occupied about half of a city block square of land.

The stones would have been moved into place with mules and block-and-tackle back then. *An amazing feat,* Oliver thought, one that would be hard-pressed to be duplicated today, even with heavy machinery. With its thick chiseled stone walls, sturdy piers, groin-vaults—Oliver reveled in old architecture—this structure added up to a near-perfect building.

Robert the Dog walked with him each circuit, sniffing the grass with some interest but never more than a few feet away from his master.

"What a magnificent building," Oliver said, his tone small, deferential, and yet the dog looked up. It was obvious to Oliver that his companion's soul—or whatever it was that dogs possessed instead of a soul—was as impressed, as filled with awe, as Oliver was.

But impressed was not the same as being enamored with the prospect of working on such a structure. Oliver was falling in love with this building. Immediately obvious to his contractor sensibilities and to anyone who had ever picked up a hammer and a nail was the reality that there would be no altering the footprint of these walls. Moving the stones would be horrendously difficult, and altering walls would require steel bracing, deep, thick cement foundations, and a huge amount of temporary supports. So the building was as big as it was ever going to be. The only possible way to expand might be with an annex, with a connecting hallway between the old structure and the new. But this existing church, the bones of this church, dictated that there would be no easy modifications happening.

Oliver sat on the main steps of the church … the *building*. Robert the Dog sat next to him and stared down the cross street.

"It's a real church, Robert. I don't know if I want to work on an historic church—like remodeling it and making it something different. Changing it into something other than a church, I mean."

Robert the Dog snorted. He snorted a lot in the morning. Oliver thought it was allergies but didn't want to subject the dog to veterinarian tests and some fancy, expensive regime of daily pills or shots. *Shots—maybe we could do shots. But pills—never.* Robert the Dog could sense any pill, no matter how tiny, and would spit it out with obvious disdain on the floor, regardless of what meat or cheese it was wrapped in. So they both were resigned to live with a few springtime morning dog snorts and wuffles.

"I know it's not a church now. But still, it was God's house once … consecrated ground. I bet He still cares what goes on here, you know?"

The dog did not look up.

"Maybe I don't want to be the one who helps … destroy an old church. Maybe *destroy* isn't the right word. *Alter? Change?* Something like that. What if she wants to make a … a … I don't know … a nightclub out of this? Would you want me to do that? Really? To a church? What would God say? Worse yet, what would my mother say?"

Oliver knew that if a stranger had come by and heard him talking to a dog … well, he couldn't blame them for thinking it was clearly an odd situation. But having Robert there, listening, or at least pretending to listen, was something Oliver really needed—an ear, a face, someone to talk to. He couldn't talk to his brother like this … and certainly not to his mother.

"I need the job, but I'm not sure about working on this church. Maybe if I don't want it so badly, it will look like I'm busy and she won't expect a low bid. Do you think that will work, Robert?"

The dog turned his head and offered what looked like a sidelong pickerel grin.

"Yeah … I don't know what I'm talking about."

It was at the moment of the dog's imagined grin of agreement that Oliver saw something out of the corner of his eye—a person coming toward him. Cars had gone past and a few pedestrians had walked by on South Aiken while the pair sat on the cold stone step, but they were anonymous cars, anonymous people, not stopping or slowing, passing on their way to somewhere else. But this singular person headed directly toward the church, as if on a mission. Oliver knew it had to be Samantha Cohen.

Robert the Dog stood up and offered a soft welcome growl.

"I think it's her, Robert."

The woman looked both ways at the curb, then jogged across, her mane of dark hair flowing behind her like a living halo of curls and waves, like some wondrous creature inhabiting an underwater reef.

Oliver normally did not notice such things, but he noticed today—she was that eye-catching and attractive, even from a distance. A tall woman, she had to measure nearly six feet, maybe even taller than Oliver, and she was smiling widely. Her dark eyes were the color of buttered rum with a swirl of cinnamon, a drink Oliver had never once consumed but had heard about in sophisticated movies featuring burly men in ski sweaters by crackling fireplaces of rough-hewn stone with rustic lumber mantels. *Artsy, for sure. Exotic,* Oliver thought, *and quite* … he didn't know how to describe this beautiful woman but tried *striking,* then *gorgeous.* Yet even those words did not justify how pretty she was.

Long legs. *Very* long legs. Like a dancer. And womanly. Oliver did not want to blush trying to think of the proper—or modest, or chaste— adjective to describe what he saw. *Buxom* flashed through his thoughts, but he banished it as quickly as it arose.

"You must be Oliver Barnett," the woman said, her voice as rich, warm, and syrupy as it had been on the phone. "I mean, who else would be sitting on the steps of a church at this time of day, unless you were a hobo or a homeless person, and you don't look like one of those at all. I'm Samantha Cohen."

She stuck out her hand—long fingers with the scarlet polished nails trimmed short, not long and witchlike, the type that scared Oliver. Even the women in church with long, curved nails would set internal warning bells ringing. This woman set none of those bells off, but a bell of a different type.

Samantha wore some sort of quilted black Asian-style kimono/geisha jacket. Although Oliver knew little about clothing styles for the feminine form, he guessed it was silk. Delicate embroidery decorated the sleeves and collar, and knot-and-loop closures, rather than buttons, marched up the front. Oliver impressed himself by noticing such detail. Then he observed her slacks—so loose and flowing that they appeared to be pajama bottoms.

He blinked. *Pajama bottoms? She walked here in pajamas?*

"And who is this fine-looking, noble dog?" Samantha said, sweet as honey, and held out her hand to Robert the Dog. Robert, as if assuming the person-to-dog introduction was to be expected, lifted his right paw and let Samantha bend down and take it and gently pump it up and down a few times. She did not adjust her geisha jacket, and Oliver could see more of her than he felt comfortable seeing. He tried not to look.

"Robert," Oliver said. "Robert the Dog."

"Nice to meet you, Robert the Dog. Did Oliver and you walk around this place? I bet he told you that this might be too big of a job, right?" She leaned closer to the dog, and Robert stood up and lifted his head toward her. "Did you tell him he's wrong? You should have."

Then Samantha stood back up, tugged her jacket back into place, and fished around in its left pocket. "Let me show you around, Oliver and Robert the Dog. Follow me."

She hurried up the steps, inserted an enormous key into a gigantic lock, and turned it with a grimace until a tumbler or two fell with an iron-like clunk. She grabbed the massive door handle.

Oliver decided her nail polish was more magenta than red.

The door hesitated, then swung open on hundred-year-old-plus hinges with hardly a squeak … perhaps simply a metallic whisper. The interior glowed, filled with the early-morning light now tinting through a thousand slivers of glass in a wall of stained-glass windows.

It was the most beautiful sight Oliver had seen in decades. Maybe even longer.

Robert the Dog entered the quiet space, lit by the dense blues and purples and reds and greens and golds of the stained glass catching the first
light of the sun, and padded slowly up the middle aisle. It was flanked by
rows of heavy, dark wood pews with blue velvet cushions and thick stone
piers supporting the arched ceiling. He made his way up to the choir,
with its elaborate woodwork facade, and stopped just before reaching
the high altar, then turned around and stared back at his two human
companions.

Samantha had taken Oliver's hand—a first time ever in his career as a
contractor that a client, or potential client, had taken his hand—and led
him around the interior. She pulled him down the side aisles, pointing
at the splendid, original, old stained-glass windows in pristine condition,
with the apostles and disciples and Jesus and Moses and virtually every
top-ten Bible story rendered in finger-thick leaded glass.

"Aren't they stunning?" she asked, not waiting for a reply but providing the answer herself. "Yes, indeed. And that big round one ... it's
glorious. Like God's eye, isn't it?"

He nodded.

"We'll have to find a way to light them to their best advantage,"
Samantha added. She pointed to the rafters. "Are they mahogany?"

Oliver stared, even as she pulled. "Probably not. Maybe oak. Or walnut. Stained to look like mahogany. Or a mahogany veneer."

She squeezed his hand (another first) and replied, "Well, whatever
they are, they're glorious. We'll need lights on them, though. We'll need to
illuminate those beauties." She ran her other hand over one of the pews.
"We'll keep these for seating. Or some of them. Have to section them up,
for sure. And the pews in the balcony will have to go away, too, because
that's where the live music will be. The organ up there, I'm not sure about
that yet. It came with the church. The pipes will stay, of course ... part of
the ambience. And then there's the altar or whatever Christians call that
area ... that will have to go as well. I'm assuming that the height difference
in the floor here, with these few steps, is not just wood framing. I would
like this area level, all at one height with the rest of the space, but I'm not
sure that can be easily done. And the ... pulpit, is it? Maybe that could be
turned into a reception desk."

They arrived back at the front of the church and Samantha let go of Oliver's hand.

"What do you think? Magnificent space, isn't it?" she said. "Can't you just see it at night, the windows illuminated, the space lit by a hundred candles?"

Seldom rendered speechless, Oliver felt tongue-tied this morning. He was caught up now, not only in the beauty of the building but in this woman's energy. The fact she had actually touched him, held his hand, was so disconcerting that he was having trouble forming a logical string of thoughts.

Church, stained-glass windows, cut-up pews, altar, pulpit, steps. Christians, holding my hand, God's eye.

Samantha looked directly at Oliver, then turned to the dog. "I've overwhelmed him, haven't I, Robert the Dog?"

If Robert could agree, or look like he agreed, he did just that with a curious tilting of his head.

Samantha smiled. "I do that a lot. My father says that's a good skill to have when negotiating, because the other side gets all … bamboozled … and that means you can then get expensive for cheap."

She sat down next to Robert on the first step of the platform and wrapped her arm around him and pulled him close. "Is he bamboozled, Robert?"

The dog leaned into this strange woman and tilted his head backward and up, to stare into her eyes.

"You're not bamboozled, are you, Robert?" she said and gave him another quick hug, which Robert obviously enjoyed.

Oliver slowly turned around, trying to take the interior in, ignoring Samantha's dialogue with his dog, as if he were listening to a soft whisper in a far corner. Not a whisper, really, but an insistent plea in a small but powerful voice. He craned his neck to the side so as to catch the voice.

There is something special about this building. I don't know what it is that I feel, but there is something here, inhabiting this space. Something … illuminating. Something exposing? Is that it? Under God's eye.

"Mrs. Cohen?"

And the truth will set you free. Maybe that's what I'm feeling.

"It's Miss Cohen. Samantha, actually, but Miss Cohen works, if you like that sort of formality. And yes?"

"It's a truly magnificent building. I've never seen anything like it or felt it ... I mean, as churches go ... except maybe in books. But when ... how ... why—"

"And you want to know what, too, right? You want to know what I plan to do to this wonderful old church filled with all these ancient mementos of God and heaven and Jesus, right?"

Oliver held open his palms, as if in supplication. "Yes."

Samantha stood, and because she was on a step higher than Oliver, she towered over him. Even Robert the Dog had to crane his neck to keep her face in view. In the glistering blue and purple and red and green and gold light, she was much more beautiful than Oliver even first observed.

"Well, Oliver, I plan on making this into a nightclub and a restaurant—maybe more one than the other. I'm not sure of that at the moment. Can't you just see it? Intimate booths, crisp white tablecloths, simple vases of blue flowers, lots of blue votives, cool jazz music. I'm still looking for an executive chef. I'm tempted to call the place *Blue*, because of that big round window. The gorgeous shades of blue in it."

Oliver had been stunned into silence with his first apprehensions coming to fruition.

Samantha broke the ice by softly asking the question that had apparently been on her mind ever since meeting Oliver. "Why did you name the dog *Robert*?"

It took a moment for Oliver to compose himself enough to answer. It was not that the scope of the project had derailed him. He was just so surprised to have made a correct guess earlier about what she planned on doing to the magnificent structure.

"Robert was the name I always wanted to have," he answered.

"Instead of Ollie?"

Oliver Barnett shook his head—he hoped not in an angry, but in a kind, bemused way. "Not Ollie. It's Oliver. But I would have liked to be called Robert. I'm not sure why."

Oliver Barnett had never really liked his name, never felt at peace with the way "Oliver" sounded as it came out of his mouth. And when he signed documents, that big initial, that all-important O, always seemed, to him—and maybe only to him—lopsided, more oval than round and perfect. A circle had to be just so, or it wasn't a circle, but something else.

His friends claimed that if anyone was an Oliver, it was he—that the roundness and the sharp finish to the name perfectly suited him. What a "sharp-finishing name" was exactly, he did not understand, but it was his given name. And what person has the right, or the audacity perhaps, to go and change it now? So he would scold himself whenever the name-changing urge came upon him.

He blamed his mother.

In time, Oliver grew bold enough to ask for the full, three-syllable rendition of his name, sometimes insisting, but insisting in a very nice way.

He could blame his mother for a lot of things … but he didn't, not really. And even if he did, it would never be to her face. Never.

A shaft of sun came in through a clear section of window and he caught a glimpse of himself in the reflection of the glass display case by the altar, to the left of Samantha and Robert.

Oliver stood a breath under six feet tall. Had he taken his baseball cap off, he would have noted that he needed a haircut ($14 at Discount Clippery, east of where the Greengate Mall used to be and where a huge Wal-Mart now stood). He wore his hair short, eliminating the need for hair dryers, styling gel, and false pride. The blond color had been, for a few years now, edging ever so slightly toward gray. The latter better matched his eyes, a sort of gunmetal gray with a heavy tint of warmth in them. He was no longer stocky, but because he had been most of his life, he still carried himself as if his clothes bore the tag *Husky*, instead of the standard *Large*. The extra pounds had come off only a few years before, after twelve months of agony, deprivation, and exercise, and he was now lean and fit. His face, previously rather round, was now not that far from angular, with the beginnings of a pair of jowls gone and his almost-double chin eliminated. It still looked odd to him—as if he were simply borrowing a narrower face from someone younger, someone better looking than himself.

"I don't have a battered self-image," he told his friends, "just a buttered one … with lots of salt."

Samantha Cohen interrupted his thoughts. "So ... Oliver, you want to hear about my plans? Or do you want to bail right now?"

His quick answer surprised him. "No. I'm very interested. Show me what you want to do."

———— ><><><> ————

Robert stayed in the truck. It was a nice morning, cool but sunny, and Oliver felt safe enough to leave the windows nearly all the way down. There was nothing of value to steal in the truck, plus he had parked right outside the coffee shop, where he sat by the window. He had to waste at least another forty-five minutes to allow the morning rush of traffic to thin enough to make the return trip home with a minimum of anxiety.

He unrolled the blueprints and placed the salt and pepper shakers in the far corners, his coffee cup on another and the large sugar dispenser on the other. The lines of the existing church building stood out in bold, and he traced them with his fingertip.

Very nice proportions.

He rearranged his improvised paperweights and flipped to the next sheet—a transparency, with the architect's rough sketch detailing the interior modifications: lighting, cabinetry, counters, tables, built-in booths, bar, serving area, downstairs kitchen—and a host of other nonmajor projects. Widening a staircase. Adding another.

I don't know. Making a church a nightclub ...

He had agreed quickly to provide an estimate, and his quickness nearly unnerved him. Being spontaneous and decisive was not his nature, and he knew that.

Do I want the job, or did that woman just get me all jangled up? Or was it the building as well? No, probably more her than stones and mortar. Yeah, it was her. Jangly.

He stared outside. Two pedestrians with earnest, going-to-work grimaces passed by, each wearing earbuds and holding a tall cardboard cup of expensive coffee.

She got me all jangled. Well, jangled *isn't the right word. Jangled is confused, sort of. She got me....* Then he started to think about Samantha, what she was wearing, and how the folds of the black silk fell in such an easy manner.

He shook his head and drank the last of his coffee. Since he had ordered a plain coffee, refills came free. Getting up for one gave him a chance to change the tone of his internal dialogue and get back to the subject of this project—the project for the woman in the black silk kimono jacket. He shook his head again.

But I need the work—we need the work. And, somehow, I feel like I'm supposed to be here.

He stood and debated on that third cup. The clerk behind the counter smiled and held up a half-filled pot. The question was answered. He walked carefully back to the table, not wanting to spill.

What if I have to stop somewhere on the way home now? Where? It's not like the turnpike, where you know how far apart the rest stops are.

She had beguiled him, he knew, because he ignored that warning in his thoughts and took an unusual third cup in one sitting. Maybe the caffeine was making him a little bold and edgy.

And these are big cups too. Free refills.

None of what she planned to do with the church was beyond Oliver's skill as a carpenter and contractor. Cabinets, booths, some knee walls, a bar, lights, bathrooms—he could do all of that. The additional stairs might be tricky, depending on the thickness of the floor. The commercial kitchen downstairs … well, for the kitchen equipment, he would subcontract that portion of the job. He knew a kitchen guy who did good work and had done a number of restaurants in Greensburg, near where Oliver lived.

Better for him—better for me.

I could do this.

A sudden furry bit caught his attention. In the truck, right outside the window, Robert the Dog had sat up and was looking out the window of the truck. Oliver could see him stretch, then circle around a few times on the seat and disappear from view.

But … I would have to commute. My heavens, commute? In that traffic? Every day? This will have to be for some big bucks for me to take the job.

At the far corner of the transparent overlay Oliver noticed, for the first time, some penciled figures nearly erased. However, because of the angle of the hard morning sun, the architect's sharp, definitive figures were still visible. A dollar sign caught Oliver's attention. The architect must have roughed out an estimate for the work. Oliver knew some architects were good at that sort of ballpark guess on costs, though some came in with dollar amounts that were laughable—like estimating labor costs at only $20 an hour.

Oliver held the page up to the light. The architect had itemized a dozen different sub-projects and assigned a figure to each one. When he saw the sum total, Oliver nearly dropped the paper. The architect had figured a total cost of over $400,000 for what Oliver had already figured, in his head, to cost no more than $150,000—a ballpark figure, sure, but a job for which Oliver would have been daring to bid a total price of $200,000.

Samantha might be expecting a bid twice as large as he was preparing

And now the job has gotten more interesting. Maybe the commute wouldn't be so bad.

He set the paper down and sipped at coffee cup number three.

Maybe I could sort of camp out in the church and not worry about commuting. There was a shower downstairs.

As this option came to mind, Oliver noticed that Robert had sat up again in the truck and was staring at where Oliver was sitting, making it apparent the dog thought it was time to go.

Whatever the traffic will be, it will be. We can leave now.

———◦◦◦———

Oliver turned onto his street, and Robert the Dog began to wiggle in a subtle but obviously excited way, realizing they were home. Oliver slowed and carefully drove along a narrow driveway and onto a narrow parking area next to the garage.

Oliver lived in an efficiency apartment he had created above the detached garage. His mother lived in the house—a not-so-big old farmhouse where Oliver was born and raised. It was nearly in the shadow of the Jeannette Memorial Hospital, recently acquired by some large health organization, though they had not yet changed the name out front. The

house lay three blocks from the high school and two blocks from the football stadium—the recent home of the most heavily recruited quarterback
in all of high school football in western Pennsylvania. Oliver did not play
sports in high school but was a football fan.

His mother would be at work, Oliver knew, so he let Robert run the
yard for a while, then whistled for him and the dog tore up the steps and
into the apartment. He felt pretty sure his mother had never liked Robert
but merely tolerated him for Oliver's sake.

For the next three hours, Oliver made lists, extensive tabulations of
everything this job might require. Miss Cohen said she was looking for
excellence and quality. Oliver made two columns for two kinds of materials.
One he labeled *Mahogany*, though the supplies listed were not mahogany;
they were materials at the top end of their category. The other list was
labeled *Pine*, designating lower-end materials. If she suddenly developed
colder feet, fiscally speaking, then Oliver would already have a clear idea of
how low the bid could go without sacrificing the integrity of the project.

He started a separate page for the staircases. He had explained to
Samantha that morning that he would not have a firm number on them
until a qualified structural engineer looked at the floor and they had a
chance to tear up either a portion of the floor or get into it from the ceiling below.

Oliver worked sitting at his kitchen table, tapping at his calcu-
lator, and scanning Web pages to check prices. While Oliver worked,
Robert the Dog slept in a cozy alcove at the end of the main room of the
apartment.

Some carpenters hesitated to show their home to clients, supporting the cliché that the shoemaker's children never had proper shoes. But
Oliver had spent a long, long winter doing the work in this apartment
and had built a stunning interior space with high, vaulted ceilings and
hardwood flooring. The back of the garage faced north, looking down a
long hill, with Jeannette some three miles distant. The town looked better from there than up close, and Oliver had carved out a covered porch
with screens and built-in seating—where Robert now slept—with a set of
French doors to the apartment that could be closed in cold weather.

His bedroom area contained not much more space than required for a king-size bed, with two eyebrow windows above. This, his inner sanctum, was as cozy as a berth on a luxury liner, with wainscoted walls. The bathroom was small but done entirely in granite and glass tiles with a waterfall shower and heated towel bars. The streamlined "bachelor" kitchen faced west, catching the afternoon light, and there Oliver had used stainless steel appliances and poured concrete counters, stained and etched (after seeing such a style in an *Architectural Digest* magazine featuring some millionaire's home in Nantucket or Cape Cod or someplace out east where the wealthy have vacation homes). Oliver liked to cook and enjoyed the extras he had put into the kitchen.

The big living space was open, with a built-in computer desk in one corner and a widescreen TV on a long wall surrounded by custom bookcases. The walls were a pale gray-blue. A scaled-down highback leather sectional in dark brown and an easy chair upholstered in a soft fabric with shades of blues and browns provided comfortable seating. A plush Berber wool area rug bordered in leather lay over the apartment's hardwood floors under the seating area, and on it sat a sleek coffee table, the home of the "coffee table book" on the great cathedrals of Europe that had been Oliver's gift to himself a dozen Christmases ago. After seeing the apartment, a few of Oliver's acquaintances had made offers to buy it from him outright— until they found out his mother lived in the house beside the garage and was not planning on moving anytime soon.

The floor was double-insulated and the automatic garage-door opener was the quietest he could find, but he still could feel the garage door rumbling below as it ratcheted itself open. He heard his mother's old Buick rattle inside. He heard a slam and the garage door wheezed shut.

He sighed, long and loud. Robert raised his head. The dog had heard the door as well. Then the dog laid his head back down and shut his eyes. Oliver thought Robert was squeezing them too tightly. He waited a long ten minutes, then stood and headed downstairs.

If I don't, she'll just call me. Might as well be preemptive.

———◦∞◦———

"I was praying for you this morning. In that terrible traffic. Getting lost. I was worried sick," Mrs. Rose Barnett said as she shuffled along the linoleum floor in her kitchen. Oliver had offered, often, to replace the old floor with tile, but his mother would not hear of it.

"The linoleum is not worn through. No need to spend money on fancy stuff. You think I can afford what you spent on your kitchen? Well, I can't. And I won't," was her reply.

Oliver knew she could afford it but never pushed the issue further than making the offer.

Rose Barnett was a few years past retirement age and looked even older, her white hair done up in tight curls once a week at Lucy's Shear Beauty Salon, reminiscent in shape of an old leather helmet that football players wore a hundred years earlier. Her face was narrow, pinched, both by time and personal inclination, cheeks not sunken in, but neither full with youth nor vitality.

Oliver smoothed the plastic cover over the threadbare tablecloth as he sat at the kitchen table. His mother rewarmed the coffee she had made that morning, before she left for her job behind the counter at the Italian grocery store a few miles down Route 30. Every day she would come home with a bag of meat and cheese ends—the last inch or so of the ham loaf or cheese brick, whatever they couldn't sell to a customer—and if she was alert, she would grab them and take them home and make soup or ham salad or melt the cheese on noodles.

"Did you get lost? You ever been to Shadyside?" she asked her son.

Oliver shook his head. "No. I found it right away. I've been through there a few times. You pass it if you go to the museums and take Fifth Avenue."

"What kind of church was it? An old rundown place like you thought?"

She poured some skim milk, straight from the plastic jug, into her coffee. She knew Oliver drank his black, so she placed the jug back in the refrigerator.

"No. Well, it is old, but not rundown. It's big. Like a real church." He tried to explain it to her, even tried to show her the pictures he had taken with his digital camera.

"I can't see a thing on this silly little screen," she complained, squinting. "What do they want to do to it?"

Oliver hesitated. *Do I tell her the truth and weather the storm now, or wait?* "Some sort of coffee shop. Maybe serve some food. You know, fancy pastries and such."

His mother's eyes, narrow and close-set, grew even narrower. "Still God's house, isn't it? Crosses and stained-glass windows? God's house. Sacred. Money changers in the temple. I wouldn't do it if I were you. Could easily bring about God's anger. You don't want an omniscient and all-powerful God angry at you, do you, Oliver? It's not the way I raised you, is it now? Turn your back on God and deface a house of worship? God's wrath is on those who curse His house. I think that's in the Bible. I'm pretty sure it is."

Rose wore knit pants with sewn-in creases and a loose-fitting floral print blouse, and she clutched at its faded pink plastic buttons. "Oliver, you're a good boy. You've always been a good boy. You've always obeyed me. You don't have to do this kind of work. I bet your father wouldn't have done it."

Oliver let the comment pass. He would not talk about his father—not now. Perhaps never with his mother. "Mom," he said, even and calm, "it's not a church any longer. It used to be a Presbyterian church when it was built—like over a hundred years ago."

His mother shook her head, as if resigned to be saddened further by her elder son. To her, Presbyterians were not real Christians but only pretended to be. It was an old argument—one Oliver would not revisit today.

"The congregation got too small, and they sold it to the Korean Christian Church."

"Koreans? Like from Korea?"

"Yes, Mom. There is a large community of Koreans on the north side of Pittsburgh."

Under her breath, she muttered, "All the more reason never to go to Pittsburgh."

"And then the church became too small for them ..." Oliver continued.

"The Koreans?"

"Yes, and they moved to a bigger building."

"Now … who bought it?"

"A very nice woman."

His mother waited. Oliver knew he would have to continue.

"Samantha Cohen is her name," he added.

His mother bent closer to the table. "That sounds Jewish. Is she Jewish?"

Oliver shrugged. "I don't know. I didn't ask. Maybe. I don't know Jewish names."

"It's Jewish, alright." Then he watched as his mother, left hand at her chest, her right cradling her forehead, said, "Jews defacing God's holy church. I never thought I would live to see the day when my own son is a part of such … heresy." She glowered at him.

Oliver knew better than to argue, at least right now, so he leaned back, tried to force down a sip of very hot and very bitter coffee, and let his mother's talk remain unanswered. There would be no defusing it, once the fuse had been lit. Oliver knew this from a lifetime of trying to quench, or ignore, that sputtering, hissing, ever-closer-to-the-explosion fuse.

———

The air had turned a springtime chilly, so Samantha grabbed a zippered sweatshirt from the hook in the hall closet. Her father would have a veritable conniption fit if she left the house without proper—meaning warm—outerwear. He insisted she carry a sweater or coat or shawl if the temperature was at all on the chilly side. Even though he wasn't home, Samantha humored him.

She walked toward the church, which was only a few blocks from her house. While negotiating the purchase, she had spent hours inside the former church building, but all during daylight hours, not having seen the interior after sunset. She needed to spend time inside, determining if the stained-glass windows allowed enough light in via the streetlights to be visible, or if they would have to install some sort of outside illumination. She did not want to have to go to that expense or trouble, knowing that any outside lamps would need zoning board approval.

No need to aggravate that starchy board more than necessary. I'll be asking for enough favors as it is.

She waited for a break in the traffic on South Aiken, jogged across the street, and from the corner, noticed a diminutive man standing in the shadow of the stone port cochere. Samantha was not a woman who could easily be intimidated, and if she ever became so, her level of anxiety depended on the size of the perceived threat.

Unless this guy has a gun, I have no need to be nervous, she told herself. *He's too tiny to be a threat to anyone.* Even though she remained calm, she reached into her pocket and wrapped her fingers around the tiny canister of pepper spray attached to her key chain. Her father insisted she carry it. She had objected some, but now was glad she had it. Her hand, hidden in her pocket, thumbed the spray canister around, so she could easily extract the weapon.

The church is on the busiest street around. Why would any criminal in his right mind pick this place to stage a mugging?

She stopped at the corner, for just a moment.

But then ... criminals are not known for their logical approach to their business, are they?

She walked at an even pace toward the church. As she drew nearer, the small man, wearing a dark overcoat that was at least five inches too long for him, stepped out of the shadows.

"Miss Cohen," the man called out. "How fortuitous is your visit."

Samantha leaned forward and, without taking another step, squinted, as if squinting would help her pierce the darkness. "Mr. Han?" she called out. "What are you doing here so late?"

Mr. Ito Han bowed at the waist, a long, slow bow, precise and deliberate. "I am honored that you recall me, Miss Cohen. Our meeting was not long in duration."

"Of course I remember you, Mr. Han. Or do they call you Pastor Han? I'm Jewish, so I'm never sure of what titles you folks prefer."

"It is your preference, Miss Cohen. I have no need for titles. And, as some churches do, I am what they call 'pastor emeritus' now. Retired. In the way. Honorable title for such an unworthy servant."

The gentle Korean man rubbed his hands together as if his bones were chilled, despite the temperate air of the evening. "Miss Cohen, I would have called, should have, of course, but I did not expect to be walking past my old church this evening. Like reminiscing and visiting an old friend. My car is in the public lot down the street. So now that I am here, and you are here, perhaps … a little favor, I may ask, but I do not desire to trouble you in any way. I planned to call this week. You are, after all, the new titleholder of this building, and I wish not to bother you. But there is one thing I believe I have forgotten inside these walls, and I humbly seek a time when I might retrieve this trifling."

Samantha hurried her reply. "Well, of course you can come in. Right now is fine. Actually, I was on my way in. I haven't been inside after dark, and I wanted to see what the windows looked like."

Mr. Han bowed slightly. "You are kind, Miss Cohen. Most kind. I must inform you that the windows do lose a certain vibrancy in the dark. But they take on a … how to describe it? In Korean, there is a word for a deeper being, a less transparent quality, and … thicker. Yes, dark and thick perhaps offers the best sense of the word. The images on the windows simply become less transparent and more real, much more so. Yes, the windows grow less visible and grow more real. It is what happens. I am sorry, Miss Cohen. It is the best this poor linguist can do with that odd word."

Samantha unlocked the door and opened it, stepped in, and motioned for Mr. Han to follow her in. She snapped on the downlights in the vestibule. They walked into the narthex, then into the main sanctuary silently, Samantha's eyes going from window to window. A car's headlights passed, illuminating a robed man, sparkling, for just a second, the image. Then he was back to being *thick*.

"*Thick* is a good word for them, Mr. Han. Visible, yes, but … thick," Samantha said, agreeing with his assessment. "So, Mr. Han, what was it that you are looking for? Could I help you find it? During the inspection, I don't think I saw anything of value that was left."

"It is such a trifle, Miss Cohen. It was left in the office."

They both entered the pastor's office area, bare except for two wooden straight-back chairs.

"It was hidden, Miss Cohen. Hidden so well that it was far from view and forgotten. Hidden from the person who had hid the item, I must confess."

Mr. Han dragged one of the chairs to the massive stone wall, flanked

by two arched windows. He climbed up on the chair with surprising agil-
ity and pulled a small stone out of the wall. He turned to Samantha. "The
mortar was loose when I moved in, Miss Cohen. I did not damage the
stone."

He reached in the cavity and extracted a glittery item—a piece of
jewelry, perhaps a locket on a thin chain, Samantha thought. Mr. Han
carefully reinserted the stone.

"I would have never known that stone was loose," she said.

Mr. Han slowly stepped down from the chair. "Then the hiding place
proved most effective, did it not?" the old pastor answered.

He looked down at the locket in his hand. Samantha could not
help but stare. Mr. Han opened the locket. Inside were two miniature
photographs.

He looked up. "This was my mother," he said softly and touched the
picture with the gentlest of touches, his finger tracing along his mother's
face. "And the little boy is myself."

Mr. Han seemed to wobble a bit, and Samantha drew close to him
and took his arm.

"Sit down, Mr. Han."

He complied, like a doll being placed in a play chair by a toddler.

"Do you want some water? I could get you a glass …"

"Not necessary. Just a momentary lapse. I will be fine."

Samantha drew the other chair close, ready to steady the old man
should he waver again.

"I always preached the truth in this building," Mr. Han said, as if
confessing some secret, hidden trait. "I think for all the years I stood
in the pulpit, God's eye behind me, I never once knowingly uttered a
falsehood."

"Is that what that window is?" Samantha asked.

"I am not certain. It is the image that I conjured up at least, and I felt
His eye upon me." He looked up at Samantha, his eyes clear, focused, but
as if in turmoil. He smiled, perhaps trying to hide his emotions.

"Really?" Samantha asked.

The old man's smile was knowing, curious. "It is appropriate to be
amused by such ideas, Miss Cohen, but I will tell you that many in my

congregation believe that this space will always be a place of truth. It will always be holy, even if those in authority above me say it has been officially 'deconsecrated.' My people, who worshipped God here in spirit and in truth, are praying that this will continue here, some way, somehow."

Samantha sat back, taking in what Mr. Han, with his beatific expression, was saying.

"I have never told anyone about my past before," he continued. "I don't know why I feel I must tell you this now, except that I may never visit this place again. Perhaps to be at peace as I close the chapter in my life here.

"My mother was a shaman, Miss Cohen. In Korea, she was called a *mudang*—an intercessor between the gods and humans. She held services, or *gut*, in order to gain good fortune for her clients and to protect villagers and to guide spirits of the dead to paradise. She alone would meet with the spirits. It is not a job anyone desires. A woman does not want to become a shaman. She is chosen, as it were, following a severe physical malady or a prolonged mental ailment, which indicates possession by the spirits."

He sighed and his shoulders sank, as if displaying how burdensome this truth, this secret, had become in its withholding, and now in its retelling.

"Before she passed, she came from Korea to visit me here once. She hated the blue color in the glass in this building—especially in the round window. Her response was immediate, visceral. She began to tremble and shake when she for the first time stepped foot inside this space. In our national flag, there is the traditional symbol of *yin* and *yang*—done in blue and red. Blue always provides negative energy. It is *t'argukki*—the balancing of *yin* and *yang*. Red, good, positive; blue, negative, evil—a sign of confrontation. Blue sums up the power of brutal awareness. She heard me preach once and then, for the rest of her visit, refused to enter this place. Except for the last day. For just a moment."

He looked down at the tiny photos in the locket, photos of a beautiful young woman and a cherubic baby. "That last day, she revealed to me a dark family secret. She said that this building possessed a mighty spirit, and that spirit—not spirits, but a single, powerful spirit—forced her to tell me the truth."

Mr. Han clenched his fist, as if summoning up the strength to continue.

"I do not want to burden you, Miss Cohen, but I feel obligated to tell you this story about this place you now possess."

He took a deep breath. "The secret was this: I was born as the result of her being taken by Japanese troops and forced to be a comfort woman, servicing the invading army during the Great War. So that moment, I knew then why I was less Korean than some. In her great shame, I was sent to America to live with my aunt and uncle."

He snapped the locket shut and stood up, as if weary from telling the story, as if having accomplished whatever mission he had. He was finished.

"That is my story, which no one ever knew. Perhaps this building, with the God's eye window, does have a way of demanding the truth and helping God change people. Perhaps it does make people inside its walls confront what they have kept hidden, for keeping secrets can prevent true wholeness. God's power can do that. It is a spiritual place, for sure. I pray that you will only be blessed and empowered by the truth that has always been spoken in this place."

He looked around. Then he reached out and touched the stone wall with just his fingertips, as if expecting them to contain some manner of electrical current. "I will miss these stones."

"Did she ever come back?" Samantha asked. "Your mother. Did she ever come back?"

"No. My mother remained agitated during her visit and died within two weeks of returning to Korea."

"I am so sorry," Samantha said.

"Sorrow is not necessary, Miss Cohen. I was told that the last words on her lips were to acknowledge God—not her gods, but my God. The one true God of Abraham, Isaac, and Jacob. It was the truth that changed her. Perhaps the truth of this place—who can know? So I buried that small locket in this church. To venerate her memory, to keep it close and protected. To keep this heart of hers close to God. Now I will bury the locket in the new Korean church."

Mr. Han slipped the locket into the pocket of his oversized trench coat. "I have bothered you for too long this evening, Miss Cohen. I must take my leave."

On the steps of the church, Mr. Han stopped. "I will pray that you will know the truth, Miss Cohen. I will pray that prayer for you every day. And, along with my congregation, I will pray that this place will always be its home."

He stopped suddenly, then looked about like a small child, as if seeing the church for the first time, blinking, eyes wide. "You know, Miss Cohen, there are stories in the Old Testament that speak of men building altars to God—to honor and praise Him. And those stories often end with the statement, 'And the altar is there to this day.'"

Samantha looked surprised. "Really? They're still there? I guess I should have paid closer attention in Hebrew school."

Mr. Han offered an inscrutable smile. "Perhaps the exact stones are indeed still there. I am not an archaeologist. But what that means—in a spiritual manner, what those stories meant to me—is that once a place is consecrated to God as a place for worship, it remains consecrated. This is a sacred space, Miss Cohen. This may be a concept not present in the American way of thinking. Of course, as owner, you have every right to do with it as you will. But I believe it will always remain sacred, consecrated. One of the last prayers my congregation offered in this place was that whoever follows us here will feel God's power—and be changed by His love."

He wiped at his eyes. Samantha thought he might have been tearing up.

"We Koreans are a unique people," he continued. "We have great reverence for *place*. The birthplace of ancestors. The burial places of parents. God's temples. They are all inhabited by memories—but only God's temple is inhabited by power, and only God's power is forever, Miss Cohen. We have prayed that this place will continue to change people, long after we as a church have departed. You need to be aware of those prayers, Miss Cohen, because they are powerful. Because this … this building … is sacred space. You will be changed as God orders His universe according to His desires."

Samantha listened carefully. After a long moment, she replied, "Perhaps God will make me slimmer, Mr. Han? That would be a change I would welcome."

Mr. Han returned her smile. "You have a good soul, Miss Cohen. I pray that you will embrace the changes God may provide for you. It would be a remembrance to my mother and an honor to her name."

With that, he grinned, pulled the coat close to his throat and, with a renewed lightness in his steps, walked away ... slowly at first, then with each step a little quicker than the one before.

As Samantha watched him leave, a dozen questions gathered, unanswered, in her thoughts.

"So, did she eat you up over this, or what?"

Oliver sat in the booth at Denny's opposite his brother, Tolliver. They had both heard every possible joke and question and had seen every shocked and puzzled reaction imaginable when they were introduced and both of their real given names presented. When Tolliver was in high school, even though he was four years younger than Oliver, he wound up growing taller than Oliver by more than five inches. Since then, everyone called him "Taller." The name started out as "Taller than Oliver" but was quickly truncated to simply "Taller."

Taller was thinner, more strikingly handsome, with a more classical face, his speech more articulate and his bearing more personable than Oliver—at least that's what Oliver thought, since Taller always received the lion's share of attention, most of it from young women who seemed to throw themselves at him. Not that Taller ever refused any of their entreaties.

And Taller quickly grew more distant from his mother, unlike Oliver, who was the good and obedient son. Taller was only three when his father died. After that, Oliver had assumed the role of head of the household and Taller took the role as prodigal son.

"No. She was ... okay," Oliver answered.

Taller grinned as he speared at his hash browns. "Come on, Ollie," Taller said, the only person to call Oliver "Ollie" on a consistent basis. "I know her better than that. A church. A Presbyterian church. A Korean Presbyterian church. And a Jewish woman. Sounds like the start of a bad religious joke. Ma didn't roll over on this one. That much I am sure of."

Oliver salted his eggs again and added four shakes of pepper, one shake at each edge of the over-medium eggs. "She … wasn't overly happy, I guess."

"Not happy? I bet she warned you about causing the onset of the apocalypse if you took the job."

Oliver cut a very square piece of egg white, careful not to open up the yolk just yet. *You have to keep the egg white and yolk and toast in the right proportions.*

Oliver knew that Taller knew their mother well. They both knew that playing out this charade any longer fell into the category of the ridiculous.

"Not the apocalypse, exactly. She nearly promised God's wrath, though. His damnation, she said, was all but a guarantee."

Taller grabbed at the dainty paper napkin on the table and dabbed at his face. He merely looked over to the counter and grinned, and their waitress hurried to the table.

"What can I do for you? Coffee? I can get you another sweet roll if you like. On the house. They don't count them or anything. Like, we don't do an inventory."

Taller reached out and touched her bare arm, almost stroking it like you would a kitten. The waitress might have been twenty, with a wholesome look and a sad—abandoned, perhaps, but not jaded—almost innocent grin.

"You're sweet—" he said, and Oliver saw his brother's eyes find her nametag without being obvious about it, "—Emily. I would love another cup of coffee. Could you get a clean cup for me, too?"

She took off, faster than waitresses were supposed to take off, and returned with coffee, cream, and a new, clean cup, pouring it eagerly.

Oliver had to raise his cup and call out, "Miss?" twice before she poured him another cup.

When they were alone again, Taller asked, "So, will you risk God's damnation and your mother's scorn to take the job? Offers big money, I bet. Good publicity. Like the job in Butler, on Alice and Frank's place."

Taller worked for Oliver. In some ways, Taller proved the better craftsman. He "listened" to the wood, he said. He became one with it, let it have its way sometimes. He lacked motivation, Oliver thought, but he had a way with wood.

"I'm not sure. I have a meeting with Samantha on Friday. A couple of questions to iron out. Then I'll decide."

Taller sat up straighter, just a bit, but Oliver noticed.

"Samantha? We're already on a first-name basis?"

Oliver hesitated. In an instant, in his mind's eye he allowed the present moment to flash forward a month into the future. He saw Taller with Samantha, Taller's charm and good looks and tallness overwhelming the woman. He saw them together, holding hands, and ... and he forced the thought away.

"No. Maybe. She said she prefers being called Samantha."

Taller let his face take on that grin that was so familiar to Oliver. "Is she pretty?"

Oliver shrugged, trying his best to be noncommittal.

Taller grinned wider. "You're terrible at poker, Brother. She must be an absolute knockout."

Emily was back at the table. "More coffee?" she said sweetly, her attention fixed on the younger brother.

Taller looked up, directly into her eyes, stared for a long second, then replied, soft and warm, "Emily, I would be delighted to have more of your excellent coffee."

She walked away, and Oliver was more torn than ever. It was a really big job, an important job. But could he stand seeing his brother with Samantha if what he thought might happen really happened—and he had no reason to doubt that it might? And then, even as the thought entered his mind, Oliver dismissed it as silly and childish.

Everyone is an adult here, he told himself.

And Oliver knew that O. Barnett Custom Construction really needed this project.

CHAPTER THREE

SAMANTHA STEPPED OUT of the hot shower, welcomed after a vigorous workout, and wrapped herself in a wickedly thick bathrobe she had bought on her last visit to the Plaza Hotel in New York City. Usually she was not susceptible to those gimmicky in-room sales pitches, like ten-dollar water bottles from hotel mini-bars. But the robe was fabulous, and Samantha loved fabulous—even if it was fabulously expensive for a simple white Turkish cotton robe.

She wiped at the foggy mirror with her hand. Her hair was wilder than it was before her shower. Water, humidity, and steam gave it a mind of its own. She glanced at her watch. There was no time to blow dry and style. Instead she pulled her hair back and held it together with an elastic band.

She quickly applied moisturizer to her face. Her image in the mirror, even without makeup—the little foundation, blush, mascara, eye shadow, and lipstick she usually wore—still pleased her. She liked the way she looked both made-up and unadorned.

A good self-image, she thought. *Maybe too good for my own good.*

She opened the robe for a moment.

I should lose a few pounds.

She tied it back up.

But then none of my gentlemen friends have ever complained, so maybe not.

She hurried downstairs. Her father would be home for lunch, as he most often was, and she needed to discuss business with him. Wearing the robe was part of her strategy.

"*Oy, oy, oy,* why don't you get dressed?" he said as Samantha entered the kitchen. Mally, their cook and housekeeper, shook her head, having heard the same discussion a hundred times before.

"Daddy, why? I'm wearing a robe."

Samuel Cohen did not look like he was obviously or blatantly newly rich, with the possible exception of the thick gold Bulgari watch around his wrist, a gift from his late wife before she died. He wore expensive clothes, but none with pretentious horses or lizards on them. Just "good quality expensive" clothes, he said, "but not so anyone can tell, unless they know quality." Great shoes were important—always Italian, always polished.

Samuel stood on the smaller side and was always impeccably groomed and well tanned—not sprayed on or from a tanning bed, either. He was tanned from sitting by the indoor pool with the giant skylights at the glitzy new health club on East Liberty, if not on the beach or at an out-door pool in Miami. He never swam, but he loved the sun. "It's my Israeli background. I crave the desert," he would explain if ever asked about his year-round bronze color.

Samantha slid into a chair at the kitchen table.

"But a robe is not what you wear in the daytime, *Bubeleh*—to lunch, for Pete's sake. You wear a robe when you come from a shower. *Oy vey.*"

"But I came from the shower," she replied, grabbing an apricot from the crystal bowl in the center of the table. "I'll get dressed after lunch."

Samuel glowered at her. She knew he didn't mean it.

"What's for lunch, Mally? Something Jamaican? Something exotic?" Samuel asked.

"I not make Jamaica food ever again, Mr. Cohen. You never eat de Jamaica food. Today is chicken salad. You eat de chicken salad. I don' be wastin' food on a man who don' eat shrimp."

"Jews can't eat shellfish," he replied. This was also a friendly argument that both pretended to dislike, but both actually enjoyed.

"A good Jew—I don' know dey not eat de shrimp. But, Mr. Cohen, you don' wear de funny hat and de long black coat. You just a man. You could eat de shrimp. You don' be one of dose Jews."

"*Slicha!*" He held up his hands in surrender. "My mother, if she saw me eating shrimp, would have a heart attack and die right there, on the spot. Do you want that on your conscience?"

Samantha loved the barbed back-and-forth. Since her mother died, now twenty years ago *(Has it really been twenty years?)* it was good to see her father laugh.

"But isn't *Bubbe* in Miami?" Samantha replied in a matter-of-fact tone.

"Beside the point," her father said. "She could surprise us. She could come for a visit. And me, with a shrimp in my mouth."

Mally placed two plates on the counter, each with chicken salad on challah bread, with a fat dill pickle, and a sprinkling of Lieber's kosher potato chips, plus an unopened can of Dr. Brown's Cream Soda. The menu changed very little from day to day.

Samuel ate slowly, keeping an eye on the muted TV screen on the counter, watching the stock-market ticker. Mr. Samuel Cohen was not a stockbroker, really, but had made a great deal of money on stocks. He was a partner in a real-estate firm and never sold real estate, but made a great deal of money in that venture as well. He also bought and sold commodities, never on a consistent basis, but more when the mood struck him. Contrary to populist thinking, his dabbling in a variety of markets was not the buying and selling of a dilettante. He simply had the ability to step in, take the pulse of a situation, react as if he had been charting the highs and lows for years, and buy and sell right. He called no one "Boss," yet worked very hard when he worked.

Samantha loved to watch him eat. He did so with grace, in an almost fastidious manner, like a bird, or a cat, eating everything just so. His dining style was in such opposition to her own frenzied business buy-and-sell manner.

"Daddy, I think I'll need a bit more … input … for the Korean church project."

Samuel looked up, appearing bothered by the interruption. "You closed on that already, didn't you? It was a cash offer, right?"

Samantha knew he had paid little attention to her latest project. "Yes, Daddy, and thank you for helping with the financing."

"No problem, Sam. Besides, it's the bank's money, not mine."

"But it's because of your name."

He shrugged. "Maybe. But my name isn't on the deed. So ... what's with more money?"

"Stan Levine ... the architect ... the one you recommended ..."

"Oh, yeah—Stan ... from the club. He's real good. And expensive. You didn't let him charge you what he charges his rich clients, did you? You told him this was a favor for me, right?"

"He knows, Daddy," Samantha said as she readjusted her robe, knowing that it made her father nervous—and perhaps more anxious to settle the deal quickly.

"He figured that the changes we want to do might cost as high as ... $300,000. So I'll need that much to do this project."

Samuel let out a slow whistle. "*Oy.* You sure you can't just repaint it and then sell it to the Baptists for a fast profit? Maybe God won't like you changing it from a place of worship for Christians into something else."

"I don't think so, Daddy."

He pushed his empty plate to the side and folded his napkin. "I'll talk to Sheldon at the bank. Give him a few days. I'll get him to drop it into your account. Okay?"

Samantha held back her grin of victory. Instead she grabbed her father around the waist and kissed him noisily on the top of his head, as all the while he was squirming and calling out, "Watch the hair, watch the hair!"

Every once in a while Oliver decided to live dangerously. Today, Friday, Samantha Cohen could not meet with him until 10:00 a.m., and Oliver did not relish sitting in his truck for hours or wasting time in a coffee shop. He could have driven around to find the nearest home-supply store to Shadyside, but with his GPS and the Internet, there was no need for that.

And if he didn't get the job, he would have wasted all that gasoline for nothing.

He decided instead to risk heavy traffic, and left home at 8:30. Robert curled up on the seat next to him in the truck. Traffic was heavier than

Oliver liked, but not mind-numbingly heavy. He traversed the distance from Jeannette to Shadyside, some twenty-five miles, in exactly the fifty-five minutes his GPS said it would take him, the device garnering an increased measure of his respect.

He parked in the covered port cochere of the church, pulling his truck up behind a very sporty, red late-model Mercedes convertible. He didn't know much about foreign cars, but this one looked expensive, lithe and agile, and luxurious.

In a hurry, Oliver almost forgot about letting Robert the Dog out, and he imagined a hurt look in the dog's eyes as he hurried back down from the steps to the truck.

It's that woman....

Robert did not run; instead he became most disciplined, and carefully and deliberately walked up the steps to the open door of the church.

In the direct morning light, the interior sang with a loud chorus of colors tinted by the stained-glass windows, almost vibrating with the hues. Oliver wondered, for a moment, if he could mount some sort of flood-lights outside, to provide this dazzling illumination after dark.

Might be an ordinance against it, but I should ask Samantha ... Miss Cohen, to check out the possibilities.

"Oliver! Over here ... in the ... dome or rotunda ... or is this the vault? Whatever they call it. Come on down ... or up."

Oliver hurried down the center aisle. Robert the Dog usually kept pace with him, or even ran ahead, but today, on this morning, he stayed back, a dozen steps back, as if he were pacing himself, not willing to fully commit to this new person—even if she had been really nice to him during their first encounter. If Oliver had looked, he would have seen the question on his dog's face: "Who hugs a dog so soon—even if I liked it?" or as much of that question as Robert could convey, in his canine sort of way.

Samantha had found a leftover square table and had placed two heavy oak altar chairs side by side at the table. With a note of apprehension, Oliver noticed that the table looked to be the sort on which Communion elements are served: of fine wood, with paneled sides, carved letters in Latin, or perhaps Greek, on the front. His church in Jeannette had a similar table, and it was reserved for Communion and Communion alone.

It's not a church anymore ... it's no longer a church.

Samantha had spread a thickness of blueprints on the table, rolling the sides backward to hold the curl. There were several sheets of transparent overlays, with bold sketches and lines and lettering all over them—as if she and her architect had been revising their initial plan.

If she changes the plan, I'll have to let her know that it will be straight time and material with the extras. That way I can't lose.

Samantha waited at the top of the step of the platform and gave Oliver a hug of greeting, which was more than enough to completely disarm him and make his cheeks burn a little.

"So nice of you to get your estimate done so soon," she said. "Let's sit down and go over it, okay?"

I wonder if she even bothered to get a second bid? She never mentioned a second estimate.

She took his hand and led him to the chairs. Oliver tried to tell himself that she was probably this casual with hugging and touching with everyone—not just with him, and not simply to make him nervous. But he was nervous.

Not nervous ... I've been around women before. I would say I am ... aflutter *... but no man gets aflutter. Who even says* "aflutter" *anymore?*

"Sit, Oliver, and show me what you've planned. Or should I show you some new angles we have—the architect and me, that is?"

To Oliver, it would not have made a big difference either way, and right now, he wasn't sure how to answer any questions. He sat down, took out his worn leather folder, and took a deep breath. "Maybe I should start with my estimate of your original plan and sketches. If you've changed things, we can discuss them after I show you what the original version would cost."

She nodded. "Sounds like a fair plan. Show me yours, Oliver."

He was nearly dead certain that she meant it as a double entendre, or whatever it is they call those remarks that made him edgy when he shouldn't be edgy, or vice versa. He gulped and hoped he wasn't obvious about it.

Robert the Dog, from behind them on the main floor of the old sanctuary, barked once—not a loud bark, more like a *Hey-get-back-to-business* bark. The dog's interruption worked, snapping Oliver back from his mental diversion.

He flipped open the estimate and unfolded his copy of the plan, then laid out the twelve sketches he had done, both freehand and by computer, of what style he thought she was requesting for booths, tables, and seating, and for adding interior alcoves and stairs and other finishing work. He used his favorite fine-point marker as a pointer, showing where all the built-ins would be and how they would fit into the existing architectural details of the church … or *former* church.

Samantha leaned close to him as he explained his drawings, closer than most clients ever got. He could almost smell her hair. No … he *could* smell her hair. Apple maybe. Or some tropical fruit or flower. A pretty smell. He observed her face, from the corner of his eye, as she watched him point to his drawings and lay them onto the main blueprint. He had drawn to scale the additions he would make to the interior on transparent paper and slid the overlays around on the large blueprint. Samantha kept nodding and agreeing and stopping only occasionally to ask a quick question, inquire as to a finish or a wood selection, ask about meeting building codes. There were no large disagreements, no major conflicts.

On the same page, Oliver thought.

After fifteen, maybe twenty minutes of explanation, Samantha leaned back and smiled at Oliver. "I've been patient, Oliver. Now you have to tell me … how much?"

Oliver never liked this part of the bidding. He knew he had to make a living. He knew that his clients knew he had to make a profit. But he never liked asking for the money. Money sullied the process somehow. Either a client became almost angry with the idea that they were being ripped off by Oliver's obscenely high rates, or grabbed at a pen in a desperate lunge to sign the contract before the contractor changed his mind and raised the prices.

Oliver pulled out his last sheet. "If we do everything with top-quality materials—not anything extravagant, but walnut or mahogany, good granite, and other high-end materials—I came up with a price of $225,000. The staircases I have kept separate—since I don't know about the floor joists and supports—but I would be pretty sure that $15,000 would cover any eventuality. I'll do that on a time and material basis, since you can get fooled. And I'll do the kitchen walls and build-out for an additional $10,000 and have a kitchen contractor bid the equipment and installation. That would be extra, and will be a significant expense, but you can get whatever sort of appliances you think appropriate for your needs."

He sat back and waited.

"That's a total of $235,000. Right? Plus or minus the whatevers, right?"

"Right. Like the stairs. In case something comes up."

"Plus appliances, cabinetry, and equipment for the kitchen."

"Right," Oliver said.

Maybe I could have bid this higher … but that's not the way to do business. The bid is fair. Really fair. I know it. And I think that she'll realize that. Maybe I could have bid higher—but … it just didn't seem right. This is an honest bid. She'll see that.

Samantha looked at his stack of papers, then directly at Oliver for a long time, just in his eyes, without saying a word. He felt something inside get all squiggly and was within a minute of lowering his price by 10 percent—and she hadn't even asked for a discount. Her eyes were that pretty, Oliver concluded.

"You think four months will be enough time?" she asked.

"Yes. Unless something happens. Like with the stairs. Or we run into a problem with the city building codes. Like if we had to upgrade the electrical on the whole building or revise plumbing. Something like that. But it could easily slip a few weeks."

"I wouldn't worry too much about codes. My father knows everyone in Pittsburgh. I mean *everyone*. We could … work out any problem."

"Not worry about codes—"

"That's what I'm telling you."

Oliver had heard that sort of promise before. Usually the person with clout was the brother-in-law of a neighbor of an aunt or uncle, and it always wound up that not one of these so-called "people in the know" had any pull at all dealing with city ordinances. Oftentimes, the simple fact that they tried to grease some wheels usually resulted in a bigger tiff with the city than when they started. But today, Oliver imagined that

Samantha's father did indeed know the right people in the right places. He imagined that any problem might simply be swept away—as in "You owe me a favor."

"If I said yes, when could you start?" she asked.

He thought he should ponder his decision, or perhaps pretend to look at a schedule or his Day-Timer, but instead of playing it cool, he decided to err on the side of honesty and tell the truth. He said firmly, "Monday."

"You have a contract with you? I want to sign now. Let's get started right away. Time is money and all that."

Robert the Dog barked, and Oliver all but shook his head to clear his thoughts. "There is one thing, though," he said.

"And that is ... you want all the money up front? I hope not," Samantha replied in her best, clipped business voice, indicating that she was no dummy and would not let herself be taken by anyone—even if they had an honest face.

"No, no, nothing like that. Twenty percent is fine. Fifteen percent would be okay, or even ten. There's not much buying needed until a couple of weeks into the project. It's not about the money. You see, I live in Jeannette, and it's a long drive here in the morning. You know, with traffic and all. I was wondering ..."

"Yes ..." Samantha said, encouraging him.

"Could I just stay in the basement of the church ... during the week? There's a shower down there. I could set up a cot or something. It would save me a lot of time and aggravation."

"Will Robert the Dog have to stay here as well?"

Oliver wondered if there was a city ordinance against it. "I ... guess so." He tried to hide his anxiety. *Not have Robert here? Who would take care of him? Not my mother, or my brother, for sure.*

Samantha grabbed his forearm and squeezed. "I didn't mean to alarm you, Oliver. You would be welcome to stay. Robert would be welcome. I was teasing."

Oliver took a deep breath and hoped she didn't notice. "Oh, sure, I knew that. So it's okay then?"

She squeezed his arm again, this time in a very gentle way. "It is more than okay, Oliver. I would prefer it that way, now that we're partners and all."

——————◦∞◦◦◦——————

Oliver had prepared a contract, perhaps a bit more detailed than a standard one. It included clauses for liabilities, for unseen conditions, and for changes in the original plan. It carefully spelled out liabilities. It was not foolproof, but a friend, who was almost a lawyer, had drawn it up and said that it would stand up in court, ninety-nine times out of a hundred.

"What happens if it's the hundredth case?" Oliver had asked.

Larry, his almost-lawyer friend, had grinned and replied in all honesty, "Then you're screwed."

Occupational hazard. Nobody can foresee every problem.

Samantha, whom Oliver was certain had really astute, and really expensive, attorneys at her beck and call, perused the contract quickly, skimming all but a few sections. She seemed to take note of a few sticking points, but asked for no changes.

"I've found that no matter what the contract says, you can find a lawyer to fight it, sue you over it, take you to court," she explained. "So it doesn't matter what sort of contract you sign. It's all a matter of trust. I trust you, Oliver. You have a kind, honest face. A handsome face, but that is beside the point. And I trusted Alice and Frank Adams when they referred you. They said you are a gem. The real deal, a trustworthy gem. A man who keeps his promises. And that's enough for me. So, where do I sign?"

A man who keeps his promises ... yeah, that's me. No matter what.

Oliver pointed to the page with his pen. She signed her name with her own black Mont Blanc pen, with sweeps and flourishes. Then she lifted her purse and pulled out a checkbook.

"Here's a check for $75,000 to start. I know it's more than you asked for, but you'll need to buy a lot of things to get started."

He took the check and carefully clipped it to his copy of the contract.

Samantha reached down to the floor and rustled in a paper bag. She sat back up and held up a bottle, displaying it to Oliver. "I know it's early, but I brought wine. To celebrate. I like to celebrate."

She produced two plastic cups and unscrewed the top of the wine. "I had to buy this bottle because I hate carrying a corkscrew. The nice clerk at the wine store said it was a very good vintage and that the industry has made all sorts of strides in capping bottles and a screw-off top is no longer seen as holding cheap wine. And he was right, since this bottle was anything but cheap."

She chattered away as she poured two healthy glasses of the red wine.

Oliver did not hesitate. At least he tried to give the appearance of not hesitating. He was well over twenty-one. He had tasted all sorts of alcohol. He would meet his friends in bars and taverns, and sometimes have a beer with them. But it was the very occasional event when he imbibed. And it was never at 11:00 in the morning.

And never, ever with a client. A very pretty client. Oliver knew what alcohol could do … and he pushed the images out of his mind as soon as they arose.

"Oh, and one more thing: I didn't want to leave anyone out and I wasn't sure he would be here," Samantha added. She reached down and pulled a gnarled rawhide strip from her purse.

"The man at the pet store said dogs love these things. They look disgusting, but then, what do I know from dogs? I never had one growing up but would love to someday. Can Robert have this? Would he like it?"

Robert had already padded up to the platform. His nose twitched as he tried to catch the new scent in the air.

"He loves them. Sure. He can have it," Oliver said, ruffling the dog's head.

Samantha bent to Robert the Dog. "Here you are, sweetie. I'll be seeing a lot of you in the next few months," she said and scratched behind his right ear.

Robert gingerly took the rawhide in his mouth and backed away slowly. Then he tossed the strip into the air, caught it, and lay down to begin his noisy chewing.

"Robert says thank you," Oliver said pleasantly.

Samantha raised her glass in the air. Oliver knew this was no time to moralize.

When someone says it's no time for moralizing—then it probably is time for moralizing.

That was something his mother often repeated.

Why did I think of that right now?

He raised his glass.

She touched his with hers. "To a wonderful partnership."

Oliver only nodded, not sure if he was supposed to add to the toast.

Samantha took a very healthy drink. Oliver sipped his, surprised at the robust taste of the wine, full-bodied but smooth, clear, tasty, and definitely expensive.

Oliver knew that for people who did not partake often, the effects of alcohol were more striking. As soon as the liquid entered his stomach, he could sense the warmth puddling in his gut, could feel the spread of the wine down his legs, down his arms, like putting on a very thick comforter.

"Tolliver? Were you sleeping? It's nearly noon. Why are you still asleep? Are you hung over? Why aren't you working? You don't believe in working anymore? It's obvious that you don't believe in going to church anymore."

Taller held the phone six inches away from his ear. His mother's voice could be shrill.

"Good morning to you, too, Ma."

"Why are you home? It's the middle of the day."

Taller wiped his face with his hand. "Why are you calling me if I'm not supposed to be here?"

"Don't get smart with me. I'm your mother."

Tolliver sat up on his bed, still holding the phone well away from his ear. He stood up and walked from his bedroom to the kitchen. He poured water into the electric kettle, measured instant coffee into a bone china coffee cup from the glass-fronted cabinet, and waited for the water to hiss and steam and boil, all the while listening to his mother, as if from a distance, debate herself on the possibility of Oliver working on a building that used to be a church.

I thought I dodged a bullet. I guess I didn't.

"Ma, I just work for him, remember? He signs the checks. If he wants to turn a convent into a gay nightclub for transsexuals, I can't stop him."

He knew what was about to happen and now held the phone at arm's length.

"Don't you dare use those filthy words to your mother, Tolliver. That's disgusting. Or talk about your brother that way."

I wonder if it was mentioning the convent or the transsexuals that got her more riled up?

"Sorry, Ma, but he's a grown man. He doesn't listen to me any more than he does you. And from what he tells me, the building is no longer a church. It's an ex-church. It has ceased to be a church. That church has expired. It has shuffled off its mortal coil."

I think a Monty Python skit went like that … the one with the dead parrot.

"Don't you talk about a church being dead."

Taller wondered why he bothered. "But it isn't a church anymore."

He held the phone away from his ear again.

"But God remembers. Do you think Christ has forgotten about that church—His bride? Do you think He's forgotten about you? He hasn't. He never will. Never, Tolliver."

"Okay, Ma. I get it. I'll talk to Ollie, but we need the work. Renovating jobs aren't exactly falling off trees these days, you know. And Ollie seems to think there's a reason he's the one doing the work. That's what he said, at least."

He took a long drink. He wondered where Emily was. Last night she said something about working the early shift and bringing him brunch today. He knew, without looking, that there was nothing in the refrigerator.

Maybe she'll get me a Grand Slam Breakfast. I like those. With extra pancakes.

There was the slightest tapping at his front door. He sniffed the air.

Pancakes. Ask and ye shall receive.

"Listen, Ma, I have to go. The … uh … landlord just came. Okay. Talk to you later."

"I'll see you Sunday, right? At church? You've been promising me, Tolliver. You promised you would come. You remember, right?"

"Okay, Ma," he said as he padded to the front door of his apartment. "I'll come. If it gets you off my back, I'll come."

As the smell of pancakes grew stronger, Taller's grin grew wider.

"I love you, Tolliver," Rose Barnett said, her voice becoming almost maternal. "I'll see you Sunday then. I'll save you a seat. I'm on the left side, halfway up. Okay?"

"Okay, Ma. Sunday."

The door swung open.

"What's on Sunday?" Emily asked as she presented him with two large, squeaky Styrofoam cartons—one smelling of pancakes, the other of bacon.

"Oh … nothing important. Did you bring extra syrup?" he asked as he bent to kiss her.

———

"So tell me, Oliver-not-Ollie, is there a Mrs. Oliver?"

Samantha Cohen had picked up her glass of wine after drinking more than half and walked down the side aisle of the church. Oliver followed, glass in hand, as if it were expected, while Robert the Dog chewed energetically on his new treat. The sound of his scraping and crunching echoed in the vast old church.

Again this was treading on virgin territory for Oliver. No client had ever asked him. Many had assumed that he was married. Or divorced.

Not that many thirty-eight-year-old contractors are still single … and in the never-been-married category.

"No. I'm not married," he said simply, without inflection.

Tell the truth … if she asks.

She did not ask further. When others asked about him being either divorced or widowed, Oliver wondered if they knew how personal the question was. Answering "Yes, I'm married" was the simple and expected response. But if as a man you answered that you were now almost four decades old and not married—and not gay, nor harboring some horrid personality issue that keeps you single—well, now that was a whole lot more complicated. People often nodded as he explained, nodded as one would nod when a lunatic was yammering away, nodding to keep their options of a quick escape open.

"And neither am I," Samantha said as she stopped beneath a window depicting Pentecost, bright fingers of flames descending on the crowd. "Married, that is. I'm not sure I'll ever get married."

"Why not?" Oliver asked.

"Too much fun being single, right? Too hard to choose."

For a second, Samantha looked as if she were unaccustomed to telling strangers that truth about herself.

Oliver felt the wine, felt it embolden him, but at the last moment stopped himself. In a second, he wasn't sure what he'd been planning to say, but was relieved that he didn't have to explain why he wasn't married.

Not that I don't want to. Or not that I haven't had … options … or opportunities. I don't know why, exactly. Just haven't met the right woman.

"Don't mind me," she said in explanation. "Wine makes me talkative. And probably too personal. I have no business asking personal questions, Oliver. I'm sorry. I should know better by now."

"No, that's okay. Don't feel embarrassed."

She laughed loudly. "Oh, I'm not embarrassed. I hardly ever get embarrassed. I just feel bad for other people who don't understand me. But I'm sure you'll get used to me over the next five months, give or take a few weeks."

She sat in one of the pews that had already been moved and finished off her glass. Oliver still had half of his left.

I do have to drive home.

"Miss Cohen, would it be okay if I moved some things into the church this weekend? That way, I'll be ready to start first thing Monday. I contacted three brothers who do demo work to see what their schedule looks like, just in case you wanted to get started right away. I've used them before, and they're good workers. They would be able to come on Monday."

"Oh, sure, anything you want to do. Here, let me give you the keys."

He pocketed them, three big keys attached to a large plain ring.

"You'll be like a caretaker here. That's nice. Looking out for the place while we work on it. I'll be here a lot as well. I always poke around the site of my projects. Just tell me if I'm in your way, okay? Promise?"

"I will."

"Four months is a long time. Or five. More than enough time to get well acquainted, right? Get used to each other's peccadilloes, eh?"

Oliver wasn't sure what a peccadillo was, but he nodded in agreement. "Sure. A long time."

Samantha glanced at her watch. "I am almost late. Well, I am late, but then I am often late. Or horribly early, like when you came here on Monday. We said seven, and I was here thirty minutes early. I don't know why I can't get an exact time down. Thirty minutes early or an hour late." She whistled. "Robert!"

Having been summoned, Robert the Dog nearly galloped down the aisle and gratefully accepted a scratch from Samantha, wagging his tail and offering his best dog grin.

"See you soon, Robert. Oliver, I will see you Monday. I am out of town this weekend. But I'll be here Monday morning."

And even though he expected it, it surprised him when she opened her arms and embraced him in a very big, enthusiastic hug, a longer and tighter hug than he thought appropriate for a contractor and his new client, but a hug that he enjoyed, nevertheless.

"See you Monday," he called after her as she slipped out the front door of the former church, leaving Oliver and Robert the Dog to stare at each other, as if understanding each other's combination of happiness mixed with a little confusion and sprinkled with a pinch of apprehension.

Which, of course, they really did not.

CHAPTER FOUR

"Mally, have you seen my swimsuit?"

Mally stood in the doorway to Samantha's room and crossed her arms over her chest. "Girl, do your father pay me to know de whereabouts of swimmin' suits? I think no, he don'."

A Louis Vuitton suitcase, its leather luggage tag elegantly monogrammed, lay open on her bed, and stacks of clothing were strewn all over the room. Samantha enjoyed a large bedroom, almost as big as the master suite in the Cohen home. It was the room in the second-floor rounded turret, with thick white moldings and a curved wall of windows nearly encircling the entire space. It had window seats with thick cushions upholstered in white, and an array of silk-fringed pillows in classic country French prints that coordinated with the shams on the sleigh bed, covered in a puffy white duvet. Off to one side were a mirrored dressing area, a walk-in closet, and a spacious spalike bathroom, complete with a long, deep English soaking tub, where, surrounded by a dozen scented candles, Samantha liked to relax away the tensions of the day. She had designed the suite herself, selecting her favorite shade of a deep peacock blue for the walls and choosing painted French Louis XVI furniture—a pair of antique dressers and nightstands with simple lines and marble tops, and a blanket chest—all of which she had found in Provence, France.

"Well, I saw it a few days ago. And now I need it. And it's gone."

Mally did not move. "I don' go takin' your swimmin' suits, missy. And why you need de swimmin' suit? Too cold for swimmin'."

"We're going up to Seven Springs. A girls' weekend. Have some fun. They have an indoor pool."

"Still too cold, girl. De trees, dey got no leaves yet. Too cold. You crazy, girl, if you swim now."

Samantha loved Mally, who had been with the Cohen family for decades. She loved the way Mally could scold her and love her at the same time. She wished her mother could have been more like that.

"So when you build dat church, Miss Sam?"

"Next week. The contractor starts next week."

Mally came into the room and sat on the edge of the bed. She pushed an errant strand of hair from her forehead then poked at a pile of clothes on the far corner of the bed.

"Here be your swimmin' suit, Miss Sam," she said as she pulled it from beneath a stack of sweaters. "Least what dere be of it."

Samantha took it and tossed it into the open suitcase. "Don't be such a prude, Mally. This is a new century. Things have changed."

Mally waved her hand in the air, as if batting away Samantha's words. "Some dings not change ever, Miss Sam. Like you. You dinkin' of fallin' for dat man who works on de church, am I right 'bout dat?"

Samantha took a seat on the large hand-painted blanket chest at the end of the bed. "Maybe. He's really handsome, Mally. Much better looking than that one who worked on the restoration on Mount Washington."

"Dat man with de black hair? He was no good. Never liked dat man, never. Don' trust a man like dat. A man like dat don' care if he be breakin' your heart, Miss Sam."

"This one is different, Mally. He is really a nice man. And he has a dog. There is something about him, Mally. Sort of a gentleness and a kindness. He seems so honest and truthful. You know when you meet someone for the first time and you can just tell that they are a special person. I felt that with this man. Kind and gentle. I know he would treat a woman with … well, the only word I can think of is *reverence*."

"What dat mean—reverence? Like for de Bible or somethin'?"

"Not like that, I don't think … but that everything would be special with him. I could tell. You could tell if you met him. There is no taking advantage of anyone. I don't know … there's just something about him. I don't think I ever noticed it about anyone else." Samantha folded her swimsuit. "And he has the nicest, sweetest dog I have ever met."

Mally burst out laughing, a rich, rolling, deep Jamaican laugh. "Missy, any man can buy de dog. Any dog can be trained to be nice. Don' mean dey a good man, just a man wid a good dog."

Samantha picked up a blouse, folded it, placed it in the suitcase then added the matching Vuitton cosmetic bag.

"You too easy with de gentlemen, Miss Sam. Don' fall for dis one. A man moons over a pretty girl and gets no work done. And you gets your heart broken. You stay away, Miss Sam."

Samantha closed her suitcase and snapped the locks. "But I like men, Mally. I like them a lot."

Mally shook her head. "Miss Sam, shame dat your mum not be here to give you what for, being foolish wid de men. She would have tol' you. You stay away. Unless dey come wid de diamon' ring, you stay away."

Samantha picked up her bag, bent down to give Mally a kiss on the cheek, then slipped out of the room.

As if that's ever going to happen.

Robert did not wiggle and dance like some dogs, like a three-year-old needing to go potty. No, Robert was different. He simply walked to the door, eyed the door handle intently, as if a dog's stare could affect the mechanism, and he might bark once, without ever adjusting his gaze.

The process—the gentle bark, mostly—might be repeated a dozen times over the span of many minutes, until Oliver recognized his dog's plight and got the message. Today, only a single bark was required.

Oliver, restless since he awoke, was glad that Robert the Dog presented him a legitimate opportunity to get out of the house. He had two bags and two boxes packed, representing the bare minimum of kitchen items (electric teakettle to heat water, plate, cup, spoon, fork, knife, toaster, peanut butter, jelly, instant coffee, sugar, and crackers) since the kitchen in the basement of the church was ancient and not operational. He also packed a rolled-up sleeping bag with bed linens inside along with a thick pillow.

There was a cot in the corner, disassembled—a deluxe unit that Oliver had purchased many years ago when he thought he might get into camping. He never did, really, and the cot, the priciest model the sporting-goods catalog offered, remained hidden in the darkness of a deep closet.

After packing, Oliver had nothing else to do … until Robert caught his attention.

Robert could easily be walked off leash, but here, in his home neighborhood, Oliver thought it best to use a retractable leash. Robert seldom pulled on it. Oliver was most concerned about the dog darting out to chase a chipmunk or squirrel and heading into traffic. There was not much traffic in Oliver's neighborhood, especially on a Saturday afternoon, but Oliver was not a man given to take unnecessary risks.

The two of them spent a happy hour, walking along the quiet residential streets, Oliver making mental notes of which house needed what sort of work, how he would adjust porches or columns or shutters or windows, noticing those houses that simply needed some form of kind correction or those whose appearance could only be improved with the use of a bulldozer.

Not more than a block away from home, Oliver heard his name being called by a feminine voice. He was tempted to pretend he didn't hear, ignore it, and walk a bit more briskly. He did that sometimes. Small talk, idle chatter, except with close acquaintances, unnerved him and made him feel inadequate. It often left him grasping at words he knew were there, but never exactly sure of just what they were.

His name grew in volume and in insistence.

"Oliver! I know you heard me!"

Oliver turned and tried to form a *you-got-me* grin, as if he had intended to be aloof for a joke. He was pretty certain he was failing miserably at his charade, but it was all he had for an answer.

He had sort of half-recognized the voice the first time he'd heard it. It was a woman, a single woman—well, sort of single.

Paula Harris came half-jogging down the street, holding what looked to be a transistor radio in her hand, but bigger, with a thick, stubby antenna. She came up to Oliver and placed her hand on his arm, not even hearing the low growl from Robert the Dog, who would not

bite anyone in a million years, unless maybe they were attacking either
Oliver or himself, but he would respond in a curious, negative way when
strangers broke into his personal space. Oliver had never been sure how
far Robert the Dog's personal space extended but imagined it to be a
foot or two.

Paula was that close.

"So, what's this church your mother says you're making a mockery of?
Is it around here? Or do I have to carry a Bible all the time now to ward
off whatever heavenly attack will come at you?"

Robert the Dog sniffed, then sat down, facing away from both Oliver
and Paula, waiting.

"No. Shadyside. The church—the former church—is in Shadyside,"
Oliver replied and tried not to look at her hand, still resting on his arm.

Paula's face grew animated. "Shadyside? Isn't that where the rich people live in Pittsburgh? Near the university? With all the cute shops and
fancy restaurants?"

Oliver shrugged. "I guess. I mean … yeah, there are some nice houses
in the area. But some normal ones too. Like anywhere. You know. Normal.
Like here."

"No. Shadyside is not like Jeannette, Oliver. Jeannette is so far from
Shadyside … like Mars. And not the Mars in Pennsylvania. The Mars out
there," she said, playfully petulant, pointing to the sky with the almost-
transistor radio in her other hand.

He looked down at his arm. Finally, she released him. He was sure she
saw his eyes dart there several times in the past few seconds.

No one spoke, and Robert readjusted his hind legs, without turning
his head one inch.

"You going to be at church tomorrow?" she asked, her voice a little
lower, Oliver imagined, a little softer. He looked at her dark eyes, just for
a moment, and her smoothly flowing hair. Oliver was not sure if it would
be called "flowing," but her dark blonde hair was not in tight curls. It was
in soft waves and down past her shoulders. He thought the waves might
be natural then decided that maybe it was some sort or perm or whatever
women do to their hair to give it that look. She was pretty, in a used way,
like a classic model of a car that was still a sweet ride, even with a hundred

thousand miles on it, he often thought. And then he would chastise himself for thinking ill of poor Paula.

After all, they once were close—very close. High-school sweethearts. And he still felt great affection for her.

His mother always called her "poor Paula," the girl with the bad luck to pick the wrong guy—not Oliver, that is—and get married to that "hoodlum," as his mother labeled Dave Harris, get pregnant, and then have her husband pick up and leave without so much as a fare-thee-well before the baby was born.

Oliver found himself half-agreeing with his mother in that moment that Paula was a poor girl for being left all on her own like that … or this.

"I should," he replied, his voice more chipper than he intended. "I'm heading to Pittsburgh tomorrow afternoon … or evening. But I guess I should be at church."

Paula occasionally attended church. "Hey, then I'll see you there. Can you come to the middle service? Will you? Please?"

She did not let him answer but placed her hand on his arm again. This time Robert the Dog stood up, because this time she pressed her palm and fingers insistently against his master's arm.

"Bridget is in child care during the middle service. She loves it there. And then you and me can sneak out for a cup of coffee. Could you do that, Oliver? It would be so swell to talk to a human being for a change. I mean … another adult. Could you? We haven't gotten together for ages. You owe me, Ollie. You do."

She squeezed. She did not pay attention to him looking at her hand on his arm. She looked straight at him.

"I … I guess. Second service would be fine."

"That's swell, Oliver. I love talking to you." She squeezed his arm. "How long have we known each other, Ollie?"

"Since we were in school together. Sixth grade? Or was it seventh? When you moved into the neighborhood," Oliver replied.

"A long time, isn't it?"

"I guess so."

"Nice to have old friends. Close friends. Friends you can count on, right? Friends that would do anything for each other."

Oliver was not sure if he would do *anything* for Paula, but she had been in his life for a long, long time.

The plastic device Paula held squawked into life. This time, Robert the Dog looked back over his shoulder—not interested, really, but maybe just a bit curious.

"Bridget. She's awake. Her monitor. I need to go. See you tomorrow," she said over her shoulder as she almost jogged back to her small three-bedroom house down the street and around the corner, the house that needed new shutters, a new stoop to replace the old one that tilted a few degrees off plumb, and probably a new roof as well, in Oliver's estimation.

Robert the Dog started walking.

I wonder if my mother set this up. It sounds like something she would do.

It wouldn't be the first time Mrs. Barnett tried to negotiate an improved social life for Oliver over the virtually nonexistent one—with women at least—that he currently possessed.

———

The din of the band died down, the jukebox in the corner whirred once, and music started to play again, softer than the live version, permitting a conversation at near-normal Saturday-night volume.

"We never see you anymore, Oliver."

"You do too."

"When? When was the last time we hung out together?"

Oliver sat in the dark corner of the booth. Guy Russo, an old friend from high school Oliver had run into, sat across from him, his eyes darting to the bar every few seconds.

"A few weeks ago. After that soccer game. With your daughter's team. Over at Lynch Field."

Guy shook his head as if a teacher was listening to the world's third-worst excuse for not doing homework. "That was nearly six months ago. Like last fall."

Oliver sipped at his drink. "You're married. I've been busy with work."

Guy finished his drink, waved his hand in dismissal, then signaled for another. "That's not what your brother says. He said it's been slow. I see him in here all the time. You … you're like a hermit or something."

Oliver did not reply. The waitress brought over another Iron City draft for Guy.

"So when do you get off work?" Guy asked her as he held a five-dollar bill between his thumb and forefinger, his other fingers extended in some odd show of bar etiquette. "I can ditch this loser here," he said, pointing his thumb at Oliver. "Have a few laughs. What do you say?"

The waitress handed back Guy's change with a withering look. "Oliver, why do you hang out with him?" she asked. "Doesn't he have a wife and kids at home?"

Oliver shrugged. He didn't know how the waitress knew his name, though she did look awfully familiar. And he didn't know how she knew Guy was married and a father.

The jukebox stopped, and for a moment, the silence sounded thick and heavy. Then a dozen conversations bubbled up.

Guy ran his hand over the bristles of his flattop—now back in style, after having maintained the same style for nearly two decades. "Hey, I hear that you and Paula have a date tomorrow. She's hot. I mean, like for being a mom and all that."

"What?" Oliver had no idea that Guy knew Paula, but then there were lots of entanglements and connections he knew nothing about.

"Paula. Patti ran into her this afternoon. Said she was all abuzz—my wife's word, not mine—about having a date with you tomorrow during church. I gotta say, Oliver, even *I* never went so low as to hit up a chick at church. But if it works … hey, maybe I'll start going to church with you. How's that sound? Can you see me in church? Looking for the ladies?"

"*Abuzz?*"

"That's what Patti said she said," Guy replied, his drink now half-gone. "But, man, you could do worse. That Paula is a real looker. Didn't you go out in high school? Like, serious and all? And let's face it, Oliver. You aren't exactly Mr. GQ of the Year. Or Bachelor of the Year. Or whatever it is. Not like your brother, with his stylin' clothes and animal magnetism. Maybe you shouldn't be so choosy."

Oliver wanted to say he wasn't choosy but knew it would come out wrong. He wanted to say he had never made a conscious decision *not* to be involved or married by now. He wanted to say it simply hadn't happened.

But he didn't say anything. Instead he watched Guy leer toward the bar, pointing with his elbow at a pair of women who had just entered the place.

"What do you think, Ollie? Should I make the move for both of us?"

Oliver didn't speak now, either, not wanting anyone to make any sort of move on his behalf. Not now, and perhaps, not ever.

The bar at Seven Springs was buzzing with twenty- and thirtysomethings, some mingling, some sitting on stools in clusters around tall tables spread around the dimly lit room.

"Listen, Samantha, can you give me some time … alone? Like me, alone, back at the room, I mean. Can you stay here in the bar for a while? He's up here from Uniontown, just for the evening. You know … I need some alone time with him."

Samantha looked at her friend. Lois, five years her junior, five inches shorter, and at least twenty-five pounds lighter, had turned back to the cluster of young men gathered at the end of the long polished wood bar. Each had spiky, messy, mousse-held hair and a world-weary, practiced insouciant look that Samantha was certain did not originate in downtown Uniontown, Pennsylvania. A jazz trio, far back into the room, or even in another room altogether, was slowly pushing its way through an odd-tempo version of "My Funny Valentine." Samantha thought it an odd choice because Valentine's Day had been nearly a month ago.

"I can give you … fifteen minutes," she said, looking at her watch. She watched her friend's face go from crestfallen to almost angry to confused.

"You're terrible." Lois punched Samantha's upper arm in a playful fashion.

"That's all it's going to take with that *putz*. You know that, don't you, Lois?"

Lois looked up at her friend, then back to the young men. She shrugged. "Only fifteen minutes?"

"That's what I'm telling you."

"So it's okay? You're okay to stay here … until I come back?" Lois asked, hopeful.

"Sure. Go," Samantha answered. "Have a wonderful quarter hour. And use protection, for Pete's sake."

Lois turned back. "I don't think his name is Pete. Something like Bryan, Bryce, or Braden—or something."

Samantha did not want to watch the rest of the tawdry details of the assignation unfold. She pushed her drink toward the bartender. "A fresh one, please. White wine. If you have good wine, then I want the expensive vintage this time."

She slid a twenty-dollar bill across the bar, appearing as if she would leave most of it as a tip if he did what she asked. He nodded to her, then, with a conspiratorial look, reached under the bar and brought up an unopened bottle of wine. He looked around as he showed her the label.

"Fine." Samantha knew it was not a truly noble vintage. A good wine—but not noble. She always mixed wine with tonic when she went out. *You can drink a lot and never do anything really stupid ... like Lois the schnook.*

She left most of the change from the twenty for the bartender, took the drink with her, and walked through the crowds, through the front of the bar, and through the huge lobby with the massive fireplace—now containing only a modest blaze, since it was at the early edge of spring. She took a single sip of the drink and stepped into the cool evening air, her skin prickling at the sudden change in temperature.

She could still hear the band and wondered how far she would have to walk to escape the noise.

Across the parking lot from the lodge was a waist-high wall of rock, holding back a pool of clear water. The wall also held two quarter-a-turn vending machines, each labeled *TROUT FOOD* and filled with brown pellets the fish obviously enjoyed.

Samantha seldom, if ever, carried metal change. She stared into the inky black water, the glow from the lodge reflecting in large cones of light. Beneath the surface, she could see silvery wisps and arrows, shooting through the water, like liquid meteors.

"I thought fish went to sleep at night," she said to herself. She raised her glass to the pond, and said, "*Mazel tov.*"

She took a sip of her wine, watched the fish for a long moment, then leaned over, extended her arm, pointed her finger, and dipped it into the cold water—an inch, no more. In an instant, a silver blast came at her finger. Samantha jerked back, heart racing, as the trout almost cleared the water, looking for the bug that broke the surface tension of the pool. Somehow she knew—understood—his disappointment, anger, and frustration as he snapped at only air, feeling nothing between his bony jaws … nothing filling his gullet.

She turned and looked back to the lodge, watching people—mostly young women and young men—ebb and flow in and out of the entry, laughing louder than their jokes warranted. Their braying and shrieking were more obnoxious in the pristine country setting than it would have been in the city—in Uniontown, Pittsburgh, or even Shadyside.

"Maybe I'm getting too old for this." She glanced over her shoulder, back into the trout pool, and thought about Monday morning.

Maybe he'll come Sunday evening. He seems like the sort of person who gets to places early. Maybe I could drop by … see if there is anything he might need.

And just as she considered it, she knew she would not.

It would be much too forward. Men read things into something like that. Like I'm looking for it, or something … well, maybe I am.

She looked at her watch. "*Oy.* Only twenty minutes," she said to the fish.

Like I'm fulfilling my fate.

She wondered if the coffee shop was still open and if they still had pie.

CHAPTER FIVE

Robert the Dog stared at Oliver, who was holding two neckties up for his companion's inspection. Oliver often placed Robert in these sorts of situations. It was obvious the dog understood there were two choices, two things, two objects, and invariably he would inspect one, carefully, with a double or a triple sniff, then turn his head and repeat the same action with the second item. If he hesitated at one or the other, Oliver would often look relieved and satisfied, toss one aside, and use the second, sometimes whistling at the decision.

Today that game was repeated. Robert sniffed at the two long bits of cloth, one with stripes, one without. He sniffed longer at the cloth with stripes, so that was the one Oliver tossed over his neck and began to fuss with, flipping it one way, then another.

Oliver leaned over, watching his actions in the bedroom mirror. He made a few adjustments, fiddled with his collar, then his cuffs, and ran his hand back over his short hair. He removed his one dress sport coat from the wooden hanger emblazoned with the name of the men's store where he'd bought it three years earlier. The store had since gone out of business, and Oliver was pretty certain the garment was still almost in style. In the past three years he had worn it perhaps a dozen times.

"Why are you so dressed up?" his mother barked as he made his way down the steps outside his apartment. They would not travel to church together. Rose Barnett often stayed later, through Sunday school and

sometimes afterward, doing whatever it was she did at church. Oliver
would go for just the worship service.

"I don't know. It's Sunday. Felt like it would be nice to look nice."

She returned a grin—not sly, but more knowing, perhaps, with a bit
of cunning. "I betcha she'll like you all dressed up like that. Like a real
professional and not some common laborer."

"Who?"

His mother reached into her purse and took out a little black box,
pointed it at the garage, pressed it, jerking her arm toward the door. She
was of the opinion that an electronic signal worked better if you gave it a
nudge. The door growled open. Oliver parked his truck outside and never
had to worry about garage-door openers.

"You know who. I saw her last night, taking her daughter for a walk.
Said you're planning on skipping church to have coffee together."

"Maybe for a few minutes. I'd still like to hear the sermon."

"Well, she's a nice girl, despite everything. And the two of you made
such a cute couple when you dated back in high school. You should have
moved faster back then, Oliver. She would have made a good wife."

"Ma, she was four years younger than me. We weren't together all that
long. And what I remember is that you didn't like her much back then.
Besides, I was too young to be that serious—just like she was. Too young,
I mean."

He thought his mother growled out some sort of dismissive reply, but
he didn't stop to ask her to repeat it.

Paula was waiting for him outside the church. Not on the steps, but
partway down the block so no one would notice them. However, her
attempt at being secretive wasn't so successful since a dozen churchgoers
waved at them as they walked away.

"I'm so glad you decided to come this morning." She grabbed his
arm. "I passed Wilkin's and they're not open—but Felder's is. They have
coffee."

Felder's restaurant was four blocks farther away. He'd never make it
back in time to hear the sermon. He would have to stay for the third service. He didn't like doing that. *Once you get past noon, the day feels almost
over,* he thought.

Paula was wearing a blue jacket—not denim, but casual—over a dress shorter than Oliver thought right for a Sunday morning. When she opened her coat once inside the restaurant, he realized her dress was also much tighter and cut lower than what he thought church-appropriate.

Maybe I just don't know what today's styles are.

"You look so nice in a sport coat," she gushed and stroked the fabric of his sleeve. "This is really nice. Must have been expensive."

He didn't want to shrug, because it was. In fact, he remembered exactly how much it cost but did not want to make a show of it. "It was on sale, I think."

Paula ordered coffee, a toasted pecan roll, and a large orange juice. Oliver had already eaten and drunk two cups of coffee, but he couldn't sit there and not order anything, so he ordered coffee as well.

As he stirred sugar into his coffee and she ate, Paula talked animatedly about a party she once went to and how the place was decorated; then she went on about her sister's wedding—how the caterer had overcharged her on the cost of the appetizers and then never delivered those liver things wrapped in bacon, not at all; their subsequent divorce (her sister's, that is); where her mother was going to move after she sold her house. Then she moved on to how Bridget was doing in day care and how she was becoming well socialized; how the price of food kept going up and if this continued she would be forced to get a second job, but that meant more child care and she didn't know how that was going to work. Maybe she would go back to school like the kind they advertise on TV about computers or art or something electronic, because they probably would pay better than just working at the insurance company.

"Don't you think so?" she asked.

Oliver nodded a lot and drank two cups of coffee as she talked. He didn't have that much else to do.

"And then there's Mindy. Don't get me started on Mindy. You remember Mindy? She was in your class. Or maybe she was year behind you. Well, anyhow, Mindy and her husband have been split up for a couple of years. She told me the other day that she's on the lookout for a friend with benefits and was thinking of joining one of those Internet dating services. Maybe even a younger friend with benefits. Like a boy toy."

Paula waited, then offered a coy, knowing smile.

Oliver had no idea what she meant. "Friend with benefits?" he asked quietly.

"Oh, you're teasing me now, Oliver."

He shook his head. "No. Really. What does that mean?"

Paula leaned in close to him, looking around the nearly empty restaurant, as if people were hoping to catch her saying an untoward word. "You know … you get to be friends … a friend like between a boy and a girl … kind of like we were back in school … you remember those days, don't you? And then there's more—friends with benefits, I mean. Everyone gets what they want. But no one gets goofy about giving it or getting it. You know … like sex."

Oliver wanted to lean back and away but thought he might look prudish again (which he probably was). It might even be a bit insulting to Paula.

"I think it's terrible, I mean," she said, as an aside, a throwaway line, Oliver suspected. "Right? But she's like that, Mindy is. I can understand why … and if the benefits were leading somewhere—like to a more permanent situation—I guess it would be okay."

She picked up the last piece of her pecan roll and popped it into her mouth. "I know the pastor always says you shouldn't do that sort of thing, but he's married. I don't think he understands the pressure. I guess the Bible says it's wrong, but it says lots of things are wrong that we do a lot and we never feel all that guilty about doing them—like gossiping, or lying."

Oliver had not said more than twenty-five words since walking from the church and even now, given the opportunity, could not find any words of response.

But that's wrong. You shouldn't think that way. Wrong is wrong, no matter the pressure.

"Don't look so shocked, Oliver," she said as she drank the rest of her orange juice. "You've been around the block, right?"

He found his voice. "People always assume I know more or have done more than I have. I'm a pretty"—*What word do I need here?*—"sheltered guy, I guess. Or maybe just dense about these things."

Paula grinned at him, as if she thought he was only being playful. "Oliver, it could work. I'm not … being Mindy-ish and on the prowl or anything. And you're not a younger guy, right? I think it would be okay, as long as it leads to something.…"

Her lingering gaze left no doubt in Oliver's mind exactly what she was offering in exchange for what.

———◦—————

Taller knew the road to the mall would be crowded today, so he was pedaling in the opposite direction, away from town, away from stores, away from traffic, heading toward his old high school, far from businesses and restaurants and people. He wasn't hiding, exactly, but he'd rather not run into any friends or family along the way. He had promised his mother he'd go to church, but he was sure they both knew he was lying.

Lying. That's an ugly word. Maybe I was just trying to keep her blood pressure down. Telling her the truth she doesn't want to hear is never a good thing.

He shifted his bike into a lower gear. Riding a bike in Pennsylvania, at least in the western part of the state, could be challenging. There were a lot of hills, some very steep hills, with narrow roads and curves and blind turns. Taller pedaled faster. He wanted to make the crest of the hill without shifting. One hundred yards from the summit, he realized this hill inclined at a steeper angle than he thought. He shifted once and knew he'd have to shift again before letting gravity do its work on the other side of the hill.

He liked the pressure of the pedals under his feet and the strain he felt in his legs and his thighs as he pumped away, seeking leverage with each stroke, the bike swaying under him. He felt the sweat on his back, liked the way the fabric clung to his skin, wet and hot, liked the tension in his shoulders, the tiny, trembling ache in his palms as they pressed on the handlebars.

He made it to the crest and leaned back, just his fingertips on the handlebars. The bike slowly gathered speed. In front of him lay a long hill, nearly a mile descent, steeper at the end than the beginning. He switched to the lowest gear and pushed hard, the bike gaining speed easily.

Taller knew he should just enjoy the ride down, that it would be fast enough without adding to the velocity, but could not resist the temptation. The wind whistled in his ears as he descended, becoming a howl that mixed with the staccato clicking of his tires on the pavement and the hushed clip-clip-clip of the guardrails as he rushed past.

Only at the very bottom did he let up, his body bent over the bike, his shoulders down, his legs tucked hard against the frame. He roared over the bridge at the bottom, the passage barely wide enough for one car. If a car had been there, the passing would be dicey at best and dangerous at least.

He let his momentum carry him down the road, up over a swell, and onto a level section, leading to the high school. Turning his head, he glanced back at the hill, glad that for those few seconds he'd thought of nothing—nothing but the speed and the danger and the wind. Everything else was gone, vanished for those few moments.

That's why I ride.

He knew Emily would be gone by the time he returned, having to work the second shift.

She's nice enough.

He pedaled slowly now, maintaining an easier pace. The high school loomed up ahead on the right, a jumble of buildings and wings added piecemeal over the years, with none of the components truly integrated.

I get free food … and other benefits.

He thought he might stop there, in the parking lot of the school, in the shade of the large auditorium, and rest for a moment. But instead he pedaled past, hardly looking at it.

That's the trouble with never leaving a place. Nothing can fade into memory. Your past is always right there in front of you.

He shifted gears again and pressed hard on the pedals, feeling the vibrations of the rough pavement in his palms and up his arms.

Oliver and Robert the Dog slipped into the basement of the former church. It was later than he'd wanted to arrive. He had stayed for the third service at his church in Jeannette, wanting to hear the sermon, but his conversation with Paula—more a one-sided monologue than a normal conversation—had left him agitated, edgy, and unable to concentrate.

I know what she wants … and what she's offering.

As he took his seat, he'd seen his mother in the narthex, buttonholing someone, gesturing with her hands, her mouth wide, her fingers pointing. She had not seen him, and that suited Oliver well.

Maybe I should take this Paula thing more seriously. She's pleasant. She's pretty. She keeps the conversation going. I could do a lot worse.

Most likely his mother would have asked how his "date" went, and he did not enjoy lying to her. He hated ever being duplicitous, but sometimes, with her, he felt he had no choice.

I never lie about big things … well, maybe a few. Mostly it's the insignificant stuff. I should stop. I should tell her the truth from now on.

He'd listened to the sermon as closely as he could but had heard nothing that penetrated his thoughts or his heart. Afterward he'd shaken a few hands, then had hurried home and hung his sport coat on its wooden hanger. He'd packed his two boxes, two duffel-bag-sized suitcases, and two hard plastic cases filled with tools into the back of his truck and had driven away with haste.

He didn't want to see Paula and was glad he didn't run into her. He wasn't sure what he would say, or if at a glance from her, a tilting of her head . . . who knew what might come out of his mouth.

Maybe it's time. Maybe that's what I'm feeling. Everyone I know is married.

When he arrived at the former Central Presbyterian Church in Shadyside, he hauled his gear down to the basement and selected which empty room to use as his bedroom. He picked the one that had probably been a classroom at one time and was closest to the bathroom, then carefully unfolded his expensive cot. As Oliver busied himself with unpacking, Robert walked to and fro, agitated. He sniffed every inch of every surface, ran down the hall to the steps, then back again, his tongue lolling out as if he were overheating.

Oliver placed the dog's water dish on the floor, filled with cold city water, and poured out a full dish of Kibbles 'n Bits. Robert sniffed both, only for a moment, then went back to his nearly frenzied inch-by-inch examinations.

"You don't want water? But you're panting. Are you hot?"

Robert the Dog did not answer.

"I know … a lot of old smells here. I bet there's been thousands of kids in these rooms over the years. Are you smelling the ghosts, Robert? I bet you are."

Oliver's soothing voice did nothing to distract his dog.

Oliver laid Robert's bed on the floor near his cot, a sort of overstuffed half-easy chair that he'd bought last year. Robert had loved it from day one, and Oliver hoped this touch of home would help settle him.

It didn't.

Oliver set up a hot plate on a counter in the next room and next to it placed his electric teakettle, filled with water, and switched it on. He had brought a jar of instant coffee and a box of teabags, thinking that a strong English Earl Grey tea would be better suited for this evening. He busied himself with that task as Robert the Dog continued his sniffings and exploration of the church basement.

When the tea was done, Oliver added a large spoonful of honey— trying to stay away from processed sugar—and headed upstairs. Maybe a breath of fresh night air would settle Robert the Dog. Oliver did not want him to be restless the entire night, and Robert could be that focused and that distracted.

He sat on the front steps, under the port cochere, watching traffic flow past on South Aiken Avenue, sipping his tea, talking softly to Robert. Eventually the dog stopped panting, circled once or twice, and laid down next to him on the stone steps, his eyes still darting back and forth, from the street to Oliver to the sidewalk. Even as pedestrians passed in the darkness, Robert remained still, his eyes following their movements.

"I think this will be a good job for us, Robert. We'll make a good profit. This is a high-profile project as well. I bet Miss Cohen knows a lot of important people. That's a good thing."

Robert snorted softly, then laid his chin on his front paws.

On the opposite wall of the port cochere, on the side that faced the street, was a circle of stone. Inside the circle, the stones were arranged to leave a cross-shaped opening in silhouette. The light of the streetlamp shone through, causing a foot-high cross to be illuminated on the inside wall, just above Oliver's head.

"I know. This is still a church. It's going to be hard to get past that. Like … that cross up there. Will she want it removed? Or covered over? I don't know. But it feels right to be here, doesn't it? Somehow I feel it's meant to be—"

A figure across the street caught his attention—a female, judging by the hair. She stopped, waited, then hurried across the street, waving. Waving toward Oliver.

No one here knows me.

"Oliver-not-Ollie!"

It was Samantha Cohen.

"I wondered if you were going to be here. And you are. How nice," she said as she stopped at the bottom of the stairs.

Robert the Dog looked up but made no attempt to rise.

"Did you walk here?" Oliver asked.

Samantha looked over her shoulder. "Sure. I live down the block."

"Really? I had no idea. I thought you lived … in Mount Lebanon, or Squirrel Hill."

She swept up the steps and sat a few feet away from Oliver. "We used to live there—Squirrel Hill," she said, pointing in the general direction of the real Squirrel Hill, not more than a dozen blocks distant. "When I was young, we lived in a pretty normal, not-so-big house. But when my father got rich, he wanted to move away from all the Jews."

Oliver wanted to ask more but didn't know the acceptable way to ask.

"Yes, we're Jewish, Oliver-not-Ollie. And my father is *very* Jewish. I guess his wanting to move away from Squirrel Hill is all part of the self-loathing that seems to run in our family."

Oliver wanted to ask what that meant too.

"So he bought a great big house down the street—an old Victorian three-story with lots of charm, packed to the gills with authentic architectural details and a million things that always need fixing or repair. Just the thing for a Jewish man who has no interest in any of that stuff—and who doesn't even own a hammer."

"He doesn't own a hammer? Really?"

"That's what I'm telling you."

Oliver nodded. It was the only gesture he felt safe offering.

"Maybe watching the parade of repairmen and contractors got me interested in flipping properties. Maybe," she added, "I wasn't really the corporate type. That's what my father claimed. So I turned to flipping properties."

Oliver seldom wanted to be social, but this evening, with this beautiful, warm, vibrant woman sitting near him, he really wanted to be congenial and polite. "Would you like some tea? I have a teakettle in the basement. And an extra cup."

Samantha looked at him, at his teacup, in his eyes, then at Robert, whose head was now up and whose eyes were on her.

Oliver was struck by how easily he could read her expression.

If she says yes, that means she'll follow me downstairs … to my makeshift bedroom … and she doesn't want to do that. Or maybe she does, but she's telling herself that she doesn't.

That knowledge, that quick interpretation, had never happened to Oliver before. Never. He could have stared at a thousand women's faces and had no idea what any of them thought. Yet somehow he knew what Samantha was considering.

"It's late," he said. "I bet caffeine keeps you up, and all I have is regular tea and regular instant coffee."

He was amazed a second time. He could see the relief wash over her, the tension in her eyes releasing, her shoulders easing.

That really is what she was thinking.

"It does. You're right. But I will take a rain check, okay, Oliver-not-Ollie?"

"Sure. That would be great."

She stood up and dusted off the back of her jeans. Oliver noticed she was wearing high-heeled black boots.

"I just wondered if you were here and if you needed anything. You're all settled then?"

Oliver nodded.

"What's the first thing you'll be working on?"

"Tearing up the carpet. Moving pews. Sort of demolition, but not that much. I've got a Dumpster coming in the morning and three guys who tear stuff up for a living. They're fast and cheap."

Samantha crossed her arms over her chest. "Good. Okay if I stop by in the morning?"

Oliver stood as she stepped to the sidewalk. "Sure. You own the place. You can come anytime."

He could see her smile in the darkness and knew it meant more than just a smile.

"Anytime? You mean that? Really?" Her voice grew deeper and slower, as if she were savoring every word.

Oliver's ability to know what she was thinking quickly disappeared—like the reverse of Pentecost and the disciples not being able to speak in strange languages.

Maybe she's kidding? Maybe she's flirting? Maybe she means exactly what she's saying.

She stepped forward, tousled the fur on Robert's head, then gently touched Oliver's forearm. "I will see you tomorrow. I hope you sleep well. Maybe we can go over the almost-final plans in the morning."

Then she turned and hurried down the street. Oliver sniffed the air. He smelled a hint of tobacco, maybe alcohol, mixed with the same sort of flower or fruit he'd noticed before.

CHAPTER SIX

OLIVER ACTUALLY THOUGHT about what he was going to wear that day. Normally, unlike Taller, he paid little attention to what he put on for work. Whatever was clean, or next in line in the closet or dresser, was what found its way onto his body.

But today he shuffled through the shirts he'd brought until he found one that was the newest and with the fewest stains or tears and without shredded cuffs. The one he selected was only a few months old, and other than a small faded paint stain on the forearm, which he covered by rolling up the sleeves, it appeared new and neat and most presentable.

The jeans he wore were the newest of the four pair that he had brought, along with one pair of khakis that he could wear out to dinner, if he went to a non-fast-food restaurant, that is.

He had gotten up early, just a shade after five, and as soon as he was showered and dressed, he roused Robert the Dog and led him upstairs and outside to a remote area behind the church, an area he'd clean up at the end of the week. He ate the six tiny powdered-sugar doughnuts he'd brought from home as breakfast, knowing it wasn't a properly nutritious meal, with all that refined sugar. But they also contained flour—and flour was healthy, right? He ate fast, quickly disposing of the evidence.

She might come early. Or the Dumpster might be delivered early. They'll need to know where I want it dropped.

Samantha was handling all the permits and other paperwork required by the city for the project. Oliver had given her a copy of his contractor's license. He didn't need a permit to remove carpet and pews and all the rest that would keep him busy for a couple of weeks. That was a good thing, because he wasn't sure where the city hall was, or if Shadyside had its own city hall or used the city of Pittsburgh's department of building codes.

He set his coffee cup down on a window ledge, just under the stained-glass window illustrating Jesus, the Good Shepherd, holding a lamb. He adjusted his carpenter's belt, the hammer on one side, a pry bar on the other, with a tape measure, a screwdriver, and a pair of vise grips in their proper places.

The beginning of a project could be intimidating.

Where do I start? What do I do first?

For the most typical additions, it was easy: clear the ground, dig for the footings, get the concrete poured, start with the framing.

But in this old church, the first move was not quite as simple.

The pews come off first. But do I dismantle them? They're historic, antique, and probably valuable. Do I try and store them outside under a tarp or something? Might be a city rule against it. Will they come apart without being damaged? And where do I stack the parts? Downstairs? There's a ton of space, but that's a lot of hauling stuff up and down. Or do we just slide them back and forth and work around them? A bigger pain—but maybe it would be easier.

Robert the Dog circled the old sanctuary several times. Then, after apparently finding the right spot to lie down, he did exactly that in a corner of the raised platform, almost against the back wall. It was underneath the spot where a cross had once hung, the space lit by the round window.

Oliver knelt by the first pew. It had been installed over the carpet.

Not the right way to do it. Should have been attached directly to the floor, and the carpet cut around it.

He nudged his screwdriver at the one edge. The screw came up easily. In less than five minutes, he had one pew unsecured and pushed it toward the center aisle.

"These are heavy. Probably be best off working around them, instead of hauling them somewhere."

Robert opened one eye, listening as Oliver talked to himself.

Then there was the loud *beep-beep-beep* of a truck backing up. Oliver
hurried out to meet the Dumpster delivery; Robert tagged along.

"Right here," Oliver yelled out to the driver, indicating that the
Dumpster should be rolled off at the bottom of the steps, just under the
port cochere outside the main door. Hauling rolls of old, dusty carpet over
a longer distance than necessary was not fun.

The metal container screeched and howled as it was levered off the
truck, the driver careful to keep the bottom entirely on the stone drive. He
edged the truck away, switched it off, and jumped from the cab, carrying
a clipboard.

"Sign here, and here, and here," he said, pointing at the form with a
chewed-on pen.

Without taking his gloves off, Oliver braced the clipboard on a but-
tress of the port cochere and signed.

"You tearing the church down?" the driver asked. "Seems too pretty
for that."

His work shirt featured the name *NED*, stitched above the left breast
pocket of the stained garment.

"No. Renovating. It's not a church any longer. The last congregation
got too big and moved."

"Really? A church getting too big? That's a new one. Huh. A church
getting too big."

Oliver wasn't the sort of person who was aggressive about his faith. If
someone really wanted to know what he believed, and expressed a sincere
interest a couple of times, then Oliver might share. But not like this. Not
off the cuff and on the street. To Oliver, this place—the workplace—wasn't
the place to talk about Jesus and his beliefs.

But this time he felt he had to say something. "It happens," he replied,
handing the clipboard back to Ned. "Churches do grow."

Ned harrumphed again in reply, then his face brightened. "Maybe
it's because I haul Dumpsters for a living. Most of the time, when I show
up, a place is getting ready to be torn down or rehabbed. I don't do new
construction all that often. Too muddy."

"Muddy?"

"Yeah, when they build new stuff, it's in a field or something and there's no roads. My truck doesn't like mud and no roads. And around here, it's mostly old stuff getting torn down." Ned tossed his clipboard into the cab. "You got two weeks on this one, unless you fill it quicker. City says two weeks is the most one Dumpster can sit outside. Worried about rats or something. Like rats are going to eat carpet."

"I'll call if we fill it early."

Ned climbed into the truck. "Who's the owner? I mean, who's doing the rehab or whatever here? Not that it matters to me. Just curious."

Oliver had to think for a second. *Did she have a company name?* "Oh ... yeah. She calls it the 2C Group," he said, happy to have remembered the name.

"2C? Like Samantha Cohen? She bought this place?"

Oliver tried to hide his surprise that Ned the Dumpster Guy knew who Samantha was. "Yes, that's her name. Samantha Cohen."

Ned leered back at Oliver as he started his truck. "She's a wild one, I hear tell. I did all her Dumpsters on a project over on Mount Washington. She's really hot. I saw her there a couple of times. The contractor for that job made out like a bandit, from what I hear, and not just in the cash-ola department, if you know what I mean."

"What?"

"You know, the owner, that Cohen lady, she paid the guy in more than just cash."

Oliver felt as if he'd been slapped, or had cold water thrown in his face, or both.

More like both.

"I ... don't know anything about that," he said in reply.

"Hey," Ned called back as he snagged the truck into first gear, "you let me know if it's true, eh? Or ask her if she's interested in dating a Dumpster guy, okay?"

Oliver stood there, in the quiet of the morning, holding a yellow copy of the Dumpster order in his left hand. As he stared after the truck that wheezed south on Aiken Avenue, he wondered what in the world he should believe.

The Pratt brothers arrived at 9:00 a.m., just as Oliver had requested, armed with sawzalls, pry bars, sledgehammers, and smiles.

"I love my work," said one of the brothers, holding a sledgehammer like a rock musician cradling his favorite guitar.

Oliver couldn't keep their names straight and wasn't sure if he even knew their first names, but none of the brothers seemed to mind in the slightest just being called "Pratt."

The three of them followed Oliver inside, bustling about, tapping at pews, knocking on old plaster walls with their knuckles, running their hands over the thick stone piers, thumping the floor with the heels of their work boots. Robert the Dog hurried from his perch and greeted each brother separately, coming to the third, and possibly the oldest, Pratt brother, then sitting with an anticipatory grin. This Pratt, the elder, grinned down at Robert, reached into his jeans pocket, and pulled out a thickness of rawhide, looking like it may have been homemade.

The Pratt brothers were like that.

Robert took his treat and trotted down the middle aisle back to his spot on the platform.

"Good dog you got there, Ollie," said the possibly senior Pratt. "Remembered that I gave him treats from the last time."

Oliver didn't mind that the Pratts all called him Ollie, since none of them minded being called Pratt.

"So whadda we got here? Pretty fancy place, eh? You lookin' for a total bust-up? Pews goin'? Any walls knocked down? Holes in floors? Whadda we gonna tear out this time?"

Oliver laid out his plans: carpets pulled up, pews moved, five walls downstairs taken down—none of them bearing walls—some badly constructed built-in bookcases in the former pastor's office removed, first-floor bathrooms gutted, every extraneous piece of furniture taken out.

The senior Pratt grinned. "This looks like a lot of fun."

One of the other Pratt brothers spoke up. "This bein' a church and all—we allowed to swear?"

"Or smoke?" the other added. "If I can't swear, I'll need to smoke. Maybe we can't do that in here. Feels like we can't, at any rate—what with all the Jesuses," he said, pointing at the windows.

"It's not a church anymore," Oliver said. "They deconsecrated it ... or it was decommissioned—whatever it is that preachers do with old church buildings to make them no longer a church. So I'm not going to monitor your language. But take the cigarettes outside. The place doesn't have sprinklers yet, and I don't want to see it go up in flames. Okay?"

Even before he was finished, two of the Pratt brothers had begun to tackle dismounting a pew, the other following closely behind, ready to drag it away once his brothers were finished. In less than an hour, one side of the church stood pewless, and the pews were carefully stacked on one another at the front of the church. They were about to start on the other side when Robert the Dog barked, just once, then immediately returned to his chewing.

"Oliver ... I brought breakfast."

The three Pratt brothers stopped and stared, a hard stare, in triplicate. Samantha stood in the doorway, holding up a large brown bag and carrying a cardboard container with a bevy of takeout cups anchored in the holder's openings.

"I hope I'm not interrupting anything," she said after a long moment of silence. "Bagels, *schmears*, *sufganiot*, Danish, coffee, and some lox, if anyone here likes lox. I like it, so if none of you like smoked salmon, I'll treat myself."

The Pratt brothers, nearly in unison, dropped every tool they were carrying and hurried toward Samantha as if they hadn't eaten or seen a very attractive woman in some time—both statements probably more true than false.

"And I brought some candles," Samantha added. "They're great for burning away the rather musty smell in here. I love candles."

Oliver walked over to the group, telling himself he was going to act natural, as if he'd heard nothing about what had happened in Mount Washington. Then he reminded himself that he really *didn't* know what had happened. Maybe Ned was a loony. Perhaps there had been no relationship at all between Miss Cohen and some sleazy contractor who should have known better than to get involved with a client, no matter how attractive she was.

"What's a suf ... sufgon—"

"*Sufganiot*," Samantha answered. "Jelly doughnut. They're delicious."

"And what's a *schmear*?" asked the senior Pratt brother, obviously posing the question because his two brothers had no idea what it was either.

Samantha laughed and leaned her head back, baring her throat. It was apparent what all four men were looking at—at least while Samantha was not looking at them.

"It's not a 'what.' Well, maybe it is. My father says it's an old Yiddish word—*shmirn*—which means 'to smear.' You take cream cheese and maybe add fruit or nuts or seasonings, like onions or garlic. That's what you *schmear*."

One of the younger Pratt brothers replied, "Sort of like peanut butter?"

Samantha touched his forearm, a gesture all the men clearly noticed. "Yes, something like peanut butter. Now, who wants to try lox—smoked salmon?"

All three Pratt brothers shook their heads. From their expressions, it was obvious none were the least bit partial to any form of disguised fish, especially at breakfast.

"Oliver? Want to try it? It's really good. It's from Kazansky's. My father never eats it but says it's the best in the city. Try some on a bagel?"

A minute later Oliver was chewing the lox and bagel thoughtfully. "Tastes like smoked fish."

"Do you like it?"

Oliver would have shrugged but remembered his mother berating him for responding to questions with a shrug. Instead he replied, "Yes, I do. I may not eat it for breakfast from now on, but it's pretty good."

Samantha appeared very pleased with herself.

The three Pratt bothers continued to stare at her—not quite as hard now, but still with obvious delighted fascination.

———

Taller Barnett arrived four days later, on Friday, in the morning, following the Pratt brothers as they clambered inside. He whistled loudly when he entered, shaking his head, staring at the stained glass.

"This is one heck of a building, big brother," Taller said. "Much more church than I had imagined. Like you're knocking down Notre Dame to the studs."

Oliver brushed the wisps of plaster dust from his forehead. "It's not that fancy," he said in his defense.

"It is too. You know it is. So don't let Ma come here. Just seeing the stained-glass windows will throw her into a religious frenzy. She'll start throwing Bibles around, I bet, and calling for hellfire and brimstone to rain on you, you sacrilegious heathen."

At the words *hellfire and brimstone* the two younger Pratt brothers stopped work and looked around, as if they were expecting the celestial pounding to start at any minute.

Taller had worked with the Pratt brothers before, so he laughed, held up his hands, and called to them, "I'm just joking. There's no brimstone forecast for this week. And hellfire has been rescheduled too."

They hesitated a moment, then reluctantly started knocking down an unnecessary knee-wall in the narthex.

Taller was dressed for work: jeans, fitted perfectly and worn in the most attractive way, spotless white T-shirt, carpenter's belt. He had not always shown up for work dressed for it, or on time, or both. Oliver understood his brother's gifts, but punctuality and consistency were far down on his list of attributes.

Oliver unrolled the final plans Samantha had brought the day before. Part of the basement would be gutted and a new wall installed around the kitchen area, so they would have to install new, up-to-code sanitary walls. The rest of the space, the former Fellowship Hall, would be used for storage. Upstairs, the pastor's study would be converted into a private dining area, separated by French doors, which required some fancy framework. There would be a long bar on one side of the main room, seating and tables spread around the rest, and comfortable sofas and chairs would fill the area that had been the pastor's platform. To get to the kitchen, two stairways had been drawn in on the plan, with new railings and steps. Both would require a fair degree of carpentry finesse to accomplish.

Taller traced the thin lines on the blueprint with his finger, almost delicately, almost dancing on the surface of the paper, looking up every so often to see what was drawn and how it matched the reality of the space. After five minutes of inspection, he whistled, a low, long sound of admiration.

"This is going to be one heck of a restaurant, Ollie. This space is magnificent. If the food is as good as the atmosphere, the owner is going to make bushels of money."

Oliver nodded.

"You bid enough on the job? You going to make enough to pay me, as well as the Pratt brothers?"

"I bid enough. You'll get paid. And, by the way, when have I not paid you?" Oliver said, his tone almost hurt.

Taller adjusted his work belt. "Ollie, you need to lighten up. I was joking. You've always paid me. See, that's the funny part. I intimated you were a deadbeat employer when you haven't been. See … humor. Funny stuff. Okay?"

Oliver would have shaken his head—not in anger, not in disgust, but more in amusement. But that's what his mother always did when she didn't understand something and wanted to show her disdain for not understanding. So he did nothing, which he felt was always better than doing something he might later regret.

"What do you want me to start on, Ollie? Laying out the wall for the kitchen?"

"No. Not yet. But you can box in the steel beams downstairs. They were all hidden in the walls, and we'll have to have them covered since they'll be storing canned goods and food down there. Then you can start the prep for the new walls."

"You bring a ladder?"

"It's down there, along with my miter saw. And the Pratt brothers hauled down most of the wood you'll need."

"Okay, Ollie, I'm officially on the clock."

Oliver did not laugh.

"It was supposed to be funny, Ollie. Like I'm punching in at a factory. You know … since I've never punched in before."

Before Oliver could answer, he heard the front door bang open, and a woman's voice call out, "Breakfast, everyone."

Every day Oliver had been on the job, Samantha Cohen had arrived at the same time in the morning, always carrying a bag of Jewish jelly dough-nuts and Danish and bagels and coffee. She stopped bringing lox after the first day, since only Oliver nibbled at it, and since she explained that it was too rich to eat every day.

The Pratt brothers had already been Pavlov-conditioned, dropping tools in midswing and hurrying to her side, digging through the bags, trying to find whatever it was that was their favorite of the day. Yesterday it had been cheese Danish, a variety of food not one of the three brothers had ever eaten. But after tasting it the day before, they had all decided it was their new most favorite taste, and nearly got into a fistfight when she had brought only two with her.

Today she brought five cheese Danish and an assortment of bagels, with just maple-walnut cream cheese, and a holder filled with five cups of coffee.

Samantha handed out the coffees, then reached into her bag and extracted a deep-yellow bagel. "It's an egg bagel—the only kind worth eat-ing," she explained as she schmeared it with cream cheese.

Taller looked at his brother and asked in a quiet voice, "She's the owner?"

"Yes," Oliver said. "And don't do anything to screw up this job, okay?" While his tone was soft, his intentions were hard and brittle.

Taller waited and stared and did not reply.

"Oliver? Are you coming?" Samantha called out.

Oliver glared at his brother for a moment, then walked down the middle aisle of the church (or where the middle aisle had been) to greet the owner. "Samantha Cohen, this is Tolliver Barnett, my brother. Everyone calls him Taller … because he's taller than me."

Taller gave the smile he reserved for "the ladies" and held out his hand. "So nice to meet you, Miss Cohen."

Samantha let him take her hand. When he held it a few seconds longer than was appropriate, she glanced down.

Oliver watched her face, hoping his ability to read her thoughts would return. It didn't.

"This is such a beautiful building," Taller said to Samantha. "I was telling Ollie the interior is simply magnificent. And your plans … very nicely done."

Samantha offered him a polite smile. "Thank you, Taller. Would you like a bagel and coffee? I like bringing food … because … well, it's what we Jewish folk do when we come visiting. Have to bring a cake or *something* when coming to dinner, and enough for twice as many people than are in attendance. Food makes my presence something work crews look forward to. That way I can easily keep track of the daily progress."

Oliver watched Taller's face. It was obvious his brother's nods and grins were all part of his practiced, successful repertoire. Oliver knew that, any minute now, Taller would touch Samantha's arm lightly—nothing invasive, just a light touch, finger to skin. Oliver had seen him do it dozens of times, and what women then did was telling: They might blush, giggle, look down at his hand, smile back at him, or all of the above, inviting him and encouraging him, even in an unconscious way, to be bolder, to extend the touch longer and move higher up the arm next time.

Watching Taller perform this calculated move with Samantha made Oliver mad but still not angry enough to say anything. *What am I going to do? Punch him? Tell him to get his hands off her? Like I have a claim? I don't.*

Samantha didn't react at all. It was as if she didn't feel his finger against her bare arm. She kept on talking without hesitation. She didn't blush, toy with her hair, and tilt her neck like so many other women did.

Taller simply looked confused. Not many women thwarted his approach.

"Well, Oliver," Samantha said as she stepped away from Taller and toward him. "Everything still on schedule? Demolition almost finished?"

The Pratt brothers, at the words *almost finished*, frowned in unison, as if being told they could no longer play at a favorite playground.

"We're on schedule. Nearly everything that is coming out is out. Taller is here to start on some of the construction downstairs. We'll box in the beams today."

"That's great, Oliver." She reached out and gently squeezed his upper arm.

For just a second, Oliver thought he could read her eyes—that she'd done it just so Taller could see her.

She leaned in a few inches closer to Oliver, toward his ear, like she was about to whisper a secret and said, "I'm out of town this weekend.

My cousin in New York—we're celebrating his bar mitzvah, a big family affair at the Ritz-Carlton. You've got everything under control, then, right? No big design decisions until next week?" Her voice grew husky, deep, and throaty. "And you know I need to be here for those sorts of decisions, right, Oliver? You'll wait for me to return before deciding anything important?"

"We'll be fine until you get back, Miss Cohen. Have a good time."

Oliver would have been happy if he'd been able to preserve the way she looked at him before she turned and left: a look of longing is what Oliver interpreted it to be.

Work continued, and the Pratt brothers hauled nearly fifty contractor garbage bags up the narrow basement stairs and outside to the almost-full Dumpster. Taller waited a long time that morning before he came to Oliver's side.

"Hey ... about your boss ..."

Oliver looked up from measuring the steps of the platform. "What about her?"

Taller offered a knowing grin with a hint of leer tossed in. "Well, for one, she's Jewish. Are you planning to kill Ma? You have the hots for a Jew?"

"What do you mean? She owns the place. She's the boss. I'm nice to her. That's all there is."

Taller looked down at Ollie. "Yeah. Sure. That's all it is."

"She's a friendly person, and I like her ... as a person. She's the boss. That's all there is."

Taller pursed his lips and shook his head, just like their mother would do. "Sure. That's all there is."

At that moment, Oliver thought about his secret, the secret only he and his mother shared. He wasn't sure why it came to his thoughts when he was angry, but it did. He realized how badly he wanted to yell it out to his smug younger brother. But he didn't.

Taller undid his carpenter's belt and hung it on a spike nailed into a bare wood frame in what used to be the church narthex. He glanced at his watch: 5:45—much later than he normally left a jobsite. What made this evening more unusual was that the Pratt brothers were still on the job well past their promptly-at-five-in-the-afternoon quitting time. Taller waved at them, called out for them to have a good weekend, then slipped out the large double front doors. The heavy doors banged shut, the sound reverberating through the jumbled sanctuary and echoing in the large open space.

The Pratt brothers, in unison, stared at the closed door for a moment. Then the two younger brothers turned to the eldest Pratt brother—the one who looked oldest, with gray flecks in his very short, dark hair and a clutch of wrinkles at the corners of his eyes—and stared. One of them said through clenched teeth, "Go on. Ask him. Now."

The oldest Pratt brother stood up with a dramatic sigh, obviously not accustomed to sighing because it sounded made-up, as if he were play-acting the father in a badly timed high-school production of *Death of a Salesman*. Yet the sigh was out there, and to his brothers, it committed him to action.

He dusted off his jeans, and the dirt that was easily removed came off in a small cloud. The rest of the dirt, permanent and solid, might not come out even with repeated washings. He smoothed his hair (what there was of it) and walked slowly toward Oliver, who was leaning over a pair of sawhorses that held a four-by-four sheet of plywood, onto which the plans for the ex-church had been stapled.

"Ollie," the oldest Pratt brother said, as if not wanting to scare Oliver, sounding his name almost as an apology, "do you think I might have a min-ute … since it's after quittin' time and you're not payin' us now, because I don't want you to think we're wastin' your time or anything."

"Sure," Oliver said. "If you're asking for your pay for this last week, I can write the check now, but I'll have to ask you to hold it until Monday. I'll have to move cash around and if I don't get to the bank early on Saturday, the check could bounce and I don't want that to happen."

The eldest Pratt waved his hand as if he were trying to erase an invisible blackboard that hung between them. "No, no, that's okay. I mean, you could write the check, but it's okay that we wait. Normally we wait a week or two to get the last payment on a job, so waitin' is okay."

Neither spoke, then the oldest Pratt brother's face changed as if he'd just realized that he had asked a question and it was his turn to speak.

"I wanted to ask … I don't know how to phrase this exactly. I'm not real good with words."

Oliver leaned back against his makeshift table, not wanting to put too much weight on it.

"What is it?"

The oldest Pratt brother stared at the floor in front of him. Oliver could see he was avoiding eye contact.

"This is a nice job. We think this is a real nice job. This is one honest job."

"And you three have done great work," Oliver replied. "There's not much more to tear out, so I can't offer you more work."

"That's what I want to talk to you about," the older Pratt brother said, now looking up, catching Oliver's eyes for a short moment. "More work. Here. Like on this job."

"But the demolition is done," Oliver said, confused. "At least all the big stuff. If there is any more, Taller or I can handle it. Or the carpentry crew can."

"I'm not talkin' about demolition," the oldest Pratt said. "I know we're done with that."

Oliver waited. "Then what? I won't be lookin' at a new project for a while. I'll keep you in mind if we need demo work, for sure."

The eldest Pratt looked up. Oliver, in one of his unexpected flashes of intuition, saw the sadness and regret and pain in the man's eyes. The oldest Pratt's hands were folded over the top of one another, like a penitent asking for absolution and forgiveness—expecting none, yet still requesting.

"I know you only think we tear stuff down. For the past five years, that's all we've done."

Oliver knew there was more.

"Like that's all we could do. No. It's not just what we could do. It's all that we were allowed to do."

"Allowed to do? I don't understand."

The oldest Pratt lowered his head and his voice, as if he did not want his brothers to hear his confession. "Demolition work … well, no one cares if you make a few mistakes. You get paid to break things, tear things apart. When the project starts, the finish guys will cover up the mistakes. Isn't that what everyone says? The framers say that the rockers will cover up a crooked wall with sheetrock, or the tile guy will square out a bad wall in the bathroom. The last guy on the job will make everything look good. That's what they say, right?"

Oliver nodded.

"We used to be the finish guys. We used to make everything right— make everything look great. Customers loved us. All three of us are really good carpenters. Trade-school diplomas, apprenticeships, union tests, all of that."

Oliver was stunned. "Then what are you doing demo work for? If you're really that good with wood and finish carpentry?"

The eldest Pratt turned and looked at his brothers, then back at Oliver. "We're not from Pennsylvania. You probably knew that from the way we talk and all that. We were born and raised in Ohio. Our father was a contractor, and we took over his business. A good life for all of us. But we were immature and really stupid. You know how it is—you get some money, and you're young and free and start makin' mistakes and doin' dumb stuff." The eldest Pratt took a deep breath. "Maybe you don't know how that is. But we do."

Oliver folded his arms over his chest, then unfolded them and let them fall at his side since he'd once read that folding your arms over your chest was the ultimate body-language sign for "I don't want to listen to you anymore," and that's not what he wanted to show.

The elder Pratt let out a deep sigh. "Two of us have been in prison, Ollie. It was a long time ago, and we tried to make amends, but no one trusted us anymore—at least not back home in Ohio. So we moved to Pennsylvania and started doin' demo work. I didn't want to risk it, bein' contractors again, bein' disappointed so badly."

"Prison? Two of you?" Oliver asked.

"Yeah. I'm not sayin' which two, 'cause then you'll treat us different."

"No ... I wouldn't."

The eldest Pratt shrugged. "Maybe not. But maybe you would. You're a real nice guy, Ollie. Nicer and more honest than most. That's why we want to work on this job with you. You're an ethical person. You keep your word. You could have brought in some illegals to do what we did here for cheap and pay them cash. I know a lot of contractors do that."

Oliver held open his hands. "You can get into big trouble if you do that."

"Yeah, and who comes in and checks for green cards? On a job like this? Nobody. You could have done that. You didn't. You've always been real fair to us, when we worked for you before."

Oliver looked down, at the edge of embarrassment. He'd never once been congratulated for this sort of decision and was unsure how to respond.

"So, would you consider havin' us work as your carpentry team on this one, Ollie? Alongside your brother? I see what you're goin' to be doin' here—this project—and I get so anxious ... or jealous. I want to do stuff like this again. Build up and not knock down. I can almost taste it. I want to use my hands for good. It would ... this would be a big deal for us. A really big deal."

Oliver hoped his expression said, "I'm thinking," and not, "Hire former convicts?" He started to speak once, then stopped, then started again, and stopped again, not sure what question to ask.

"You want to know what for?" the eldest Pratt said softly. "Why two of us were in prison and all that?"

Oliver nodded. "Yes. I'm not sure if it makes a difference or not, but I guess I need to know."

"One was for stealin' ... from a homeowner. Jewelry. Some cash out of a safe. Not much, but enough to get arrested." He shook his head. "Stupid."

Oliver waited.

"The other was for manslaughter. Ten years, reduced down to seven, and five served."

Oliver wasn't certain what manslaughter meant, exactly, other than someone winding up dead. He wasn't sure of the legal definition, how it was different than murder, and how guilty a person was who was convicted of manslaughter, and if they had to get counseling or something for that, and whether or not they could still be bonded, even though most clients never asked if every worker was bonded. Miss Cohen had not asked, either.

"Manslaughter?"

The eldest Pratt nodded. "I know. This is sort of a surprise. I don't want you to answer now. But I'm just askin' you to think about it. And … well, we really want to work with you. Especially here. Somethin' about workin' in a church makes it all feel right, somehow. At least, this church makes me feel right. Maybe it's the windows—and the big old stone walls and the rest. All the goodness in here. You go to church, don't you?"

"I do," Oliver replied.

"Well—think about it," the elder Pratt said softly. "It's okay if you say no. We'll understand." Silence filled the church until the eldest Pratt bobbed his head. "Just mull it over. We'll come back on Monday to get the rest of our tools. My brother drove today 'cause my truck is in the shop, so we all came in his wife's itty-bitty car."

Oliver watched as the three Pratt brothers picked up their lunchboxes and left the church without saying another word.

Now what's my weekend going to be like? Thinking about ex-convicts …

CHAPTER SEVEN

THE ROBE IN THE CLOSET at the New York Ritz-Carlton was nowhere near as plush or as well tailored as the robe from the Ritz-Carlton in Maui that Samantha had at home. She decided that the owners of the New York Ritz had bought economy—something no one ever expected when they stayed at a Ritz-Carlton hotel—and the disappointment saddened her more than it should have.

Samantha did not like to travel. She liked being *at* places, but she hated getting *to* places. New York was on the top of her list for places she despised getting to and was not all that fond of actually being there. Sure, there were a great many wonderful sites to visit, awesome shopping and fabulous restaurants, exciting theater, but on this trip, Samantha felt no thrill, no tingling from anticipated experiences.

Her father was off meeting a business associate—or that's what he told her. She didn't think he did much business in New York, but he did know a great many people and perhaps there was someone he had a legitimate reason to meet. Or he could have arranged a meeting with a paid "escort." That's what Samantha had first thought, then chastised herself for thinking such bad thoughts about her father.

She loved her father. She knew he was a good man, or a mostly good man. But he was a man, after all, and she couldn't fault him for still having needs. It had been twenty years since her mother's too-early death and that many years was a long time to mourn alone.

Samantha's relatives lived on Long Island and would not arrive in Manhattan until the following afternoon. She and her father had arrived too late this evening for arranging a dinner way out on the other island, so now with her father gone for the night, she was on her own.

In the past, being alone away from home had caused some anxiety. But as she grew older, being by herself—even in a big city or a strange city—was nothing that she couldn't handle.

She sat at the edge of the bed, in her not-quite-as-fluffy-as-she-was-used-to robe, with the television remote in her hand, flipping through the channels. At least the hotel management had not skimped on the cable offerings; there appeared to be several hundred different channels, as well as several hundred movies that could be rented at the touch of the button, and the obligatory selection of "adult" entertainment. Maybe that's what her father was doing—watching dirty movies by himself in his hotel room. Samantha almost laughed at the thought, then was angry she wasn't more upset at the image.

She flipped past sporting events and a plethora of religious talk shows, complete with hosts sporting bad hair and copious makeup, teary-eyed, pleading for money—at least that's how Samantha viewed them. She flipped past old movies with far-from-believable dialogue and accents, new movies with depressing stories, crass situation comedies, horrid reality shows, and a dozen all-news-all-the-time networks where groups of talking heads competed with each other to see who could shout the loudest and drown out whatever opposition they faced. She stopped at an old black-and-white movie with Steve McQueen as a bomber pilot in World War II. And as she watched, she reached over to the nightstand, took out the room-service menu, and dialed the number. She ordered the "Surf and Turf"—a petite New York strip steak, medium rare, split lobster tail with drawn butter, with a baked potato, loaded with whatever it was they had, a salad with the house dressing, a piece of New York–style cheesecake with strawberries, and a carafe of coffee with cream.

I should go out. It is New York after all ... a tad more cosmopolitan than Pittsburgh, that's for sure. But I don't want to dress and take a cab and all that. And I really have a taste for steak and lobster, although I won't tell Daddy I ate shellfish.

The movie was interrupted by a shouted commercial for some miracle cleaner being sold by a man with a horrid English accent and offered only on TV and not in stores, as if that made the product more valuable, effective, and tantalizing.

She walked to the window, adjusting her robe more tightly around her waist even though she was on the nineteenth floor looking out over Central Park and was certain no one could see her. The streetlights glistened through the first buds of leaves on the trees as cabs and cars jockeyed for position on the street below. She was so high up and well insulated that the angry traffic was only a whisper to her.

She stared up at the darkness, or as dark as the New York sky gets, wondering what Oliver had accomplished today on her project. She wondered if he planned to stay there, in the church basement, over the weekend. She'd told him that he could, that she would not mind, even if she herself would find it very creepy, sleeping alone in a big, empty old church basement like that. But having a caretaker would be a good thing. What he didn't know is that she would pay him for the time he spent there, protecting her investment.

She wondered if Robert the Dog liked being in the city, where noises were bigger and lasted later into the evening. She wondered if she should call Oliver, just to check on things.

She grabbed her purse and took out her cell phone. The little clock in the corner of the phone's face read 6:35.

"Six-thirtyish. Too late to call him?"

She scrolled down the list of phone numbers saved in her contact list until she came to Oliver's name. She placed her finger on the *Send* button, then hesitated.

No. I shouldn't call him. Not tonight. Mally was right. If I get involved with him, his work suffers. And I don't want a repeat of the Mount Washington fiasco. Even if the physical part of the deal was fabulous.

She paced the room, stopping to watch the movie, carefully taking in the scene where a wounded Steve McQueen fought against the vibrating airplane controls in a heroic effort to bring his badly damaged bomber back to England, only to die in a huge, fiery explosion as the plane lost altitude and crashed headlong into the White Cliffs of Dover.

As the debris rained down to the sea below, Samantha found herself weeping. Tears rained down her face and great sobs tightened her chest, as if she and Steve McQueen were fighting the same battle—the same desperate attempt to bring in a wounded plane before spiraling to earth to face a horrible, preordained fate.

And as she cried, berating herself for being so emotional over something so stupid as an old movie, a tap sounded and a voice with a foreign accent called out, "Room service." She wiped her face on her robe and headed to the door.

The Pratt brothers stuffed themselves into the decade-old compact car with the youngest Pratt, Steven, in the driver's seat. He was not the most intuitive driver and clutched at the steering wheel, his hands at the ten-and-two position, with a white-knuckle grip. He had to drive, he claimed, for he was the only Pratt listed on the car's insurance policy, other than his wife; "And none of you look anything like my wife, so I have to," he'd said.

Gene, the middle Pratt brother, the most nervous, asked the question. "So did Oliver say anything that might mean we'll get the job?"

"He didn't say anything like that," the eldest, Henry, replied. "But he didn't say no, either. Most people say no right away. Prison gets them nervous, and when manslaughter comes up—well, that sends them over the edge."

Steven called out, "But it wasn't my fault. Everyone knows that."

"Even the judge knew it. It was accidental, but the fix was in for a manslaughter charge," Gene added.

"Doesn't matter," Henry replied. "No one cares. Besides, we all said we're not goin' to talk about that anymore. It's ancient history. Either he'll give us the job or he won't. And if he doesn't, we'll keep doin' what we're doin', okay?"

The other two Pratt brothers remained silent.

Henry did not speak for several miles. *It's not that this job is so much different than all the other jobs we didn't get. But it's time to start buildin' things again. A man can only do so much tearin' down. It's time. We paid our debts. We did wrong, and now it's time for us to do what we do best again, for sure.*

"They goin' to sell beer and stuff at that church restaurant? I mean, isn't that against the Bible?" Steven asked.

"Would be if it were still a church," Gene replied. "I bet there are churches out there that allow for drinkin', even though they're still a church now. I heard some churches have kegs of beer for their picnics and stuff."

"That so?" Steven replied. "Why don't we go to a church like that, then?"

Gene shrugged. "I dunno. I guess I never could tell what churches serve beer from the outside. I mean, I heard people talkin' about a church like that, but I never thought of goin' to church just for the beer."

Henry stared out the window. *Workin' in a church ... maybe we should start goin' to church again. It's been a long time. Maybe here, where people don't know about our pasts, after all the years that have gone by, it's time again to start. Oliver goes to church, and he's an okay sort of guy.*

Henry rolled the window down a few inches, letting the air flow against the side of his face. *Maybe we'll do that. Maybe goin' to church is a test or somethin' ... like if we go, we'll get the job. And workin' in that church feels different somehow. It's makin' us more honest. Maybe we should start goin' to church to prove somethin' to Oliver.*

He took a deep breath. *I don't think it works like that. But still ... it wouldn't hurt to go.*

Steven interrupted his thoughts. "How do you decide on a church to go to? There are a lot of churches out there. How do you find the good ones?"

Gene spoke up. "Maybe you get some sort of sign when you're ready. Like somebody comes and tells you about it. God works that way, don't He? Like in all those movies?"

The eldest brother snorted. "Naw. It don't work that way. No one is goin' to walk in off the street and tell you about God and all that. Don't work that way at all."

Oliver pulled into his driveway a few minutes past seven that Friday night. He felt as if it had been a long week. The first week on a new job often felt the most overwhelming. He was not sure why, just that it was. Robert the Dog leapt from the open window when the truck was at a complete stop. He ran in circles around the small backyard, sniffing and wuffling as he went, making sure this was indeed the same backyard he had left five days prior.

From the looks of his mother's house, she was gone, the windows all dark, the shades all pulled. Oliver grabbed his duffel bag, now filled with dirty clothes, and dragged it up his stairs.

It'll be nice to have a home-cooked meal for a change.

Taped on the glass of his front door fluttered an entire page from a yellow legal tablet. It was not a note from his mother—of that he was sure. She reused old envelopes and paper bags and grocery store receipts to leave notes, never wasting an entire sheet of paper for something as short as a note. That the note was not from his mother provided a visceral sense of relief.

He whistled for Robert, who immediately tore up the steps, his nails clacking like castanets on the wood. He unlocked the door and tossed his duffel bag inside. Robert tore around the apartment, making sure everything was as he had left it. Oliver retrieved the note from the door and switched on the recessed lights by the entryway.

The note was written in pencil, with great swoopy curves to the letters. He glanced at the bottom before he read a word.

It was signed *Paula* and the *P* was nearly four lines high, with a spiral flourish on the top left of the letter, like a feminine John Hancock signature on the *Declaration of Independence*.

He looked back to the top. She had written *Friday afternoon* on the right-hand side of the paper.

The note read:

Dear Oliver,

Your mother said you would be home this afternoon. My mother has offered to babysit for Bridget tonight, which leaves me free for the first time in months. I know this is being very forward (your mother said it was okay and that you wouldn't mind), but let's go out tonight—dinner, a movie?

Some drinks afterward … and then, who knows what? What do you say? Call me as soon as you get in. I'll be waiting.

(Your mother said you would call me back and let me know, because you're a "good boy.") ☺

I'll be waiting.

Yours,

Paula

Robert the Dog was nosing his water dish along the kitchen floor. He did that when his bowls were empty. Oliver put the note on the counter, ran the water till it got cold, filled the dog bowl, and opened the pantry door and pulled out a half-filled bag of Kibbles—not the off-brand from the warehouse store, but the good brand advertised on TV as recommended by vets. Robert seemed to like the cheap brand better, but Oliver thought it might be loaded with all sorts of chemicals. So in order to keep the peace between him and Robert concerning diet and nutrition, he mixed it half and half, the good with the bad—or, more exactly, the expensive Kibbles with much-less-expensive "kibbles."

Robert set to both bowls with gusto, as if the trip back from Shadyside had left him famished and dehydrated.

As Oliver kicked off his shoes, the phone rang. He knew he should have bought caller ID, but he hadn't. It might be Samantha. So he picked up the phone.

"I saw your truck pull up. Did you get my note?" Paula asked, her voice perky.

Oliver shut his eyes. *So much for my home-cooked meal.* He didn't want to go out but felt out of options even before this conversation started. "I did. I just got in."

"I know that, silly. I saw your truck, remember? I wanted to catch you before you got naked and jumped in the shower or something."

Oliver had planned on doing exactly that. The shower in the basement of the old Presbyterian church in Shadyside didn't exactly meet spa-level qualities in terms of water pressure, ambience, and cleanliness. But the fact that Paula mentioned showering, without clothes, made him feel awkward because of the intimacy it suggested.

Awkward and a bit ... peculiar. He felt a prickling inside him—a feeling not unpleasant, but more unplanned and unexpected.

"Well, I do need to get cleaned up."

"I know. But men don't take long, do they? I mean, getting ready—you don't take long, do you?"

Oliver sensed she had layered her words with a secondary meaning ... then wondered if it might be just innocent chatter. Paula could chatter on, seemingly, without effort. That was so far beyond his abilities—like dunking a basketball or running a marathon.

"Since you don't take long, I'll call Angelo's for dinner reservations—say, in forty-five minutes? That's long enough, right?"

Oliver would have sighed loudly but didn't, because again it reminded him too much of his mother's responses. "Sure. Dinner will be fine. I'll be ready in twenty minutes."

"You are such a doll, Oliver. I mean that. This is my first date in months and months and months."

This is ... like a real date? Is that what it is?

"I love having Bridget and all that, but I sure miss having a good time, too."

Well ... we're having dinner together. And Angelo's is a place where people take dates. So I guess it is a date. Sort of.

"You'll come get me, then? In twenty-five minutes? I'll be waiting ... unless you have another way in mind to start the evening."

This time Oliver was certain she meant something else altogether but decided to completely ignore any implication of impropriety on his part. "Sure. I'll see you in twenty-five minutes."

Taller unlocked his door, as quietly as he could, opened it a crack, and listened. His apartment, the first story of an old, intricately decorated, devotedly maintained Victorian mansion on Greensburg's north side, only a few blocks from the art museum, appeared dark and blissfully empty. The owner of the home was curator at the art museum and a near fanatical homeowner.

Taller slipped inside and listened again.

Nothing.

He switched on the light and carefully set his keys into a bowl on the carefully arranged table in the entryway. It also displayed two candles in tall, straight glass pillars, a clear low bowl filled with bits of polished blue seaglass, and a cobalt blue dish he had found digging in an abandoned farmstead in Somerset County three summers ago. He slid it over two inches, back to its proper place.

From where he stood, he could see the living room, large and spartan, with a huge section of an old Mail Pouch advertisement, taken intact from a derelict barn in Franklin County, several miles north of Pittsburgh, hanging on the wall. Taller had cleaned the dirt and cobwebs off the wood and encased it in a sleek Plexiglas covering; a center section of the faded paint was caught midflake on the ancient cedar boards. Most visitors couldn't guess what the abstraction was until Taller explained it. Abstract and concrete at the same time—Taller loved the tension, the juxtaposition of reality and absurdity.

Taller padded toward his bedroom. He had forgotten if Emily possessed a key to his home. In moments of weakness, Taller was often expansive, handing out keys too early, when the advent of a physical relationship was the only criteria for key-dom.

If she has one, I need to ask for it back. She's easy on the eyes—not gorgeous like that Samantha woman, but nice enough to look at—and pleasant and all that ... but I don't want her sneaking in here and moving any of my stuff. That will never do. And she already said the place needs plants. I don't want plants in here. I don't want their happy little leaves turning brown, dying, and falling on the floor and then having to feel guilty when I pitch them out in the trash. I don't want dead things on my conscience.

Taller had a one-foot-square, short metal box filled with grass, or what looked to be grass (artificial, of course) placed on a very expensive Stickley Marlborough lamp table next to his bed. The table's wood glowed nearly red when the light hit it just so, with its ebony inlay in stark contrast, on the south wall of the room, catching both the morning and afternoon sunlight.

That's enough green in the room.

He walked into the adjacent bathroom with its pristine vintage black-and-white marble tile floor and walls, turned on the deluxe water-fall showerhead with a brushed-nickel finish from Restoration Hardware, waited until the water was almost painfully hot, then proceeded to stand under it, with his skin turning red for a half hour until the water began to cool, having used all forty gallons the water heater held.

He dressed carefully: jeans, long-sleeved fitted black T-shirt first and dark gray short-sleeved T-shirt on top, with just the right amount of the bottom T-shirt showing through. He donned a pair of black slip-ons—not that he wanted to appear trendy or upper class, but Taller hated the way sneakers and running shoes looked with jeans.

Everyone looks like they've got bad aching feet when they wear running shoes and they aren't running—an awkward sort of tension that's unsettling.

After wiping down the marble walls of his shower with a squeegee, he sprayed a new product that promised to clean shower walls without scrubbing, placed his wet towel in the plastic-lined wicker hamper, closed the lid, and switched off the lights. He walked slowly back into the living room, savoring the silence and luxuriating in the dim ambience. He saw the outlines of objects, catching only a glimpse of their true color, and was comforted by the precision of their placement. In the gathering dark he sat in the overstuffed Baker box armchair, covered with a soft plush fabric, and listened to the subtle creaking and groaning of the old house and the traffic three blocks away on Main Street. He waited, enjoying the near quiet, the solitude, and wondering where he might go tonight ... debating if he would bring home whatever conquest he might meet out there.

And asking himself if it might be time to simply come home alone.

———⊷∞⊶———

Oliver didn't have much time to deliberate on any of his alternatives for the evening. He took a short shower, dressed quickly in khaki pants and a polo shirt, and shaved in a hurry, since he had not done so that morning. He checked his wallet—four twenty-dollar bills and a few singles.

If all we do is have a quiet dinner, that eighty bucks ought to be enough. But if she really wants to go someplace else afterward, then I'll have to use a credit card for dinner.

Oliver didn't like using credit cards, but some situations almost mandated their use.

Angelo's is a nice enough place. I guess I could go for Italian tonight instead of the plain grilled chicken breast I was planning on having.

He attached his cell phone to his belt and grabbed a golf jacket from the closet.

Robert the Dog was on the leather sectional sofa, where he was not supposed to be. It was a familiar game they played. Robert would climb up on the cushion, like a mountain climber scaling a sheer ridge of ice and snow, clambering upward, struggling to gain a foothold. He would seldom jump, but rather, climbed. And even though Oliver would scold him, or pretend to scold him, Robert the Dog realized that Oliver was not being serious and would always allow him to stay up on the sofa—unless he had company and the company did not like dogs. And that seldom, if ever, happened, except with relatives.

Oliver patted the dog's head. "I won't be late. At least I'll try not to be late."

Robert stared at him obediently then laid his head back on his front paws, his eyes big and saucerlike, as if he intentionally wanted to appear abandoned.

Oliver closed the door to his apartment, making sure it was locked behind him, and hurried down the stairs. He went to the passenger side of the truck first and removed a couple of woodworking magazines, his Thermos, and his carpenter's belt. He placed them all on the first step of the stairway up to his apartment, in the shadows, so no one could see them. He patted at the seat, wiping off any dust or crumbs or dog hair that might be there. Oliver wasn't obsessively neat, but his truck was never excessively dirty, so having a human passenger didn't require a wholesale cleaning.

If she hates a little dog hair, then, well, we could take her car.

He wondered what sort of car she drove. He tried to remember if he'd ever seen a car in her driveway, but for the life of him, could not recall its color or make.

He pulled up to her house, switched off the engine, and opened his door. The door to the house slapped open, a burst of light pouring out.

Paula, hurrying down the stairs, called back to her mother who remained in the doorway, "Don't wait up, Mom. I'll let myself in. You go to bed, okay? I know you're tired."

Paula was wearing some sort of stretch sweater or knit top under a different jacket than the one she wore to church, and jeans. *Dressy jeans,* Oliver thought, tight enough for him to notice that they were.

"Oliver, you stay there," she called out when she saw him, "I can open the door myself." She hurried around to the passenger door and hefted herself inside, sliding closer to him than he expected, more than midway across the bench seat.

She smelled of something … not fruity or flowery … but more earthy. Oliver was bad at identifying smells, but this aroma was more pronounced, more invasive and clunky than the subtle scent Samantha wore.

Now why in the world am I thinking of Samantha and the way she smells?

It may have been the first time in his life that he compared the scents of two different women.

"I'm so hungry, Oliver, you can't believe it. I would have had lunch, but Bridget was fussing this morning, and it took everything to keep her happy and get her fed before I had to leave for work. After I dropped her off with the sitter, I remembered I didn't pack my lunch. I know I could have bought a sandwich or something, but I hate spending five bucks on a crummy sandwich at the 7-Eleven.… "

Oliver nodded as he drove, and she talked, thinking maybe it was okay she talked a lot because then he didn't have to worry about carrying on a conversation with her.

Like I would with Samantha. I don't have any idea what I would talk about with her. Maybe something about construction or renovation? With Paula I can just listen and nod, and it's all okay. Guess that's something good I could say about Paula. Things would never be quiet with her around.

By the time they reached Angelo's in downtown Jeannette, Paula was describing her day and had only made it to her morning break. Oliver parked the truck and hurried around to open Paula's door but only made it to the front bumper by the time she jumped down and slammed the door behind her.

"Do I need to lock it, or does your truck have one of those fancy remote-control locky things on the key?" she asked.

"It does, Paula. I'll lock the doors."

"I wish I had a fancy car too. I hate locking the car doors by hand. I never have anything inside, maybe the carseat, and who would steal that, right? And nobody's going to steal a beat-up old Toyota, are they? Maybe some kids out for a joyride, but even then."

A Toyota.

He held the door of the restaurant open for her.

"Why, Oliver, thank you," she said.

Angelo's was dark, darker than Oliver remembered. The two of them followed the maître d' farther into the darkness to a table by a window with a view of the municipal parking lot and the old train station up on the hill.

"This is so nice." Paula grabbed a breadstick. "I haven't been here in ages. Remember when we dated—way back when? You took me here once."

"I did? That I don't remember so much," he replied.

"We were in high school—after prom. I was so impressed."

"You were?"

She patted his hand. "That's okay. I remember all of it. Really."

The waitress came and handed out menus. Oliver glanced at the prices first.

Credit card. Definitely credit card here, and cash later.

Midway through their meal (Paula had the veal parmigiana with a Caesar salad, minestrone soup, and two glasses of the house Chianti, and Oliver selected the traditional spaghetti and meatballs with Bolognese sauce, a house salad, and a diet soda), Paula paused and laid her fork down on her dish.

"I'm so happy we can do this, Oliver. I know I'm being way too aggressive since it's the man's place to do the asking and all that, but your mother said you don't go out all that much. She really encouraged me to call you—and since we went out before ... I don't want you to feel bad or awkward or anything, but there's nothing wrong with the two of us having a good time, is there?"

"No, it's okay."

"That's good. Neither of us is getting any younger, right? Not that I want to rush things, but we had such a good time last Sunday and I've known you forever and can talk about anything with you—you know what I mean? We've been together before."

Oliver paused in midtwirl of a mound of spaghetti. "I think I do."

She took a long swallow of her wine, nearly draining the glass. "I'm not asking for anything long-term or a commitment … not really. But I do like being with you. Your mom said you haven't been involved with anyone for a couple of years and that it's about time you settled down. She said you wanted a person who went to church and believed in God and Jesus and all that, and that's something I do—I think all that religion stuff is real important. And she said that if anything was going to happen, I'd better be the one that starts it 'cause you were usually so shy around women. So that's what I'm doing, Oliver. I hope it's okay with you."

Oliver didn't say anything since he hadn't been asked a question, nor had he found an appropriate comment to interject.

"Going to church is nice and all, but I guess I could take it or leave it. But your mom said it's real important to you. It is, isn't it?"

Oliver chewed and swallowed and took a drink. "I like church. I enjoy going. I try to be the best Christian … believer … that I can be. You know, treat people nice, don't cheat or steal, help others, all that sort of stuff. Love God and tell people about Jesus when you get the chance. It is important. The most important thing. Otherwise, life isn't all that much. And if you want to get into heaven, you know …"

"Oh, sure. No one wants to wind up heading in the other direction. Duh! Going to church. Sure. I can do that. We could do that. Bridget loves her little Sunday-school class. She always comes home with something cute pasted together with Cheerios or macaroni or cotton balls. They're all over the refrigerator—so adorable. She needs to be raised in a house that knows something about God and Jesus and heaven and all that, right?

Oliver nodded. "It's important to me. I may not talk about it all the time, but it is. Knowing who God really is."

Does Samantha know who God is? Jews know all about God, don't they? I'm sure she's heard about Jesus, too. But they don't believe He's the Messiah—

"That's good, Oliver. I'm glad we're on the same page about this. If it's important to you, then it's important to me."

As Oliver speared a piece of his meatball, he wondered how she got to where they were so quickly without him noticing the speed of the trip and its ultimate destination. And as he considered the where and why and how, Paula raised her hand to the waitress, pointed at her wine glass, and offered both the waitress and Oliver a very big, almost lopsided grin.

Samantha finished her meal quickly. It seemed as if dining alone made her hurry, speeding through the food like a sprinter. She devoured the steak— petite, but fabulous—and thought the lobster very fresh. She consumed the entire baked potato, the crispy skin included, slathered with too much whipped butter, sour cream, bacon, cheese, and salt.

Dr. Rosen would kill me if he saw me killing myself with all this sodium and fat.

She poured a third cup of coffee, emptying the carafe, and slid the room-service table back into the hall. Samantha hated the way empty plates, dirty cloth napkins, and food scraps looked. Even if the plates had covers, she hated passing the used trays in the halls of a hotel, so she called room service again and instructed them to retrieve their delivery apparatus as soon as possible.

The TV had been left on, the chattering volume soft, the blue glow filling the room with flickering images. Samantha retrieved a packet of architectural drawings from her soft Gucci leather briefcase. She had let the architect know that she hated the long rolls of blueprints, the sort that always curled up and flopped about when trying to read them, so she instructed him to reproduce them, reduced, on legal-sized sheets that fit into a folder.

Flipping open the folder, she paged through the drawings, trying to visually construct a restaurant from the elegant, sharp lines on the page. She flipped the pages, staring at the basement reconfigurations. She could see the existing structure—the large open space labeled *Fellowship Hall* and the room where Oliver had set up his temporary quarters, next to where the shower was located. She wondered where he was this weekend, what he might be doing now, and if he had ever stopped and thought of her.

She shook the image out of her head, likening it to what she and lots of her friends used to do in seventh grade, writing a boy's name over and over on a diagonal in her notebook, like the repetition of some romantic rosary.

It's not like we really know each other, but I love talking to him. I know we've only been working on the place for a little while, but we've still been together a lot. I can tell he's interested. I can always tell if a man is interested. But it's not that sort of interest. Most guys just want to jump in the sack, but I think Oliver enjoys just being with me. He lights up. That's what I see in his face. There's something about him … so kind and gentle and passionate about his work. Sort of a bottled-up passion. Maybe that's why I'm attracted to him … because I want to uncap him, let it out. And he seems so … reverent about his work. Like it's a sacred thing, a promise he needs to keep. He takes care and time with everything he does. I don't think I've ever seen so much care—even in the demolition—as what I see with him.

She glanced up at the TV, staring at the muted action—some car-chase movie with people firing pistols out the windows at each other. She watched until the thoughts of Oliver cleared from her head then flipped the notebook to the second section. Here she kept the designer's renditions of the logo of her new venture—different approaches, different names. She had gravitated to the simple name: *Blue.*

If we want it to make sense, we'll have to backlight the windows from the outside. At night, that blue will look like compressed ice, so blue it looks translucent, pellucid.

The name was done in ovals in one, in squares in another, and one was placed inside a cross—stylized, but still recognizable as a cross. That, Samantha knew, would be pushing the connection to the old use of the building and might be seen as verging toward bad taste.

The oval rendition, the letters done in an elegant 1930s font, had been her favorite. Here, in New York, the capital of all things sophisticated, the name still worked. The style still rang true, yet it was edgy in a nice way, not pushy and all in your face like cutting-edge design can sometimes be.

It'll be Blue. *I like that. I can hear people saying, "Where do you want to go tonight? Blue?" And, "Did you hear about the new place in Shadyside: Blue? It's so cool."*

She picked up her phone and thumbed through the numbers. She stopped at Oliver's number, hesitated only a moment, then pressed *Send*.

He won't be answering his work number this late at night. I just want to leave him a message, that's all.

She heard the call connect.

And this time will be different. I can change. I don't have to be ... what she said I was. I can change. It's not my fate—no. I can choose.

CHAPTER EIGHT

"Hello?"

"Oh … oh … Oliver? What are you doing answering your work phone so late?"

"Samantha?"

"I didn't want to bother you. I was just going to leave a message. I'm sorry for disturbing you."

"I only have the one phone with the one line, so … you can always know where I am, I guess." A packet of silence, a clipped staccato, filled the phone. "What's up?"

"Oh … uhh … what was it? … Oh, yes … the name. I settled on *Blue*. And I think I showed you the oval design. I'm not sure why I needed to tell you that now, this late, but … I really thought I was going to get your voice mail. This would have made much more sense as a voice-mail message. Then you could simply have hit *Erase*, and it would all be gone."

"No, this is no bother. I like *Blue*. I think the oval design is great."

"Okay then. Have a good weekend, Oliver. I'll see you Monday."

"Yep, Monday. You have a good time in New York, too … at … the—"

"Bar mitzvah."

"Yeah … bar mitzvah. Have a good time. I mean, if you're supposed to have a good time. I guess I'm not really sure what a bar mitzvah is. Do you have a good time at them?"

"That's the plan. It's a coming-of-age ceremony for a thirteen-year-old boy, but it's really about the party afterward—lots of food, lots of drinks, lots of loud people. A good time if you like that sort of thing."

She listened closely to the phone. She thought she heard music in the background but couldn't be certain. She didn't hear the noises of a party, though.

"Well, okay then, Miss Cohen. I'll see you Monday."

Miss Cohen? And his voice sounds a little strained. He's with a woman.

"You will, Oliver. Have a nice night."

She flipped the phone shut, almost angry, then wondered why she was almost angry. She knew why, of course, and wondered why she raced into these feelings, wondered why she was always arriving at emotional destinations before the person she might be with arrived there ... or even started the journey.

"He was with a woman."

And now it starts. Just like always.

———

Paula did her best not to appear upset, but her lips were narrower, tighter, more pursed than they had been all evening. She watched as Oliver snapped his phone closed and clipped it back onto his belt.

"No one ever calls me—that's the funny thing about it," he said, grinning.

Paula dabbed slowly, deliberately at her lips with her napkin. "Who was that? A client? This late? Isn't that sort of ... unusual? On a Friday night?"

Oliver again remembered his mother's warning about shrugging. So he simply said, "A little. Sometimes clients have funny hours."

"Does this one?" The looseness in Paula's voice had disappeared, replaced with a very tight, very even tone.

"I guess. She's in New York. At a bar mitzvah."

As soon as Oliver said the words, he realized he shouldn't have said them. He could read Paula's thoughts from her expression: *And just how do you know she's in New York? And attending a—what? Do the two of you have intimate talks while you're working? Or maybe over drinks after hours? Is that it, Oliver?*

"Oh," Paula replied, making it clear she had a lot more to say than the single word she'd offered.

"She mentioned it to me in passing, I guess," Oliver said, not really knowing why he felt an obligation to explain. "She talks a lot."

Paula nodded. Displaying great control, she reached for her wine glass and took a small swallow. "What's a bar mitzvah, anyhow?" she asked, her tone almost dismissive.

This time Oliver did shrug. "I don't know. Some sort of Jewish thing. I think it's kind of like being confirmed or something."

"Jewish?"

Apparently that was the only word Paula heard.

"Yeah."

"Did she go with her husband?"

"No, I don't think so," was all Oliver answered.

Paula finished her wine, set the glass down, and pushed her plate a few inches away. Oliver noted she'd only eaten half of the veal and knew Robert the Dog would love the rest but didn't think this was the most perfect time to ask if he could have a doggy bag.

Oliver drove back toward Paula's house. She didn't ask to go elsewhere, for drinks and dancing or whatever she might have had in mind before Oliver's woman client called and interrupted the mood.

And it is a little late. Dinner took longer than I thought.

He waited for a car to cross the intersection at Gaskill Avenue.

It was only a phone call. And it's not like we're dating … really. I like Paula and all; she's a nice person, and she's pretty, but this is sort of fast … isn't it? Maybe being past thirty and single means you don't spend as much time playing games. Maybe it's better that you just go after what you want … or what would be best for you. Settling down wouldn't be all that bad. Have someone to be there when you came home … besides Robert the Dog, that is.

His truck labored up the hill by the rubber works.

I am thinking about settling down. Maybe this is the right time. Maybe with Paula. She's nice. I'm ready, right?

Paula turned to him as he downshifted into second. She slid closer on the bench seat, much closer than she was on the trip into town, her knees just touching him, and placed her hand on his forearm. Oliver glanced over but did not want to stare.

I don't need to be choosy. No ... I have no right to be choosy. I'm not like Taller, who can have any woman he wants. Paula is nice. She works hard and is a good mother and all that. She's pretty, too.

He downshifted into first and the truck lurched.

I could do worse. And she's here. She's available....

"Oliver, I didn't mean to go all silent on you back at the restaurant. I didn't expect a phone call from a woman during our dinner, that's all. I know she's a customer and that you have to be nice to customers. My mom's second husband was a builder, and she always said they were interrupted at all sorts of times by phone calls or people at the door and whatnot. So it's okay. I don't mind that you get phone calls or anything like that."

He stopped at the stop sign just past the crest of the hill.

"So ... I mean, let's not go home to my place right now. My mom is there and everything."

Oliver was glad she wasn't upset but surprised at her mood and its quick turnaround. "Where do you want to go?"

Paula drew closer to him and slipped her arm into his, even though he still had to use it to steer. "We ... we could go back to your place. I'd really like to see it. Your mother said it's gorgeous—like out of a magazine."

She snuggled even closer. "Please, Oliver. It's not that late yet, and I don't want to go home. I know you're not a drinking man, being a church-going man and all. So can we? Just for a minute?"

Oliver pulled around the corner and slowly drove past Paula's ranch house. The blue flickering light from a TV filled the living room.

"She's still up. My mom's a sort of night owl, so we can't go to my place. And Bridget might wake up, so even if I sent my mom home ... you know."

Oliver did not know but turned the corner and slowed down as he neared his driveway. He felt that prickly feeling again and decided it was not entirely unwelcome and not entirely uncomfortable, but more like that tingling, slow-to-awake feeling after a stiff leg falls asleep and then wakes up.

"Please, Oliver. Just for a few minutes. I haven't been out for months, and I don't want to go home right now. Okay?"

And with that she dropped her head onto his right shoulder. It was obvious she didn't mind him moving beneath her, steering the car, and she let go of his arm and instead used her right arm to almost encircle his chest, holding him close.

"Please, Oliver. What do you say?"

Shadyside never grew completely dark; few places within a city ever did. There were streetlights and stoplights and house lights and cars, so darkness—losing-your-hand-in-front-of-your-face darkness—was instead reserved for the country, far away from buildings and people. Barth Mills held tight to his dog Rascal's leash and walked slowly along South Aiken Avenue. He liked the absolute darkness of a moonless night, far away from houses and cars and cities and even villages. He liked sitting in a tent, staring at a cloud-filled sky, with darkness as a blanket. All the chatter that lived in men's heads disappeared in that darkness. It was a solitude that offered peace, comfort.

But he hadn't been in such darkness for over five years now, not since being removed from his final—so far—pastorate way up in Kane County. Some of the congregation had deep suspicion and anger over trivialities; it had fermented for years. Then it exploded, taking Barth and his pastorate with it. Now past the government's recommended age for retirement and nearing most denominations' mandatory retirement age, he figured he'd never have the chance to darken a pulpit again.

He missed the dark quiet of the forest. He could have gone camping, but it all seemed like so much work. His tent was probably not in his cozy apartment—more likely in the storage space on Negley Avenue that he had to rent when he returned to Pittsburgh. But at this moment, in the semidarkness, he couldn't locate in his head just where that tent might be.

I couldn't have sold it in that blasted garage sale, could I?

Rascal tugged at the leash, like he always did. Rascal was a small, low-to-the-ground basset hound with loose skin. His fleshy jowls, larger than they should be according to the standards of the breed, were wet with hints of saliva and slapped back and forth as Rascal and Barth walked.

When the dog jerked ahead, Barth stumbled on a break in the sidewalk. He caught his balance at the last moment, causing nearly as much pain due to stretched muscles as the fall would have caused with scraped knees.

"Hold, Rascal, blast you," he barked out. "Hold. Stay. Sit. Stop it, stop pulling!"

Since it was late and almost dark, he didn't want to shout as loudly as he felt like shouting. He had no desire to be classified as one of those almost-crazy people wandering the streets, nor thought stranger than he already knew he was.

Barth vowed at that moment to have Rascal's ears checked next time they visited the vet, which was proving more frequent than Barth's own visits to one of his doctors.

"Maybe he can't hear me anymore. Maybe that's it," he muttered as the two of them set off again. He stopped at the corner where Central Presbyterian Church used to stand. The building still stood, of course, but it was no longer a church—that he knew. He saw the hulking shadow of the Dumpster by the port cochere.

"They're not tearing it down, are they?" he said aloud to Rascal, his words nearly shrill. "They can't. It's too beautiful. Not this church too."

Rascal yanked at the leash, and even though Barth was better braced this time, he nearly tipped over again, yanking back as Rascal began growling. He no longer barked. At fifteen years old, the ancient basset could only rumble, a sort of phlegm-clearing *hark-hark-hark* that Barth found endearing, or at least, not completely aggravating. He did this when near the presence of other dogs.

Barth listened closely and heard no other dogs nearby. "Rascal, shut up. There's no one here. No dog."

They came closer to the Dumpster. Barth could see the building permit tacked to the door but knew he couldn't read any of it in the dark with his eyesight. Though a building permit normally didn't provide any details, Barth felt reassured because it usually meant renovating, not demolition.

"That's the problem, Rascal. All the relics, all what was once good and noble and beautiful, is being lost and trampled by progress."

Rascal waffled and harked his reply, his nose lifted up high as if placing a wet finger in the air to determine the direction of the wind.

"Like anyone cares," Barth grumbled to himself. "Maybe I don't care so much anymore. A church isn't walls; it's people."

The two of them shuffled down South Aiken Avenue, Barth wondering if he should stop at the Giant Eagle farther down the street and buy some dinner—maybe a roast chicken—then remembered he had Rascal with him. If he tried to tie the dog to some fixture outside the store, the dog would turn apoplectic in Barth's absence, attempting to summon up the strength to manage an actual bark.

"No … too late for shopping."

As they turned on Summerlea, where they lived now, Barth remembered that he still had half a loaf of bread left and that toast and coffee might be all he'd need to feel satisfied this evening.

He ran his hand through his hair, now a silvery gray.

He was pretty sure Rascal had a full bowl of food as well.

"What more could either of us ask for?" Barth said almost too loudly, without sarcasm or self-pity, to no one but himself and his dog in the almost darkness on the short, and not entirely pleasant, Summerlea Street. "Dear God, what more could I ask for?"

"For just a little while, Paula, okay?"

It appeared that Paula suppressed a giggle. "Most guys want to get me into their place, and here you are, being so cautious about it. It's like you're nervous about what I might do to you. Are you nervous, Oliver? Think I might be able to overpower you and force myself on you?"

Oliver's laugh was indeed nervous, but he hoped Paula didn't notice. "No. I don't mind you coming up. Really. I just don't want to … you know … start rumors or anything."

"Well, aren't you sweet? I mean that," Paula said as she squeezed him tighter. "Most guys could care less about that. You know, a divorced woman with a baby."

Oliver navigated his truck into the driveway. The windows on his mother's house were still dark. She went to bingo at the Catholic church, which lasted until 10:00 and often went out with friends—usually to Denny's, she said, where they had coffee and pie and talked. Oliver suspected the group may have coerced his mother into going to a tavern with them once or twice, but not a tavern in Jeannette where she might be recognized. It would have to have been over in Latrobe, or even Ligonier.

He switched the engine off, jumped from the cab, and hurried around to the passenger side. This time Paula waited for him, extending her hand so he could help her down to the driveway.

"Careful on that first step. I put some tools and stuff there earlier."

"I see it. No problem."

Oliver could hear Robert the Dog jump down from somewhere as he turned the key—bed, sofa, or easy chair. The dog's black nose poked itself into the door opening.

"Back, Robert. Back up."

Robert eyed the stranger with great intensity and slowly came to her side, sniffing loudly, his canine eyes focused upward.

"Oh, you have a dog. I knew that, didn't I? What a cute doggy," Paula said, not bending down, not offering to scratch his ears, not leaning in to accept a doggy welcome. Not at all.

As soon as the dog backed up, Paula entered the center of the main room and twirled about. "This is so beautiful. Your mother was right. This *is* out of a magazine—one of those architect magazines that are way too expensive to buy. I can't believe this is built over a garage—and in Jeannette. Just beautiful. You are full of surprises."

Oliver's home hadn't received that many visitors and guests. It wasn't large enough for a party, really, so only his closest friends ever saw his work. Paula's compliments felt nice, warming.

"And you're neat. That's unusual. For a man, I mean. But then, you were neat back when we dated, weren't you?"

Paula looked into the bedroom area and into the bathroom and swirled to the screened porch.

"The town almost looks too pretty from up here," she said, then came back in and dropped casually on the sofa, not appearing to care about manners. "Maybe a bit too much wine, Oliver. I think it was deliberate.

You were giving me too many drinks because you wanted to take advantage of me."

She looked up, tilted her head, and patted the seat next to her. "Are you going to take advantage of me, Oliver? Like old times?"

———————————

Taller unlocked his door and slipped in sideways, closing it firmly behind him, latching the lock, then setting the chain into the slot. The streetlight across the way was bright enough. He set his keys in the cobalt bowl on the table, slipped his shoes off, picked them up, and walked into his bedroom without touching a light switch. He came back into the kitchen in his socks. Underneath the microwave was a light, which Taller switched on from the keypad on the sleek, stainless steel unit. The commercial stove glistened underneath, all six burners immaculate.

Taller hesitated. He wanted tea but debated whether he should use the microwave or the gas burner and a teakettle to heat the water. He had an electric teakettle on the counter, providing yet another option. He looked at each one and decided that making tea with hot water boiled on the stovetop felt the most authentic—maybe because he rarely used it. He let the water run till cold, then filled the kettle with more than enough water and turned the dial on the stove. The blue flame flickered on, and he set the kettle exactly on the middle of the burner.

He took out one mug, one tea bag—Russian Royalty, advertised as the choice of discriminating chefs. He waited at the stove until the water boiled, then filled the cup and poured the remaining hot water down the drain and set the kettle on one of the unused burners. He added two scoops of sugar to the tea, opened the cabinet over the sink, took out the dish that was just the right size for a teabag, and carried both the cup and the dish to the kitchen table.

Taller had visited the Point Bar for a while that evening, then Mr. Toad's, and the Touchdown Club in Latrobe. He had purchased three draft beers, one at each establishment, had drunk no more than a third of each glass, and now sat at his kitchen table with four phone numbers scrawled on the backs of his business cards. He set the four cards on the table, in a row, top to bottom.

He tried to remember which number was which, which woman was which woman, and failed. No one had made an impression deep enough to last through the dark of the evening. He piled up all four cards into a thin deck and turned them over, so his name was facing up, and slid them to the center of the table.

He sipped at his tea, hot, sugary, almost thick with flavor, nothing herbal or fragrant about it. "I like the Russians," Taller said to himself. When one lives alone, talking aloud is not so odd, at least that's what Taller told himself. "No pretense. Tea like a fist."

Afterward Taller rinsed his mug and teabag dish, placed both in the dishwasher, walked to his bedroom in the dark, undressed, placed his clothes in the hamper, slipped on a pair of running shorts, and lay on his bed, from which he could see the sky through an eyebrow window across the room. He saw no stars that night, only a muddy darkness.

Maybe I'm just tired of the women around here. Maybe I need something else ... something a little exotic. Maybe someone like Samantha Cohen.

He folded his hands behind his head, his eyes open in the dark, unseeing.

And how do you think my mother might react? Or my brother? Mister Perfect. Who might be the most livid? Wouldn't that be a wonderfully complicated situation? Serve them right.

He closed his eyes and smiled. Then the pleased expression faded, replaced by nothing, and he simply waited for sleep to free him.

Barth carefully inspected the remaining slices of bread, checking for the tiny blue clouds of mold that formed, sometimes in a matter of minutes, it seemed. He turned the plastic bag over and over, holding it close to his eyes.

"I think we're penicillin free, Rascal."

It took the dog a minute to lift his head and look at Barth, almost understanding him.

Barth slipped the bread into the toaster, pressed the lever, and waited. He could see his reflection in the glass of the microwave. He could see the etched wrinkles about his eyes, deep and furrowed, and the increasing cloudiness in his eyes, the cloudiness that stole his acuity. He lifted his chin, turning from one side to the other.

"Not all that bad for an old man, I guess. Could be worse, Rascal. Could be dead, right? Or that might be better. Maybe time to go home to Jesus."

Rascal did not move.

Barth never liked the name Rascal. It had been his wife's selection, since it had been his wife's dog. She had been gone for nearly ten years.

"Ten years, Rascal," Barth said aloud, acutely aware of the passage of years since his wife's death. An aneurism had dropped her as cleanly as if she had been hit by a sniper's bullet while on a camping trip. She had been in the soup aisle of Wegman's Grocery Store in Williamsport, Pennsylvania, with a can of the store-brand tomato soup in her hand.

The toast popped up, and Barth slathered both slices with peanut butter and apricot jelly, both Rascal and himself a fan of each flavor. The water in the kettle was boiling, and Barth spooned in the instant coffee, added a packet of sugar, and two spoonfuls of powdered creamer.

He sat at the kitchen table, slowly eating his toast, listening to the whir of the refrigerator. Rascal sat at his feet, not begging, but offering his best plaintive and expectant stare, and gratefully receiving a few torn corners of each slice.

I wonder where that tent is. Maybe I did sell it. I got rid of too much stuff. Ellen never liked camping, I bet, but was too nice to tell me how she really felt. Maybe I could go for a drive some weekend, up to Venango County … maybe get a hotel room, watch spring spring. Maybe Rascal would like a change of scenery too.

Barth chewed his last piece of toast, knowing he wouldn't take a drive to Venango County—not this weekend, not anytime soon.

Doesn't seem worth all the effort.

He put the plate and the cup into the sink and shuffled into the living room, picked up the remote control for the TV, and switched it on, hitting the mute button immediately. The cold flickering glow filled the room. Rascal climbed up on the couch next to Barth, circled twice, and flopped on his side. Barth flipped through the channels until he got to the weather station. He set the remote on the arm of the sofa and watched, in silence, as the perky weather—weather*woman?*—pointed at a cold front building up over Saskatchewan and a low-pressure system over the plains. Barth wondered what might happen when the two of them collided.

———————

Whenever someone patted furniture, Robert the Dog assumed it was a personal invitation for him to join that person at the exact spot the patting took place. And that is what Robert the Dog did when he thought Paula was inviting him to sit next to her by patting on the cushion.

Paula, obviously surprised at his gallumping up next to her, didn't shriek, but she didn't treat Robert's intrusion as welcome, either.

"Robert, get down," Oliver all but shouted. Robert looked at Oliver, apparently hurt. "Down. Now!" he called again, and Robert slunk off the couch as snakelike and humiliated as a dog can be.

"Sorry about that, Paula. I guess Robert isn't used to guests," Oliver said, moving between the dog and the sofa, as if Robert might try to jump up again, though Oliver knew he wouldn't.

Paula offered too broad of a smile in reply. "No problem, Oliver. We never had a dog when I was a little girl. I think I must have wanted one, but my mother said they were too much trouble and would chew stuff up and make a mess. So we never had one. She said that my dad—my real dad, not my stepfather—liked dogs. I don't know why she told me, but I remember her saying he had a soft spot for helpless creatures like dogs and rabbits."

Oliver sat next to her, almost where she had patted the cushion, but not quite so close as she had indicated. He tried to think of a cogent response, but he could summon up no reply that fit.

The recessed lights over the coffee table were on, the lamps at both ends of the sofa were on, and the tiny halogen spotlights on the wire track lights over the sink were on. Undeterred by the brightness, Paula scooched closer to Oliver. She snuggled in next to him and, almost in self-defense, he placed his arm over her shoulder—on the top of the cushion, not really on her shoulder. She leaned into him.

"This is nice, Oliver. You're so sweet. I mean, taking me out to dinner after I was such a hussy, asking you out first. You don't mind that, do you? Old friends can do that, right? It's not like we never dated before, is it?"

"No. Not at all. This was … real nice. Or is. I mean, it is real nice. And we are old friends."

Paula leaned in even closer. She turned her face up to his, her eyes half shut with a deliberate seductiveness.

"I'm glad, Oliver. I'm glad you had a good time. And maybe … maybe we can make it even nicer." She moved up and her face came closer to Oliver's. "I remember how it used to be, Oliver. You remember, don't you? Back then. When we were young and wild and … you know … excitable?"

Just then, at that suggestion, at that tipping-point moment, the garage door rumbled into life, clanking and rolling, the electric motor slightly off-center, vibrating through the frame of the garage.

Paula stopped, eyes wide, and asked, "What's that?"

"My mother's home," Oliver replied. "Don't worry. She never comes up here."

They both waited. They could hear the car door slam and the rumble of the garage door closing. Then, instead of footsteps on the concrete driveway, they heard the creaking and groan of wooden steps, the steps leading to Oliver's apartment.

"Oliver! Oliver!" his mother called out, and immediately both Paula and Oliver jumped to their feet, as did Robert the Dog. Rose Barnett's words were not accusatory but offered more as an early warning.

Oliver opened the door even before she made it to the top of the steps. "Mom, what are you doing here? I didn't think you'd come up."

"I wanted to hear about your date. With Paula." Mrs. Barnett, holding the handrail tightly, pulled herself up to the landing.

"Hi, Rose," Paula called out from over Oliver's shoulder. "We had a wonderful dinner at Angelo's, and I begged Oliver to show me his place. After you said how gorgeous it was, I just had to see it. And Oliver has been the perfect gentleman. We had such a nice time."

Oliver expected something dramatic from his mother, but he was disappointed.

"That is so nice, Paula. And I love Angelo's too. What did you have?"

Paula and Mrs. Barnett spent ten minutes discussing the meal, the menu, the prices, the waitstaff, the state of fine dining in Jeannette, how difficult it was to find a good person to date these days, the fact that living with a dog produced all manner of objections, that Oliver was a genius when it came to contracting and decorating, and that Rose Barnett was most apologetic for interrupting their time alone.

Oliver was nothing short of flabbergasted.

"Oliver, what time is it, anyhow?" Paula asked.

"Almost half past eleven."

She grabbed his hand. "Then you have to walk me home now. My mother will be worried."

The three of them made their way down the steps, Mrs. Barnett exiting quickly toward her back door. Both Oliver and Paula bid her good night and began walking down the block, turning the corner toward Paula's house, midblock.

She stopped him at the corner. "My mother will be up. So … let me thank you here for the best night I've had in a long time."

She grabbed him, pulled him into a surprisingly forceful bear hug, and mashed her lips against his for a period that might be appropriate for a tenth date, Oliver thought. She made it obvious that she would have preferred more, was offering more, and was frustrated their alone time had been interrupted.

She relaxed her arms around him and leaned back with a victorious look. "We'll do this again, won't we, Oliver? Take it up where we left off. Okay? Tell me we will."

He nodded, knowing there was no other answer to that question, at least not this night. "Sure, Paula. Sure we will."

CHAPTER NINE

THE ORGANIST PRESSED at the organ keyboard with an earnest harkening, the bass shivering the foundation of the church as Oliver hurried to the balcony, knowing his mother would never sit there, and that mothers with young children had to sit on the main floor to see the "wild child" number-alert system. He felt safe in the balcony, even though it rendered him feeling more like a spectator than a participant.

Sometimes watching is okay, he told himself as he climbed the stairs and selected a seat well toward the back, just under the large, oval, beveled-glass window. There no one would notice if he didn't sing along with the hymns and choruses, and he could dispense with the miming—moving his mouth as if he were singing. He could simply stand and listen, which he often told himself was more worshipful than singing badly—at least that was his self-evaluation of his vocal abilities.

The pastor's sermon involved something about creation and our response to it, but Oliver couldn't stay focused. Thoughts raced about, all competing for attention, none of them finding a preeminent position.

Afterward Oliver took his time coming downstairs. He had not seen either his mother or Paula in church that morning. Sometimes Rose Barnett came to the third service. And sometimes Paula never came at all. Today Oliver wore his more standard church outfit: khaki slacks and a blue shirt. He felt no need to overdress.

The crowd around Pastor Dan Mosco had thinned. A few people still chatted with him, most of them familiar, all with post-sermon comments. Oliver had hoped to have three minutes alone with Pastor Mosco; that's all the time he figured his question would require.

"Oliver, how are you?" Pastor Mosco boomed. He boomed even when it wasn't required. "Working hard? I hear you have a big job in Pittsburgh. That's a long drive, isn't it? All that gas eating up your profits?"

Pastor Mosco lived in the parsonage behind the church, a pleasant house in which Oliver had replaced the outdated kitchen before the current pastor had been called.

A man who can walk to work has no understanding of what an aggravation it is to commute.

"It's not bad. I'm staying there during the week. At least for now. There's a shower and all that. I brought a cot with me. So it's been okay."

"Being in the big city like that," Pastor Mosco added, "would drive me to distraction. You know—the crime, the noise, sirens, and drunks and prostitutes in the alley."

Oliver shook his head as nicely as he could. "It's not like that ... really. Maybe a little more crowded, but not bad."

Pastor Mosco offered his best pastoral grin, signifying that he didn't believe a word of what Oliver said but was much too polite to carry on that segment of the conversation any longer.

"I have a question for you about my current project, Pastor Mosco."

"Remodeling question? I'll be of no use to you with remodeling. All thumbs with a hammer."

"No, not remodeling. More like ... more of a spiritual nature."

"That I'm expert at," Pastor Mosco boomed out again, maybe even louder than before, this time adding a laugh. People were now arriving for the second service, and Oliver felt hurried to get the question out and answered so he could slip out unnoticed.

"Well, I have three brothers working for me ... or they worked for me. They're sort of done now. They do demolition and are real good and fast at that. But the oldest brother asked me last Friday if they could do carpentry work for me on the rest of the project. I'll make a long story short here: He said they used to be carpenters a long time ago, but two of them were arrested—one for stealing and one for manslaughter. They served time in jail, and it's been over ten years since it happened. My question is: Is it okay … Bible-wise, I mean, if I hire them? Should I hire them? What does the Bible have to say about that?"

Oliver figured that Pastor Mosco must field questions like this on a regular basis.

At the words *stealing and manslaughter*, the pastor's grin disappeared like a frog diving into deep water. He stood up straighter and leaned backward an inch or two. "Stealing? Manslaughter? That means somebody was killed, right?"

"Yeah, it does. I had to look it up. You can have a car accident and if someone gets killed, that can be involuntary manslaughter. But even Wikipedia made it confusing. I didn't ask if it was voluntary or involuntary."

"Killing is wrong, Oliver. So is stealing."

Oliver nodded. He knew that already. The morning sun glinted from the thick gold cross that Pastor Mosco wore on his lapel. Oliver wondered if he had only one cross and switched it all the time to his various suits, or if he had lots of crosses and kept one on each suit.

"Oliver, in the Good Book, you can find this question: Can an Ethiopian change his skin or can a leopard change its spots? That's in Jeremiah … 12 or 15 … if you want to look it up later. And in the Good Book, the answer is no. There is no changing spots."

Oliver nodded, pretending as if he was going to look it up later. "So … are you saying that it's impossible for people to change?"

"Not impossible, but very difficult." Pastor Mosco looked over Oliver's shoulder and nodded to a cluster of arrivals at the front door.

"So should I hire them, or not? They are really good workers, and they've never stolen from me."

"Personally, I would say not to hire them. You have to be so careful about who you associate with. What would it look like for a believer to be unequally yoked with an unbeliever in business—especially as a boss—and you're the boss there, right? We need to be *in* the world, but not *of* the world. We can choose to stay away from all unclean elements, to stay clean and pure in our work life as well as our home life. As a Christian employer, you don't want people to look at your employees and base what they think of a Christian business on how those employees behave, do you? And knowingly subjecting your clients to a criminal element—well, I think you would be making a big mistake."

Oliver nodded, not surprised by the pastor's answer. "Thanks, Pastor Mosco. Thanks for the advice."

Pastor Mosco was already slapping at his shoulder in dismissal and moving on to the new group of parishioners, booming out "Good morning!" to them so loudly that several people turned their heads, thinking the pastor was welcoming them as well.

Oliver hurried out the side door, the door facing Third Street, along which he had parked, a few blocks from his normal spot up by the funeral home. Apparently he was successful at slipping away unnoticed, for no one called out his name as he made his way down the street, past the shuttered Third Street bar, and to his truck.

—————

Rose Barnett wore her slippers—pink half-slippers, actually, the kind that made a person shuffle when wearing them—even though she was venturing outside the house. She hoped the pink fur around the top of the slippers wouldn't get dirty on the sidewalk.

It's just around the corner. No one will see me.

She was wearing an ill-fitting, well-worn brown velour athletic suit as well, which was more obvious to the casual observer as to her fashion standards but less so to Rose, who never wore it for exercise. Its function was purely as lounge attire.

It is Sunday afternoon, the day of rest, and I have every right to be comfortable.

She shuffled and slapped down the street and around the corner. The sun filled the afternoon air, a hint of warmth to come. Instead of ringing the doorbell, which Rose knew would wake Bridget if she were sleeping, she tapped at the door as lightly as she could, no more than a heartbeat of a tap. If Paula was awake, even with the TV turned on, she would hear her.

Rose could see the top of Paula's head, movement, and then an eye in the rectangle of glass on the door. The latch was undone, and the door swung open. If Paula was surprised at Rose's unexpected appearance, she did well in hiding that emotion.

"Mrs. Barnett," Paula said, gesturing the older woman inside.

"Rose, remember. Not Mrs. Barnett."

"Oh, sure. I'm sorry. Rose. I forgot. How are you?"

Rose entered and took two shuffling steps, now halfway into the living room. "We need to talk, Paula, about my son. Is your daughter asleep?"

Paula hurriedly nodded. "Always takes a nap in the afternoon. She's a real good sleeper."

Rose looked around. The sofa was cluttered with a rumpled comforter, a stack of magazines, and a Kleenex box on one arm. Two cans of Diet Coke were on the coffee table. The TV was on, turned down very low, and was playing reruns of *American Idol*. Rose didn't like that show, didn't like the title, thought the judges were mean-spirited, but knew the original episodes happened at night, not on Sunday afternoon. The small dining/kitchen table had two boxes of cereal in the middle—one of a very sugary, unhealthy variety, Rose noticed—and two empty bowls with spoons still in them. There was one oversized chair that might be a recliner sitting adjacent to the couch. It was empty, so that was the seat Rose took.

Paula tried to apologize. "The place is a mess, Rose. I just sat down for a minute after Bridget went down. I was about to start cleaning when you tapped."

Rose decided to accept the lie as truth and offered a forgiving smile. "I remember what it's like to be on your own with a little one. Oliver's father—a wonderful Christian man—passed when he was seven and Tolliver was three. It wasn't easy to keep up after things—that much I know. So no apologies are needed. A little clutter isn't that bad, Paula. Really. Don't think twice about it."

But Paula's face gave away her conclusion that Rose wouldn't forget about it so easily.

In that moment Paula vowed, one of many such vows over the past couple of years, that from now on, she would keep her house neat and tidy—just in case.

"Did you see Oliver at church?" Rose's question was much more than just a question, Paula thought—more of a command.

Paula tried not to appear flustered. "No. I mean, I didn't get up in time. I'm sorry, Rose. Bridget sleeps later than normal on the weekends. During the week, when I work, I have to get her up and I hate doing that on Saturdays and Sundays when I don't have to. She was still asleep when I checked, then it got too late to go. I'm really sorry I wasn't there."

Neither woman spoke.

"Did I miss something?" Paula finally asked, breaking the silence.

"No. Not really. They sang too many choruses today. Drives me batty. Over and over and over. Like God is hard of hearing or something. And the pastor's message was okay, but nothing to write home about. It didn't hit home with me. I didn't see Oliver, either. I thought you might have. Or that he might have come over here. But his truck is gone, and I bet he went back to Pittsburgh."

"I didn't see him today. Just on Friday night. And I waved to him Saturday afternoon as he drove past."

Rose adjusted the sleeves on her velour top. They came down past her wrists, and she had cuffed them twice, but the cuffs were uneven, Paula noticed.

"You had a good time?" Rose asked. "On Friday night. On your date. With my son."

Paula nodded energetically. "We did. He is such a nice person. We get along really well. We always have."

Rose nodded this time, much like a lawyer nods to get a witness to continue talking.

"I like him a lot, and I think he likes me. I mean … we're older. So maybe relationships are different now. It seems like we'll spend less time playing games. And we've known each other for a really long time. I mean, we dated way back in high school."

Rose looked hard at the young woman. "You weren't going to have sexual relations with my son when you went up to his apartment Friday night, were you?"

The words were flat and even, but Paula felt as if she had been punched in the stomach. "Goodness, no, Mrs. Barnett. We wouldn't have done that. I mean, Oliver wouldn't have. And I wouldn't, either. No. We were just talking. That's all. And I wanted to see his place."

Rose sniffed, almost testing the air. "And that's the truth?"

Paula leaned forward. She was wearing a very loose V-neck top and, in an attempt at being modest, pulled it close to her as she replied, "That is the truth. We were just there for a minute or two before you got home. Not enough time to do any fooling around, really."

"Don't worry about it," Rose said, indicating with her tone that Paula should indeed worry about it. "I trust my Oliver to do the right thing. A boy who is born again and has Jesus in his heart will not sin against God like that."

Paula nodded in agreement, though she had no idea what Rose was talking about.

"You do know what *born again* means, don't you, Paula? To know Jesus? You've been born again, right? You attend church. The pastor talks about it sometimes. You pay attention, right?"

Paula nodded, feeling like a used-car salesman answering a customer's questions. "Sure, I understand. Born again. That's important. Oliver knows how I feel about church. He knows that I agree with him on religion and all that. We talked about it."

Perhaps for the first time since stepping inside Paula's home Rose smiled legitimately. "You talked about religion with him? During your date? Really? Already?"

"We did. I said how important it was to me."

"You did?"

"Yep," Paula answered, trying not to sound too triumphant.

"Well, if you two are talking about religion, that's a really big step. You can't be talking about religion and then fool around willy-nilly, right?"

"Yeah … or no. You know. I agree with you."

Rose slid forward and took Paula's hand. It appeared unnatural for Rose to do so and was uncomfortable for Paula to experience.

"Listen, Paula, Oliver is a good boy. He'll make a wonderful husband. And it is way past time for him to settle down. I know you're a few years younger, but if Oliver sticks with a woman his own age, well, I might never have any grandchildren. Now you, Paula, I know you have Bridget, and she is a sweet child, but you're young enough to have more, aren't you? There are no female problems, are there?"

Paula shook her head, indicating no, but feeling unwilling to give voice to the answer.

"So you be nice to Oliver. You make him happy. I can see that. He's a shy boy, and he needs someone like you to bring him out of his shell. You can do that, can't you, Paula?"

"I think so. He seems happy when he's with me. We were happy before, too."

Rose squeezed the young woman's hand and stroked her forearm in a motherly way. "He'll come around, Paula. You are a beautiful woman. Any man would love to have you. And Oliver is ready to settle down. I know that. I talked to Pastor Mosco and asked him about it. He said that since you were abandoned by your husband, it would be okay for you and Oliver to get married in the church."

There was a moment of silence. Paula appeared surprised by the word *marriage*. Then she smiled modestly, as if what she wanted was now out on the table, visible—something that would unite both women with a common cause and leave Oliver with few, if any, other options.

"That's good. Religion is important," Paula said, reaffirming her stand.

"Born again, right?" Rose repeated.

"Sure. Born again. That's right," Paula reasserted.

"And you have to keep him away from that Jewish woman. That's not right. He knows it. He needs a nice, clean Christian woman—like you, Paula. Right? Like you."

Rose squeezed her hand again and, as if by magic, Bridget started to cry, loudly.

Rose stood and said, finger to her lips, "You're busy. I'll let myself out."

And she did, shuffling back home in her pink slippers with a very purposeful expression.

CHAPTER TEN

THE PLANE BANKED LEFT, roaring out of LaGuardia, sweeping over Long Island Sound, then kept banking until it was pointed due west, on its way to Pittsburgh. Flying first-class helped minimize the aggravation of traveling, Samantha realized, but she still found all the security checking and removing of shoes and belts and whatnot to be invasive and unsettling, allowing total strangers, often rude strangers, wearing white latex gloves, to paw through one's personal possessions that you had to schlep through the long line. The Sunday-night flight was only three-quarters full, yet the first-class section was entirely occupied. Samantha knew most of the people now squatting in the section were there because of free upgrades, people "paying" for the privilege with some sort of frequent-flyer mileage account—not money out of their own pockets.

She thought there should be two first-class sections: one in which it recognized the passengers who actually paid hard personal cash for the luxury, and another section, with fewer amenities, for the *knakers,* the uncouth masses who happened to be forced to fly a lot for work or spent too much on their credit cards and were given the upgrade for free.

Behind her was a pair of construction workers, she imagined, whose union bosses had negotiated first-class travel for all their members when on business.

They obviously did not pay for these seats themselves.

The bar mitzvah had been lovely, very nice. The food at the Ritz-

Carlton was uncommonly tasty—for banquet food, of course. The boy's parents, one a stockbroker, the other a plastic surgeon, had spared no expense: a very smart, sophisticated jazz trio during dinner, a plethora of waiters circulating about the large crowd with full trays of elegant appetizers, a seven-course kosher meal, a dessert bar, a bar for adult drinks (all the best liquor, no cheap house brands, of course), and the bar was open all evening; plus there were wonderful personalized parting gifts for all the guests.

Nothing schlocky—premium all the way.

Samantha estimated a total event tab of nearly six figures for a celebration honoring a thirteen-year-old boy—a nice boy, but with an air of expected privilege that edged toward distasteful.

The seat-belt sign blinked off. Samantha sat in the wide leather seat by the window next to her father and watched New York disappear, while sipping at ginger ale, in a real glass, with a lime slice floating in the bubbling drink. The flight attendant tried to sell her on dinner, but neither she nor her father wanted the evening fare offered.

"But it's steak. It looks really good," the young woman asserted. "Just try it."

Samantha's father appeared pained. "Honey, I betcha that it's the best airplane steak ever produced by your chefs back in the New York commissary, but both of us have spent the last two days fending off relatives who think we never eat properly. *Oy,* I gained five pounds and I don't want any more heavy food. Just another drink. Make it a Virgin Mary this time, okay?"

"And another ginger ale with lime, please," Samantha added.

The flight attendant took her time leaving, not understanding at all why a sane person would turn down a free meal—or rather, a meal that they had already spent part of a thousand dollars purchasing, since it came with the first-class seat.

"So, did we have a good time at the bar mitzvah?" Samuel asked.

Samantha shrugged. "I guess so. Too much food. Too many loud relatives. Too much everything. I've forgotten how exhausting family can be."

"Being the black sheep of the family and living six hundred miles away has its advantages," her father said. "I love them, but I'm so glad to be leaving them."

"And they all asked me, about a hundred times, when I'm getting married and settling down with a nice Jewish man. At the end, I was telling people I was gay just to keep them quiet. Didn't stop any of them, though. 'A nice gay wedding would be wonderful,' they said."

Her father laughed along with her. "I heard you talking to my sister about it. Such a *shadchen,* she is—loves matchmaking and planning weddings. Doesn't seem to matter who is getting married, as long as it's a wedding."

The flight attendant brought back fresh drinks. "You sure you haven't changed your mind about the meal? They're up there waiting for you, nice and warm."

"No, we're fine, doll. Really. But thanks for being concerned. Really," Samuel repeated.

They both glanced up at the movie, some action-adventure epic starring someone who might have been a wrestler or a rap star at one time. Neither of them wanted headsets to listen to the warbly soundtrack.

"So, Samantha, when you got all those marriage questions, did you really mean it when you said that you're probably never going to get married?"

"Daddy, now you're at it too?"

"Just curious. As your father. You know your mother would be pushing you in that direction. Find a real *mensch,* some nice Jewish doctor or lawyer or CPA and settle down. She would have wanted that for you. Shalom. Contentment. Stability. Everything that comes with having a husband and a family."

Peace? Contentment? That's the impossible dream. Remember, Daddy? I'm destined to fail at love. Remember?

She wanted to tell her father about that last conversation with her mother … when she found out that she was doomed to failure. But she didn't. She didn't then, and she didn't now.

Samantha stared at her father's face, still tanned and relaxed, but she could see the care in his eyes, a parent's concern—concern that he had not adequately been both father and mother these last twenty years since his wife's death, that Samantha's growth and maturity had suffered because her mother was dead, even though Samantha was nearly an adult when her mother passed away.

"Daddy, you, too?"

"Sam, *ani ohev otach.* I want the best for you. Someone to take care of you when I'm gone."

"I love you, too, Daddy. You're not going anywhere. You're as healthy as an ox."

"*Halevai!* I hope, but you know what I mean. Don't become like Aunt Lydia, poor thing, living all alone in that rat-hole apartment."

"She's not a poor thing. And it's not a rat hole. It's a nice place. Small, but nice."

"And still. You know what I mean. You'll be richer when I'm gone. But being rich is worse if you're alone. Being rich is hard, *Bubeleh.* People look at you different—like thinking what they can get out of you. That's no fun. You wonder about who is really your friend, and who thinks they'll get your table scraps. You need someone, Samantha, someone to be with, to grow old next to. Someone who appreciates you. That's what I'm saying."

"You don't have anyone, Daddy. You're growing old alone."

Her father scowled, just a little, just so the lines around his eyes deepened.

"What?" she asked as she turned to face him.

"What what?" he replied.

She leaned close to him, then backward again. "You're seeing someone. Who? Where? In Pittsburgh?"

He shook his head.

"In New York?"

"Maybe."

"A relative? You'll have deformed babies."

Her father laughed out loud, so loud that the person in the seat in front turned around for just a second, just to show annoyance.

"No. A friend of a relative. That's all I'm saying. That's where I went the first night. Just dinner. She's nice. She's going to visit soon. She's coming to Pittsburgh. She's never been there. Can you imagine that? A cultured person who has never been to Pittsburgh. You'll meet her then. And there'll be no gossip allowed. I already reserved a nice suite for her at the Marriott."

"Who? Who is it? Tell me."

"You'll meet her soon enough. It'll be a surprise."

"Is she that young? Younger than me? Is that why you're not telling me?"

Her father placed his half-consumed drink on the tray in front of him. He smoothed at his hair. "No. Not that young. But younger than me. *Oy,* everyone is younger than me."

Samantha could only manage to stare in reply. She was a little angry, a lot amazed, but also perplexed because a new sort of ache and emptiness entered her soul.

Oliver woke up early Monday morning—way, way early, sometime just before 4:00. Robert woke to his master's rustling, padded over from his dog bed, and nosed at Oliver's hand.

"I know it's early, Robert. I know."

Oliver squinted at the clock, then sat up. Once awake, he would not attempt to go back to sleep. Not at the beginning of the week, anyway. Too many questions and problems and situations humming about his subconscious.

Work and women, he thought to himself. *The first I could expect, but not the women part of it.*

He hurried to the shower and was dressed and ready by 4:15. Too early for hammering, Oliver found his sweatshirt and Robert's twenty-foot retractable leash. Robert made a grand show of stretching and yawning and stretching again, both back legs and front legs, twice each, as if he were pretending to be some sort of Olympic runner getting ready for a long practice session.

Oliver knew there were two or three coffee shops in Shadyside, only a few blocks away, that would probably be open this early. At least he hoped they would be open. Two of them had sidewalk tables. Oliver could get a coffee, a newspaper, and a sweet roll or something and sit outside with Robert.

It was dark and almost still as he walked down South Aiken and onto the main shopping street of Shadyside. The stores populating the area were the type that Oliver would never shop at—fancy jewelry stores, fancy women's clothing stores, fancy "stuff" stores—all items overpriced and not at all practical. Oliver passed a men's accessory store featuring a Rolex in the window—or at least it did when the store was open. All that was left on the velvet podium taking center stage in the display was an elegant sign, announcing a Rolex Daytona wristwatch and the price tag: $15,000.

How could anyone in their right mind pay that much for a watch? I can buy a car or an entire house in some neighborhoods for a little more than that.

Robert nosed along the sidewalk but kept his enthusiasm low. Some dogs, Oliver noted, when walking in an area with lots of dog traffic, would get agitated and nervous and bounce about, as if there were too many scents available for interpretation. Robert appeared above all that and sniffed only occasionally. And when he did, he did so in an almost delicate, detached manner.

In the middle of the block, a pool of light filled the sidewalk, coming from the Coffee Tree Roasters, the one coffee shop that Oliver had hoped would be open. On warm days, like this Monday portended to be, the store would roll up its front windows, exposing everything to the elements. A few tables and chairs sat outside; more were inside, and Oliver gently tied Robert to a chair, saying, "You stay here, Robert. I'm just getting coffee. You can see me inside, okay? No whining."

Robert apparently understood as he sat down on his haunches, watching Oliver enter the shop. A few minutes later, his master returned with coffee and a tray with a bagel and a Danish with pats of butter and a hunk of plain cream cheese in foil, napkins, a plastic fork and spoon, and a glass of water. Oliver sat down and prepared his breakfast, Robert sidling next to him, positioning himself for the optimum amount of begged food. The dog was quickly rewarded with a piece of bagel with a hint of cream cheese.

Oliver wasn't sure if cream cheese was good for dogs, so even though Robert seemed to enjoy it, he tried to limit the amount of non-dog-food items Robert consumed every day.

Oliver unfolded the newspaper. He didn't have to purchase one after all, since the shop had a stack of papers, already discarded from even earlier customers. He read through the front page and the editorials, then hurried to the last section and the comics. As he had aged, he had stopped reading every single comic strip and now focused only on the half-dozen he really liked and found consistently amusing. He felt guilty about abandoning the rest of them but hoped it might be a sign he was finally becoming a mature adult.

He sipped at his coffee. A stooped, older man with white hair made his way to the outside tables and pointed at the empty chair at Oliver's table.

"Anyone using this?" he asked, his words coated with early-morning phlegm.

"No. Go ahead," Oliver replied.

The man put his hand on the back of the chair, then looked about. One of the other two tables was occupied by a man and a woman, apparently at the end of their day, not at the beginning, and at the other table a man had spread out his newspaper, laptop, coffee cup, and bagel in a wide array, as if clearly saying the entire table was occupied.

The old man shrugged. "Okay if I park it here?"

"Sure, that's okay. We're alone. Me and the dog."

"What's his name?"

"Robert. Robert the Dog."

The old man nodded. "Robert the Dog. A nice noble name for a pooch. I like that."

Robert sat up straighter and leaned toward the newcomer. The old man reached out, tentatively, and patted Robert's snout. Robert replied by brushing his tail back and forth on the sidewalk.

"I'm Oliver."

"Barth. Barth Mills. Nice to meet you."

Both men hesitated, and both took drinks from their paper coffee cups.

"Up early, Oliver. You on your way to work, or just an insomniac?"

"Both. Sort of. I'm almost at work. But I woke up real early, and when that happens there's no way I can get back to sleep. So Robert and I went for a walk and are enjoying the nice weather and a little breakfast."

The old man seemed to nod along with Oliver, stopping when Oliver stopped. "Would have brought my dog too. Rascal. Never liked that name. Rascal. Sounds like I'm a fan of the old *Little Rascals* movies—which I'm not—or like I'm stuck in one of those horrid motorized wheelchairs. Either way, it sounds stupid. But he was my wife's dog. She's gone, and I couldn't bring myself to change the name on her, sort of behind her back. And Rascal's old and was still asleep. The dog sleeps like a log, and I'm up and down a dozen times. Don't seem fair at all. Sorry. *Doesn't* seem fair. Live alone and your grammar goes to pot. No one there to worry about sounding right for. Or to. Or whatever."

"Well, the next time you come, bring Rascal," Oliver said. "Robert loves meeting new friends."

"I'll do that. I live down a few blocks that way. Top half of an old house. Summerlea."

"I don't really live around here, but I am staying at the church around the corner while it's being remodeled."

Barth stopped and glared at him. "The big stone place just around the corner? The beautiful old stone church? The one no one should be messing with? You're tearing that apart? You should be ashamed, young man, of desecrating not only God's house, but an architectural treasure."

Oliver was stunned but pretty sure Barth really meant what he said. He certainly wasn't joking; he actually looked angry.

"The outside will be the same. Nothing's changing on the outside," Oliver said, his defense quick. "And the inside will be very nice. I'm only the contractor. I don't own it or anything."

Barth's scowl softened as he tore off a piece of his scone. "So the outside stays the same?"

"Might be a new name on the building, but basically it'll be the same."

"Restaurant?"

"Yes," Oliver replied, leaving out the nightclub aspect.

"How come it's not a church anymore?" Barth asked, his tone more suited to an attorney on cross-examination.

Oliver calmly explained the series of owners and what had happened.

Barth harrumphed at the end. "Presbyterians. Back when I was preaching, I rarely found much common ground with 'em—theologically speaking. And the Koreans." He harrumphed again. "My father served in that war …"

Oliver thought for a second and realized that he didn't know any Presbyterians—or Koreans, either. He figured he might have known a Presbyterian, but maybe they were just quiet about where they went to church. Oliver was pretty sure there was a Presbyterian church in Jeannette, but growing up, his mother had never found much good to say about the big Protestant denominations.

Oliver decided that discussing Presbyterians might not be the most edifying early-morning conversation. "You're a pastor?" he asked instead.

"Was," Barth replied, his voice more rumble than most and graced with the hint of pastoral verve. "I'm not from a big, fancy denomination. In my humble opinion, God doesn't like big and fancy. Retired five years ago, after my wife passed. Lived up in Kane. Kane Church of the Savior. Good people. Mostly good, I guess. Rile up the wrong people in a church and the pastor don't stand … *doesn't* stand a chance. I was done with the fighting by then, so I came back to Pittsburgh."

Oliver nodded as he spoke, wondering why the man was sharing so much with a complete stranger. "Did you grow up here?"

"I did. A few blocks from here. No one's left, though. Just me and Rascal. It's enough." He took another bite of his scone and chewed slowly. "Breakfast is the best meal of the day. The rest of the meals are just for refueling. Breakfast though, light of dawn, a new day … I like it the best."

Barth held out a piece of scone. "Okay for the dog?"

"Sure. I give him treats like that all the time. I figure if it won't kill me, he'll be okay with it."

Barth leaned over and opened his palm with the corner of the scone cupped in it. Robert the Dog sniffed, and with canine gentleness, picked up the scone with his teeth and appeared to chew with deliberation. Barth put his hand on the dog's head and ruffled his fur.

"You got a good dog here, Oliver. Some dogs see something special and they snap at it, like a wolf, and that scares the person doing the offering. Robert was right gentle about it. I like that."

Robert sniffed at the old man's hand nicely, hoping to find another bit of scone, wagging his tail in a slow show of excitement.

The old man stood up, grabbed what was left of his coffee, and took a step toward the sidewalk. "Rascal is probably awake by now. Need to get him outside." Barth was on the sidewalk, then turned back. "I'll bring Rascal tomorrow. I'll get him up early. What's he have to sleep in for, right? If you're here, we'll have coffee."

He waved, and Oliver waved back, wondering if Barth would be able to get Rascal up in time.

Oliver was alone in the church, the morning sun a few hours from being strong enough to illuminate the colors of the stained glass. The once nicely stacked pews now lay about, not exactly scattered haphazardly, but not exactly following a tight formation. The Pratt brothers had discarded a few of the pew sections—those with broken arms, split seats, cracked backs, missing supports—all of which would prove too costly to repair. As it was, there would be a surplus of pews at the end of the job. Of that Oliver was sure.

We'll need a dozen or so to use as booth seating, as incorporated into the space plan. Maybe Samantha can sell the rest of them on eBay or at an auction or something.

Oliver would be alone this morning. Taller had a dentist appointment. The Pratt brothers wouldn't be early. Maybe only one of them would come, or maybe all three, to collect their tools. Oliver still wasn't sure of his decision on hiring them for the job and was glad to have a bit more time to think about it.

I know that they did wrong. I wish I knew which one did the more wrong thing ... but the eldest Pratt brother was right—I probably would treat them differently. I know what Pastor Mosco said about hiring people with a criminal past, what the implications are for my business. But I don't believe bad people always stay bad. That's what the church is for, isn't it? To be an agent of transformation in people's lives ... to help turn bad people into good people by helping them find God and grow in their faith. If we isolate ourselves as Christians, how can we ever make a difference in the world?

The more Oliver thought about it, the more frustrated he became.

Maybe it's time to look for a new church.

This morning, instead of wallowing in his frustration, he decided to putter about the project, maybe not diving into a specific task, but assessing where they were on the timeline, what needed to be tackled now, what subs might have to be lined up in the next few weeks. Contractor "busy work," Oliver called it, a task that he secretly enjoyed. He walked through the church with a clipboard in hand as the sun came up, making notes as he went, ticking off projects that needed to be buttoned up before other work could progress.

The support beams in the basement needed to be covered with wallboard, and just before that, conduit had to be extended, and lighting fixtures would have to be installed. A few more days of work would be required before the kitchen could be started.

Upstairs, in the former sanctuary, the work appeared to be simpler—a sign that Oliver always considered to be an omen foretelling of complications and headaches. What might be most troubling was providing electrical service throughout the building. As it stood, there was exposed conduit attached to the thick stone walls, almost at floor level. Oliver made a note to double-check with the architect about the current electrical code. He imagined that the outlets would have to be higher off the floor, in spaced increments, and if that was the case, it would require a lot of extra work.

I'll call him today. And I'll need to talk to Samantha. If all the electrical outlets need to be revamped, it could cost a lot more than I estimated.

Instead of worrying about what might be, Oliver spent a half hour tidying up a row of pews, lining them up straight, at right angles to the wall. Then he heard the front door of the church bang open.

That's one thing we'll have to fix. New doors have not been specified, so we'll need some sort of hydraulic open-and-close system for them.

He stepped out of the shadows and smiled. Samantha stood alone in the now-sunlit space, holding a cardboard tray with six coffees and a large brown paper bag.

"Breakfast!" she called out.

Oliver made his way to her. "I'm afraid I'm your only company today. My brother's at the dentist, and the Pratt brothers aren't scheduled to work today."

If Samantha was at all disappointed with the less-than-full crew, she was expert at hiding it. "Well, that means more for us then, doesn't it, Oliver-not-Ollie?"

That's like a nickname for me, isn't it? I sort of like it when she says it like that.

"How was New York?" he asked.

Samantha found an accessible empty pew, set the coffee container down, laid out a napkin, and began to unpack the paper bag. "I hate New York. Too big. Too busy. Too many Jews. That self-loathing thing again. But seeing the family is fun—in short doses."

Instead of using a knife like she had done every other morning, spreading cream cheese on her bagel with some delicacy, this morning, Samantha just tore off a healthy chunk of bagel and swiped it through the open cream-cheese container.

She caught him staring and grinned. "This is the single woman's way to do it. Fast. Easier. But don't tell my father."

"It's the single man's method as well. Saves washing utensils."

They ate in silence for a moment, Oliver considering it a very pleasant silence and not the sort of awkward silence he felt when he was around most women.

"I thought you would be the sort of person who would love New York. You know—shopping and theater and going to clubs and all that sort of thing," he said.

Samantha held up her finger, indicating a needed pause, then pointed at her closed mouth as she exaggerated her chewing and swallowing. "Shopping I can take or leave. With the Internet, I can find anything I want from anywhere, so walking down a crowded street in New York is no longer a thrill. And Broadway shows? If you don't mind spending a few hundred dollars on a ticket, it's okay—but I can wait. Eventually one of the touring companies from every Broadway hit shows up in podunk Pittsburgh."

Her face tightened up, as if she was remembering something, then brightened. "You mentioned clubs. I don't do them much anymore. There is little charm to being groped by strangers in the dark ... if you know what I mean."

Oliver did not. His experience was limited, and groping anyone, even in the dark, seemed to him almost criminal, if not downright rude.

"There are enough bad clubs here where I can get hit on by half-*shikker* married men who think they are God's gift," Samantha added.

"Shikker?"

"Drunk."

Again, Oliver had no frame of reference for her comments. He was not married, had never imbibed to even half-drunkenness, and never once considered himself as God's gift to anyone.

Samantha brushed her bushy hair back from her face, the morning light catching her eyes and cheekbones. "You understand, Oliver-not-Ollie?"

"No, I really don't," he admitted in a rush. "I don't go to bars very often. And I don't think I've ever been to a bar that could be described as a club, other than the Elks Club. But I don't think that's what you mean."

Samantha laughed and put her hand on his knee. "You are such a dear, Oliver. I mean that."

She let her hand rest on his knee for a longer moment than was called for by his cute remark, but not as long as he would have liked.

Then what he did next would astound him later on as he thought about it, and astound his brother Taller even more when he heard about it. Occasionally, Oliver let himself do what his gut wanted him to do, instead of thinking about how and why and should he and what might happen if he did. He simply acted on impulse, on what his heart was urging him to do and not what his brain was saying.

Something about this building …

He turned a bit, to face her more directly. She had the prettiest, deepest brown eyes he had ever seen. He wondered, in that splinter of a moment, if all Jewish people had brown eyes. He didn't think so, and maybe he would ask her later, if everything worked out just so.

"Samantha," he said without hesitation, and with as much verve as he could muster, even though he was not a man to have a lot of verve to begin with, "I can't say I have ever been in this position before."

He thought she might be ready with a funny comeback, but she must have seen something in his face so held her words.

"I know you're the boss here and all, but do you think you might like to go to dinner with me? Maybe tonight? Or this week sometime? If you're available."

She looked down at her hands, then up to find his eyes. "I would love that, Oliver. I'm free tonight. We could go out tonight." She smiled.

Oliver bobbed his head, as if setting the appointment down permanently. "Okay then. Good," he said, his words unwinding from a spool under great tension.

"Seven?"

"Seven is good. Casual?"

"Casual is all I have with me, Samantha."

"I like casual. Should I meet you here?"

Oliver shook his head. "No. A gentleman picks his ..." As Oliver felt the word in his mouth and realized what that meant, he wondered, in a sort of terrified way, if she felt the same way. But he had marched too far down this road to take a detour or retreat. "A gentleman picks up his date at her house. Yours is the big Victorian with the second-floor turret, right? I drove past it last week. It's really beautiful."

"That's my house. I'll be ready at seven, then, Oliver."

It was then that Robert the Dog started his gentle barking, as if he had urgent business to attend to somewhere else, and Oliver excused himself to take his dog outside. Samantha said she had an appointment this morning, so they both left the church at the same time.

Oliver watched her walk down the street. She turned back three times and offered a cheery half-wave, seemingly happy that he was staring as she headed home.

Oliver wondered if his heart was beating fast because of what he had done or because of what he was anticipating.

———◦◦◦———

Of course, Oliver was no good for anything the rest of the morning. He sat outside the church with Robert the Dog for at least a half hour after Samantha had disappeared into her house. Oliver could barely see the house from where he sat, and could barely see her, but he had stopped seeing movement, so he knew she had gone inside. Robert the Dog must have thought it odd to be outside so long and began, at some point, to nose against the church door, as if telling Oliver that break time was over and someone needed to get back to work.

Oliver did not take the hint.

"Why did I do that, Robert? Why did I ask her out? My mother would say that she's a horribly wrong choice. There's the 'experience' end of things. I mean, she has probably been with other men. That's what the Dumpster guy said. And I think he's probably right … sometimes you just sort of know. Then there's the religion stuff—her being Jewish."

Robert looked back over his shoulder. He was standing with his nose to the door but felt he needed to listen to Oliver go on about something or other.

"I have never done this before," Oliver said. "I mean … she's the boss. Who asks their boss out for a date? And she's probably really rich. What business do I have asking her out? Who am I to think that she might be at all interested? Maybe she's just being nice. Maybe she didn't know how to say no without hurting my feelings and she's worried about me finishing this job on time. I bet that's it."

Robert stopped staring at the door and slowly circled to stare at Oliver instead.

"You know what I mean, Robert?"

Robert, on occasion, did appear he understood what Oliver was saying. But not today. The dog even tilted his head to one side, like he really wasn't tracking with Oliver at all.

"I know, Robert. None of this makes sense."

He stared at his hands.

Especially since the thing with Paula is getting a little more serious. She's expecting me to call her, too.

He hoped his shocked expression wasn't apparent to Robert the Dog.

Good grief … Paula. And Samantha.

Oliver didn't say her name aloud. He didn't want to upset Robert with this potential duplicity. It was better the dog not know.

Oliver got up slowly, as if the sudden change might disorient him further. He braced himself on the rough-hewn stone wall, and slowly made his way back into the church and the cool blue interior.

Oliver's phone buzzed, and he slapped at the phone holster on his belt like a twentieth-century cowboy in a staged gunfight in a cheesy black-and-white movie. Since he wasn't really working but wandering about the church, he felt almost virtuous about getting a call, since a phone call meant he was doing some sort of work.

It was the eldest Pratt brother on the line—Henry Pratt. He sounded harried and at the edge of anger.

"Listen, Oliver, I won't be able to make it to the worksite today like I said I would. I'd have to borrow my neighbor's car and I don't want to do that—even though he borrowed my truck to pick up a refrigerator at his mother-in-law's place and got it stuck in the driveway and I'm on my way there to get it unstuck. If it's all the same to you, could I just come by tomorrow mornin'? My neighbor promised up one side and down the other that he'd be back by one this afternoon and now it's two. I know it'll be a couple of hours before we get everything straightened out. So is tomorrow okay? Don't tell me yet if you made a decision or not. Just let me wait till I see you in person. Okay?"

Oliver, almost overwhelmed by the barrage of words, rocked back on his heels a bit, then calmly replied, "Tomorrow is fine. And I haven't decided yet, so an extra day would be appreciated."

"That's swell, then," Henry replied. "I'll see you in the mornin'."

Oliver snipped the phone shut and returned it to its holster.

Robert was at his side, staring upward. "I know. I have to come to a decision on this. But it's hard, Robert. I don't know what to do. Not really. Maybe I'll feel better tomorrow. Right now, I'm too nervous."

<hr />

After walking around the church awhile longer, looking at loose ends to tie up here and there, Oliver opened his phone and checked the time.

4:00.

He knew it was absurdly early to start to get ready, but he didn't know what else to do, so slowly he made his way downstairs and spun the dial on the shower. Hot water took a long time to reach this specific outlet in the old building. He kept his hand under the spray until he felt a hint of warmth.

"Okay, Robert, you can go now."

Robert stood up and slowly exited the room, head down, as if he had done something wrong. Oliver never liked showering when the dog was standing around. He had the weirdest stare when he inadvertently entered the shower when Oliver was in it.

Oliver dressed carefully. He took out the few articles of clothes that were dressier than most of his work clothes—clean, almost pressed, and not made of denim or flannel. He combed his short hair carefully and applied a few drops of Old Spice, the only aftershave he'd ever bought—one bottle every year or so had been sufficient.

Heading upstairs, he sat in a pew near the area where the pulpit had stood. He opened his phone. *4:30.*

Good grief. What am I going to do for over two hours?

Taller walked out of the dentist office feeling like a stroke victim. A large cavity had required filling, and his current dentist apparently loved pain-killers, inserting a whole series of shots into his gums and the roof of his mouth. He checked in the mirror before he left, and while his face didn't look different, it felt semi-paralyzed.

He climbed into his truck and wondered what to do next. He didn't have any food at home—at least no soft food. He didn't want to go to a restaurant, knowing he'd slur his words for another hour and probably dribble water all over his shirt or bite his tongue.

He could go to the supermarket, but he wasn't the sort of man who felt at home there. He only shopped for the barest minimum of supplies—coffee, tea, sugar, cream, popcorn, lemons—and lots of cleaning supplies: paper towels, ammonia, vinegar, three kinds of Fantastic, spray kitchen cleaner with bleach, Comet, Windex, Lemon Pledge, plus laundry deter-gent (preferably unscented Tide), and a few other items.

He started the truck. Only one person he knew would have soft food and not require him to talk much for a few hours.

In ten minutes he pulled into his mother's driveway. The light over her sink was on, which was all the evidence he needed to know that she was home. He switched off the engine, pushed in the emergency brake, and checked his face one more time in the rearview mirror. He looked normal but still didn't feel normal.

He was deliberate with each step up to the back door, debating if he should continue or silently slink away. But then he was at the door, tapping gently at the glass. He heard shuffling inside, then a thumb's width of curtain was pulled aside and he saw his mother's left eye, peering out back at him, almost sideways, as if she were trying to minimize her exposure to a potential stranger. When she recognized her son, the curtain flapped down, the door locks clacked open in rapid succession, and the door was yanked open so fast that his mother held onto the handle for balance.

"Tolliver! You're here! Come on in. I haven't seen you in weeks. Why weren't you in church? You said you were coming to church. I looked for you. And the pastor said you weren't in the first service."

Taller had his story set. He pointed to his cheek. "Toothache. I just got back from the dentist. I'm full of novocaine. Can't feel a thing."

Taller's mother grabbed his arm and pulled him inside. "They don't use novocaine any more. Alice at the store—her nephew is a dentist—said that he said they use all sorts of new-fangled drugs now."

Taller shrugged. "Whatever. I'm numb. I dribble when I drink. You have anything soft to eat?"

She hustled him to a chrome and vinyl chair, patched in two places with duct tape that almost matched the original color but was peeling off and sticky at the edges. He sat gingerly, glad he'd worn an older pair of jeans, soon to become work jeans.

"Soup? Grilled cheese sandwich? Meatloaf? Scrambled eggs? Jell-O? Applesauce?"

Taller was more certain now that he had made the right choice in coming back home. "Scrambled eggs. I could eat scrambled eggs. And maybe some white bread toast? With lots of butter so it's kind of soft?"

Rose hurried to the refrigerator and unloaded eggs, butter, cheese, bread, ketchup, and jam onto the counter. She took a frying pan from off the stovetop where she stored it, much to Taller's chagrin, and began to cook. She began talking to her son without turning away from the stove.

"How's work? How's your brother?"

"Fine. It's a nice job. And Oliver is fine."

"He's desecrating a church, if you ask me. And doing the dirty work for a Jewish woman. That's asking for spiritual warfare. I bet the Devil is licking his chops over this one."

Taller didn't roll his eyes and reply "Mother" in an elongated, exasperated tone like he wanted to, like a petulant teenager. Instead he massaged his cheek and jaw. "Maybe. I haven't run into the Devil on the job—yet. Just the Pratt brothers. And I would imagine the Devil would inhabit brighter people than them if he wanted to vex us."

"You can laugh at this, Tolliver. But evil is real. Evil is all around us."

Taller mimed saying "Even here," knowing his mother wasn't looking. He grinned, reminding himself that fighting with his mother was a lose-lose proposition.

"I know, Ma. But I need to work, and Oliver has the jobs. So I do what I'm told. And the Jewish lady who owns the place is a very nice person. I think Oliver might be sweet on her."

Rose swung around so fast with the spatula in her hand that some of the scrambling eggs flipped onto the floor. "Don't you even joke about that, mister. You know it's a lie, and you tell it for laughs—or even worse, to upset me, your mother. Don't you dare make fun of something like that. That's evil, Tolliver. Straight from the pit."

His mother's snappish, angry response immediately told Taller that this wasn't an open subject for discussion—ever. "Okay, okay. Bad joke. Won't mention it ever again."

Rose stared hard at him, then pointed the egged spatula at him like a laser pointer. "Besides, Oliver is dating Paula. Or, rather, dating her again. You know, Paula from around the corner. Wasn't she in your class in school?"

"Yeah—and you didn't like her a whole lot back then. You complained the whole time Oliver was dating her. I remember."

"Well, she wasn't from a churchgoing family. And now she's changed. Anyhow, I think it's time Oliver settles down. And Paula is a very nice girl."

Taller wasn't used to being surprised at his mother's house. He thought he knew what to expect most of the time. Apparently, he was wrong.

"Paula? Paula with the baby? The divorced Paula?" he said, testing his mother, knowing Paula had a baby and was divorced, but wanting so much to see how his mother handled this dilemma.

Rose did not turn around. "Yes. Paula with the baby. I know what you're thinking, Mr. Smarty Pants. Just to aggravate your mother, I bet. And you know, as well as I do, that it's not her fault that no-good bum of a husband left her. She's young. She can have more children. She's pretty. Oliver likes her. Pastor Mosco said it was okay if they were to get married. He even said he would love to officiate at the wedding."

"What? A wedding? They're talking about a wedding?" Taller felt the earth move slightly.

"It's too early to talk about a wedding. But they have been out a few times and both of them have nothing but good things to say about each other. They talked about religion and God. She's born again, you know that, Tolliver? Born again. I'm sure Oliver is thinking beyond just having a good time with a woman."

Mr. Perfect again.

Rose scraped the eggs onto a plate and added two well-buttered pieces of toast. "Unlike some young people I know who think more about their private parts than they do about obeying God's laws."

"Mother," Tolliver replied plaintively, holding his petulance at bay again.

"You know what I mean. Oliver is a good boy. He needs to have a wife. Paula needs a husband. Her daughter needs a father. I think it all works out perfectly," she said, easing herself down in a chair at the table.

And what am I? Chopped liver?

She opened a jar of strawberry jam, bought at the local discount store. Tolliver disliked generic food but had little choice.

"Coffee? Do you have any coffee, Ma? Real coffee?"

She jumped back up. "Of course I do. I'll make a half pot. You'll drink more than one cup, right? I don't want to throw any away."

Taller waved at his mother. "I'll drink it all, Ma. I need coffee with eggs."

And as she busied herself with measuring water and grounds, Taller wondered about Paula, wondered what she might be doing tonight since Oliver was nowhere in the area, and wondered if he might take a walk over to her house later, just to chat, to find out about this woman who apparently had beguiled both his brother and his mother.

Yes, he thought, *that's what I'll do after I eat. Go on a visit to see Paula. Just for a minute or two.*

Immediately he regretted not wearing his new Diesel jeans, the ones that were cut leaner and closer to the hip than the ones he was wearing.

I still look good … regardless.

He slowly chewed on his eggs and toast, wondering if the pain shots would be worn off by then.

CHAPTER ELEVEN

"I THOUGHT WE might eat at Enrico's," Oliver said as they walked down the steps of the great wraparound porch of Samantha's home. "I've never eaten there, but the people at the coffee shop said it was really good. Great Italian food."

"I like Enrico's," Samantha replied. "They're a member of the 'Slow Food Movement.'"

"What does that mean?" Oliver asked.

"It means they support local provisioners by using local and seasonal ingredients—you know, pastas made in Little Italy, meat from local butchers, produce grown locally. Fresh and natural, with no preservatives or fillers. Even the wood they burn in their oven comes from local hardwood and fruitwood trees. I'd like to do the same at my restaurant, if I can find the right chef."

"Wow," Oliver replied. "I guess I made a good choice, then."

"A very good choice, but anywhere would be nice. I mean … with good company, *noshing* at McDonald's can be a good experience."

Oliver didn't rise to the bait. Once, in the past, a long time ago, a woman had said that to him in almost exactly the same words (but without the word *noshing*) and he'd changed his plans and actually went to McDonald's. It was a big mistake. He would not do that again, although he pretty much believed Samantha when she said it.

"McDonald's is okay," he said. "But the eating part of the meal is over in ten minutes. I think it would be nice to have the opportunity to talk a bit longer."

She smiles like an angel, he thought as he opened the door to his truck for her. If she was surprised by his show of manners, she did not let on. He waited until she had her feet inside before solidly closing the door.

She smells really nice tonight.

He hopped up into the cab. "The restaurant is almost close enough to here that we could walk," he said as he pulled away from the curb, "and I'm not saying that because I want to save on parking."

"I would have never thought that," Samantha replied.

"Besides, they have free valet service. I drove past earlier."

Samantha grabbed at his right arm, not to laugh, though she looked like she was about to, and slipped her arm through his.

Two valets met the truck, opened doors, and handed Oliver a claim ticket. Oliver escorted Samantha inside. The walls of the long, narrow dining room were lined with lush color photographs of scenes in Italy, highlighted by droplight fixtures. Cast-iron details gave the space a rustic feel, warmed by its exposed wood-burning oven. A short, stubby man in a tuxedo shirt and black tie escorted them to a table by the window. It had a white tablecloth covered by a paper topper.

Oliver leaned into the table, and Samantha leaned to meet him.

"This is a lot fancier than I expected," he whispered. "Am I dressed well enough?"

Samantha took a quick look around. "The only people that get dressed up to go to restaurants anymore are the waiters and the maître d'. No one else does. You look just fine the way you are, Oliver-not-Ollie."

The prices were not as steep as Oliver had feared. In fact, the cost of a dinner here was less than he'd paid at Angelo's in Jeannette.

Samantha closed her menu quickly.

"You've decided?" he asked.

She shrugged. "It's a gift. Or a curse. I can get to a dish that sounds good very quickly. Why torment myself with a hundred choices that I can't have? I like deciding. I don't like an indecisive *schnook*."

To Oliver, this was a first. Any girl he'd dated (and the number was not all that large, of course) had never made a dining decision that quickly, unless it *was* at McDonald's. But Samantha seemed to have no trouble finding the perfect meal. He liked that.

"I know Jewish people have a lot of rules about what they can and cannot eat," Oliver said, "so I'm glad you found something you like."

"Oh, I don't follow the kosher laws. My father does, most of the time. And my mother always kept a kosher kitchen. But after she died, well … lots of things changed. She was the religious one, but I decided that it wasn't for me. I mean, all those years she tried to keep all those laws—did you know there are 613 of them? A lot of good it did her."

"Six hundred and thirteen? Really?"

"Really, although there's actually only about 77 positive laws and 194 negative laws that the rabbis say can be observed outside of Israel today."

"That's still a lot of laws."

"That's what I'm saying. Not only rules about what you can and cannot eat, but rules about what you do when you wake up in the morning, what you can and cannot wear, how to groom yourself, how to conduct business, who you can marry, how to observe the holidays and *Shabbat*—the Sabbath—how to treat other people, and animals."

"That sounds exhausting," Oliver answered.

"It is. It was. Although my father only keeps the basics and only insists I participate in observing the holidays—Chanukah, Rosh Hashanah, Yom Kippur. Well, he doesn't insist, but I do it out of respect. We still light the Shabbat candles, and he prays after meals. He goes to temple religiously but doesn't demand that I go. I consider myself an 'observant' Jew. Although I think I'm a very spiritual person."

"And he's okay with that?"

"He would like to see me a bit more devout, like he is. But in my opinion, it reduces the religion to a set of rituals devoid of spirituality. Our rabbi says that, on the contrary, observing the laws increases the spirituality in a person's life, because it turns the most trivial, mundane acts—like eating, getting dressed—into acts of religious significance, because you are constantly reminded of your relationship with the Divine, and it becomes an integral part of your entire existence."

"That's interesting," Oliver said. "So everything in your life can be an act of worship."

"It would be nice to think of it that way. But mostly, I think it makes everything in your life an act of guilt."

Oliver had so many things he wanted to say, but as he was puzzling over them, the waiter appeared to tell them about the specials of the evening. Oliver ordered something he had never heard of before called *osso buco,* but it was the chef's specialty, and the waiter went on and on about it, claiming it was delicious and had veal in it. While Oliver was not always big on veal, and never cooked it for himself, this time it sounded good.

Once the waiter departed, Samantha changed the conversation to the church project before Oliver had a chance to respond to what she'd said about her faith—or lack of faith. Soup came (Italian wedding soup), salad and rolls—not standard bread, but some sort of flat, hot, crispy bread flavored with garlic and rosemary—then both enticing entrees. Oliver and Samantha agreed that what they had chosen was perfect.

Oliver was greatly relieved when she didn't ask for a bite of his, nor offer him a bite of hers. *You should be satisfied with what you order. Otherwise it could lead to being disappointed with having to eat your own meal.*

Oliver watched Samantha's eyes light up when she spoke of her ideas for the restaurant and watched her hands as she drew quick sketches of a tile design on the table's paper topper. He had never spent time with a woman who was so … vibrant, so passionate. He couldn't help but compare her to Paula, who talked a lot, sure, but rarely said anything he'd remember afterward. But Oliver knew he'd be thinking about his conversation with Samantha long after the evening was over.

To Oliver, the time slipped past like a spot of mercury held in your hand. Even though you were never to touch the silvery liquid metal, he knew what it looked like and remembered poking at it in a beaker during a science class in high school. All of a sudden, the meal was over, the second cup of coffee—named *caffè latte*—was consumed, and he was presenting the valet with the ticket that would claim his truck. Even though the service was free, he slipped the valet five dollars. He always felt sorry for people who had to work so hard for tips.

On the way home, neither Oliver nor Samantha spoke much. In the past, Oliver would have felt all twisty and tense inside, knowing that his date was probably wondering why he wasn't talking, thinking he was busy crafting an excuse to cut it off early, regretting the fact that she had said yes to him in the first place.

But tonight, Oliver felt none of that—no tension, no projecting deep regret on Samantha. In fact, the silence felt good, normal. Both of them were smiling. It was obvious to Oliver that she was enjoying herself, even when not talking.

"You don't mind silences, do you, Oliver?"

"You read my mind," he replied.

"I didn't," Samantha said, "but it's nice to be with someone who feels assured enough not to chatter on about nothing, just to fill up the blank spaces. Some guys I've dated liked to *vort* on and on about sports. It's not that I don't like the Steelers or the Pirates, but I don't necessarily need to hear an inning-by-inning, or quarter-by-quarter, recap of the last week of ball games."

"That's good," Oliver said, "because I don't think I could do that. Don't get me wrong, I like sports, but I'm not obsessed with them."

He walked Samantha to her front door, the whole time wishing the evening would last longer than it had and wishing he was the type of person who knew of a cool club they could go to where the music was soft and they could talk into the night. But he also knew that he had to work in the morning and figured that Samantha did too.

"Well, Oliver-not-Ollie, I had such a nice time tonight. It was so sweet of you to ask me."

"My pleasure," Oliver replied.

Samantha stood in the doorway and opened the door a few inches. The gentle yellow light from inside glowed over her shoulder, backlighting her hair, making her eyes luminous even in the shadow.

"Would you like to come in? My father isn't home, and even if he was, he wouldn't care. I've had visitors before. We could … get better acquainted. I'd like that."

Suddenly the gift of interpreting expressions returned to Oliver. He stared at her eyes. He knew what she meant. But then another look in her eyes struck Oliver as incongruous.

She wouldn't mind if I came in. I may be inexperienced, but I'm pretty sure. Yet I think she wants me to say no. And I want to say no. I just would never do that.

"I would love to … but maybe some other time. I have some things to do to get ready for tomorrow. And Robert the Dog will need to go out. Is that okay?"

Relief flashed in her eyes. "Sure."

She leaned toward him, maybe only an inch, and tilted her head even less than an inch. But even the inexperienced Oliver knew what that meant. He leaned too, and they met for what Oliver thought would just be a hug … but quickly it turned into something else altogether. He felt her lips on his—more than a good-night-and-thanks-for-dinner sort of kiss, more substantial and meaningful. Oliver did not show his surprise and let the kiss last as long as Samantha let it last. Finally, she leaned back and blinked, showing her surprise … and a sliver of satisfaction as well.

She touched his lips with her two fingers. "I look forward to seeing you again, Oliver-not-Ollie. And not just at breakfast. Okay?"

Oliver struggled to get his power of speech back. "Okay. Sure. I … I will see you tomorrow. But we should do this again. Dinner, I mean. And … you know …"

She kissed him again, a short peck, a kiss of agreement, then slipped inside and closed the door.

Oliver walked back to his truck in the driveway, wondering how in the world he would stop thinking about the feeling of her lips on his.

Tolliver stayed at his mother's house for a while that evening, watching the early edition of the news with her, ignoring her angry comments on most of the subjects covered by the newscasters and her one-sided, incensed monologue at the world's ills and foibles. He even sat through an entire episode of *Dancing with the Stars,* a show Taller found horribly insipid, but one his mother seemed to enjoy, despite her dismay at the racy outfits and her disapproval of everything Hollywood had to offer.

"I like it when those movie-star big shots get taken down a peg or two," she said.

Tolliver would have explained that very few bona-fide stars ever participated in the show—more like a catalog of B- and C-level almost-celebrities—but the effort wasn't worth his time.

He said his good-byes, got into his truck, backed out of the driveway, and drove down the street, driving away from her house, then circling back, going a few extra blocks. He then parked a half block away from Paula's home, well out of view of his mother's windows.

There's someone else I'd like to take down a peg or two.

He sat back in the truck and tapped his fingers on the dashboard.

I'm sick of always being thought of as the bad son. "He's such a good boy, that Oliver. Just like his father." If I hear that one more time, I think I'll puke.

He locked the truck and brushed off his shirt and pants. An errant toast crumb wouldn't fit his image.

If I can't have Samantha, then maybe I can have Paula.

He walked up to Paula's door and tapped ever so lightly.

From inside he heard a rustling and a TV being muted or turned off. The door opened a few inches.

"Taller!" Paula exclaimed, opening the door wide. "This is a surprise."

Taller waited outside, just on the landing, knowing that any eagerness on his part would be seen as suspect. He knew when to play situations on the cool, almost detached, side.

"I was at my mother's. She was talking about you and Oliver and you two dating again. I thought I'd just stop by and tell you how wonderful the news was. I mean that. Really."

Paula appeared to stop, midaction, for a moment. Taller could tell she was thinking. Then she stepped back, opened the door farther, and said in a warmer, more accommodating tone, "Come on in. Can you stay for a second or two? I don't get that many callers. *Gentlemen* callers are even more rare." Her giggle was muted.

Taller waited, as if he were truly considering his choices. "Sure. If it's okay, and if the baby's asleep. I don't want to intrude or anything. I only wanted to say how happy I am for you."

"No, it's okay. Come on in. The baby has been asleep for hours. Sleeps like a log, that one. I was watching TV."

Taller stepped in and, without trying to be too obvious, took in the stack of dishes in the sink, spilling over the drainboard, the rumpled comforter on the couch, the empty pizza box on the kitchen table, and a quartet of empty beer cans in a jagged semicircle on the coffee table.

"Well, just for a minute, to catch up a bit. It's been years since we've talked, hasn't it?"

Paula switched off the light in the kitchen, the light over the dining-room table, and then the TV. "It's been years, Taller. I see you around all the time, but we really haven't talked or anything, have we?"

Taller waited. The recliner in the living room had a stack of laundry, all in a tangled heap, apparently long out of the dryer, waiting to be folded and put away. There was an empty laundry basket on the floor next to the chair.

"Come, sit on the couch. It's more comfortable than that chair. My husband, or my ex, I should say, bought it right before he took off. I never liked it—yet I'm still paying for it."

Taller hoped his expression showed great concern and sympathy. It was an expression he'd practiced. He knew she saw it and considered it genuine.

"I bet it's been hard on you, Paula, hasn't it?"

She nodded. "Harder than you can imagine. No one asks about it. Like it never happened and no one really cares. Especially the guys. They just see a single woman … and I guess you know what that means, don't you?"

Taller nodded, his face still grave. "I don't understand it. Why people don't care. Why men, especially, can be so … insensitive."

Paula showed a brave smile. "But you understand, don't you, Taller? You know how hard it can be. I can see that in your eyes. That's such a dead giveaway—a man's eyes. He can lie with his mouth, but his eyes tell the truth. I heard that in a song. I think I did anyhow. Some country-western song. But I bet you don't listen to country stuff, do you?"

He offered a shy grin. "Don't tell anyone, Paula, but sometimes I do."

She waved her hand at him in a good-natured, friendly dismissal. "You're just being nice. But—"

He waited long enough to show he was really interested in what she was saying and thinking, then said, "No … go on. Tell me."

"Being alone. It's hard sometimes. Being responsible for everything. I get so tired. I get tired of not having an adult to talk to. But maybe the biggest thing I get tired of is not being hugged." She looked down, then said quickly, "I love Bridget and all that, but hugging her is not the same as being close to someone else. You ever wonder why little old ladies go to the beauty parlor every week?"

Taller shook his head.

"It's not because they need their hair done. It's because they don't have anyone to touch them. They miss the physical touch. That's what I think it is."

"Paula, you're not only pretty but smart, too. Observant."

Paula blushed.

Taller leaned in a little closer.

"You're sweet," she said. "Like your brother. He doesn't talk much. But I think he understands. You understand, too, don't you?"

He moved an inch toward her and saw that she moved an inch toward him. He held the smile that he felt. He put his arm up and around her shoulder. "I do understand, Paula. I do. A hard life. A hard time. Alone."

Paula hesitated, then leaned into him until her shoulder nestled in his open arm. "I don't like being alone, Taller. Remember back in high school? Remember how much fun we had in that class we were in together? What was it? English?"

Taller had little recollection of that class and none of Paula being in it but agreed anyway. "Sure. English. Mr. Marino, right? I always thought you were special back then, Paula. I can see why Oliver is interested in you."

"Really?" she replied.

"Oh, sure. A pretty woman like you. Desirable. I'm jealous of him. I really am." He reached out with his free arm and touched her forearm delicately with his finger.

She placed her hand over his and leaned harder against him. He gave her shoulder a gentle pull, bringing her closer to him, and felt her grow soft against him, on the couch, with the comforter bunched on one side.

Her head fell against his shoulder, and he pulled her even closer. She let him, even encouraged him by turning to him. Tilting her head back, she presented her waiting lips to him, her eyes all but closed, her palm open and relaxed on his thigh.

———⧫———

Oliver returned to the church, parked his truck under the port cochere, and unlocked the front door. Robert the Dog was sitting just inside—not barking, but waiting to be excited when his master returned.

"Hey, Robert," Oliver said as he bent down. Robert bounced a bit, whining a little. He only whined when he was really excited. He sniffed at Oliver's chin and face as if he wanted to know what he had eaten.

Oliver snapped open his phone to see the time. "It's not even 10:00 yet. Do you want to go for a walk, Robert? Maybe stop at the coffee shop?"

Robert recognized the word *walk* and did his four-legged happy dance all around the vestibule of the church in anticipation. Oliver had hung the dog's leash on a coat hook inside the door in the vestibule. Snapping the closure on the dog's leash, he set out. He planned on taking a very long route—heading north on Aiken, south to Fifth Avenue, then west to the University of Pittsburgh area, past the Cathedral of Learning and the Heinz Chapel, both lit dramatically against the dark night sky, then back again to Negley, and up Walnut Street. Oliver wanted time to decompress from his dining experience—and more so, from what happened during the good-bye on the porch. A walk seemed like the perfect end to a most remarkable evening.

Robert took the lead, never pulling hard at the leash, walking a few feet in front of Oliver, waiting at curbs for instructions. Oliver would point, and Robert would head off in that direction. The circuitous route took about thirty minutes to complete. Oliver was not walking fast, and Robert the Dog even gently tugged at the leash once or twice to speed things up. The pair turned onto Walnut at the light and walked up Shadyside's main shopping street.

The sidewalks had cleared for the most part, though a number of people were doing just what Oliver was doing: walking, taking advantage of one of the first mild evenings, a hint of the real warmth of spring in the air. Robert the Dog would walk closer to Oliver when the sidewalks were crowded, not wanting to interfere with others or unwilling to have his paws stepped on by some nonlover of animals.

Oliver stopped outside the Coffee Tree Roasters shop, snagged Robert's leash to an empty chair, and hurried inside to order a *caffè latte* and something sweet that he and Robert might share. He heard a bark, then another from outside, grabbed his coffee and scone, and hurried outside, thinking Robert might be the cause of the disturbance.

He found Robert, standing up, tail wagging in a most friendly manner, and a very round basset hound on the sidewalk on its back, tongue lolling out, being as submissive as a fat, old dog could be. His master was barking at him, "Rascal, get up! Get off the sidewalk! He's a friend. Get up, you silly old mutt."

"Barth, it's Oliver. You brought your dog."

Barth was near to falling, his nonretractable leash wound around one leg and a parking meter. "Stupid mutt. Does this with every dog. Like he's a doormat or something. Get up, Rascal. It's okay."

Rascal finally got the message and wheezed over to one side, his short, stubby legs scrabbling to gain purchase on the ground. With a mighty galumph, he rolled onto his belly and stood up, appearing as if he considered it an event of monumental and satisfying proportions.

Oliver pulled out a chair. "Will you join us for coffee?" he asked, surprising himself, since he was not the sort of person who was all that chummy even with old friends.

Barth succeeded in untangling himself, snorting as he did. "I guess. But no caffeine for me. Too late. These people have anything without caffeine, do you think?"

Oliver assured him that they did. "I'll watch Rascal for you. He seems to be okay now."

Barth repeated "Stupid mutt" one more time, then headed inside. Rascal looked up at Oliver, sat down with a wheeze, and then shifted his limpid, watery stare between Robert, whom he recognized as a dog, and Oliver, who smelled like he had food with him.

Barth returned with a cardboard cup and sat down heavily in the chair. "At this time of night, my knees let me know they've had it. Getting old is a ... well, getting old is never as pleasant as those blasted AARP magazines make it out to be. They never ask me how it feels to turn seventy. If they did, I'd tell 'em the truth. Not like those fancy Hollywood types who can afford to have people do everything for 'em."

Oliver sat quietly, listening.

"Meant to tell you that I apologize for being crabby about your business the other day. You have to work. I know that. And if the building … I mean, if you're okay with the building not being a church anymore, then who am I to tell you what to do? I'm just an old pastor. I can be pretty old-fashioned and thickheaded. I know God ain't … *isn't* only in religious buildings. He's inside each one of us. Or He should be. Or He wants to be."

Barth sipped at his cup. Oliver smelled cinnamon.

"You a Christian, Oliver? You believe? I didn't get around to asking."

Oliver nodded. "I am, Barth. I guess I've always been one, but I understand what it means. Forgiven. Redeemed. Following Christ."

"Yep. That's good. Since I don't do pastoring anymore, I have to remind myself to be … up front about it. Ask folks. If they say they don't know, why then, I've got an opening."

Oliver broke the scone in half. "You want some, Barth? Too much for one person."

Barth waved it off while drinking. "Give some to the dogs. They'll enjoy it a sight more than I will, I bet. Something about watching how much a dog loves food gives a fellow encouragement."

Oliver broke pieces off the scone and tried to give both Rascal and Robert an equal share. Robert was well behaved as he accepted his piece, but Rascal snorkled and shoveled at the food as if he had not been fed in weeks—yet the dog's ample belly proved that false in an instant.

A few cars whirred past as they sat. A clutch of pedestrians, well into their cups, jostled along, laughing and slurring. Both dogs looked up and followed the crowd intently, Rascal sampling the air like a machine.

"Old habits," Barth explained. "At one time, Rascal was a great bird dog. Bassets don't usually make for good bird dogs, but Rascal was. I didn't hunt, even back then, but we both liked watching pheasants clear out of a patch of grassland, their wings clattering in the air, those squawks following them as they flew off. Old Rascal would stand there, looking back at me, with a grin of accomplishment on his face. He never figured out that

a dog should chase them. And once he heard a gunshot, he drop
ground, shaking like a bunny. Had to carry him home."

Rascal turned around as Barth talked about him, almost adding a rue-
ful nod at the end of the story as if to say it was all true.

"Barth, what sort of pastor were you? Back when you were pastoring,"
Oliver asked.

"A good one." Barth laughed. "Well, maybe *decent* is a better word. I
was okay. If you mean what denomination—it was an independent church.
It didn't grow that much. But then, Kane is a small town, not many people
to draw on, and once they get settled in a church, not much moving takes
place. Not like here in Pittsburgh. People pick up and move all the time.
In all of Kane County, there were maybe a dozen churches, so there was no
place you could go where they didn't know you."

Oliver sipped at his coffee, never liking to sip the hot liquid through
that tiny opening in the cup's lid. But if he left it off, he ran the risk of a
bug drowning in the milky foam.

"Getting back to the church building," Barth continued, "if you're a
true Christian, Oliver, then you also must know that *we* are the church.
In the New Testament, the Greek word *ekklesia* appears over a hundred
times—and never meant a place. It always meant a group of people who
followed Christ, who said He would build His church, and the gates of
hell could not prevail against it. In those days, they didn't have buildings to
worship in. They met in homes, or outside. They didn't have all the fancy
trappings and fancy denominations—all that came later. And look how
Christianity spread in the first century without all that. That's what happens when the Holy Spirit comes down. Don't get me started."

"Barth, can I ask you a question? Sort of a church-and-pastor kind of
question?"

"Ask away. Be good to keep my theology sharp, right?"

"I've got a chance to hire three brothers to work on the old church
with me. Hard workers, pleasant, good carpenters."

"So far, Oliver, I don't see any theology in this one. You're not doing a
good job of stumping me."

"Not at the hard part yet," he replied and handed each dog another
thumb-sized chunk of scone. So far, Oliver had not tasted it himself.

"Two of the brothers have a criminal record. Served time in jail. Since then, they've been law-abiding and all that. My question is: Should I hire them? Being ex-criminals and all?"

Barth leaned back and stroked his chin. "A lot of different ways I could answer this. Stay away from bad influences. Avoid fools. Surround yourself with like-minded people."

Oliver listened closely. "So … I shouldn't hire them?"

Barth bristled. "No. That's not my answer. Do they deserve a second chance? Will they do a good job? Are they a danger to anyone?"

Rascal wheezed a bit and lifted his front legs on Oliver's knee, staring up at him, snuffling the air, trying to determine if there was any more of whatever it was he had been eating. Oliver tore the last remaining piece of scone in two and gave one to him. Rascal inhaled the tidbit.

"Get down, you mutt," Barth softly barked out. "You've had enough."

Oliver tossed the last bit to Robert, who hardly moved his head and snagged the piece in midair, gulping it down.

"You know, when God wanted to use a man, didn't matter what he was—only what he had inside and what he might become. He picked Paul. Most bosses would see his résumé and toss it out. But God saw something inside. That's the hard part, Oliver. Do you see something inside these men? Something good, or honorable, or a willingness—something that's beginning to change? If that is there, go ahead and hire them. Who knows what kind of influence you may have in their lives? Ellen, my wife, used to quote an old Swedish proverb: 'Love me when I least deserve it, because that is when I really need it.' And remember—God is the God of second chances. And we need to be that way too."

Oliver let his relief show on his face. "Thanks. That's the advice I needed."

Barth grinned. "It's not like you're marrying these fellows. It's only a job, right?"

Oliver nodded. At that moment, he realized that the second question he was letting form in his thoughts might best be left unasked, at least for now.

Samantha climbed the stairs to her bedroom slowly, as if not wanting to call an end to the evening. Once she reached her bedroom, her date would officially be over.

She tossed her sweater into a corner of her closet and dropped her blouse and slacks on top of it, grabbing at a nightgown. She knew Mally would scold her about the pile in the morning, a familiar yet comforting admonition.

Dropping onto her bed, she pushed the gathering of decorative pillows and shams into a deep pile and lay back against them. She grabbed her cell phone and scrolled through the numbers once, then again.

There's no one to talk to about this.

She stood up, grabbed her robe, and slipped down the hall, the back staircase, the long hall toward the kitchen, the three steps, and then the short hallway that led to Mally's quarters—a large bedroom, bathroom, and cozy sitting area. Samantha seldom entered this part of the house. Her father had scolded her once, as a young teenager, for bothering Mally at night.

"You let her be after hours," he warned. "She needs her time away from us. And if she gets too much like family, then I can't be her employer. You understand?"

Samantha didn't, but she obeyed, most of the time. And so tonight she ignored what her father said years ago, because she needed someone to talk to, and her father was of no use with questions about men and women—especially if the woman was his only daughter.

Samantha tapped softly.

"Dat be you, Miss Sam? I hear you comin' in before. Come on in, child."

Mally was still fully dressed. The TV was turned to a Spanish soap opera.

"I didn't know you speak Spanish," Samantha said.

"Oh, child, I don'. I pick out words sometimes. I likes to guess at what dey be sayin'. More fun than dose dancin' shows. Dey be a foolish waste of time."

Samantha let herself fall onto the loveseat opposite where Mally sat.

"You be out with de new man? De one from de church?"

Samantha nodded.

"He not come in? You not ask him in? He dat bad?"

As Samantha shook her head, she realized how well acquainted Mally was with Samantha's history in dating. All too often Samantha let her dates become overnight guests, well before they had earned that privilege—at least according to Samantha's preset rules on dating and intimacy. Mally had grumbled to Samantha many times in the past that she let her desires get in the way of her brain.

"You not be dinkin' with your head, child, but wid somethin' else altogether," she often said.

"No," Samantha answered, "he's a really sweet man. I invited him in, and he said no. And you know what, Mally? I was happy he said no. I don't know why I was happy, because he's really cute and treats me … well, like a lady. Like he really respects me, likes me for *me*. I just feel … safe with him."

Mally moved from her chair to sit beside Samantha on the couch. "It be de proper way, Miss Sam. A real gentlemen, he don' be goin' fast because he can. Take his time. Dat be de right ding."

"You think? It's not because he finds me disgusting, is it? Or he's gay?"

"Child, you have de most crazy thoughts. He sound like a gentleman, dat be all. A gentleman gets to know a lady. You got time. He got time. Plenty a time, Miss Sam."

Samantha took a thickness of her hair and twisted and twirled it in her fingers.

"So, what dis fellow like? You need to bring him to Mally so I can get to what he be made of."

"I will, Mally. He's as tall as me. Almost. Maybe a half inch shorter. He has blond hair, short, but not too short … no annoying buzz cut. He has a kind face and gray eyes. Nice hands, too—especially for a contractor."

"He be dressed nice?"

"Nothing fancy, Mally. Khakis. Blue shirt." Samantha giggled. "I think he was wearing Old Spice aftershave."

"Dat be bad?"

Samantha held open her palms. "I don't know. It's the stuff I used to buy for Daddy at Chanukah … when my mother was alive.…"

And as soon as the words were out, Samantha knew what would happen. If she didn't talk about it, the pain wouldn't be there. If the name wasn't mentioned, her loss wouldn't seem as great. But there it was, and for that moment, Samantha felt alone and lost and adrift. There was a catch in her throat and a tear in each eye.

When she turned to Mally and held out her arms, Mally tenderly embraced her, stroking her hair and whispering, "All be okay, child. I know you miss her. It be hard, Miss Sam. It be hard on all of us left back home."

Sam let herself cry—not because she missed her mother, but because she didn't miss her at all. That absence of feeling scared her and made her feel so very guilty—just like her mother's curse scared her and made her feel bad.

Taller entered his dark apartment and didn't turn on a single lamp. The light from the streetlamp at the end of the block was enough illumination to navigate. He placed his keys in the cobalt bowl, then readjusted the bowl's position an inch to the left.

Walking into his bedroom, he took off his shoes, placing them in the empty spots on the shoe rack in the corner of the walk-in closet. He took off his still-clean shirt and placed it into the hamper. Removing an old sweatshirt from the top of his dresser, he slipped it on, then padded out, barefoot, into the kitchen. He stood in front of the sink, debating between tea and coffee, and decided on neither of them. Taking a new bottle of water from the middle shelf of the refrigerator, Taller walked slowly out into the living room and took a seat at the end of the high-backed sofa. He carefully cracked the seal of the bottle, making sure he didn't spill any liquid on the sofa's fabric, and drank deeply, nearly consuming half the bottle in that first long drink.

He screwed the cap back on and placed it on the coaster at the edge of the end table.

Why did I do that?

He leaned back and let his head loll on the back of the sofa, his eyes open and focused on the darkness above him.

It was too easy. She was too easy. It was all too easy. And I'm only going to hurt both of them—Ollie and Paula.

He closed his eyes and breathed in deep.

And it will simply kill my mother.

That's when he found a look of pleasure on his face but quickly wiped it off. Sitting up, he picked up the bottle of water, moved the coaster back into its place, and marched into the bedroom, knowing full well that sleep would elude him this evening.

It will kill her.

He opened his eyes to the darkness.

And it will drive Ollie crazy.

———◦✧◦———

Paula opened the door to her daughter's bedroom only an inch to peer into the room. It was barely lit by a nightlight in the shape of a frog, casting a green color over the room. Bridget lay still, the blanket nearly off her tiny form. Paula slipped into the room as silently as she could, lifted the blanket, and settled it carefully over Bridget's shoulders. For several minutes, Paula watched as her daughter's chest rose and fell, rhythmically.

As Paula's hands rested on the side rail, her grip tightened, harder and harder, as if she were hanging on to some dangerous thrill ride, with the passenger car careening down the tracks. With all the blind turns and dips and curves in her path, if she let go, she would be hurled out into space.

Why did I do that? Why did I let him do that?

She rubbed her hand under her nose, thinking that tears might accompany her thoughts. So far, they had not.

I like Taller. I always have. Why did he come over tonight? Why?

She looked down at her child. Bridget rustled a bit and kicked her legs, jostling the blanket from her shoulder again. Paula retrieved it and backed out of the room, not fully closing the door, knowing that the latch clicked loudly and might waken her child.

She stepped out into the darkened living room and walked over to the kitchen table. Picking up each of the four beer cans in succession, she shook them gently. They were all empty. She opened the refrigerator, sliding items about one way and then another. Disappointed, she closed the door. Walking over to the pantry, she switched on the light. Up on the top shelf, behind the sack of flour she never used, was an amber bottle, half full. Retrieving it, she poured two inches of the liquid into a plastic tumbler, added some cola from a two-liter bottle that was in the refrigerator door, and swirled the contents to mix them. She took one swallow, and then another, until the cup was almost empty before setting it on the counter.

Picking up the comforter that was spread out over the couch cushions, she walked it back to the laundry room and threw it toward the washing machine.

I'll get to it tomorrow.

Once back in the kitchen, she swallowed the rest of the drink and pulled out a kitchen chair. She sat down heavily, pushed the empty pizza box out of the way, folded her arms on the table, and laid her head on her arms. Closing her eyes tightly, she tried to think of nothing—nothing except the darkness and the stillness of the night.

———

Rose waited at the back door, her key in the lock, until the garage door fully descended. Then she turned the key and slipped into the dark kitchen. The light on her stove, the kind of stove they don't make any more, was more than enough light to see. Rose poured cold coffee into a pan, placed it on the gas burner, and turned the handle. The pilot light whoofed and the burner ignited. She could have used the microwave, a gift from Oliver several years earlier, but she didn't want stray, leftover waves of energy scattering out when she opened the door. Their cumulative effect might cause some manner of brain injury.

She sat at the kitchen table and took an envelope out of her purse. She extracted a thickness of U.S. currency and fanned the bills out—nearly seven hundred dollars. She had not won the grand prize at bingo that night but had won one of the two semigrand prizes. She tapped the bills into a stack, carried them with her to the stove in one hand, poured the now-hot coffee into a cup with the other hand, and went back to the table. This time she counted the bills twice, just to be certain.

While Rose considered gambling a sin, as well as playing the lottery, she felt bingo a fine activity. After all, it was played in the Catholic church, or at the VFW hall—for a good cause, probably—and the veterans wouldn't do anything that was illegal.

It was the first time in months that Rose had won one of the final big-money games. *It's almost enough to pay for a bridal shower. Paula could use a few new things, and it would be nice to give her something special.*

She tucked the money back in the envelope. She would place her winnings in the dented gunmetal gray lockbox tucked into a corner of the guest-room closet.

A tinny, sharp thought poked into Rose's musings. *I know this might be putting the cart before the horse, but I'll sit down with Oliver soon ... tell him it's time. He knows he needs to be married, and Paula is a good girl. She'll make him a good wife.*

She sipped at the coffee, not minding the bitterness. *He's a good boy. He'll listen to me. He's always been a good boy. Just like his father, but not disappointing and weak. And not like Tolliver, who lies to his own mother. A good boy. A good boy who will obey his mother.*

Oliver checked his watch: *past 10:00 p.m. now.* He stood in the former sanctuary of the church. It was dark, silent. He scrolled through the numbers on his contact list. He came to *Pratt Brothers,* then hit *Send* and waited. The eldest Pratt had said they let all calls go to voice mail after dark.

"Don't like pickin' up the phone after the sun goes down," Henry had admitted once.

A most curious affection, Oliver thought, *but no worse than anyone else.*

The connection clicked, and Oliver listened to the familiar instructions before he said, "This is Oliver Barnett. I know you said you'd be here tomorrow, Tuesday, but I wanted to let you know tonight. I've decided to use you on the job in Shadyside. I know what you did way back when in Ohio—but like you said, you've paid your debts. You've always worked hard, and you've always been honest with me. That's more than I can say for a lot of the subs I've had over the years who *haven't* been to prison. So ... come on in, plan to start. I think we've got maybe three months of solid work ahead of us. Maybe four, or even five—depends on what we run into. So ... I'll see you tomorrow."

He clicked the red *End* button, disconnecting the call, and snapped the phone back into its holster on his belt. Robert had been watching him as he spoke. Robert looked full, and after half a scone, Oliver was sure he was. The two of them headed downstairs, switching off lights as they descended.

In a moment, Robert was curled up in his bed. Oliver lay on his cot, his hands behind his head, staring into the gentle darkness. From the corner of his eye, he could see his wind-up alarm clock: *10:24*.

Closing his eyes, he tried to picture Samantha's face just as she turned her head and let her eyes all but flutter shut. He could still feel her lips—welcoming, inviting—and smell the soft scent that entwined the very air around her.

He blinked, trying to focus on nothing, and Paula came to mind again. Peering toward the clock, he realized that, tonight, sleep might be hours away. From the end of the bed, he heard the canine whistle and snore from Robert and wished, for a moment, that *his* life might be that uncomplicated.

CHAPTER TWELVE

PAULA ROUSED HERSELF from her disturbed sleep in the recliner in the living room. The sun had not even broken the horizon. Her head felt tight, almost painful, as she shuffled to the kitchen sink for a large glass of cold water. Blinking several times, she swept the empty cans into the trash bin kept under the sink, folding the greasy pizza box in half and sliding it in as well. She grabbed the clean laundry off the floor by the recliner where she had tossed it, placed it back in the plastic basket, and carried it to her bedroom. After dumping it all on the bed, she pulled on a pair of jeans and a sweatshirt.

She listened closely at Bridget's door.

Still asleep. Such a good sleeper.

Rather than wait for the percolator to work, she switched on the electric kettle and found the near-empty jar of instant coffee she kept on hand for situations like this.

I'll need to get more coffee, and I'll need to get another "emergency bottle" for the pantry. Maybe I should get a regular-sized bottle. It would probably be cheaper that way. The liquor store always has something on sale.

Paula had always bought the small bottles of alcohol, usually inexpensive whiskey, figuring that a full bottle might encourage her to drink more, and more often.

As she placed the last dirty dish in an already-full dishwasher, she heard what might be a tapping at her door. The clock above the refrigerator indicated 6:45.

Who could that be ... so early?

Paula pulled the window blind out a bit. If you stood just so, you could see the front step.

Rose Barnett stood on the stoop, clutching the lapels of a large, wrinkled raincoat tight to her throat.

Paula opened the door quickly. "Rose," Paula said in a loud whisper, "is something wrong? What's happened?"

Rose slipped inside without being asked. "Nothing's wrong," she whispered back, "but we need to talk. I knew you'd be up. I saw the lights on in the kitchen."

"I'm making coffee. Do you want some?"

"Okay," Rose replied, opening the raincoat to reveal yet another faded and ill-fitting exercise outfit that never saw the inside of a gym. "Black is okay. If you have milk, that would be okay too. I bet you have milk, with a little one in the house."

Paula placed two cups on the table, both pale with milk, some artificial sweetener, and two spoons. Rose ignored the sweetener and took the closest cup.

"You said we needed to talk, Rose. About what? Is Oliver in some sort of trouble?" Paula asked.

"Heavens, no," Rose replied. "Other than desecrating a church, Oliver is fine. He's a good boy. But we do need to talk about him, you and I."

Her thinking still fuzzy, Paula waited for Rose to explain herself, knowing she couldn't do a thorough job of interrogating the older woman.

But Rose paused, as if she were waiting for Paula to ask more questions, as if giving her fuzzy thinking a chance to clear. Rose took a long drink, placed the coffee cup down, and folded her hands in front of her. "We need to get Oliver to commit."

Paula resisted the urge to blink in surprise. "Commit? To what?"

Rose sighed, an almost-frustrated sigh. "To marry you, of course. He's ready. You're ready. Why should you both waste time dilly-dallying? He needs to know that it's time to commit. Time to get married. I know this may not be the most romantic approach, but Oliver is a good boy. He'll listen to me. And he respects you. He likes you. He really does. I'm sure of that. But maybe he's too nice of a boy—if you know what I mean. Too nice means too kind and that means not enough courage. He's the kind of a boy who always needed a nudge or two to get into action. It will all fall into place with the proper encouragement. The right guidance."

"Marriage?"

Rose sighed again, loudly, as if she was explaining something very simple. "When Oliver's father and I got married, we knew each other for less than a month. You and Oliver have known each other since high school. You dated for a long time. Now when Oliver's father and I decided to get married—well, it was on the spur of the moment. But I knew it was right and pushed him. I had to. Otherwise, he would still be trying to decide. And that was how it was back then. Oliver is like his father. A wonderful man, but needs a lot of encouragement. He needs a big push. He knows that being married is a good thing. He needs us both to … all three of us have to … be on the same page. He's a good Christian boy, and he needs a wife. And you need a husband."

Rose glanced around the room. "You don't want to live like this for the rest of your life, do you? In a tiny house with no one to come home to and no future? You want to be married, don't you?"

Paula nodded. "I guess. I mean, I do. I just don't want to force Oliver. We were close way back when, but even if I wanted him to … ask me, I'm not sure if—"

Rose waved off her concern. "Please," she said a little condescendingly. "You've known each other forever. You two dated for years and years back then. You know each other better than most people who get married. Oliver needs a good Christian woman, a woman who has been born again. You *are* born again, right?"

Paula nodded. "Sure. Yeah. I'm born again. Of course."

"That's what he needs. A good Christian woman. You're pretty, attractive, a nice person. And you like Oliver, right? You need to treat him right, Paula. You have to be a good girl, but you have to get his attention. Do you know what I mean? Men like … well, they like things that maybe a good woman thinks are disgusting. I know how it is. Men are different than women. This whole sex thing is something I never cared much for. But I guess men do. Sometimes even a good girl has to get a man's attention. Sometimes you might have to … you know. You do like Oliver that way, don't you? I mean … you find him attractive … that way. Right?"

Paula felt as if the house had been caught up in a tornado that was spinning everything out of control, changing everything normal into what wasn't so normal, and making the expected the unexpected. "Sure, Rose. I like Oliver a lot. He is such a sweet guy. And handsome."

Rose snorted softly. "Handsome doesn't last. It doesn't pay the bills. Oliver's brother—Tolliver—you know him, right? He's the handsome one. And he uses women like shoes. God hates him for that. I know He does. Women fall all over him. You are much better off with a man like Oliver. Solid, dependable. Stay away from men like Tolliver. Nothing but trouble."

For a split second Paula panicked, wondering if Rose had seen Taller enter last night, had somehow peered through Paula's windows and seen what had transpired in the dark, with Bridget roundly sleeping in the next room.

———◦◦◦———

Oliver held a clipboard in his hand and placed a tick mark on one line, halfway down on the third sheet of a yellow legal pad, the edges curled and wrinkled. It was several weeks into the work schedule, and the first and second pages were heavy with tick marks, each indicating one part of the project that had been completed. The basement was nearing completion—or at least Oliver's part of it. Kitchen walls were framed, drywall hung, taped, and primed. The electrical conduit had been installed. A sprinkler system ran along the ceiling. A nonslip sanitary flooring would be laid last, covered with a protective layer until all the appliances were installed.

The new stairway to the basement was under construction. The building engineer located a spot, just off the kitchen, and below the east side of the platform, where the rafters were not bearing any floor load and where four beams could be installed for stability. The Pratt brothers had cut through the floor, placed support beams, and built railings around the opening on the first floor. They were in the middle of constructing a double-wide staircase, with wider-than-code-called-for treads and risers. Bringing food upstairs would be taxing to a waitstaff, and Oliver wanted to make sure the steps were safe and easy to climb—even though the city's code of building did not call for it.

Oliver's kitchen contractor was scheduled to start the following Monday.

There was a large empty space in the basement that would remain untouched—the former Fellowship Hall. Samantha had decided to let the next owners do with it what they wished, and for now, it would be used for storage. So Oliver didn't have to worry about it.

The upstairs looked more and more like a restaurant every passing day. The bar, where the platform had been, was almost complete, except for the long polished walnut top—due in any day. Plumbing had been tricky to accomplish, pipes being snaked and jimmied along steel girders and basement rafters. It had been roughed in to support multiple sinks in the bar area, for faucets and wastewater.

Every project Oliver had ever worked on had its own set of peculiarities and challenges, and regardless of how meticulously planned, each one progressed at its own rate. With some jobs, everything went right, and schedules were easily met or exceeded. Some projects seemed as if conceived in a black cloud, and no matter what Oliver might aspire to, the schedule lengthened and then lengthened again, much to his dismay, as well as to the consternation of the owner.

Some parts of the current "Blue Church" project, as Oliver had begun to refer to it, were completed faster than Oliver had imagined; some resisted completion. But, overall, he was well within his projected schedule parameters, plus or minus a week or so.

And to make the job more gratifying, Samantha Cohen was satisfied with the work Oliver was doing. The Pratt brothers were proving to be an inspired choice—hard workers, creative, and each with what Oliver called a "servant's heart."

"'Servant's heart'?" Samantha had asked, puzzled, when he first used the term.

"I'm pretty sure the term isn't in the Bible," he explained, "but it talks a lot about the trait. Preachers use the term a lot. It means that people are willing to listen and do what they're asked to do joyfully. When I first started out in the business, I worked for a couple of fellows who always knew more than their clients, would argue about the right way to do things, and insist that the client was stupid for wanting a project the way they wanted it."

"I know people—builders mostly—who do the same thing," Samantha said wryly.

"I told myself that if I ever had my own business, I would do what the client wanted me to—you know, unless it was against code or dangerous or something. I wouldn't argue with them just because I'd have done it differently. I might discuss it, but I'd never argue. Well, the Pratt brothers do what I ask, they do it well, they find ways to make things better, and they're always cheerful. Hard to find those qualities in the world of contractors."

"Amen to that," Samantha answered.

This particular morning, Samantha had appeared, as usual, around 9:00 with a bag of breakfast treats and a tray of coffee. The Pratt brothers were all in love with her, perhaps because they had begun to associate her with food and a welcome pause in their work. They clamored about her when she came in, polite as fifth-graders trying to pass an etiquette class; their normal, more boisterous language and demeanor subdued. They each had their new favorite items, and even though Samantha would try to get them to taste some more "exotic" Jewish bakery items, they were all creatures of extreme habit.

Oliver, as was now his custom, would continue working while Samantha entertained the Pratt brothers, waiting until they were finished so he and his client could talk uninterrupted.

"I'm just going to have coffee this morning," he said as he refused the bakery box. "I usually lose weight when I'm working this hard. But on this job, I'm pretty sure that hasn't happened."

"A proper Jewish mother is not happy unless everyone is well fed, Oliver-not-Ollie. You're willing to let a little pudge upset my religious, maternal instincts?" She tried to sound hurt, but Oliver knew, and she knew, that her facade was paper-thin.

"I guess so," he replied. "I hope you also have a tradition of forgiveness, Samantha."

She waved off his apology and explanation. "You know, O-not-O, I often wonder how much of what we do depends on our parents and how they tried to imprint us. Like a swan. Remember that documentary on TV where a bird guy—ornithologist?—raised some baby geese or swans or whatever kind of bird they were, and wore a goose mask and used an ultralight plane to teach them to fly? That's what my parents did with food. Being full, having a more-than-satisfied stomach, is very important. Food is love."

Oliver sat in the pew opposite her and watched her as she spoke, the way she used her hands to color the air, the way she tilted her head back when she laughed, the way her eyes were lit when she felt passionate about a subject. He would have liked to sit next to her but wondered what it would look like to the crew. Since their one dinner out, they had not been alone together—not for a lack of trying, but due to circumstances. Samantha had asked him to lunch once, but Oliver had to be in court fighting a parking ticket he felt was undeserved. He'd asked Samantha out to dinner a second time, and she'd begged off with great sorrow because of a Passover event with her family, scheduled weeks prior.

"Oliver, can you slip away for a few minutes this morning?" she asked. "I want to show you some glass tile I saw at the Molto Bella store on Walnut. I want to ask your opinion of how it might look in that backsplash idea for the bar I told you about. These design details can be overwhelming, and sometimes I can't sort out what's best without the opinion of someone I trust."

"Sure," he said. "We're pretty much on schedule. I can spare a half hour or so."

"We can walk down. It's not really raining, just sort of misty."

"We won't melt," Oliver replied.

He grabbed his coat, told a most disappointed Robert the Dog to "Stay," and called out to Taller that he would be back in a few minutes. Taller acknowledged his departure with half a wave, preoccupied with marking the dimensions on a series of risers for the new basement stairs.

Samantha didn't bother buttoning her coat. She twirled about, once, on the sidewalk.

"I just love spring," she said. "The air is just so perfect—even in the city. Everything smells ... so fecund, you know what I mean, O-not-O?"

Oliver didn't. Samantha often used Jewish words and other odd words that he'd either never heard of or had no clue of their meaning. *Fecund* was a new one. He imagined it had something to do with the hint of new birth, or buds, or new leaves on plants. He tried to force himself to remember the word so he could look it up that evening in the dictionary he'd brought from home, specifically to respond to Samantha's larger-than-his vocabulary.

Molto Bella Ceramica was one of those stores Oliver would never have entered by himself. Upscale, elegantly designed, and intimidating, the store held a cornucopia of tiles and mosaics and hand-painted ceramic pieces imported from Italy. Samantha took him by the hand and pulled him down one aisle, pointing out a selection here, and down another aisle, pointing at another variety there. After looking at a dizzying array of choices, Samantha paused, put her hands on her hips, and inquired, "So, what do you think?"

He took a chance. "I like the blue ones over there. With the coppery glaze. It wouldn't show any water marks."

Samantha ran over to the stack of tiles, held that sample up to the light, turned it vertical, then horizontal, and finally declared, "You're right. These, with their almost-iridescent finish, would be beautiful. How much do I order?"

Unaccustomed to such decisive action, Oliver replied, "I don't know exactly. We'll need to measure the area. Will these people take back any overage? I'd estimate that we need at least sixty square feet. Maybe more, depending on how high up you want it on the wall."

Samantha was off to find a clerk, and within minutes, she returned. "We buy it, we own it, he said, so we'll need to measure close. They have it in stock, so we can order it at any time, I guess."

Once back outside, she grabbed his hand. "Let's get coffee. I know you already had some. So maybe some tea. Or water. Okay?"

Samantha pulled him inside Jitters, a tiny coffeehouse, where the owner/barista greeted her warmly and by name. Samantha ordered a large complicated mocha—coffee-caramel-chocolate-decaf-with-whipped-cream affair—and Oliver settled for a simple coffee with cream.

She took a seat by the window. "I owe you money, Oliver. I didn't get you your check last Friday."

"No problem, Samantha. I've got a little bit of a cushion. You can get it to me tomorrow or whenever."

She dug at the whipped cream on her drink with her straw. "No. We have an arrangement. I'm late on paying."

"Now this is a first," Oliver said. "A client insisting that I get a check."

Samantha playfully slapped at his hand. "I have errands all afternoon. Why don't you come over to the house after work? I'll have the check then. We can talk. Maybe have a drink or something."

"Sure. What time will you be back?"

"Six. Can you do six?"

He nodded. "Six is great."

After Samantha and Oliver left the coffee shop, Samantha spent the rest of her morning and early afternoon meeting with her banker, her architect, and a very unpleasant man from Pittsburgh's zoning board, who had angered her by threatening to pull her construction permit on a technicality. She had almost used, in defense, the line she never used: "Do you know who you're talking to?" But she didn't, biting her tongue, making sure that her project would not receive undeserved, extra scrutiny from some underpaid and resentful zoning-board clerk.

The day had become increasingly gray, and a heavy mist now hung over the city. She drove her red Mercedes slowly back from city hall along the Allegheny. Threads of low clouds hovered over the water as she took the longer route back, allowing herself time to unwind a bit and lose some of her anger. Samantha did not enjoy being angry, while some of the people she worked with seemed to thrive on it, letting their anger fuel their drive.

I'm a lover, not a fighter.

She signaled her right turn and sped through the familiar neighborhood just north of Shadyside—Little Italy, they called it—but it was anything but little. Block after block of interesting stores and wonderful restaurants, butcher shops, and bakeries beckoned.

So much good food. So little time.

She pulled into the drive of the church. There was only one truck in the drive—and it wasn't Oliver's. She wondered if the door would be locked.

It wasn't.

She stepped into the large space—that "sacred space" as the old pastor described it. On this late afternoon, the light coming through the windows was minimized by the shroud of mist outside. It was so ethereal, so peaceful, despite the jumble and clutter of renovation. To Samantha, few things felt really sacred. But even with the mess, this place was beginning to feel that way to her—and more so on days like this than when filled with the light of a bright afternoon. It was almost still and timeless.

She sat down on one of the pews.

This reminds me of foggy afternoons in Paris, when I'd wander into Notre Dame and sit alone in the very last pew, gazing at those beautiful windows ... with all the candles flickering in the smoky darkness. Sometimes I was lucky enough to hear the organist rehearsing that beautiful César Franck piece or a Bach. So inspiring, in a way that was poignant, yet peaceful.

Samantha's reverie was interrupted by footsteps. Before she could become alarmed, though, Taller came around a corner, saw her, and presented her with a charming, disarming, welcoming, and flirty smile. *He could be even more handsome when he tried,* she thought.

"Where is everyone?" she asked.

"Besides me, who else do you need?" he replied. His remark wasn't cocky but at the edge of self-deprecation, trying hard to be engaging.

He's good at it.

"Taller," she said, "I didn't mean to imply that I didn't want to see you, too. But Oliver and the Pratts? Have you done away with them? All of them don't leave early too often."

Taller ambled toward her. "The Pratts weren't scheduled this afternoon. And Ollie headed over to a mill shop in Aspinwall. Somebody said they had a huge warehouse filled with the end runs of special millwork. Ollie always looks for bargains, Miss Cohen. My brother can squeeze a penny in half."

Samantha laughed at the remark, then almost scolded herself for doing so.

"I like your laugh, Miss Cohen. It's very hearty—but lilting at the same time."

He is good.

"Call me Samantha, Taller. Miss Cohen sounds like I work at a bank or something."

"Sure thing, Samantha," he said, coming even closer than a workman would stand to an employer, a closeness that seemed to fit Taller to a T.

Samantha could see in Taller's eyes a calculation of sorts, a mental checklist of moves and actions and touches he had at his disposal—all the things he could call up when dealing with a woman.

He holstered his hammer in his tool belt and let it fall against his thigh, drawing attention to his tight-enough jeans and muscular legs.

"Samantha," he purred, "I know you know this area a lot better than I do—me from the boonies like I am. I wonder … no, you're too busy and much too sophisticated …" It was an incomplete question that begged Samantha to ask for clarification, all the while being wound up in flattery.

She had to rise to the bait. "No, Taller, ask me. I'm not all that sophisticated. Just a small-town girl from Squirrel Hill."

Taller reached out and touched her forearm, casually, as if he had been touching her forearm for weeks and weeks. He didn't even look down as his fingers rested on her skin. "You are not a small-town girl, Samantha, but I appreciate you making me feel at ease." His fingers waited, then slid slowly and deliberately down her arm. "You're sophisticated, regardless of what you might say. And very beautiful as well. My question was … I would love to have a woman like you accompany me to some quality nightclubs in the area. But what makes it difficult for me is that I don't know any quality clubs in the area."

He waited, smiling gently. "Are you free this weekend, Miss Cohen? I think we could have a good time together."

Samantha watched his eyes dance with possibilities as he stared into her eyes without apparent guile. But somewhere deep inside, Samantha knew better.

He is good. And I am tempted.

She found herself clenching her fist, her hand hidden in the pocket of her coat. "Taller, I'm flattered. But … I am going to say no."

She was about to say why when Taller held up his hand.

"Don't tell me why," he said, soft and easy, as if expecting that answer. "If I don't know, then I can ask you again, when you're not so strong. When my charm is stronger. Is that fair, Miss Cohen? I'll take a reluctant rain check on my request, and not your answer. Is that okay with you?"

He said it in such an offhand, disarming way that Samantha nodded her head, almost in admiration.

"Sure, Taller. Ask me again sometime."

And with that, she offered him a sort of half wave and walked away, past the gallery of stained glass.

—————

The cold light from the windows subtly caught Samantha's hair as she passed each window.

Taller knew women, and he had the experience to know that some nos meant no for both now and well into the future. Samantha's no was one of those long-term nos. He had seen her eyes darken as he asked, seen her grow tense before she'd replied. He knew exactly why she was saying no.

It was Oliver. He was the one she wanted.

Only God knows why, he thought. *And she's picking the wrong man. I'm the one who can truly appreciate her passionate nature.*

Taller stood there, still and alone, for a long time after she'd left.

Oliver always gets the good stuff. He's always the good boy. He always does the correct thing. He always says the right thing. I'm tired of him always being the good boy—and I'm always the bad one, the bad seed.

Despite the fact he had work to complete, Taller did not move.

He's everybody's favorite fair-haired boy.

He took in a deep breath.

And now ... even Paula.

Then he smiled.

Paula ...

He put his hand on his hammer and removed it from his belt.

Paula ... now there's an interesting topic. Hmmm. Samantha is a lost cause, but what about poor, abandoned, mistreated Paula? She's beautiful ... and as needy as they come.

He went back to the ladder, climbed up, and began to hammer. *And then we'll see who the good boy really is.*

———

"You're staying here tonight, right?" Taller asked Oliver when he returned from Aspinwall. He removed his tool belt and tossed it onto one of the broken pews. "You're not coming back to Jeannette, are you?"

If Oliver thought the question and his brother's tone were odd, he made no mention of it. "No. I'm staying here. Too much trouble to go back and forth. I don't see why you don't do the same. There's plenty of room."

Taller grinned. "Share a room? Like when we were kids? I don't think so."

"Save you a lot of aggravation—rush-hour traffic and all."

"The traffic isn't as bad as you think, big brother. And ... I have things to do back home. Things I can't do with you staring over my shoulder."

"Suit yourself," Oliver replied and continued to measure out the area behind the bar, wondering aloud how much space he needed to allow for the granite countertop and the mirrored display area above it.

Taller waved and the front door banged shut.

———

When Taller left, Oliver stopped and checked his watch: 5:35.

He had plenty of time to run downstairs, take a shower, and iron the one nice but wrinkled shirt he had brought with him.

At 6:02, he tapped at Samantha's door.

He was most often very precise, so the two extra minutes were intentional, thinking that Samantha most likely would expect any guest to be a polite minute or two late.

The door swung open. An older woman with dark skin and dark hair invited him in. "You be de church fellow," she exclaimed. "I be Mally. You be Oliver, right?"

"That's me."

"You call me Mally, okay?"

"Sure," Oliver replied, a bit off balance. He knew Samantha and her father had a maid but didn't know she would be answering the door and greeting people as well.

"Miss Sam be upstairs. She run late today, but den you most likely know dat she run late at times. She said she be done in a moment. She say meantime I be offerin' you a drink. We have wine and beer and whatever else you like. I don' know much 'bout mixin' dem fancy drinks, so you ask for beer or wine, okay?"

"I guess a beer is fine. Whatever you have."

"I don' know beer either. I close my eyes and pick one. Whatever it be, you tell me it's okay, okay?"

"I will, Mally," Oliver said with a laugh.

She returned with a bottle of Iron City and a glass. Oliver was a bit surprised, since Iron City carried a definite blue-collar connotation; he would have expected Mr. Cohen to buy only the best. But he accepted the drink with a sincere "Thank you."

Mally eyed him critically for a moment, then stepped closer. "You treat Miss Sam good, Mr. Oliver. She a good soul, and I don' want nobody to be hurtin' her, okay?"

Oliver agreed, nodding emphatically, not sure of how entangled Mally thought the two of them had become. Oliver was pretty certain that he and Samantha were not entangled enough to warrant anyone's concern.

There was that kissing after our dinner date, Oliver thought. *Since then, though, we haven't even been out together … until this afternoon. But looking at tiles for the project doesn't really count, does it?*

"I would never hurt Samantha," he said.

"Dat be good den. You be a man of your word, yes?"

Samantha flew down the steps, apologizing from halfway up. "Sorry I'm late, O-not-O, but everything took longer than I expected. Oh, good, you've got a beer. Iron City? Did he ask for that, Mally? Or did you give it to him just to see what he would do?"

Mally shrugged—an impressive shrug that dismissed Samantha's concerns.

"Well, I'll take one too, then, so Oliver won't suffer alone."

When Mally left the room, Samantha whispered to Oliver, "Actually,

I like Iron City. I just like giving her the business. And I'm sure it was intentional on her part. She's tricky like that."

Samantha made a show of pulling a check from the breast pocket of her blouse and handing it to Oliver. "There. As promised, Oliver. Now all accounts are current."

"Thanks, but I could have waited," he said as he folded the check and slipped it into his pocket.

The living room of Samantha's huge Victorian house had inlaid hardwood floors, Oliver noticed, with floor-to-ceiling windows and elaborate moldings, all painted white. It had been decorated in a way that somehow shrank its immense size and provided an intimate feel. None of the furnishings were Victorian, but classic modern, without being overly sleek—rich and earthy, of leather and expensive wood, with a few expensive-looking antiques mixed in.

Style that never went out of style. Classic contemporary, Oliver would have described it if he had been asked.

A large marble fireplace at one end of the room, where they sat, was flanked by two matching coffee brown leather sofas. The low glass and chrome table was set on a huge Oriental rug in deep reds, blues, and browns that looked authentic and very luxurious. One end of the room was done entirely in bookcases, packed with bound volumes, each of the books appearing to have been read (there were small tears in the dust jackets) and not purchased just for show. A scattering of paperbacks, some stacked vertically, some horizontally, were mixed in with decorative pieces and a few framed photos. The walls were done in a pale coffee color above the wide chair rail with a darker shade below.

"Did you measure for the tile?" Samantha asked as she shifted her position on the sofa, now more or less facing Oliver head-on.

"I did. If you buy seventy square feet, that should be enough. If we're short, we can add a few pieces from the store's stock. If it's a different dye lot, no one should be able to see the difference if we add it on one end."

"I'll call them tomorrow."

They both remained silent—but it was a comfortable silence.

"I'm really happy with the project," Samantha said after a long moment.

"That's good. It's coming along well. Have you found the chef or whoever it is you hire first for a restaurant?"

"A chef. If he's expensive, he calls himself an executive chef. He's been on board for a couple of weeks. A really, really nice guy. Young, very creative. Busy planning menus and stealing away other cooks from the places he's worked before."

"Is he a member of the 'Slow Food Movement,' like you told me about at Enrico's?"

"Ah—you remembered. As a matter of fact he is."

"Is he from around here?" Oliver asked.

Samantha offered a puzzled look. "I'm not sure. I mean, he works up at Seven Springs now but can't stand living so far out in the country, so I guess he's a city boy … from somewhere nearby. And they don't cook 'Slow Food' there. He's very, very good. C.I.A. trained and all."

It was Oliver's turn to be surprised. "Like a spy?"

"No," Samantha replied with a laugh. "Culinary Institute of America. It's in New York. I remember someone saying it's on the Hudson River."

"Oh," Oliver replied. "I'm glad you're pleased, and that everything is on schedule then."

"It is. He has all the china ordered, as well as the flatware and tablecloths, the small kitchen equipment, and everything else we'll need. He's got a friend who will be in charge of the bar, and all those supplies are on order as well."

"That's good."

She placed her glass on the coffee table, not even looking for a coaster, then reached over and took Oliver's left hand in hers. "I like you being here. I was serious when I said I wanted us to do dinner again … or get together again … in a social setting, and not just business. This is okay with you, too, isn't it?"

Oliver told himself not to be eager. He told himself that he liked her company. He told himself that Paula was waiting for him back in Jeannette. He told himself that he and Samantha had so many differences between them, including their faith, that anything more than friendship would be foolish to imagine. He told himself that he was not the sort of man who could overlook, or ignore completely, a woman with a tarnished background, who'd had all sorts of intimate encounters with other men. Even though she hadn't said as much, it was what Oliver imagined to be true.

"Sure, I like being here. I like being with you."

Samantha squeezed his hand in response. "Good. I'm glad." She didn't let his hand go but released it to a degree so she could entwine her fingers with his. "Strong hands."

"Have to use them for work."

"And other things, Oliver? Do you use them for other things?"

Maybe she's just being funny. Maybe it's her sense of humor. But he saw her eyes—deep and glowing. *No, she's not being funny.*

"I guess," he replied.

"I'm making you nervous, aren't I?" she said softly.

"Well … maybe a little."

Samantha squeezed his hand again. "I like that. *Ata chamud*—you're so cute. A man who admits to being a little nervous is a good thing. Charming. Innocent."

Oliver knew this required more than just a nod. Words, actual words. "Samantha—" he said.

She looked up at him.

"—you said *innocent*. I know that's a corny word to use to describe a guy. Of course I know what goes on and all that. With men and women, I mean. Maybe *inexperienced* is a better word. *Pure*, even. I'm that sort of man."

Samantha's eyes grew wide. She sat up a bit straighter, her shoulders back in surprise. Oliver knew he had to continue before she started asking questions and getting him entirely flummoxed.

"I've dated some women. I mean, I've *always* dated women. It's not like I just started."

Samantha offered a sweet, considerate, kind laugh. "Oliver. I know you're not gay."

Oliver breathed a sigh of relief but still had something to explain. "Okay. So I've dated women. But I've never … I want to be pure when I get married, Samantha. So I haven't, you know, with a woman."

Samantha lowered her head and peered in closer at Oliver. "Never?"

Oliver shook his head.

"Never?" she repeated.

He took a deep breath. "I've had chances, opportunities. I'm not like an angel or anything. But my faith, being a Christian, is really important to me. And the Bible says it's wrong to ... to act like you're married when you're not. So I never did."

Samantha kept hold of his hand but leaned back into the sofa cushion.

Oliver waited. "So you have to say something, okay? I don't mind the silence when we're together ... except that I mind it now."

Samantha shook her head. "That is a speech I never anticipated, O-not-O. It may take a little while to sink in. I had thought you were going to say something about me being a nice Jewish girl and you not being Jewish, and I was going to say that it was okay because I've dated Christian men before, and everyone went away happy, if you know what I mean. But I guess they weren't the sort of Christian man that you are."

Oliver did not speak.

"*Oy.* Wow," Samantha added, nodding to herself.

"Is that a bad *oy*, or a good *wow*, or a maybe-we'll-see sort of *wow*?"

Samantha laughed, dropped his hand, and in a sweet, quick move, embraced Oliver harder than a hug should be. When she broke the embrace, Oliver patted at his ribs.

"I thought you might have cracked something," he said, smiling.

She playfully hit his shoulder. "I don't know why I did that. But I have to tell you: I've never been more attracted to someone than I am to you right now."

And that's when she grabbed him again and held him tight, at least until Mally banged against the door to the kitchen. She came back into the room, carrying a tray of cheese and crackers on a plate, and stared hard—angry hard—at both of them.

※

Back in the kitchen, Mally put the empty tray down, then leaned against the counter and folded her arms across her chest.

*Dat one, he gonna fall fast and hard. De real nice ones … dey always do.
Dey always do.*

———— ⟩∘∘∘⟨ ————

Oliver made it back to the church and to a very angry Robert the Dog just
before 10:00. Robert stared up at Oliver, his dog eyes narrow, staring over
his shoulder as he trotted outside. He moved with great deliberateness that
evening as Oliver waited at the top of the back stairs, not wanting to call
Robert and cut short his outdoor time.

Robert trotted back up the steps, right past Oliver, not stopping for a
moment, and kept on walking down the steps to the basement and out of
sight. He went straight to his sleeping pad, ignoring their usual nighttime
petting and talking.

Oliver had known, in advance, that leaving Robert alone for an evening was more than enough to set him off.

He switched the lights out in the main sanctuary, or more accurately,
the main *dining room,* and as he did so, his cell phone warbled. He grabbed
at it.

"Oliver," Paula said, her voice sounding as if she were trying her best
to combine sweet and sultry in one tone. Her effort was not entirely successful. "I know you're busy, so I don't want to call you all the time—but
I do miss you. I have an opportunity for you. Maybe a surprise you might
like."

"What sort of surprise?" Oliver replied, wanting to sound pleasant.

"Well, my mom has the week off of work and she volunteered to
stay with the baby. She suggested that maybe I could come visit you in
Shadyside. I haven't been through there in ages, and I bet there are all sorts
of great new restaurants and shops and stuff. I wouldn't have to spend the
night. I know you don't have guest beds or anything, although I wouldn't
mind snuggling if you wanted to.…"

Oliver would have found the situation amusing if he hadn't been
the one *in* the situation. If it happened to someone else, Oliver would
have laughed. Now, with two women in his life—two entirely different
women—he simply felt like the walls of the room were slowly moving in
on him. Like that scene in *Star Wars* where the heroes are in some sort of

garbage-disposal system and are slowly being crushed. That's what it was—having nowhere to go and no escape. That was the feeling that troubled Oliver.

"That sounds great," he said, trying his best to sound truthful. "But this week is not so good. Wednesday I have the kitchen people coming at seven—in the evening—to do final measurements. And Thursday, the architect is coming after work to figure out a couple of snags in the design and then Friday ... well, Friday, I'll be in Jeannette."

Oliver was surprised at how easy it was to stretch the truth.

"Oh. I understand," Paula responded. "I just thought—since I haven't seen you in a while—that I could surprise you. We could go out and have a good time."

Oliver heard the disappointment in her voice, and it was more than that: not just disappointment, but something deeper, maybe edging toward rejection. Oliver knew she'd had enough rejection in her life already.

"Listen, Paula, I don't want you to make the drive down here when I can't focus on you and spend time with you. That's not fair. Can your mom babysit on Friday? Or Saturday? We can go back to Angelo's. Or any place you like."

"That would be nice," Paula replied. "I'll ask my mom. I think she could be free one of those nights. Friday would be good, probably. We can both sleep late the next day."

It was obvious to Oliver that she meant more than she said.

"And on Saturday, maybe we could just get a pizza, and I could come over and we could rent a video," Oliver said. "Can Bridget stay up that late? We could start early, and I could get a cartoon movie or something."

"That is so sweet, Oliver. That would be nice. I'll find out when my mother is free. I bet that she could do it for both nights. I'll call you and let you know for sure, okay?"

"That would be great. Good night, Paula," he said, snapped his phone shut, and wondered why he was so eager to agree with her desire to go out. Now he found himself committed for the entire weekend.

I imagine there are worse ways to spend a Friday and Saturday night.

Paula is a nice person. And she does go to church. That's important. That's more than I can say about … and I have to let Samantha know that we can only be friends. That's all. Just friends.

———✦———

Paula didn't expect the gentle tapping at her door so late in the evening, but she wasn't surprised by it. Without either of them saying a single syllable about it, she knew he'd be back—and soon.

"Hi, Paula," Taller said as he slipped inside.

She looked out. His truck was nowhere to be seen.

"Did you walk here? You live in Greensburg, don't you?"

"I parked a block over. My mother has a spy network. Like the KGB. Informants all over. No sense in getting on the wrong side of the commissar, is there?"

Paula could feel her excitement rising, in spite of the fact that he was back in her house, standing before her, as handsome as he was before and dressed better this time, with a sharply tailored sport coat over a trim blue shirt, with the first three top buttons undone.

On Taller, she decided, the look fit him well, accentuating his chin and mouth and broad shoulders in relationship to his very trim waist—with those muscular abs in between.

"You're looking very nice, Paula. You're more dressed up than the last time."

Paula narrowed her eyes at him. Even though she was a little angry with him for complimenting her like this, and angry with herself for letting him, the attention felt good—very good.

She found herself turning halfway and looking down at her hips. "This old thing? This is a before-the-baby outfit. But at least it still fits, right? Haven't had all that much chance to wear it—or a need to."

He reached out and took her hand in his, just like she knew he would. "Well, happy for me, then."

Both of them stood a few feet apart, Taller close to the couch, Paula closer to the kitchen.

"You want a drink?"

Taller waited.

"I have some beer. I could do a whiskey and soda if you'd like. We could talk. Old times, right?"

Taller extended his other hand, opened his palm to her, and tilted his head just so. From his eyes she caught a glint or something. *Passion? Desire?*

She found her other arm raising, almost by itself, without her giving it motion. Taller took her hand and pulled her to him. She felt him embracing her, encompassing her with his arms.

"Do you enjoy this?" she asked, her mouth at his shoulder, her words breathless. "Do you? Taking advantage of needy women like me?"

If Taller felt injured by Paula's question, he didn't show it. "Paula, I really enjoy this. Being with you, I mean. You bring out the best in me. You're not needy, just desirable. A man would be a fool not to notice how desirable you are."

She felt his strong hands on her back. "So I'm not some sort of conquest?"

"No. Of course not."

"And you're not using me to get back at your mother?"

She felt his body stiffen.

"What? What did you say?" His words were harsh, brittle.

Paula knew she had hit a nerve. "Using women to get back at your mother? Is that part of this?" Her words came out as if she weren't forming them herself, as if they came from somewhere outside her.

Taller grabbed her shoulders and pushed her back. His eyes were narrow, angry. "No," he said, and with that he spun her around and pushed her hard toward her bedroom, following her, his hands on her shoulders still. "It has nothing to do with her." And with that he pushed the bedroom door shut.

In the darkness, Paula closed her eyes tight, knowing his anger would soon be satiated, and she would soon feel back in the place that she deserved—in balance once again.

CHAPTER THIRTEEN

THE PRATT BROTHERS worked well as a team and finished the staircase over the course of two days. They left the rough temporary railings in place, not wanting to install the elegant dark walnut railing yet, knowing that it most likely would get nicked and battered by the ongoing construction.

While they were finishing that project, Taller and a team of workmen completed the installation of the thirty-foot dark walnut bar, with a hand-polished top and a thick rounded edge, inlaid with light ash wood. It was fastened with copper fittings, and would complement the Italian blue glass tiles used on the backsplash of the bar with their matching coppery cast. Even Oliver, not a real fan of bars, thought it looked fantastic.

Downstairs, the sounds of hammering and drilling echoed upward as the kitchen subcontractor was busy finishing the installation. Oliver had installed an adequately sized freight elevator on the back side of the church, building it in an old window well, and planned to hide the machinery behind a stone wall. The elevator was perfectly suited for delivery of food and supplies—straight to the kitchen. But for now, for bringing in large equipment, the wide staircase proved perfect, allowing for an easier-than-expected delivery of the kitchen components—commercial stoves and ovens, refrigerators, dishwashers, stainless steel prep tables, and the rest. The freezing and cooling equipment came in sections and had been assembled on site, in the basement, rather than arriving as a single complete unit.

Oliver felt more like an air traffic controller on these workdays, coordinating the different teams, arbitrating minor disputes, answering questions, settling design and installation issues—and he had not lifted his hammer once in two days. While the complexities of the project required it, Oliver often felt ill-used, and he yearned, just a bit, to be able to point to his own completed building task at the end of the day, instead of a series of tick marks on a clipboard.

Just before noon on Thursday, Samantha showed up at the jobsite. The weather outside must have warmed some, for she was wearing dark jeans and a simple, long-sleeved blue blouse, with some sort of ruffle along the place where the buttons were. She had tied the top half of her hair back from her face with a thick blue ribbon. And her hair was unusually tame. Oliver figured that she must have done something to it or been to the beauty salon to have them style it, but couldn't even offer a guess as to what it would have been. But her hair was smooth and sleek, amplifying her face somehow, making her beautiful eyes and lips more prominent.

She came over to him and asked, "Are you grinning at my hair?"

He shrugged. No other expression would have worked. "It's different. I like it."

"I set it last night. Spent several uncomfortable hours with my hair in rollers and under a hair dryer—the big kind on wheels with the hood that raises and lowers. Do you believe I have one of those things? Like at the beauty salon. It was my mother's. Every once in a while, I'll use it. Brings back fond memories of women in curlers, Salem cigarettes, *Vogue* magazines, and bloodred nail polish."

Oliver stepped back, hoping that he was not being obvious and that no one was paying attention to their conversation. "Well, your hair looks very nice. Different, but very nice."

"Good," she declared emphatically. "I'm glad you like it, because I've come to take you to lunch today. You can sneak away for a bit, right?"

He looked around, as if expecting someone to scold him and tell him that he was indispensable and should not think of leaving the jobsite—ever.

He was glad no one came forth. "Sure. I can get away for a while."

They walked out into the warm spring sunshine.

Samantha's hand brushed against his as they descended the steps, and without thinking of who might be looking and without thinking of what someone might say, he took her hand in his. He knew he didn't want to lead Samantha on, or promise something he shouldn't, but holding her hand felt so right and so natural. She glanced at her hand in his, just for a second, then over at him, her eyes level with his, and grinned like a young girl finding pleasure in such a gentle and innocent action.

"Where to?" Oliver asked.

Samantha all but skipped.

"Cappy's Café? Not gourmet, not expensive, but nice. Quiet. We can talk. They have malts, too. Real malts, made with homemade ice cream and malted powder spooned into the mixer. What is malt anyhow? It sounds like it might be good for you. Is it? And they have really good egg salad. Not many places have *really good* egg salad. Not too much mayo. I think that's their secret. And dill. Or tarragon. Or one of those herbs I love. Do you like egg salad, O-not-O?"

Oliver walked with her, simply happy to be with her. "I guess. I don't get it very often. Once in a while I think about making it, but it means I have to boil the eggs and then cool them and shell them and do all the other stuff. I like to cook, but that's a bit too time consuming for me."

Samantha stopped him, pulling on his hand. "Then let's both get egg salad today for lunch. What do you say? Like a pact, okay?"

Cappy's Café, a mom-and-pop restaurant on Walnut Street, was nearly filled, and Samantha and Oliver were given one of the two remaining empty tables. A waitress brought menus encased in a clear plastic binder. Samantha waved them away.

"Egg salad sandwiches—for both of us. Right? On white bread. Not toasted. Lettuce—but only a little bit—a leaf or two at most—and tomato. French fries, of course. And two chocolate malts. Nice and thick and malty with lots of whipped cream." She raised her eyebrows at Oliver, as if forming a question. "Okay?"

Oliver opened his hands in surrender. "It sounds like the perfect lunch to me."

Oliver had his hands on the table, and this time, Samantha reached over and placed hers on top of his. It was obvious to Oliver that she was watching him carefully to see if her move caused any negative reaction. It did not.

The waitress hurried off, and Samantha grabbed at Oliver's hands again. She cupped them both in hers, tilting her head in that way women do when they're interested in what a man is thinking. Hoping perhaps that men, being like dogs, will somehow blurt out their innermost feelings without being tortured to do so.

Oliver smiled back, just thinking how pleasant this day had become.

Then the egg salad sandwiches appeared, and Samantha grabbed hers almost before the waitress removed her hand. She took a great big bite, mumbling "Delicious" through the filling and the bread.

Oliver tasted his as well. "Hey, this *is* really good egg salad. You're right—not too mayo-intensive. With dill. It's perfect."

"I would order another one right now if it wouldn't make me look like a pig. I saw how the waitress gave me the eye," Samantha answered.

As Oliver chewed, he tried to remember what the waitress looked like, but couldn't, and wondered how Samantha could have seen all that in the short glance she gave the waitress.

I guess women are better at those sorts of things, distinguishing one little look from other little looks.

Samantha finished her sandwich and most of her fries before Oliver had consumed half of his, and started in on the huge dollop of whipped cream on top of her malt.

"So, O-not-O, tell me more about this religion thing. No one I've talked to understands any of it."

Oliver swallowed hard. "Did you talk about me to your friends?"

Samantha took a large gulp of her malt, tilting the heavy glass up, wiping the excess from her lips with a series of paper napkins from the dispenser. "Why, Oliver? Does that scare you?"

Oliver thought about it for a second, and since he was still chewing, he shrugged. This was one time when shrugging felt like a most appropriate answer.

"Well, it shouldn't. I didn't discuss anything personal. But no one knew much about what being a true Christian was all about. I mean, none of us are *shlemiels*, but, well, I had to explain bar mitzvah to you—and my family would consider that really odd. You know what I mean?"

"I do. I guess. And, no, talking about me to friends doesn't scare me. It's just that … some of what I told you about myself was kind of personal, and I'm not sure how—"

Samantha suddenly grew very serious and reached over and took his free hand. "Oh, no, Oliver, I would never do that. I just asked if they understood Christianity and your beliefs. I never said a word about … you know, what you told me. That *is* personal."

Oliver slid his plate away and pulled his malt closer. "It would have been okay if you had said something. I'm not ashamed of being a virgin. It's just that in this day and age, with someone my age … people assume things. Or it's the first thing they think of when they meet me."

"That's perfectly understandable," Samantha replied. "But again, the thing that has me confused is this purity thing. I guess the Torah says the same thing, but it doesn't seem to be as big a deal to Jews. Or maybe that's just in my family."

Oliver drank some of his malt. "You're right. This is a wonderful malt. Malt-a-licious," he joked.

Samantha beamed at his approval.

"I guess the same could be said for Christians," Oliver said. "There are some who don't seem to think intimacy before marriage is a big deal. I've heard people say that as long as you're in love, or engaged, or committed, then having sex is okay."

"And is it? I mean—why not, then?"

Oliver drained the last of his malt. "You know, if the waitress hadn't given you 'the eye,' and I don't think she did, I would be tempted to order another one of each."

Samantha shook her head. "She did give me 'the eye.' And you. You would be hog number one if you ordered a double. But go on about this sex thing. You've got my interest."

"Well, the Bible says that sex is great—but only between people who are married."

"Really?"

"Sure."

"No, what I mean is … does the Bible really say that sex is great for married people? It says that? Really? I thought it was against it. Turn the lights off and close your eyes and only once in a while, mostly to have kids, and you better not have fun doing it."

"Nope. Just read the Song of Solomon. But the catch is—you need to be married," Oliver explained. "That's what makes it special, almost holy. It says the marriage bed is undefiled."

Samantha said with a grin. "There is always a catch, isn't there?"

"I guess. Maybe. But it's God's rules and standards. And if one really believes, and takes the Bible as the truth, it's not that hard to follow."

"So … you'll wait until you're married?"

Oliver had never, ever talked to a woman about this and never imagined he could do so this freely, without stammering or embarrassment. He wondered how in the world he was doing it today. "I will," he stated.

Oliver had trouble reading Samantha's oblique expression. He thought it might be a worried expression—or simply devious.

"So … how far can you go and get away with it?" she asked.

Oliver took her hand gently. "I've heard the question before. Not from a woman. I think it was in a sermon or something. It's a question that doesn't have a simple answer. It's not about seeing how close you can come to stepping over some magic line without God zapping you. It's about Him wanting me to be as obedient as I can to what He says because I love Him more than anything and because He knows what's best for me, for my good. God's principles work."

With eyes wide, Samantha replied, "You mean, we've gone as far as we're going to go?"

Oliver thought for a moment. "Sort of."

Leaning back in her chair, Samantha said softly, "*Oy.*"

And in her face, Oliver saw not disappointment or disgust, but something akin to a woman keen on facing a new, unexpected, yet novel challenge.

And that look scared him a little.

———

Reluctant to leave work on Friday, Oliver wandered about the project, touching piles of raw wood with his fingertips, staring up at unfinished

electrical outlets, testing the sturdiness of the temporary basement railings, debating if there was a project he could begin that late at the end of
a workweek. He decided, with regret, that there were no simple projects,
no I-can-get-it-done-in-an-hour sort of tasks. He could sweep up. That job
always needed to be done, but Oliver didn't really like sweeping up. He
could have patrolled the area, looking for debris, but that was not much
more appealing than sweeping.

The middle Pratt brother saw Oliver moping about and called out to
him, "Why don't ya just leave? You're the boss, right? Ain't no good in bein'
the boss if ya can't take off a bit early on a Friday afternoon."

Oliver was tempted to argue with him, thinking the discussion would
eat up another fifteen minutes or so, then decided the middle Pratt was
correct. "You're right. I can beat the traffic if I leave now."

And with that, Oliver called for Robert the Dog, hung up his tool
belt, and instructed the middle Pratt to be sure the door was locked behind
him when they left. He knew Samantha would be in on Saturday, just to
check up, and wanted to make certain the place was secure.

"We'll lock it. Don't worry. Have a good weekend."

Robert fell asleep halfway home. The traffic, lighter than usual, let
Oliver make the trip in less than an hour.

As he pulled into the driveway, careful to park far enough over so as to
not block his mother's path, he was surprised when her back door banged
open.

"Oliver," she shouted, much too loudly for the distance her voice had
to carry.

Robert the Dog nearly cowered in his seat.

"Come on, Robert," he whispered. "It can't be that bad."

As they exited the truck, Oliver replied, "I need to let the dog out for
a minute and get him upstairs. Then I'll come over."

His mother scowled. "You clean up after that animal, you hear?"

Oliver wanted to count to ten, but didn't. "When have I not cleaned
up after him?"

His mother's scowl didn't change. Instead of replying, she simply
slipped back inside and snicked the door shut. Almost immediately, it
popped open. "Do you want coffee? I could make some. Real coffee.

DeLallo's discontinued some Italian brand and was selling it for half-price. So I bought a can. Real good coffee. I know that you'll like it. Is that okay?"

"Sure, Ma. That would be great."

Since when does she buy real coffee—even if it was half-price?

Robert tore around the apartment, making sure it was exactly as he'd left it, all the smells and dog toys in the same place as they had been. He found a rawhide bone, gnarled and bitten, grabbed it, clambered up on the sofa, and began chewing, looking as happy as Oliver had seen him all week.

"Good to be home, isn't it, Robert?" Oliver said. "Hard to be away from everything familiar."

Then he grimaced and looked out the window, down at his mother's place. "Well, maybe not all that hard." He patted the dog on the head, and Robert appeared a little annoyed at the interruption. "Be back in a few minutes."

Moments later he sat at his mother's kitchen table and waited for her to cease her fussings.

"Here you go. Nice hot fresh coffee," she said. "What else can I get for you? Toast? A sandwich? I have some doughnuts from yesterday. They're still fresh, mostly."

Oliver held up his hands. "No, I'm fine. Besides, I'm going out to dinner in an hour or so, so I don't want to eat twice."

His mother took the chair next to his, not her usual seat across the table. "That Paula—she's such a nice girl."

Oliver stirred a teaspoon of real sugar into his coffee. "She is," he agreed. "A nice girl."

"And pretty, too. She's a real pretty girl."

Oliver sipped and nodded. He was beginning to get an uncomfortable feeling in his stomach, like the start of the flu, the kind you can't take antibiotics for but simply have to let run its miserable course. "I guess. Yeah, she's pretty."

His mother appeared ready with a checklist of questions. "Why did the two of you stop dating after high school?"

Oliver was certain his mother already knew the answer and remembered she had been happy about the breakup. "I don't know. She wanted to stop, I guess. It wasn't me."

His mother took his hand for a moment and patted it, a gesture Oliver had not seen her do since … since forever. "I know," she said. "She told me. She said it was her biggest regret. She said she never should have let you go. And now you two are dating again. I can't tell you how happy that makes me."

Oliver wondered, for a moment, if his mother had had a stroke this week, because she was acting in a way that totally unnerved him. Not only was her opinion of Paula totally different from what it was when he was in high school, but she was also acting civil and kind … almost compassionate.

"And Paula said she's happy now too," Rose added. "Happy you're back in her life and all."

Whatever bearings Oliver had before this afternoon were now gone; he felt like a little ship in the middle of the ocean with a typhoon on the horizon and the rudder snapped off by a freak wave.

"Well, that's good. But I wouldn't go that far. I mean … putting us back together permanently and all."

It was at this moment that Rose stiffened and almost stood erect.

"Oliver!" she said with a snap. "You are not getting any younger. Or haven't you noticed? Paula is a wonderful girl. A good Christian girl. Born again. I know she was married before, but he was a bum, and good riddance. She's a Christian girl now, she's changed, and I'm not going to let you twiddle your thumbs while she gets away this time. You're old enough, Oliver. You're my firstborn; maybe I held you too close and didn't let you become independent early enough. But I did the best I could, without a husband to help. I worked three jobs back then. Three! And when I wasn't working, I was with you. And your brother, but he didn't need me like you did. I gave up my life for you. And for Tolliver. Now that I'm getting old, you want me to die without grandchildren? You want that curse on my life?"

She waited for Oliver to speak, almost as if daring him to defend himself. He did not.

"Paula is a wonderful catch, Oliver. You're just like your father—slow to make decisions. I had to push him when we got married, you know. He still would have been living at home, or by himself today, if I hadn't pushed him. That's no life, Oliver. You need a wife. Paula needs a husband. I want grandchildren. I can't think of a more perfect match than you two—and *now*, Oliver, not a year from now. You need to let Paula know that's where this is going. That you want to be with her."

She waited again. Oliver did not look at her eyes.

"You hear me, Oliver? I don't want you to be alone. I don't want you to end up like me. Old and alone. You don't want to be alone, do you?"

Oliver shook his head no.

"Then good. Be a good boy, Oliver, and listen to your mother. You've always been a good son and a good follower of Jesus. Do what I ask, and bless the few years I have left on earth. You'll do that, won't you? Say you will, Oliver. Please?"

The torrent of her words flooded over him like a river overflowing its banks—rushing, tumbling, pushing, and not letting anything stand in its way. Oliver had no defenses. She was alone. She had little in this world to show for her life, save two sons—one a wastrel, the other obedient. Oliver had always been obedient. He had always honored her, just like the Bible instructed.

"Ma …"

"You know what the fifth commandment says—to honor your parents. The only commandment with a promise attached, that you'll live a long life."

Oliver was beginning to tune her out, having heard this tactic before, used for a variety of situations.

"You need a wife, Oliver. Paula is pretty. And sexy."

Oliver looked up. That was the first time he'd ever heard his mother use the word *sexy*—and the first time she ever implied that physical attraction was a good thing.

"She is, Oliver. Very sexy, don't you think? I bet all the boys wanted her in high school. And if she was your wife, on your arm, everyone would be jealous. She's that pretty … has that sort of shape, doesn't she? Don't you think other men notice those things? I see where they look and what they look at. Don't you notice those things?"

Oliver had to make her stop talking. He had to make her stop push-ing. "Okay, Ma. I'll … I'll think about it. She is pretty. And, yes, I have eyes. I can see."

"And?"

"I'll think about it. That's what I said. I'll think about it."

When she picked up his hand again, he almost snapped it back, out of her clutches.

"You are such a good boy, Oliver. Not like your brother at all. You are such a good, obedient Christian boy, just like your father, who loves Jesus and will make his mother happy … after all these years. I'll finally be happy, and it will all be because of you, Oliver. Won't that be such a special gift?"

Oliver could not taste the coffee going down. It might have been sweet, but it just as easily could have been a bitter poison.

———

Oliver didn't even get his hand on the handle of his truck's door before Paula's front door slapped open. She hurried down the steps, hardly waving to her mother, who stood in the doorway, holding Bridget, both waving good-bye. Oliver did notice what his mother mentioned earlier: Paula was indeed a very alluring woman, more pronounced now perhaps because of what his mother had said, and how she'd said it.

She bounced into the cab, slid close to Oliver, and planted a firm and affectionate kiss on his cheek. He imagined the greeting would have been even more intimate had her mother and daughter not been staring from the front steps.

"You look nice," Oliver said. "Blue is your color."

Paula looked pleased. "Aren't you sweet? This is an old dress. I haven't had many chances to wear it since Bridget was born."

"Well," Oliver said as he shifted the truck into gear and pulled away from the curb, "you should wear it more often."

Paula slipped her arm into Oliver's and hugged it. "You're sweet, and I'm famished," she declared. "Any idea of where you want to go? After working hard all week, you deserve to treat yourself. I'm just along for the ride."

"But you did say you were famished. Anything in mind?"

She squeezed his arm against her. "Nope. You decide. You're the boss. I want you to be happy."

Oliver thought about returning to Angelo's but didn't want to be thought of as a person who gets stuck in a rut. He considered, then decided against a number of nice, but typical, chain restaurants in the area.

"How about The Nest? They have good seafood. Are you up for seafood?"

"Sure, Oliver, that would be great. I like shrimp. They have shrimp, don't they?"

She leaned against him. There was a strong scent of flowers in her hair. It was nice, Oliver thought, nice and pleasant. He liked The Nest, though he didn't go there often. It was even more expensive than Angelo's but served more than just pasta dishes.

They drove to the restaurant in silence. While Oliver had steeled himself for a more talkative Paula, this quiet, reserved part of her personality was beguiling. She didn't speak until they were inside the restaurant and seated.

"And how was your week at work?" she asked, placing the napkin on her lap, then demurely adjusting the neckline of her blue dress. Oliver thought her adjustment didn't serve to cover more skin, but actually showed a bit more. He told himself that he would not stare, but he did notice.

"It was fine," he replied and told her about the progress they had made and the quirky things the Pratt brothers had said, and how Robert had seemed to be so relieved to get back home. "I miss being home too. I like having my things around me. I may not have a lot, but I like knowing I can get to them."

Oliver expected Paula to launch on a discourse of material things, but she simply said, "And I like having you home as well, Oliver."

They gave their order to the waiter. Oliver ordered crab cakes. Paula ordered shrimp, as she had hinted, and only an iced tea.

"I've been going to church during the week," Paula said. "To the Wednesday-night service. And there's a women's Bible study on Tuesday nights. I'm learning a lot."

"Really?" Oliver said, surprised.

Paula nodded as she broke a breadstick in half. "I know you know so much more about the Bible and all that than I do. I figured I needed to do a little catching up. And Bridget loves their child-care people, so I don't have any excuse. It's good to learn."

Oliver had no reply.

"And you know what one of the things I asked the pastor about this week?"

"No," Oliver replied, knowing she wasn't really asking him to guess.

"I was trying to figure out a way to say it politely, but I couldn't. I asked him about remarrying and all that. Obviously I've been with another man. But the pastor said that since my ex abandoned me, it would be okay to remarry. I mean, as believers and all that. Born again. Right?"

The pressure was slowly being turned up, and Oliver knew it.

"He went on to say that if a woman made a mistake in the past, and if she stayed away from making the same sort of mistake now, then she's like … well, he called it being a 'born-again virgin.'" Paula averted her eyes as she said the word *virgin*, as if she would blush had she stared into Oliver's eyes as she said it. "So he said if I'm not with anyone now, I guess that means I'm sort of like a virgin again. I mean, I know I'm not, but—"

Oliver stopped her. "I know what you mean, Paula. I've heard about this before. And I'm proud of you for making that decision. I know you've been with another man. But God makes sinners pure again. And so, if you're right with God now, then, well, that makes you pure again too."

When Paula averted her eyes again, Oliver assumed she was at the verge of blushing or crying or however it was that women responded when talking about these sorts of personal issues. Oliver was surprised she had brought the subject up, but was, in one way, happy that she had. It was important to Oliver that any serious relationship he had would be with a woman who was right with God.

An image of Samantha flashed in his thoughts, and he realized with a start that, perhaps, she would never be right with God. *Never.*

Paula looked up and took his hand. "I'm so happy that you understand, Oliver. You don't know how happy that makes me feel inside."

After dinner, after a long, pleasant conversation over coffee and tiramisu, Oliver ran out and brought his truck around to the restaurant's entrance. He hurried outside to open Paula's door. This time she accepted his offer with a sly grin.

He parked the truck outside her house.

"What time is it, Oliver?"

"Nearly ten."

"I wish we could stay out longer, but my mother said she needed to get home tonight, and I don't want to keep her up too late. And I can't invite you in while she's here."

"It's okay," Oliver replied. "I had a great time tonight, and we'll see each other tomorrow."

Paula slid over to him and wrapped her arms around him, under his arms, and held him very tightly. She lifted her head, obviously expecting a kiss, and he didn't disappoint her. She reached up and put her hand on the back of his head and pulled him close, moving even closer to him, if that was possible. She slid her hand down past his shoulder and on his side and then to the outside of his thigh, where she let it rest.

"I'm here for you, Oliver," she whispered in his ear. "I'm here for you. If you ever need anything, just ask me. I mean that. Anything."

And with that, she slowly leaned away from him, kissed him once more, then slid out of the truck and was on the landing in front of her house, waving good-bye, even before Oliver could find the handle to the door.

Samuel Cohen was not the most intuitive behind the wheel. Had he been just a bit richer, he would have hired a driver, but since he was not exactly to that level of wealthy, he was forced to drive himself to most places. His preferred cars for the past decade (much to Samantha's chagrin) had all borne the Cadillac nameplate—big, plush, not horribly ostentatious nor pretentious, but expensive enough to make a statement. The trouble, he thought, was that Cadillacs were not built for some of Pittsburgh's narrower streets. Concentrating hard, holding onto the steering wheel with an almost-white-knuckle grip, he maneuvered the big white auto into the parking lot of the Marriott hotel. There were no valet-parking attendants there: a suburban Marriott offered simply a large self-parking lot, meaning Samuel would have to park the large car by himself.

Beside him sat Judy "Pixie" Allen, a short blonde woman, attractive in a past-middle-aged, well-worn manner, with a snappish laugh and an eager, pleasant smile. A neighbor of Samuel's cousin Grace, from Long Island, Judy had been divorced for over a decade, had no children, and worked as a buyer for Macy's in Manhattan. She was dressed very well in an exquisitely tailored pantsuit, and everything matched just so, down to her brick-colored alligator shoes and handbag.

Samuel found a stretch of four empty spaces and pulled in without having to worry about finessing the car into a narrow slot. He hurried from his side and opened the door with a flourish.

Judy exited and slipped her arm into his as they walked toward the front entrance.

"Dinner was lovely, Samuel. Pittsburgh is much more cosmopolitan and cultured than I would have imagined. Us New Yorkers think that nothing exists west of the Hudson."

She drew out the words *New Yorkers* into almost a caricatured turn on a clichéd New York accent. Samuel found it charming.

"I know. The rest of my family thinks we're *Yankels,* living in the wilderness out here. But Pittsburgh has its charms, for certain."

"So far, I really like it," she said, "but I can't imagine how anyone finds their way without getting lost. If you dropped me off, I'd have no idea how to find my way home."

Idea became *idear*. Samuel liked that, too. "Once you're here for a while, you get the hang of it, Judy—"

"Pixie, remember. People call me Pixie."

"Pixie, right, I keep forgetting. Pixie … you up for a nightcap?"

"Sure. We're still on New York time."

They found a table in the nearly empty bar off the lobby of the Monroeville Marriott. Samuel waved at the cocktail waitress who was seated at the end of the long bar, uncluttered with patrons, each bar stool setting exactly equidistant from the next.

"Now, when am I going to meet your daughter?" Pixie asked as she stirred her drink with a narrow plastic straw.

"Sometime soon," Samuel answered.

Pixie made a face like someone tasting a raw lemon.

"I know it's silly," he explained, "but I wanted to spend some time here with you and not have her worried about things. Maybe it's a Jewish thing. Parents keep secrets from the kids and the kids keep secrets from the parents. Keeps everyone safe. And everyone is happy."

Pixie nodded as if she understood, but her eyes gave away the fact that she didn't, really, and wasn't too happy about it. "Maybe it is. But in my family, once the child is out of college, they leave. It's for the best that they become independent. Like a bird who has learned to fly. We don't want them to be *shlumps*, staying in the nest any longer than necessary. Don't you think your daughter should be out on her own? Establish her own life? She's old enough, isn't she?" Pixie asked.

Samuel drank and nodded. "Of course she is. And she's got a lot of *chutzpah*, that one. Maybe you're right. Maybe it is time to encourage her. Since my wife … well, since then, I think she feels obligated to stay with me. I think she thinks her dad can't handle being alone."

Pixie reached out and took his hand. "I know. That I understand. But … maybe you don't have to worry about being alone. A handsome man like you. You should never be alone."

When she offered the come-hither smile that most middle-aged women would give so freely to a past-middle-aged man, and then some, Samuel knew exactly what she meant.

CHAPTER FOURTEEN

OLIVER NEVER HAD SAT this close to the church organist. Not that he had anything against sitting so near the front, but he had allowed Paula to pick the seats. It was just that he hadn't ever seen the organist move his feet so much, attacking the row of wooden pedals underneath the massive keyboard. In fact, Oliver wasn't sure if he had even known there was a keyboard for feet under the keyboard for the hands. It had taken him by surprise and was enough to keep his mind off the songs and the sermon.

Instead of mentally focusing on the pastor's subject, he reviewed the activities of the night before. He had brought a huge half-cheese, half-cheese-and-sausage pizza to Paula's, along with three animated movies—one about dinosaurs, another about talking cars, and the old Disney classic *Cinderella*.

The evening did not start well. Bridget had examined all the movies carefully, turning the video cases over and over, not being able to read, but pretending to. And then she'd declared, very emphatically, "I don't like these stupid movies," and threw them on the floor.

The child's mini-tantrum brought an immediate rebuke from Paula, who had reminded her firmly that those sorts of words were not used in this house, and Bridget had yelled that the movies *were* stupid. No pizza was consumed until a time-out was completed, and by then, Bridget had been in no mood to eat anything.

Oliver had felt out of his league. He'd only occasionally spent time with children, so he was in no position to expect or demand any sort of behavior. Paula had appeared at the edge of being distraught but had remained calm and even in her tone. Just before Bridget's bedtime, she'd relented and offered both Oliver and her mother a mumbled, near-to-angry apology and had managed to eat a whole slice of cheese pizza without once uttering the word *yucky*.

By the time Paula had gotten her daughter to bed and asleep, it was nearly 10:00—hours past her regular bedtime. The two of them had sat at the table and eaten ice cream, talking softly for another hour until Bridget woke, came out into the hall, and complained of a stomachache.

Oliver had taken his leave then, not willing to make a tense situation any worse, knowing that a male visitor was bound to increase the anxiety.

Paula had given him a good-night peck on the cheek, apologizing over and over.

"It will take time, Paula. She's a good girl. I know that. But it's hard for her—me being in your house. She doesn't know how to say that she's upset, other than acting out, right?"

Paula had shaken her head, her expression filled with admiration. "You know how to make a mom feel better. I just wish I could have had you alone for an hour ... you know what I mean? I could have made the end of your week a lot better."

Oliver tried not to ponder here in church what she'd meant by that offer.

And now the two of them sat in the front pew together. Bridget was safely and happily ensconced in the child care downstairs. Paula was next to him, wearing a demure black dress that buttoned almost to the neck, though the fabric was more clingy and tight than might be standard for a "church dress."

Oliver never liked standing for hymns, but with Paula next to him, it was better. She had a sweet voice, clear, and always on pitch, if that was the musical word for it, Oliver thought. She could have been an alto, but Oliver was never good at those musical identifications. He really liked listening to her as she made her way, with the rest of the church, through all four stanzas of a hymn that Oliver found impossible to sing.

They did not leave hand in hand, nor arm in arm, but together walked down the side aisle, greeting people, saying hello, waving. Oliver noticed something that morning—a confirmation of what his mother had said a few evenings ago. The women who looked over to them, seeing them as a couple, all seemed pleased and nodded, as if their being together was the most natural thing in the world. The men, on the other hand, offered sidelong glances, keenly aware of Paula's attributes. Oliver could see it so clearly—perhaps because he himself had been the author of many of those sidelong glances in the past.

In the narthex, Paula went off in one direction, chatting with a group of ladies that Oliver imagined were in her Bible study, which left Oliver to shake Pastor Mosco's hand. The pastor's grip was much tighter and more vicelike than Oliver thought necessary.

"Oliver," he boomed, even though no one was near since the crowds had thinned out. "How are you? How's the latest project coming? Schenley Park, was it?"

"No. Shadyside. An old church. Used to be a church."

"That's right. Things going well?"

"They are, Pastor. We're right on schedule."

Pastor Mosco looked about the entryway, just his eyes moving. "I see you came in with Paula. She's a nice girl. Started coming to service on Wednesday nights. And my wife tells me that she's attending the women's Bible study on Tuesday nights. Asks lots of questions. That's a good thing. Shows that she's growing. Growing in her faith."

"It is."

The pastor leaned in close to Oliver, closer than he liked, and Oliver wanted to step back. Then he wondered how that would look: two men, one of them dancing backward. He decided to stand his ground.

"You're okay with her having been married, aren't you, Oliver? I mean, it's not her fault that she's alone now. If you two were to … get together … you'd be doing her an honor. So don't be worried—from a spiritual standpoint, I mean."

Now Oliver did lean backward. "Thanks, Pastor Mosco. I won't be worried. I guess I wasn't. But knowing the church thinks it's okay … that makes it easier."

"That's my boy," the pastor called out, louder than he needed and slapped Oliver on the shoulder, a behavior Oliver did not like but tolerated.

Paula came back with Bridget in tow.

"You two ready for breakfast?" Oliver asked. "Eat 'n' Park? Mickey Mouse pancakes?"

Bridget didn't say a word. She merely smiled, her smile growing broader as the three of them descended the church steps.

They arrived at Paula's car, and as Paula strapped Bridget into her carseat, the little girl called out, pointing at Oliver, "He's coming with us, isn't he, Mommy? I want him to come with us!"

"He's coming with us, sweetie. Don't worry," Paula answered.

And as she handed Oliver the keys to her Toyota, she whispered to him, "You've made a friend. She's never done that with anyone else."

"It's the Mickey Mouse pancakes," Oliver whispered back. "Drives women crazy."

Paula looked back at her daughter and gave Oliver a quick peck after she decided that Bridget was not watching.

Oliver arrived back in Shadyside late on Sunday. He had spent most of the afternoon at Paula's watching the Pittsburgh Pirates through the static and dancing fuzz on her cranky old analog TV. Bridget had gone for her nap, and he and Paula sat comfortably close to each other on the sofa.

"We need to be careful. Bridget sneaks out of her room sometimes during a nap. I don't want to upset her," she had said.

Now it was dark, and back at the "Blue Church," and during the drive into the city, Robert the Dog appeared almost irritable, perhaps owing to the fact that he had been alone most of the day.

"I'm sorry, Robert. Next time I'll take you along. Or have Paula over at our place."

But I couldn't have Bridget there. It's not childproof, or whatever they call that. Too many things she could get hurt on.

Oliver parked his truck under the port cochere, grabbed his duffel filled with clean clothes, and Robert ran to his spot at the back of the lot.

Oliver placed his key in the door and was about to turn it when he heard muffled noises inside.

Didn't the Pratt brothers lock this door? Do I call the police?

He pulled his key out and was about to open the door, just a crack, when it swung in and opened all the way, seemingly by itself.

"Oliver!" Samantha called out. "I thought that might be you. I thought I heard your truck."

Oliver was so surprised he nearly fell backward, off the steps.

"I scared you," Samantha said, apologizing, putting her hand over her heart. "I should have rung a bell or something—to warn you."

"It's okay," he insisted as Robert the Dog bounded in, sniffing and grinning, accepting Samantha's effusive greeting with glee. "It got my heart started again."

"I was just in checking some dimensions for the architect. Apparently his time is more valuable than mine."

Robert the Dog chased around the church, snuffling loudly.

"Anything important?"

"Not really," she replied. "Well, at least to me. He wanted to make sure of the width of the back hallway, so I said I'd run over here and measure. Something about the building code being different if there is access to an exit door from the hallway or not. I didn't really get the implications—just left the numbers on his voice mail. I told him to check with you first thing tomorrow morning if you needed to make changes."

"Thanks," Oliver replied. "I've never heard of that sort of rule, but Pittsburgh codes are a bit different than the ones in Jeannette."

Samantha stood to his side, appearing a little awkward, perhaps the tiniest bit ill at ease. "How was your weekend?" she asked.

"Fine," Oliver said, not wanting to go into any detail about being with Paula, feeling just a bit duplicitous at the moment, trying to think of a good cover story if she pressed the issue. "And yours?"

She shrugged. "Nothing special. Saw some friends on Saturday night. Went to dinner. Slept late today. Read the paper. Did a little shopping. Standard stuff. And you?"

Oliver hoped his face would not give him away. "Pretty much the same."

Samantha nodded, as if making a mental checklist. "Are you hungry now?"

"No, I sort of ate before I came. Are you?"

She shook her head no. "I ate too, but if you were hungry, I would come with you and have a little *nosh* if you were going out."

"I wasn't planning on it."

The two of them stared at each other, silent, for what seemed to Oliver to be a long time. Robert rattled between them, tossing around a large section of a rawhide chew toy, grinning as if he had uncovered a lost treasure. But he did not break their face-to-face, silent dialogue.

It may very well have been her lips, Oliver thought, that so attracted him to her, or that he'd first noticed. But in those few moments of looking, he amended that thought, adding her eyes—the something deep and accommodating and sensuous in them that clearly showed her innermost being more than anything else.

He resisted looking elsewhere on her, knowing that elsewhere was just as attractive to him as her finely defined face.

And then she moved, took a step forward, one hand still cradling her cell phone, as if being too preoccupied to place it back in her jeans pocket where she always kept it. The step forward was enough of an indication, enough of a first move to blur what had happened this weekend, to place it in another box within Oliver and fold the top down so the contents couldn't escape.

He moved as well, taking a longer step. Robert the Dog passed near them, noisily mangling his chew toy, and then they were in each other's arms, in an *I-couldn't-wait-another-minute* sort of embrace, hard and almost fierce.

She leaned into him and kissed him. The kiss was long and intense and nearly took Oliver's breath away.

After a minute, she whispered, "Let's go downstairs."

Oliver shut his eyes and tried not to elaborate on what she had said or was offering to him, struggling not to add a visual picture of what would come next. It took all the strength he had to open his eyes and say, "No. I can't."

To Oliver, it was obvious that was the answer Samantha expected. He wondered, though, in that second, having previously considered both the question and his response, how what might happen next would feel with her. That he had not previously considered.

"Why, Oliver? Why not? I know you have your rules and all that … with the Bible stuff you talked about. You're not going to hurt me, Oliver," she said in a soft, forgiving voice. "It would be okay if this … between us … was just physical. I'm not asking for anything more than that. Really, Oliver. It would be okay with me."

He did not let go of her, not yet, not wanting to release her from his arms. "It's not that, Samantha. I mean … it's not *just* that. It's that I can't … or won't do what the Bible says I shouldn't do."

Her eyes narrowed. Oliver licked his lips, which had suddenly gone dry.

"It's because of my past, isn't it?" she asked, then backed out of his embrace, only a step, but out of his arms. "It's because I've been with other men. That's why you don't want to be with me."

"That's not it, either, Samantha."

In that second, he realized her admission meant there were many men in her past, many men who had known her, shared the ultimate intimacy with her. Oliver saw the faces without knowing the faces, saw the numbers without knowing the numbers, and felt the knife prick just below his heart.

"It isn't. Really."

Samantha took another step back. "It is, Oliver. Why would your God deny you something that was offered to you out of love? Why would your God want you to turn your back on a beautiful thing? It doesn't make any sense to me, Oliver, none whatsoever. Rules! I hate them! We're two adults. We want each other, and you've just said, 'No thanks, Samantha.' Why? I have to think it's because of me. My past."

Oliver had never imagined being in a conversation like this, in a situation like this, where he would be faced with turning down the determined advances of a beautiful woman—a woman he cared deeply about and felt some sort of spiritual connection with—not in the biblical sense, but in the sense that she understood him without his having to explain himself, something so wonderfully unique, so wonderfully special.

"It's not that, Samantha. It isn't. It's more than just a set of rules."

She waited, only a moment. Oliver had no more explanation to offer that evening.

"I'm sorry, Oliver," she said. She turned from him and walked quickly to the door. By the time she got there, she was running, and even Robert the Dog looked up from his chew toy and watched as she banged through the door and entered the warm spring night.

———

Had Samantha been fifteen again, she would have thrown herself onto her bed and muffled her cries into the duvet, perhaps even flailing her arms and legs. The last time she did that, her mother had stood in the doorway, a clean set of sheets in one hand.

Instead, this night, Samantha sat on the window seat under the wrap-around windows in the turret, with darkness sweeping in to blanket her bedroom. She listened. Only the traffic noise filtered in and maybe a snippet or two of the television program her father watched downstairs in the living room. Her mother had hated the television and everything on it, leaving her husband to watch it alone most nights.

Samantha closed her eyes. She could see it all again, as if it were happening before her, like some old movie, flickering on an old black-and-white movie screen, the images blurred and indistinct, the dialogue scratchy, and the volume turned down. Yet Samantha felt forced to watch and listen to the ghosts in her head.

In that scene, that horrible scene nearly two decades earlier, there had been a packet of birth-control pills, in a tidy plastic oval, the foil backing peeled away on half a month's supply, lying on the middle of the bedroom floor, thrown there when Samantha's mother had discovered them, hidden between the mattress and the box spring.

Samantha, fifteen, was sobbing on the unmade bed.

The grown Samantha wanted to look away, wanted the vision to change, but it remained, as persistent as a dark cloud on a windless day.

"How long have you been on the pill?" her mother had hissed, still carrying the clean set of pink sheets in her hands.

Samantha had raised her head, just an inch. "A few months. That's all."

"Where did you get them? Did Dr. Rosen give them to you? If he did, there'll be hell to pay."

"No. He didn't," Samantha had shot back. "I got them … at the free clinic in Wilkinsburg."

It was a lie, but a convincing one.

"You little hussy," her mother had whispered. "Why? Who is it—one of those juvenile delinquent boys from your class? Who?"

"It's nobody," Samantha had shouted back. "Nobody you know."

Her mother had carefully placed the stack of sheets on Samantha's princess-style chest of drawers and had walked to her daughter's bed. That night Mrs. Cohen, taller than her husband, more elegant, more sophisticated than Pittsburgh society warranted, had seemed like a person Samantha did not know. She had grabbed her daughter's shoulder with one hand, flipped her over and upright, had raised her right hand across her body, and brought it down, fast and severe, hitting Samantha hard enough to knock her backward on the bed.

"You're lying!"

She had waited.

"Who?"

She had waited again.

"Who is it? Who are you having sex with?"

She had waited a third time, pulled her daughter upright once more, and hit her again, this time with the palm of her hand. The young Samantha had fallen backward, tears and sobs colliding, freezing what words she might have spoken in her throat.

"Shut up," her mother had whispered, her words more chilling than if they had been screamed. "You're a liar. Maybe you have your oblivious father fooled, but not me. You're nothing better than a common whore— giving in to any man that asks. You disgust me."

"I'm not a whore. It's just one guy, and I love him."

"Love? What do you know about love at your age? I know what you are. Mark my words, Samantha. I can see this in your future. There is no denying it. I know one when I see one. If you're this way now, as young as you are, then that is what you will always be. You'll never keep a man."

And with that, Samantha's mother had turned and walked away, stopping only for a moment in the doorway, where she'd turned her head and repeated, "Disgusting."

Samantha had been left alone in the darkness of her bedroom that night, crying herself to sleep in an unmade bed.

Two nights later, without having spoken a single word to her daughter, Mrs. Samuel Cohen had slit her wrists and died, without a murmur, sitting fully clothed, wearing her new Versace outfit, in the great marble tub in the master bathroom.

CHAPTER FIFTEEN

WHEN THE PRATT BROTHERS arrived at the worksite in the morning, they took one look at Oliver and asked, nearly in unison, "Are you sick?"

The eldest Pratt added, with concern, "You look terrible, Oliver. You're not comin' down with somethin', are you?"

At that, the two younger Pratt brothers took a full, deliberate step backward, as if whatever germs Oliver was infested with wouldn't be able to take the journey to find them.

Oliver acknowledged their concern and fear with a wave. "No, I'm fine. I know I look bad, but I don't think I slept for more than ten minutes last night."

Oliver saw the youngest Pratt brother relax. "Well, don't you worry at all, Mr. Oliver. Miss Cohen's coffee and those Jewish jelly doughnuts will fix you right up. I don't know where she gets it, but it always charges me up."

Oliver shook his head. "She won't be here this morning. She left me a voice mail saying that she had an appointment. We'll have to get our own coffee and jelly doughnuts."

All three of the Pratt boys appeared crestfallen. Even Robert the Dog, to some canine degree, looked hurt. The humans, instead of whining, hesitated just a moment, then all started to work without further conversation.

At 9:00, Oliver decided he did indeed need something to help him wake up and volunteered to go to the Coffee Tree Roasters on Walnut to buy coffee for the crew. He picked up a dozen Danish rolls—"Surprise us," the Pratts had said—and a tray of coffees, a bag filled with sugar packets, fake sugar packets, dozens of little plastic jugs of cream, and a handful of stirrers. He almost ran into Barth Mills as he exited the store.

"Where's Robert?" Barth asked, as if Oliver had abandoned him somewhere in an alley.

"Back at the jobsite. Waiting for his breakfast, probably."

Oliver could see Barth was disappointed at the news. He held his cup close to his chest. "Oh. Okay …"

Oliver wouldn't mind the company today. "Why don't you come back with me?" Oliver offered. "Have you ever been inside the church?"

"No. But I'd like to. You sure I wouldn't be in the way?"

"Not at all. Come on. Walk with me."

When Oliver opened the front door of the church, Barth gasped. On sunny mornings, like this day, the light exploded through the east windows, setting the interior aglow with pungent reds and purples and blues and golds, nearly vibrating the mote-filled air with color.

"This is … magnificent," Barth said solemnly. "I-I did not even begin to imagine."

Oliver stepped inside. "I know. After a while, I guess we've gotten used to it. But it really is breathtaking."

Robert hurried over to greet the old man, wagging and dog-grinning in recognition, looking toward the door, several times, as if expecting to see Barth's dog enter.

"Sorry, Robert the Dog, but Rascal looked a bit peaked this morning, so he's home snoozing."

The Pratt brothers hurried around Oliver, taking the coffees and Danish, all eyeing the new person in their midst.

"This is Barth Mills," Oliver said. "He used to be a pastor. Well, I guess he still is … sort of. Do you ever stop being a pastor? From up in Kane County. These are the Pratt brothers: Henry, Gene, and Steven. That's my brother, Tolliver, over there on the ladder. And that's Kevin and Bob over there working on the electrical."

Barth waved at them all.

"Really? A pastor?" Gene, the middle Pratt brother, asked. "Like a pastor who preaches?"

"Like we shouldn't swear now?" Henry, the oldest brother, added.

"Yep."

"And like one that … what do they call it … hears confessions and stuff like that?" asked Steven Pratt, the youngest.

"Well, not exactly. You might be thinking of the Catholics. They have priests who hear confessions. I never did that—at least not in an organized way. People confessed. But they didn't have to. Not to me, anyhow. To God, yes."

Steven took this in, nodding as the old man spoke, as if needing confirmation about some odd doctrinal issue. "But … if someone wanted to confess, then you'd listen, right? I mean, if this person didn't know how to do it by himself."

Barth took a drink of his coffee. "I suppose I would. Offer guidance. Offer support. Pray for them. Whatever."

A happy look appeared on Steven's face—not in a joyful sense, but in an *I'm-glad-I-figured-that-out* sort of sentiment.

Oliver had his hand on a cherry Danish. "Barth, help yourself. And feel free to wander around, as long as you're careful. This is a construction zone, you know? Make yourself at home."

"Thanks." Barth found a spot on a pew that leaned against the west wall, then sat staring at the big eye window. He watched as the Pratt brothers began assembling the pieces of a corner booth, just under the stained glass of Jesus holding a lamb, wearing a much-too-elegant robe, complete with gold tassels. As He gazed heavenward with a beatific expression, His thumb and two fingers of His right hand were raised, forming a turn-of-the-century benediction.

Barth stuck around, watching the work, until lunch. "I have to go home and feed Rascal," he explained to Oliver. "But would it be okay if I come back and bring him? I forgot how nice it is to be around people. I won't get in the way. I promise."

Barth had simply sat and watched all morning, the Pratt boys going to him on occasion, speaking to him for a moment or two, then letting him be.

Oliver shrugged. It was the right response. "Sure. Come on back. Nice to have an audience sometimes."

Barth sat in the same pew for the rest of the afternoon, after lunch, with Rascal snoozing on the floor beside his feet, the old dog not even waking when a circular saw whined through a two-by-four or when someone pounded nails into recalcitrant hardwood.

―――――

At 5:00, the Pratt brothers began to set aside their tools. They were nothing if not prompt and very conscious of the clock.

"Start on time, leave on time," Gene had said at the outset of their work—and that is what they did.

But this evening was different. The two younger Pratt brothers, after hanging up their tool belts and cleaning off the table saw and offering some rudimentary cleaning, walked over to where Barth sat, their hands folded, like dusty acolytes, and sat next to him. Rascal looked up, pushed himself to his feet, wheezing, and sniffed at both of their legs. He sneezed once, probably because of the sawdust.

"We know you're not a priest," Steve, the youngest Pratt, said.

"Henry, our older brother, knows all about religion and stuff, and he explained it to us at lunch," said Gene, the middle brother.

"But we haven't been to a church in a long time," Steve added. "And I think that things probably changed since we went last."

Gene added, "We keep talkin' about going to church—since Oliver goes to church and talks about God and Jesus sometimes, just like the chaplain in prison did. It all sounds so nice, so peaceful, you know? And this place—it's like that. A special place."

"And we heard about churches that serve beer," Steve added. "Did your church serve beer?"

Barth knew better than to laugh because the question was asked with pure childlike innocence. "No, not as a rule. But sometimes, at church picnics, some of the members would have beer in their coolers. I don't partake, but I don't mind anyone who does—just as long as they don't get drunk. Unless the little man in the bottle gets too big, then I guess I don't see no ... *any* harm in it. Although there are pastors that do."

Gene waited patiently until he was finished. "So you're not mad if I have a beer when I get home?"

"Nope," Barth replied. "Just make it one. Maybe two at the most."

"Deal."

No one spoke until Steve broke the long silence. "We want to confess."

Barth answered, "You don't have to confess to me, Steven. Like I said, you just have to confess to God."

"Yeah, well, I heard that all right. But like Gene said, we're not in the habit of goin' to church. And seein' as how we are in one now, and, like, you're a pastor, we just figured it would be okay."

Barth had decades of service to God under his belt. He had heard all sorts of strange requests and demands and opinions about God and the Bible, and the Pratt brothers fell into the "really innocent" category. He could see in their eyes, on their faces, their sincerity, their lack of guile, their absolute belief in the power of a pastor. Barth had been so long out of the pulpit that this belief came as a jolt to his system, a nearly tangible, palpable current that ran from his head to his heart, down through his fingers.

"Boys, I want you to know that I don't need to hear anything."

The youngest brother spoke up. "I bet Jesus is pretty busy. And I bet you can help get Him to listen to us. If He needs to listen to us, I guess. We don't want to push ourselves on Him, 'cause I know He's a busy guy, like I said. Bein' a pastor and all, I think it would be a good thing, like bein' our attorney or somethin'. You know?"

Barth decided not to offer any more argument or discussion. If these boys had something to confess, then land sakes, they should be allowed to confess it.

Barth noticed that the oldest, Henry, waited, almost at the other end of the room, where the platform had been. Oliver came upstairs, and Henry motioned him over, speaking to him in a whisper.

"You know I can't give you forgiveness," Barth said quietly. "Only Jesus can do that."

The youngest Pratt nodded enthusiastically. "Yeah, we get that part, mostly. I just want Him to listen. And I bet He'll be more likely to listen to you than me."

Barth looked at both men. "You have things you need to confess? To get off your shoulders?"

They both nodded.

"I don't need to hear what they are, but God does."

"I stole some jewelry," Gene said softly. "And some money. It was a long time ago. In Ohio. That's where we're from. Ohio. West of here."

Steve added, "And I had this car accident, and someone got killed. They said it was involuntary manslaughter—even though it was his fault and he was sort of askin' for it—but I shouldn't have done what I did."

"We both spent time in prison," said Gene.

Neither spoke.

Then Steve said in a mouse-quiet voice, "We hated what we did. We wished it never happened. It made us feel like people that we really weren't."

Barth waited. "And you want to be forgiven for your past sins?"

"Yes," the two said in unison.

"You want me to pray for you?"

They both answered quickly. "Yes."

Barth put his hands on their shoulders. He would not offer high-church, fancy praying—that was often more about those listening to the prayer rather than a real prayer to God. Instead, he'd offer something much simpler, much more direct, much more childlike.

"Dear God, here are two of Your children. They have sinned. They both have said that they are sorry for what they did. And they want Your forgiveness, for You have said that if we confess our sins, You are faithful and just and will forgive us. That is what they ask today. They have both paid their debt to society and now they want to acknowledge their sin to You."

Barth waited. He could feel the tension in the shoulders of each Pratt brother, as if they were straining under a large, awkward, and invisible load. "Hear our prayers, Lord."

He waited more, then closed softly, simply, and with power. "Lord, we are grateful that You have forgiven these two brothers because they both have asked and have shown their faith like a child. You have taken their sins upon You. You have paid the debt for their sins. Thank You. Give them a brand-new start. And help them to find a church and to grow in their faith. And now let them go and sin no more."

He breathed in. His heart was beating faster than it had in years. "Amen."

When he watched the two brothers open their eyes, he saw forgiveness on their faces, a lightness that was not there before, a new joy, an innocent happiness.

"That's it?"

"That's it," Barth said. "If you agreed with all your heart to what I said, then God has forgiven you."

None of them moved. Then Steve said, voice trembling, "This feels good. I haven't felt this good since … since forever."

Oliver guessed at what was transpiring—more or less—filling in the blanks with the hushed tones, the facial expressions, and the Pratt brothers' repentant posture on the pews. Oliver knew Barth didn't possess magic spiritual powers, or some hidden, private roadway to God and to forgiveness, but he knew, just as certainly, that ritual—especially biblical rituals, like the laying on of hands by elders, performed over and over through centuries of Christendom—did have power and made an impact on people.

After the Pratt brothers gathered their coolers, each stopped to shake Oliver's hand on the way out, thanking him for letting them work on this project, thanking him for bringing a man of God onto the jobsite, and thanking him for being the sort of person he was—all undeserved praise, Oliver felt, with maybe the exception of being wise enough to hire good men and trusting enough to take a chance when others would not.

Barth waited, sitting silently on the pew until everyone else had departed. He stood up, Rascal waiting on the floor, unwilling to waste energy standing up until Barth got closer to the door.

"Oliver, thanks for having me here today."

"My pleasure. I take it that the Pratt boys asked for some spiritual assistance?"

"They did. They've been carrying around a full sack of guilt for a long time. I just showed them where they could unload it. Simple, I guess, simple to people like you and me who understand. But to the person lost in that thicket of brambles, finding the way out is anything but simple."

Oliver nodded. "Thanks, Barth. Thanks a lot."

"No, thank *you*, Oliver. This is the first time in a long, long while that I've felt useful—and needed. It means a lot to me, son, to feel connected—even in this small way. Thanks again. And maybe …"

"Maybe what?"

"Maybe I could stop by tomorrow? See how Gene and Steve are doing. I won't get in the way."

Rascal wheezed to a standing position and walked toward them, the creaky stiffness in his legs almost visible to the human eye.

"Stop by at any time. It would be my pleasure to have you here."

For a second, Oliver wondered if Barth was going to cry. Instead, the older man turned to his dog and, clapping once, called out, "Come on, Rascal. We have to get home for supper. That sound good? Supper?"

———

The women sat at battered gray round folding tables, the sides nicked and scuffed from being rolled back and forth, in and out of the storage area at the rear of the multipurpose room in the church basement. Forty women, plus or minus a 10 percent standard deviation from week to week, gathered there, in the basement of the Christ Community Church, on the north side of Jeannette, drinking murky decaffeinated coffee from white foam cups, nibbling on the "variety pack" of cookies from a large round tin—the sort of tin one buys at discount or dollar stores—listening to the pastor's wife, teaching weekly about the attributes of God and what makes one a proper Christian woman.

Paula held her book open with her left hand and cupped her chin in her right hand, her elbow on the table, much like the posture she had favored all through high school. She tried to listen to Mrs. Mosco—"Barbara! You have to promise to call me Barbara!"—and tried to figure out how all this knowledge of the building of the tabernacle might actually apply to her life outside of this stuffy, with-a-hint-of-mildew room, but most often she felt plain stymied.

To her left sat Lisa Olsen, a woman her age, but who had attended Jeannette High School instead of Hempfield Area Senior High like Paula and Oliver and Taller. Lisa wore sweatpants and sweatshirts exclusively to these studies, apparently owning a cornucopia of various colors and styles. Her thick brown hair was tied back with a yellow band with the ponytail sticking out from her head at a pronounced right angle. She leaned close to Paula and whispered under her breath, "Does any of this make sense to you?"

Paula glanced at the speaker to see if she was looking in their direction. When she saw that she wasn't, she whispered back, "No. I thought I was the only stupid one here."

Lisa scrunched her face tight, like some manner of insect, and murmured back, a little louder than a whisper, "Not likely. I hardly ever understand it."

At this point, Mrs. Mosco did look over and arched her right eyebrow, a gesture that accompanied every question from the floor. Paula bit her lip to keep from laughing, and Lisa looked at her like she was the one with the question.

When Mrs. Mosco heard nothing, she turned back to her notes and continued speaking.

Lisa turned slightly away from the front and pantomimed being relieved at escaping getting caught.

After the study ended, Lisa said to Paula, "Sorry for almost getting you detention."

Snickering, Paula answered, "No problem. It's just nice to know I'm not the only one confused."

"Not by a long shot. I come here because my son likes the child-care people, and it gives me a two-hour break. Even though I get confused, it's still a break. A single mom needs all the help she can get."

"Me, too," Paula agreed. "It's nice having a break—regardless."

Lisa slid her Bible into a quilted cloth cover and zipped it up.

"Maybe next week I could get my sister to watch the kids for a while and we could go out for a snack afterward."

"Yeah, that would be fun," Paula replied. "Call me. I'll pitch in to pay a babysitter if she could watch Bridget as well."

As Mrs. Mosco hurried toward them, Lisa slipped away, in a hurry as well, calling over her shoulder, "I'll call you."

Mrs. Mosco grabbed Paula's free hand and held it tightly. "I'm so glad you've joined us," she said with bright cheer. "Having young women is so important."

"I like … coming here," Paula replied, a little intimidated by speaking one on one with the pastor's wife, a woman always immaculately made-up—not in a flashy way, but precisely, with her blonde hair set just so and a strand of pearls always around her neck, like an updated June Cleaver with a spiritual spin.

"I've been talking to Rose Barnett, and she goes on and on about you and her son Oliver. Says she's so proud of you being a 'born-again virgin.'"

Paula must have appeared badly confused, because Mrs. Mosco said, "You know, Paula, obviously, with a child, you can't get that 'pure' status back again, but Rose says you're staying faithful now. That's such a noble thing for you and your child—and for any man you might marry."

Paula tried to make her expression radiate enthusiasm.

"I know my husband has talked to Oliver too. About how you were wronged—being abandoned and all. How it would be okay for a good Christian man like Oliver and you … well, if you two got together. The church, or I should say, Pastor Mosco, would be perfectly fine with it. Some other churches may not be as gracious as we are. It's just so nice that you've found Jesus. I've known Oliver forever … for at least as long as we've been here. That feels like forever. And Oliver is a good man. He seemed so pleased when Pastor Mosco passed on his blessing for you two dating … and, you know, whatever. Genuinely pleased. Like a burden was being lifted from him, the pastor said."

In that instant, Paula wanted to poke the pastor's wife hard with her finger—hard enough to push Mrs. Mosco backward for referring to her husband, the pastor, as if he were not her husband, but some well-known third party.

"Well, that's nice, Mrs. Mosco. I'm happy that he and Oliver had a chance to talk. I know how busy he must be."

"Never too busy to answer questions or to help out. Or to help two people get together," she said.

There was an odd, self-congratulatory smile on Mrs. Mosco's face, Paula thought. When Bridget came running down the hall, calling out happily for her mother, this time Paula was very happy for the interruption.

———⊷∞∞⊶———

Oliver stood in the dark, quiet Blue Church. There appeared not to be a bad time to be inside the building. Mornings were filled with light and color, and in the afternoons, the sun gave the more muted colors of the west-side stained-glass windows voice, and the room became serene. And at the edge of evening, when the light inside became stronger than that outside, the windows seemed more sculptural than transparent. Yet when a car drove down the street opposite, the windows appeared as if they were moving, arms and legs and robes illuminated for a moment, then dark again.

Oliver liked every moment inside. He had come to love this building. Robert clambered up on a pew near the door and watched as Oliver walked the large room, stopping at an unfinished booth, examining the joinery, and counting the two-by-fours stacked against one wall. He ran a finger across the pebbly glass and thin lead fingers holding the windows together, then headed back to the bar, trying to imagine it filled with people and music, the aromas of food, laughter, and the clatter of glasses and silverware. Pools of light radiated from the miniature spotlights hidden in the ceiling, creating the drama of light against dark, making dining an intimate experience.

Even though he could see the transformation now and could tell that it would be wonderful, he still worried that something bad might happen because of his involvement. *Sacred remains sacred,* he knew. Yet at the same time, he still had the strong feeling that he was here for a purpose—that it was meant to be.

Robert hopped down off his perch and trotted over to Oliver.

"I know it's foolish," Oliver said, assuming Robert had been privy to his thoughts and was entering the conversation fully aware of what had preceded his spoken words. "But at the back of my mind there's a little fear that something will happen because of what this place once was and what I've done to it. And I won't like it. But there's also a lot of hope that something good will come out of it instead. Foolish, right, Robert?"

Robert sat down and looked up expectantly.

"And then there's Samantha."

Robert swallowed.

"And Paula."

Robert snorted, and then again, as if clearing his nose of an unpleasant smell.

Oliver sat down next to his dog and put his arm around the animal. Robert appeared neither happy nor unhappy—just distant, as if he didn't want to discuss this particular subject with Oliver at this particular moment. Then Robert sighed once, resigned to the discussion, regardless of what he wanted, since he was, after all, only a dog.

"I like Paula a lot. She is very, very pretty. She's easy to talk to. I mean, since she does most of the talking. That's okay with me. She's pleasant, most of the time. I would have said that she was too good for me—looks-wise—a few years ago. And then my mother—she really likes her now. That's a real turnaround. I could do worse, I know that. I bet she would do her best to make me happy. And maybe that's what it's all about. At my age, anyhow. It would make my mother really happy. That's a big part of it. My mother sacrificed so much to raise me and Tolliver. Maybe she deserves for me to treat her well, now that she's older. And is there anyone else on the horizon, Robert? I haven't dated that many women. Virtually none in the past few years.

"And now Paula. Maybe that's what God wants me to do. Pastor Mosco seems to think it's a good thing. And my mother—she's definitely for it. Maybe that's what I should do, Robert. Maybe I should just go ahead and make the leap. That's what they did in the old days. Found someone who was acceptable and went ahead and got married. I heard somewhere that a great percentage of arranged marriages work. You learn to be together. Like you and me, Robert. We learned how to be together. We didn't know each other when I found you. I had no idea if you would be a good dog or not. And you didn't know if I would be a good person for you. You just went with me. You go where I go—that's from the Bible, isn't it? Something about 'Wherever you lodge, I will lodge.' But it's true. We both took a chance—and see how well it has worked? Maybe that's what I should do. Maybe I should just go for it."

He and Robert sat for a long time in the growing darkness, watching the car headlights play against the windows of the Blue Church, watching the God-eye over the platform come alive, Samson in front of the pillars of the temple, and Jesus in the garden, His face inclined toward heaven, praying for guidance for all those who believed and were willing to follow where God was leading them.

When Oliver's phone squawked, he nearly jumped up in response, his quiet reverie suddenly snapped closed by the electronic chatter. He unholstered the phone.

"Hello, Oliver. Samantha. I'm not interrupting you, am I? I can call back or talk to you tomorrow."

"No, it's okay. Robert and I were just sitting here watching car head-lights on the stained glass and thinking about taking a walk. It's pretty nice out, and we haven't gone on a walk in days."

"Well, I'm here, just lying in bed. Thinking. Maybe you could throw pebbles at my window when you pass by. Do people still do that, or do they just text each other?"

Oliver let out a short laugh, wondering what she wanted.

"I think texting is the way the young people would do it. I might still use pebbles."

"You're a traditionalist, Oliver-not- … I mean, Oliver. I like that."

Oliver felt a pang of loss at her interruption in using his nickname.

"Listen, I want to apologize for making you feel bad, or nervous, the other night. I had no right to do that."

"It's okay, Samantha. It really is."

"I still feel bad for getting upset. I just want to say that I accept who you are. I really do."

"Well … thanks."

"And I like the way you are."

"Thanks."

"I like you. You like me. Right?"

Oliver knew he could think about this one for a long time and not come up with a clever answer. "Sure. I like you."

"Well, then, it's settled," she said, her voice happier than it had been when they last spoke. "Let's just see what happens. Maybe nothing. Maybe something. Okay?"

Oliver felt no relief at all. "Sure. That's okay with me, too," he said with more enthusiasm than he felt.

CHAPTER SIXTEEN

PAULA HEARD THE familiar tapping. She checked on her daughter—sound asleep—and hurried to the door.

"I was hoping you would stop by," she said.

Taller hurried to close the door. She watched his eyes as they went from window to window. All the blinds were down, tight to the windowsills.

"I was hoping you were hoping. A lot of hoping," he said.

"Did you have dinner? I have half a sub sandwich. Some diet soda."

He shook his head, took her hand, and led her to the sofa. He tossed her knitted afghan to the side. "It's scratchy," he said.

"It's okay. I only use it when I'm cold."

Both of them knew what Taller would say next. Paula could see in Taller's face that he hated himself for being so predictable.

"I'll keep you warm." His words were honey, slow and presumptive.

"I'd like that," Paula said, whispering in his ear, leaning against him, her hand against his hard chest. "I like being warm. I like your sort of warm, Taller. Keep me warm as much as you want."

"I'll keep you warm all night," he said.

She knew he was lying to her, lying to himself.

To Gene Pratt, the brightness of the lights at the Eat 'n' Park on Route 30 was all the reason he needed to keep his baseball cap on indoors. His mother, dead now nearly fifteen years, had been an absolute stickler for hats off indoors. She would have been driven to distraction by the new sense of etiquette, of how proper, respectable manners might be ignored.

His younger brother, Steve, and older brother, Henry, sat opposite him. The restaurant, more or less equidistant from all the brothers' homes, was Gene's suggestion. The bright lights were cause for him to mentally note that he would not make the suggestion again.

Three cups of coffee were delivered, and the Pratt brothers all made a lemony grimace when they first tasted the beverage.

"Good Pittsburgh coffee from Miss Cohen has ruined us, hasn't it?" Gene said.

"Yep," both brothers agreed.

Henry stirred another creamer into the coffee, knowing it would not improve the taste. "So you two want me to find a church for us?"

His brothers nodded.

"And you'll go?"

They nodded.

"And what you and Pastor Barth talked about made you feel better?"

Steve spoke first. "I guess I knew I didn't need a church pastor to do it, but Gene and I talked about it. It was time to give it up. Oliver started it by givin' us the job. It was the first time that somebody knew what we did and took a chance on us. And then we knew that we had to do somethin' about it. Maybe there's somethin' about that church we're workin' on that's changin' us somehow—makin' us better. More Christian or somethin'. Then there was Pastor Barth, like it had been planned. If that's the way God works, then we better stay right with Him. I don't want to be on His bad side. I mean, He could just as easily kept us confused. Or does the Devil do that? Well, whatever. We need to stay right. And that means goin' to church, right, Gene?"

Gene sipped his coffee, grimaced, then muttered, "That woman has ruined coffee for me forever. That ain't right. It just ain't."

⎯⎯⎯⎯⎯

Rose grabbed for her glasses. She squinted at the clock—almost 10:30 p.m. She had been in bed for nearly an hour, knowing she would probably not find sleep for hours more. There was nothing on TV, and Rose had never been much for reading or for crafts.

She padded downstairs, pushing and patting at her hair as she did. A few clean dishes rested in the drainboard. She put them away and wiped clean the counter with a dishcloth. She walked to the front room and peered out to the street, watching two cars as they passed her house. She picked up the TV remote, pointed it at the TV, then put it back down. She walked back into the kitchen, took out an old envelope from the shoebox filled with scrap paper and a pencil, and walked to the refrigerator. She opened the door, stared, shut the door, then scrawled: *butter, milk, cottage cheese, orange juice.*

The phone rang, scaring her a little, and she squinted at the clock again.

Who could be calling this late? I hope it's not Oliver.

"Hi, Ma." It was Taller. "Sorry to call you so late, but I haven't talked to you for a while."

If her younger son had been in the room with her, Rose would have shaken her head in rebuke, tightening her lips and narrowing her eyes. But he was merely a voice on the phone, so she waited a moment, then replied. "Are you in trouble, Tolliver? Do you need money or something? I hope you don't, because I can't give you any. Lord knows, I've given you enough in the past. And you've never paid me back, Tolliver, do you remember that? Never? And I have never asked you for it."

She heard him take a deep breath, a loud, deep breath, and then loudly exhale. It took a long time.

"Well, what it is then, Tolliver? Why are you calling?"

"I can't call to say hello? If this was Oliver, would you ask him why he was calling?"

"He'd never call this late. Unless it was an emergency or something. He's a good boy."

She heard him mutter something.

"What? What did you say?"

"Nothing, Ma. I didn't say anything."

Silence over a phone always proved to be very silent.

"Then what?"

Taller inhaled again. Rose imagined that he was in trouble again ... and was trying to figure out a way to tell her without making her angry or upset.

He's had a lot of practice. Wrecked a couple of cars. Got picked up for drunk driving. What else could he do to give me heartache?

"It's not me, Ma. Not this time. I know I gave you some troubles back then. But not for years now, right? And as for paying you back, yeah, well, I want to—but like I said, put it in your will that I owe you money and Oliver will get it from my share. Unless you really need it now."

"No. I don't need it."

"This time, it's Oliver, Ma. Not me. He's in trouble."

"Trouble? Is he hurt? Tell me, Tolliver, tell me!"

"Hold on a second, Ma. Nothing like that. But ... he *is* in trouble."

"What do you mean, *trouble*? Why? How?"

Rose heard Taller take another breath and exhale, in dramatic fashion.

"That woman."

"Paula?"

Taller answered quickly. "No. Not Paula. Good grief, not her. That woman in Pittsburgh. Samantha Cohen. He's ... dating her. They've been out to dinner, he takes her out to lunch, and she's always at the jobsite. I thought you should know."

"Oliver?"

"Yes, your son, Oliver. He's dating that Jewish woman in Shadyside. I know they've been out to dinner a bunch of times. And he's gone to her house and spent the evening. To me, that's dating."

"My Oliver? I don't believe it. He would never do that. Never. Not to his mother."

"Ma, I can't make you believe anything you don't want to. And I didn't want to tell you about him and Samantha. But I thought you deserved to know. You deserve better than him lying to you."

"Oliver?"

"Yes, Ma, he's dating a woman of another faith. And from what I hear, she's a loose woman, with a lot of men in her past. *A lot of men,* I hear tell."

"My Oliver?"

Rose couldn't believe her ears, couldn't believe Tolliver was telling the truth, even though it sounded like he was.

"Just don't tell him that you heard it from me."

After they had hung up, she wondered if the note of glee she heard in Tolliver's voice was real or not. She told herself that it was only something she imagined hearing, the news being such a shock to her system and all.

Samantha dialed the number she had on her cell phone for Cameron Dane Willis and the office of Three Rivers Restorations. Samantha had met Cameron through her friends Alice and Frank Adams years earlier, when one of her property flips on Mount Washington was used for a short segment on the television show *Three Rivers Restorations*. The show had planned to feature Samantha's current project—not just a ten-minute "before and after" report, but a full-blown half-hour piece. The television crew had shot the "before" footage just after Samantha had purchased the church.

"Hello? This is Cameron."

Surprised at hearing the television host's voice, Samantha stumbled on her words. She had fully expected to have to leave a message on voice mail after a certain hour. Samantha's bewitching hour was 9:00—unless the caller ID indicated the caller as someone she might want to talk to, regardless of the late hour.

"Who is this?" Cameron asked.

Samantha marveled at how pleasant the host sounded even though it was late at night. "Samantha. Samantha Cohen," she managed to say.

"Sam! How are you? I was going to call you tomorrow. Really. How funny that you beat me to it," she said.

"You mean I didn't wake you?"

"Good heavens, no. Peter, the baby, just went down. Chase is over at a friend's house. Ethan is out giving an estimate to a potential client. And Riley is still up, jabbering on in her bed. So that means that Mom is still up."

"I don't know how you do it—a baby, a toddler, a teenager, and all the rest. When do you sleep?"

"Sleep is highly overrated. And once they're all in college, I'll catch up. What's on your mind? You ready to have us come back and do the 'after' photography on 'Blue'? You said summer, and I have yet to hear of a renovation that was finished ahead of schedule."

"No. We're not done. Getting there, though. Things are really starting to shape up. It's actually beginning to look like a restaurant inside. Maybe a month. More likely two. You weren't planning on doing any in-progress shots, right?"

"No. Not on a project like yours. Not that it's not a wonderful project, but viewers seem to like watching homeowners in the middle of chaos. On commercial projects, no one has to live in it, so there's not as much drama. No dose of reality."

"Well … there is someone living there. In the church. Sort of."

"Who? How?"

"You met him—Oliver Barnett, the general contractor."

"The cute one? From Frank and Alice's job in Butler? He's the general on this project? The cute cabinet-and-booth guy—with his real handsome brother?"

"That's him."

"He lives there?"

"Well, sort of. During the week, he stays in the basement. With his dog. Goes home on the weekends. But … I know that's not what you mean."

"No," Cameron replied, obviously relieved.

"But I do have a question for you. Not a building question. Not about the show, either."

"Then you've got me," Cameron replied. "That's all I know about. Unless you want to talk about diapers and how to get baby puke off your most favorite cashmere sweater."

"No, not about that either. But … well … you know when you talked to me about faith and church and finding Jesus as the Messiah and how I was real polite and blew you off."

"You didn't blow me off," Cameron replied.

"Yes I did," Samantha said. "And unless you want me to lose all respect for your judgment, your memory, and your personal code of ethics, you'll agree with me, because we both know it's true."

Cameron's laughter was the type that could not be disguised or silenced. "Yeah. You did blow me off. I remember. You were nice about it. But you did."

"Of course I did," Samantha replied. "But since you're smart about this religion stuff, I have a question."

"Shoot."

"Well, that cute contractor is the same sort of person you are. I mean, like a real Christian or whatever it is you call yourselves. Born again, right?"

"Some of us use that term. Christian or Christ-follower is okay too."

"I really like the guy, Cameron. I mean, I really, really like him. He's very special—unlike anyone I've ever known. We've been out a few times. And we've never gone all that far. You know …"

"Like to California?"

It was Samantha's turn to laugh. "You know very well what I mean."

"Yeah, I guess I do."

"And he says he won't, because of what the Bible says. And, of course, that just makes him all the more desirable."

There was a pause. "So what's the question, then?" Cameron asked.

"What can I tell him so that he'd think it would be okay for him and me … for the two of us to be … together. You have any advice?"

Then there followed a much longer pause, as one of the parties tried to quickly figure out the right words to say.

Rose jabbed hard at the buttons on her phone. She had hated giving up her old rotary phone. Somehow dialing when angry was a much more satisfying experience than merely jabbing at buttons. Yet this was the only option she had.

She looked at the clock. Nearly 11:00.

Way too late for making phone calls … except for now.

"Hello."

At least he doesn't sound sleepy … like I woke him up.

"Oliver? This is your mother calling."

Rose nearly always identified herself when calling her sons.

"Ma? What's the matter? It's … what?—past eleven. Are you okay?"

She loved hearing his voice, but her anger made her ignore that pleasure. "You know why I'm calling," she said, her words icy and clipped.

There was a moment, then Oliver responded, "No, Ma, I have no idea. Unless it's the church-project thing again. And that topic is closed. I'm sorry, but I need the work. So does Taller. And it's not a church anymore. I don't want to upset you, but this is nothing that can be changed. So I guess you'll just have to live with it."

"Oliver," Rose said after waiting for him to finish, "it has nothing to do with that. All my life you're the good son, the son I can trust, the son who never did one thing to hurt me. You were always such a good boy. And now it's like the Devil is using you, Oliver. Yes, you heard me. The Devil. How else can I explain it?"

She paced back and forth in the kitchen, tethered to the wall in the hallway where the phone was hung. She didn't want to pay for the extra-long cord or a cordless phone so her walk was abbreviated—three steps forward, then three steps back.

"Explain what?"

"You're dating that woman. That Jewish woman. How can you do this? How can you kill your mother's dreams without even a hint of remorse? And what about Paula? Are you just using her? Are you having sexual relations with her, Oliver?"

"No!"

"No to which one, Oliver? With the Jew? Or with Paula?"

"With neither one."

Both of them were quiet. Rose knew that Oliver was a smart boy and had figured out who had told her about his social life. So she lied … just a little.

"Tolliver didn't say a word about this, Oliver. I figured it out on my own. And I want to know if you enjoy hurting me."

Again, no response. Rose waited.

"Ma, I'm not going to talk about this with you. I am not. And I don't hold Taller responsible. You have your ways of getting information. So this conversation is now officially over."

The line went silent and dead.

For the first time in her life, her dearest son had hung up on her, leaving her with an acrid taste in her throat—a taste she didn't like one bit.

After a moment or two, the silence on the phone was broken when Samantha, never the most patient at waiting for anything, said, "I'm sorry, Cameron. It's late, so maybe we can talk about this some other time. I should let you go...."

"No, Sam, it's okay. I think Riley's finally asleep. I was just thinking that maybe you should be asking a different question."

"Different question? What do you mean?"

"Well, there is the whole issue of faith, an issue larger than your physical attraction to Oliver, and his to you. How do you feel about the difference in the way you two view God—specifically Jesus?"

"Oh, that doesn't bother me at all," Sam answered quickly. "I mean, I'm Jewish, but I'm not orthodox or anything like that. My mother always took a very serious approach to religion. My father—not so much. He keeps the *Shabbat*—the Sabbath—and some of the other traditions, but not like my mother. And even though I went to Hebrew school and all, I'm more of an observant Jew. After college, when all my Jewish friends were making their pilgrimages to Israel, where did I go? To France, of course. Paris was much more alluring than the Wailing Wall. My attendance at temple has been, shall we say, sporadic at best."

"Observant Jew?" Cameron asked.

"Yes. I mean, I believe in God and observe all the holidays, but it doesn't really affect my daily life. It's more of a cultural thing. And I respect other people like you and Oliver, whose religion is more important. Everyone has their own path. Live and let live, I always say."

"But, Sam, you have to realize that for people like Oliver and for me, our faith is the most important thing. And believing the truth of the Bible does affect the way we live each day—including our moral decisions."

"I'm an okay person. I follow the Golden Rule," Samantha answered.

"It's not about rules, Sam, but about a relationship—with Jesus—that changes everything," Cameron answered. "God is not an irrelevant, distant being, but inside us and all around us."

"You really feel God's presence?"

"Yes. Yes, I do. All the time. Can't imagine life without the love and peace He brings. And what is so attractive to you about Oliver could well be that very thing—Christ in him, and the hope he has. You have to understand that there may be nothing you can say or do to Oliver to change his mind on what he believes or how he behaves—including in the romance arena."

"I've never known anyone like him before—a guy who really believes. I know guys who believe in the Steelers, maybe, or the Pirates, but not in God, and not like this."

"I get it, Sam. I've been there. When I met Ethan …well, let's just say his stand on such things was at first frustrating, yet impressive. I didn't have the Jesus factor to process through, since I had always been a Christian who sort of dabbled at being a true believer, but there were plenty of ways that my faith needed attention before I came to a clearer understanding of Jesus that changed my life."

"We talked about this before, I know, but I still don't know what you mean by 'understanding of Jesus,'" Samantha said. "Wasn't He just a rabbi, a good man who wanted to help His people when they were under Roman oppression?"

"Jesus was a Jewish rabbi, but so much more. It goes back to the beginning … to creation, really. You know the story: Adam and Eve in the garden and how they were banished from God's presence because of their sin. The Old Testament, the *Tanach,* is the story of God working to restore His presence to His people through the burning bush, the pillar of fire, building the temple for the ark of the covenant, where His presence resided, which they feared. Jesus, the long-awaited Messiah, fulfilled all the incredibly detailed Old Testament prophecies. He was the culmination of God's plan to bring sinful people—all of us, Sam—back into right relationship with God, without fear. Not through following a set of laws—the Torah, or any other religious rules—to perfection. No one can do that. The Bible says that leads to death, because God is holy and can't tolerate even the smallest sin. So we are separated. But if we believe Jesus is the Messiah, who by grace took on our sin and paid the penalty for it, and we trust that through His sacrifice on the cross we can be saved from eternal death, then we can live in His presence and have an eternal future in heaven. That restored relationship leads to life."

"So by believing all this, that's how you changed your life?" Sam asked.

"*I* didn't change my life, Sam. God did. I was a mess—believe me. I had so much baggage from my past, was in denial over it all, and looking for love in all the wrong places. Ethan, too, was struggling through pain from the tragedy in his life. Ultimately, we both found peace in God, through Jesus. Only He can fill the void in our lives."

It was Samantha's turn to be silent.

Then Cameron spoke softly. "Sam, if you really think Oliver is special, maybe the best thing you can do is look into *why* he's so different, in a good way, than all the other men you've known. Investigate how his life is unique because of his faith in Christ. Talk to him."

"But I know so little about Christianity … I wouldn't even know where to start."

"Hey—you own a church. There must be a Bible around there somewhere!" Cameron said with a laugh.

———∘◇∘———

Cameron put the phone down and began to ask God to allow her words to penetrate into Samantha's heart, praying that she had said enough, but not too much.

And then she remembered Sarah.

Cameron looked at the clock on the kitchen wall.

Too late to call tonight. I'll phone her first thing in the morning.

———∘◇∘———

Paula peeked into her daughter's bedroom. Bridget, sleeping soundly, was nestled up to the pillow, the blanket drawn to her neck, her angelic face illuminated by the moon. Paula stood by the bed for a long time, watching the rise and fall of her daughter's chest. She crept out of the room, closed the door, and walked to the guest room on the other side of the hall. She could hear the subdued garble of a late-night talk show on the TV. She tapped twice, with a soft hand, and cracked the door.

"Mom? You're not asleep?"

"Oh, honey, I never sleep well on this bed. It's a little too soft. But I'll make do. Really. You get to bed."

Paula sidled into the room, halfway. "Mom, thanks for coming. The babysitter has the flu, and I didn't want to get Bridget up an hour early in the morning to get her to your place. You sure you don't mind staying overnight?"

"Honey, it's okay. A few days of some missed sleep is no big thing. You get older and you don't need as much sleep. That's what everyone says."

Paula had heard the same thing from Rose Barnett, but Rose was much older than her mother.

"Listen, Mom, would it be okay if I ran out for a few minutes? Lisa, a friend from church, wanted to get together. Her daughter is with her ex, so she's free. Is it okay? We're going to meet at the Eat 'n' Park in Greensburg." Paula hoped it sounded like the truth.

"Honey, that's so far. And it's so late."

"I know. But I never get to have adult conversations anymore."

It was a tactic Paula knew would work.

"Well, okay. But don't stay out too late."

Paula hurried to her car and started driving. She punched at her cell phone. "Hi. Can you meet me at the Eat 'n' Park? I know it's late, but I need to talk to you. Okay?"

———◦◦◦◦———

In fifteen minutes, Paula had taken a booth facing the highway, in the back of the restaurant. She had combed her hair using the rearview mirror in her car and hurriedly put on a thin sheen of lipstick.

This is all the makeup I have in my purse, so it will have to do.

Taller walked in slowly, his shoulders moving in time with his hips, the movement both languorous and tempting. Paula eyed him as he came closer. He offered a short but knowing smile.

"Hi."

"Hi yourself. You're lucky that I don't go to bed early," he said.

"Sometimes you do," she said coyly.

"Yeah. Well, sometimes. But not when I'm alone. Why did you call?

Aren't you afraid that someone will see us together and tell Ollie about it? How would you explain that?"

"You're his brother. And what would they tell? We know each other. I stopped on the way home from a Bible study. You were here. We decided to have a cup of coffee together. Pretty harmless, right?"

Taller leaned back in the booth, his head nearly hidden from the other customers. "You've thought about this. Prepared. I like that."

"Among other things," Paula replied.

Why am I doing this? Why am I risking a good man like Oliver?

"You want to go back to your place?" Taller asked as he stirred a third sugar packet into his coffee.

"We can't. My mother is staying with me. The babysitter is sick, so she's helping out."

Paula looked at Taller, her eyes searching his. "We could go back to your place."

Taller's smile wavered just a bit, as if he were briefly considering the offer, then immediately discarded it.

Paula decided the wait was answer enough. "I know. It's late. And I do need to get back in a few minutes. My mother is already worried."

Taller, eyes fixed on her, sipped his coffee. She squirmed under his gaze, like she was some sort of butterfly, or caterpillar, about to be pinned to a display board.

Paula knew she had to ask the question. It was why she'd invited him here. It was why she'd called. There were doubts and tensions, worries and suspicions, and Paula thought she could live with that ambiguity, that uncertainty. But now she realized, in a stab of awareness, that maybe she couldn't; she had to know more than Taller had ever told her.

"Do we have a future, Taller, you and I? I need to know. Well, maybe *need* is the wrong word. But I … I really like being with you, and you seem to have a good time with me. So I guess I want to know if you're doing this because you really want to be with me … and find me attractive and sexy and all that … or are you just …"

Taller sat up straight and pushed his coffee cup to the side. His smile had disappeared. His hands were folded now, in front of him, and his knuckles appeared taut.

"Just what? What am I just doing?" His words were not tender, not comforting nor inviting, but angry, hostile.

"Are you doing all this to get back at your brother?" Paula asked.

His eyes narrowed and his hands jerked, just an inch. They moved involuntarily, Paula thought, as if some current had struck them, a charge that caused a recoil of muscle and tendon.

"Oliver has nothing to do with this," he said evenly, calmly … almost.

"And you're not getting back at your mother, either—really?"

It was a question Paula had not anticipated asking again, but once she had spoken the words, she knew it was the question that would answer all her other questions.

Taller's right hand pulled back in a snap, with his fist suddenly clenched. Paula flinched—as if he would swing at her out in public like this, in a restaurant, in front of the trio of customers at the counter and the brace of waitresses, milling about the coffee pots, whispering and laughing amongst themselves.

Then his body relaxed, and he settled back into the booth, his shoulders almost slumping, as if overcorrecting and relaxing too much, just to show they were at peace. He smiled. Paula didn't believe the change in his expression, though she smiled back at him, encouraging him, wanting the truth.

"Nothing to do with my mother, Paula. Nothing at all."

She waited a moment. "Okay. If you say that's the truth."

Taller didn't take her hands, but he leaned close. His words weren't angry, but there was a scent of malice in them.

"And why are *you* doing this, Paula? You and me, I mean. It's not like I've ever said I love you. But I do love what we do. So why? To get back at your lousy ex-husband? That would be enough reason for me. Leaving you like that. Unless you did something to push him away. Did you, Paula? Or are you getting back at *your* mother? Don't daughters do that sometimes? Pick the wrong man just to make their mother crazy? Or are you just angry at having a baby? What? What drives you, Paula? What makes you and me work? We do work together, don't we? Have you been to a therapist to find out why? Have you? Do you understand why?"

Paula said nothing. His words became a deluge, submerging her, drowning her ability to speak, to respond.

"I thought as much. Hey, do me a favor. Stop thinking about it. Stop. You and me work—on some level. Let's just leave that as it is. Okay?"

She nodded, still unable to reply.

"Then that's settled." Taller stood up, reached into his pocket, extracted a twenty-dollar bill, and tossed it on the table. "You can keep the change," he said softly. He turned, took a step, then turned back. "I'll call you tomorrow evening. We'll see what happens, won't we, Paula? We'll see what happens between you and me."

And then he walked away, toward the exit, slowly, with the same sort of walk that he had when he came in.

CHAPTER SEVENTEEN

OLIVER GOT UP EARLY, took Robert for a walk, then wrote a long note listing a score of different tasks he wanted Taller and the Pratt brothers to work on that day.

At the end he wrote,

> I have a lot of errands to run. If I'm not back by five, lock up. I have my key with me.

> Oliver B.

He didn't want to talk to Taller today. He didn't want to talk to the Pratt brothers. He didn't want to see Samantha. He would have liked it if he could have packed up his truck and driven into the Allegheny Mountains and hiked up in the woods for a few days without talking to anyone, leaving his cell phone off and even Robert the Dog at home.

But Oliver couldn't do any of that. A day missing from work would be bad; two or three or four would be a disaster. The Blue Church project was now a couple of weeks behind schedule as it was, so his emotional turmoil couldn't push it further back. He would be leaving money on the table, and he was in no position to do that.

It's always been this way. I always have to do what other people think I should do. I've never been able to be myself, to decide on things by myself, to determine what's good for me. I want to believe my mother wants the best for me, but I don't know what I want anymore. Not at all.

He parked the truck off of Walnut Street. He might be stressed, but he still wanted his morning coffee.

What I want. That's a laugh, isn't it? Like I know. Or ever knew. I wish I could make a decision for me … just once.

Jitters Coffee Shop opened early, and Oliver truly preferred their brand of coffee, creamy with only a hint of chocolate. The Pratt boys liked Coffee Tree Roasters' coffee, so that's where he usually went.

Even buying coffee I'm pleasing others. Not today. I can get whatever I want, he told himself, at the same time realizing that choosing between coffee shops didn't exactly constitute an emotional breakthrough.

Oliver knew perhaps three people in all of Pittsburgh, and he kept running into them, over and over. He and Barth nearly collided in the doorway of Jitters.

"You're up early," Barth said with great cheer. "You don't start until eight. And it's only—what?—a little after five."

"Couldn't sleep, Barth," he said, as the two of them took a table for two by the window.

"And Robert was fine with being left back?"

"No, but sometimes if I'm running errands, he gets confused. He wants to get out at each stop and not every business wants a dog inside— even if they are good-natured."

Barth poured a heaping spoonful of sugar into his coffee, stirred, tasted, then added another. "You don't mind if I stop at the church later this morning, do you, Oliver? I promised the Pratt brothers a basic book about the Bible. They could use some instruction."

"Sure. Feel free to stick around as long as you want. You seem to have a calming influence on them. And I'm glad they got the whole guilt and forgiveness issue settled."

Barth sipped, as noisy as a garbage disposal. "Not settled, entirely, but on their way."

"Speaking of instruction," Oliver said, "I've got a question for you as well."

Barth brightened, as if he were a grade-school child being praised for a good spelling paper, his expression revealing he both deserved the praise and was taken aback. "Shoot. This is good for me. Keeps me active. They say that thinking prevents Alzheimer's."

"It has to do with sex," Oliver said, lowering his voice, so the steam from the coffee machine would drown out his question from other nearby ears in the store.

"Sex ... hmmm," Barth said. "If it gets real complicated, I'll let you know. Didn't get a lot of calls up in Kane County for sex advice. Discussing sex and money was pretty much off limits to most people. And if it involved ... women's issues ... I usually let my wife talk to the other woman about it."

"Not that sort of complicated, Barth. I don't think so, anyhow."

"Well, go ahead. I'll give it a try." Barth resettled himself in the chair and shook his arms to limber them up, like a prizefighter waiting for his opponent to throw a punch.

Oliver took a deep breath, then let it out. "I'm seeing this woman. I really like her. It's not serious, at least not yet. We're really, really different. But ... oh, well, here goes ... she more or less asked if we could go to bed together."

Barth coughed into his coffee cup, held his hand over his mouth and coughed again, waving his other hand, indicating, Oliver hoped, that he was okay and just coughing and not having a seizure of some kind.

Oliver waited an anxious moment while Barth's coughs subsided.

"I'm okay. Took me by surprise there. Go ahead," the older man sputtered.

"Well, she would have and I said I wouldn't, because of my faith and what I believe in. I don't think she understood. I think she took it as an insult. I told her firmly that I'm waiting until I get married. Like the Bible says to do."

Barth puckered his lips. "And ... what's your question?"

"I guess I just want you to say that it's okay."

"Okay to do it?" Barth asked, sounding a little shocked.

"No—saying no. As a believer, I don't think I have any choice, do I?"

Barth sighed, a world-weary sort of sigh. "I don't preach anymore, Oliver, but I read a lot. There are some churches out there that seem to think it's okay now. Like everything's changed. But it hasn't—not God's morals, at least. So I wouldn't. I never would. You know, if she can't under-stand that about you, then maybe that's God telling you she isn't 'the one.' I had one love in my life: my wife. Once she died, it was like I lost my reason for living. And if Rascal dies, then I won't have anything left of hers. It will all be gone."

The old man sniffed loudly and looked away, out the window, at the early-morning traffic on Walnut. Then he pulled himself together.

"Anyway, Oliver, that's been my counsel whenever a young person asked if God had only one special, unique person they were supposed to find and whom they would be happy with. I'm not sure God is in the matchmaking business like that. Maybe there are any number of women out there who you could be happy with. Women who love God, of course, and who will try and love you, women who believe in commitment. I don't think God plays hide 'n' seek games with the perfect mate, where you have to find the one and only person for you somewhere out there in the whole wide world. I believe He brings people across our path. But this is the most crucial piece of advice I can offer you: Don't rush things with … you know … sex. I would tell you to wait. Sex before marriage might ruin whatever chance you have to be happy. If this woman can't understand that concept, then maybe you need to move on. I know it's hard, as a man, but that's what I believe is the truth."

He looked straight into Oliver's eyes. "And, deep in your heart, I think you do too."

———

"Are you free for lunch?" Oliver asked, holding his cell phone awkwardly against his left cheek while he steered with his right hand, knowing that he should stop the car. But traffic was slow and he felt in no danger of being distracted. "Sorry I wasn't on the jobsite this morning. I had some errands to take care of."

Samantha didn't hesitate. "Sure. Where?"

"How about the Carnegie Café?"

"Where? Where's that?"

"At the Carnegie Museum of Natural History. By the university. You've been there, haven't you? Over on Forbes."

"Of course. With the dinosaurs? Sure. Like a million times. Twice a year with school. It was a sacred pilgrimage. I loved their spooky displays and all the stuffed animals. But I never ate at their café. Brown-bag lunches and all that."

Fifteen minutes later, Oliver hurried down the massive steps in front of the museum as Samantha exited a yellow cab.

"I knew I wouldn't be able to park close," she said, as if she needed to explain the taxi. "And I was pretty sure you would give me a ride back home."

"Sure," Oliver said as he stopped in front of the revolving doors. "Do I go first, or do you?"

"You go first," Samantha said. "If the door is hard to push, then the man is supposed to bear that heavy burden."

Oliver pretended that the door was indeed very heavy and recalcitrant, which it wasn't, but he enjoyed hearing Samantha laugh at his acting.

They found a table overlooking the dinosaur hall, only a half wall separating them from the entrance. They could both see the head and tiny, disproportionate forearms of the T-Rex bathed in the spotlights that washed over the bones, casting ominous shadows on the floor that provided a nervous pause to a packet of grade-school children as they walked through the exhibit.

"I remember being so scared by all the bones," Samantha said. "I was sure, at least once, that I saw them move. All those huge skeletons with their big, toothy grins. Scary stuff for a little kid—especially since I didn't understand it."

They both ordered lunch. Oliver wouldn't have ordered anything if he had been alone, except coffee and maybe a piece of pie, but Samantha ordered chicken salad on wheat toast, a cup of the soup of the day (cream of broccoli), and a salad with the house dressing ("dinosaur vinaigrette") on the side. Oliver didn't want this lunch to be more awkward than it needed to be, in case she felt self-conscious eating alone, so he decided to order something.

As she neared finishing her food, Oliver, who had only picked at his chef's salad, put his fork down and lifted his coffee cup toward the waitress, who quickly brought a refill.

"Samantha," he said, "I need to explain something to you."

She took another bite of the second half of her sandwich and looked up, her beautiful eyes wide with invitation.

"It's about what we talked about the other night. When you came to the church. And when … you know …"

She had not swallowed completely when she started to reply. "I know, Oliver. It made you nervous. I understand. I can give you time. I know we're wired differently. But I can be patient. Really."

Oliver didn't respond immediately.

"That's the guy speech, isn't it?" she asked. "I don't think many women get a chance to say that."

"You're probably right about that," Oliver said.

A group of squealing children raced past them and pointed at the bones ahead. Some of the boys were making dinosaur-growling noises, all the while a quartet of harried teachers and aides chased after them, calling to them to be reserved and quiet.

"I know what you were offering … that night," he said, looking at her evenly.

Samantha wasn't the sort of woman Oliver thought could ever blush, but he saw her cheeks flush for a moment.

"And I was flattered. A little guilty for feeling so flattered. And very, very tempted," he added.

"Well … thank you," she replied, obviously not knowing if that should be considered a compliment.

"But I couldn't."

"I know," she said. "You explained why. Your faith. The Bible. But I said I would give it time, Oliver. I know sometimes love doesn't happen … not *love*. I didn't mean that word, exactly. But two people, being together … well, sometimes it takes one of them longer to feel ready. That's okay."

Oliver waited as the waitress cleared the empty dishes, asking if he wanted to take home what was left of his salad. He shook his head.

"No. It's not a time thing," he continued. "I'll always be tempted—believe me. But I won't ever be ready. Unless I'm married."

Samantha wrinkled her face. "Never?"

"Not without being married."

"Really? Really and truly?"

"That's what I believe."

They both sat still, not speaking, looking into each other's eyes. Oliver tried to discern what she was thinking but couldn't.

"We have to believe the same thing?" she asked. "I mean, like being married first. I have to believe what you believe?"

Oliver narrowed his eyes. "Yes."

Samantha's expression went from puzzled to angry and puzzled. "You mean, I would have to change who I was if we were to be together? No other man in my life has asked me to change myself like that."

Later, Oliver would berate himself for his next question. "And just how many men have there been in your life?"

Samantha no longer looked puzzled at all, just angry. Maybe angry and hurt. "You don't have the right to ask me that."

"I do have the right," he replied.

"Just because you haven't had sex doesn't mean I shouldn't have had sex," she flared back.

At that moment, Oliver began to realize the truth: He didn't have a future with this woman. That realization was beginning to break his heart—more than a little.

How could I forgive this? How could I overlook what she has done with her life? How could I overlook the fact that she has slept with—what?—a dozen men? Maybe even more than that?

Samantha sat still, her eyes hot and fiery. He had never seen her like this before.

And she is a Jew.

"It's not a matter of changing yourself," Oliver said.

"I don't know what you mean," Samantha replied.

"People can't really change themselves. That, only God can do."

"He didn't change my mother. For all her keeping of the laws, God didn't change her."

Samantha stood up, grabbed her purse, and turned and walked away, every step a bit faster than the one before. But just as she turned, Oliver saw her eyes and the welling of tears starting to spill from them.

"I won't be home until later tonight," Oliver explained. "I know it's Friday, and I said we would go to a movie tonight, but the air-conditioning people won't be done until … maybe six tonight. They want to button it all up before the weekend, so that's why they're working late."

"Oh, Oliver, that's okay. Just being with you for a while is enough," Paula said. "Late is okay."

"I'll hurry home, get cleaned up, and call you. Your mom still fine with babysitting tonight?"

"She is. She's spending the night, so we can stay out a little later," Paula replied, a hint of hopefulness in her voice.

By the time Oliver made it home, fed Robert the Dog, and took a shower, it was nearly 8:30. Robert looked as grumpy as a dog can look when Oliver left, and he almost had to shove the dog's snout out of the way to get the door closed. Paula was ready, of course, and before Oliver had a chance to get out of the truck, she was hurrying down the walk, pulling on her light jacket, juggling her purse between her arms as she climbed into the passenger side. She leaned over and kissed him lightly on the cheek, her hand resting on his arm and giving it a light squeeze.

"I'm glad you're here," she said, and Oliver believed her. "It seems like ages since we've been together—and I know it's only been a week. I miss you when you're not around."

Oliver put the truck into gear. "Where to? I'm kind of fried, so tonight is your choice. Whatever you want."

She sidled closer to him and took his arm in hers. Her perfume was stronger than he'd have preferred, but mostly pleasant.

"Are you hungry?" she asked. "Really hungry?"

"Well …"

"You had a candy bar on the way home, didn't you?"

Oliver turned for a moment to stare at her. "How did you know?"

Paula leaned in and gave him another kiss on the cheek. "The wrapper is on the floor over here. Your truck is always so neat, so I figured it had to be recent."

Oliver's grin was sheepish.

Paula grinned back. "What about Eat 'n' Park? Big food, little food, no food, whatever you want."

"You want to go there?" he asked. "It's so—ordinary."

She shrugged. "It doesn't matter to me. As long as I'm with you."

They were seated in the last booth, farthest from the door, the booth facing the highway, in the back of the restaurant.

"This is nice," Paula said. "You remember how often we came here back in high school when we were dating? I loved being here with you."

"Yeah, I remember. We would split a strawberry pie and order two glasses of water. I think the pie cost a dollar back then."

The laughter came easy between them, and Oliver began to relax. He hadn't been relaxed in a long time or at least it felt like a long time. When she took his hand in hers, her action didn't feel awkward or forward. It was pleasant.

"I talked to Pastor Mosco this week," she said.

"When did you see him?"

"No. I mean, I didn't talk to him—not exactly. I talked to his wife. She said that you and he had discussed ... you know, me and you dating. What it all means. What it might lead to. That sort of stuff. She was so helpful."

"She was?" It amazed Oliver that he was ever the topic of other people's conversations.

"Mrs. Mosco said Pastor Mosco said you'd asked about us, and that he'd said we would be okay. You know, us being in church, and me being born again and all that. She said he said it was okay with the church and that you seemed pleased by it all. That means a lot to me, Oliver, that you're happy with the way things are, the way I am, the way you are, and how we are with God and everything. That's important. Like she said, me being a born-again virgin was important. Like I'm not doing anything that God doesn't like ... until the right man comes along. She said it was important to do that, and that's what I'm doing. I'm waiting. Me and Bridget are waiting. She said that God will provide."

Oliver was happy when the waitress came over with her green order pad. He scanned the menu. He knew what was on it, but the examination bought him some time.

Paula ordered the sesame chicken dinner; Oliver selected the Superburger and a Diet Coke. Neither spoke until their drinks were served.

"I didn't mean to go so fast, Oliver," Paula said. "I guess I just get anxious because I don't see you during the week. I know your mother is pushing you. I don't want her to do that, but you know your mother. I know Pastor Mosco is pushing you too. And I know Bridget would love to have you around all the time."

Oliver took a long drink. "I know. I know everyone wants to see us together. At least it seems that way."

"What about you, Oliver?" Paula asked as she speared a lettuce leaf. "What do you want? I know what I want, and that's to be with you. But what is it you want?"

Oliver hated the question. He really did. When people asked him what he wanted, he never knew how to reply. Did he tell people what he thought they wanted for him, or what his mother wanted, or what *he* should want? Wasn't he in the business of giving people what they wanted—even if he hated it? Make the customer happy—that was the most important part of his business. If his heart wasn't in it, so what? The customer would be satisfied. People would be happy. No one would be unhappy. That's what motivated Oliver, that's what drove him—everyone happy and content and not sad or depressed or … whatever. Give the people what they want.

And tonight, Paula looked so earnest and needy, so pretty and inviting, too. She looked like she really needed him. Her daughter needed a father … Oliver could see that. Paula needed someone to be her rock—to keep her safe, protect her, and prevent her from being lonely. Oliver knew that. He wanted to do right by Paula, as well as his mother and the pastor.

"Do you want to be with me, Oliver? Like that? Like your mother wants? Like I want? You need to be honest with me." She speared another piece of lettuce and chewed carefully.

"I think I do, Paula," he said, letting the words slowly leave his mouth, as if it were a test to see how they felt and how it sounded when spoken aloud. *That wasn't so bad. The words sounded okay. I felt … okay.*

"You do?" she asked, placing her fork on her empty salad plate, sliding it to the edge of the table to make room for her main course. "Are you sure?"

"Sure. I guess I'm sure," Oliver said.

The waitress placed both their orders on the table. "Anything else I can get for you?"

"Everything looks great," Oliver replied. "Just great."

"Then you two enjoy."

"That's great, Oliver," Paula said. "I'm so happy."

She patted his hand, then reached for her knife and began to cut through the chicken breast, nearly hidden under a beige sesame sauce with a large sprig of parsley like a forest on the north side of the dish. "That is just so great."

———

After dinner, Paula suggested strawberry pie, for old times' sake, and Oliver politely declined, claiming the Superburger and the mound of french fries had left him stuffed, unable to eat another bite, even a forkful of dessert.

"It's too early to go home," Paula insisted as Oliver pulled out of the restaurant parking lot. "Let's drive over to Twin Lakes. We can watch the moon on the water. Remember when we used to go parking there back in high school?"

Oliver nodded. He did remember but didn't want either of them to elaborate on those memories.

He pulled into the dark parking area. He had remembered the lake as being larger than it was. It had been years since he'd visited the park. Clouds obscured the moon, but the air was warm, and they both rolled their windows down. Oliver switched on the radio and found the one classical station in the area. He liked it, not for the music so much as it was listener-supported, so there were no commercials unless it was pledge week, and it wasn't.

"This is so nice, being with you like this," Paula cooed as she snuggled against Oliver. Crickets and katydids and spring peepers filled the night air with their calls. After a long piece by Mozart, Paula turned to Oliver and kissed him, full on his lips. As she did, she placed her hand on his knee, and slowly began to move her hand, waiting for his encouragement. After a few inches, he placed his larger hand on hers, his palm thick with calluses, and pushed her hand slowly away, trying not to be obvious or dramatic about it.

She pulled her hand away. "What's the matter, Oliver?"

"Nothing," he replied. "I'm just tired. I need to get to sleep."

Paula slid away from him a few inches. "Are you feeling okay?"

"Sure. But I'm tired tonight. It's been a long week."

He tried to interpret what she might be thinking through her eyes, but the moon was still hidden, and the faint glow from the radio wasn't strong enough to dispel the darkness.

On the road back toward Route 30, he felt more awake than he had in weeks, his mind racing.

She would not have stopped. She would have kept going.

CHAPTER EIGHTEEN

IN THE EARLY-MORNING HOURS of Monday, well before the sun, well before the traffic, even before the coffee shops opened, a sleepless Oliver was at work. Even Robert the Dog slept on, curled up on a pallet of painter's drop cloths over by the basement steps.

Carrying a hammer and a pry bar, Oliver meticulously removed a series of trim and molding from around the mirror behind the bar. One of the long pieces of trim was the slightest bit warped, and every time Oliver laid eyes on it, it disturbed him, bothered him. He stripped it all off, then compared each piece with a long metal drywall level.

Your eyes can fool you, he told himself. *But if you compare it with something you know, a true piece, then you can be sure.*

All but two of the pieces possessed some slight curvature or bend. Oliver knew he could use extra nails and perhaps get every piece to lay flat, but that wouldn't be right. Eventually, the curve, that built-in warp, would pull away from the wall or leave a gap around the mirror. By then, changes would be too late. He couldn't leave it as it was.

Like I left my signature on a flawed, bad piece of work. I can't do that. I'd never be able to live with myself. It wouldn't be the end of the world, but I don't like leaving an error in a place like that where everyone can see it.

So, alone in the church, he set out to remedy the situation.

Here he was, at three in the morning, facing a trimless mirror and a stack of a more substantial style of trim piled in the middle of the room.

Oliver wouldn't charge Samantha for the time or the materials. This had been his decision. She might not have even noticed, but he did. The plan called for a two-inch surround, a stock profile, for the trim. The finished product would be fine, but not special. When plans were drawn, when it was only paper and pencil and T-square, the relationship of pattern to surface to wood to paint to geography in the room—none of that was real. Instead, the room was imaginary. Now that the dimensions were here, now that there was a reality to the bar and the lighting and the way the mirror reflected the colors from the stained-glass windows, Oliver could see the original specifications for the trim were woefully insufficient. Two inches of wood was lost in juxtaposition to the massive full-wall reflective surface of the mirror.

The lumberyard in Aspinwall, not the Home Depot just down the road that supplied most of their needs, had the perfect trim in stock. It had been delivered late Friday. The trim, the remainder from a high-end custom job, had been milled for the private residence of an investment banker and was nearly as thick as both of Oliver's outspread hands, thumbs touching. It was done in hardwood, not pine, and would be stained dark later, but he was anxious to have it installed before anyone else arrived. He did not want to explain his need to see this changed, nor try to defend his design decision.

I'm not sure I could explain it. I just know that it looks better this way. It has to be this way. Right is right, and truth is truth.

Instead of using the screaming electric miter saw, Oliver carefully measured three times, then cut the wood slowly with a Japanese-style saw, cutting on the pull stroke, rather than the push. The blade was narrow, almost delicate, and each cut could be the thickness of a heavy sheet of paper.

The rasp and hiss of the saw filled the silent room. Robert the Dog looked up, almost as if the human-powered saw was such an unusual sound that he needed clarification of the source.

Oliver maneuvered the long board to above the mirror, one side resting on the top of a ladder, Oliver holding the other. He gently tapped at his edge with the cushioned handle of his hammer, nudging it into place. Once the position was perfect, he pulled a thin, glistening finish nail from his pouch and gently tapped it into place, catching a stud beneath the plaster. He hurried to the other side and did the same at the far end. He removed the ladder and stepped back a few feet, then a few feet farther.

Absolutely perfect, he told himself. *It's what that space required. An honest frame around this reflection.*

With deliberate patience, he cut the remaining three pieces and tapped them into place in the same manner. On the bottom rail, he was forced to make two rectangular notches in the trim to allow access to electrical outlets, and as much as he didn't enjoy cutting into the long expanse of wood, moving the outlets would require a return visit of the electricians and a return of the city inspector, all adding too much to the cost and completion time.

Once we stain this, no one will see the slight imperfection.

He went back to the trim, tapping in a long finish nail at each stud. He liked to nail by hand, not with a nail gun; the pneumatic sniffing sound felt too machinelike to Oliver. He liked the tap-tap-tap sound of metal on metal. He liked using a nail punch to personally countersink each nail, a tiny, perfect round hole that hid the nail under a small encasement of stainable wood putty.

He looked at his cell phone. *6:30. Not bad. Not a bad morning's work.*

—————◦◦◦◦◦—————

Barth sat at a table almost in the dark, in front of the Coffee Tree Roasters. The air was still chilled, almost too chilled to sit outside, but it was an empty table and Barth was wearing his down jacket—normally too heavy for spring, but not too heavy for this dark spring morning, he had decided. He fussed with the plastic lid on his cardboard coffee cup, muttering to himself as he tried to get the lid properly sealed.

"Can't they design these blasted things so normal people can use them?"

After a few more tries, he managed to snap the lid into place, then remembered he hadn't added sugar to the coffee yet.

"Blast."

He stared at the cup, now with the lid, and the four sugar packets on the table, staring back at him, mocking him.

"I'll drink it without," he said to himself after thinking about and immediately rejecting the possibility of pouring the sugar into the slit in the top of the lid.

"Better for me without," he harrumphed.

He heard his name being called out, not middle-of-the-day loud, but six-thirty-in-the-morning loud, and looked up.

Oliver and Robert the Dog were striding toward him—Robert with a grin, and Oliver wearing a baseball hat with a tool company emblem on the front. He waved.

"Sit down," Barth insisted. "I'll take care of Robert. Get your coffee and whatever."

Oliver returned with coffee and a paper bag, too full for one person. "He likes scones now," Oliver explained, as if the full bag required a defense.

"That's why Rascal is at home. He's fatter now than ever. I guess I'm too soft of a touch."

Oliver grinned. "Maybe. But what good is having a pet if you can't spoil him a little? I know all about keeping them healthy—and yourself— but if I had nothing but rice cakes to eat for breakfast the rest of my life, why get up in time for breakfast?"

"You are a scholar after my own heart," Barth agreed as he bit into his cinnamon Danish, drenched in icing.

The two sat, eating, drinking in silence, until Oliver spoke. "Barth, how are you at tough theological questions?"

Barth rubbed his hands together not to warm them, but to rid them of excess cinnamon and Danish crumbs. "Depends. If you're willing to take my word on things, then I'm pretty good. Like asking a carpenter for advice on how to … I don't know, build a bookcase. They can give you all sorts of pointers that sound good, but then if they walk away, you're on your own …" Barth let his words fade off. "Well, that doesn't make any sense, does it?"

"Yes. It does. You have to put it into practice. That's what you're say-ing. See if the advice is applicable. I understand what you mean."

Robert sidled up closer to Oliver and almost put a paw on his leg in supplication, something that the dog never did, but the scones were that good. Barth knew firsthand.

"Okay. Okay. Here's another bite." Oliver put the paper bag on the table. "Barth, this question … it's about suicide—if it's an unpardonable sin. I asked my pastor, but I came away more confused than before. What do you think? What happens in that situation?"

Barth didn't show his alarm at the question. He calmly sipped his coffee. "There are people on both sides of that question."

"I know that, but what if the person is a believer? Christian all their life, but struggling. You know, overwhelmed by things … that sort of scenario. Life just got too much to bear. But without a doubt loved God to the last moment."

"What did your pastor have to say about it?" Barth asked.

"I want to know what you think."

"Oliver, I don't claim to have all the answers, but I would say that once we're saved, there's no sin we can commit here on earth that Christ's death didn't take care of. The atonement was complete. He can forgive anything. We're most likely all going to die with some unconfessed sin. And God knows the heart. Knows what's going on inside a person—if they're mentally ill or whatever. Our God is a big God. His ways are perfect. He is love and justice in perfect balance. Some people … well, I don't know anyone personally who has taken their own life. I guess I'm sheltered. But maybe they're not in their right mind at that moment. Maybe they can't help where they are. God never says that if that happens, then you're out. The Bible only talks about one sin that is unforgivable—and that's apostasy."

"I've heard that as well. Means what? Turning away from God?"

"Sort of," Barth said, "but more than that. Like actively campaigning against God. But there are those people, like my Presbyterian friends, who say that once God elects you, there ain't … isn't … anything you can do to escape from His calling. And they believe a person who campaigns against God was never a believer in the first place."

"So that's the unpardonable sin? Not suicide?"

"I don't know of a passage in the Bible that speaks to it directly, although the Old Testament records a half-dozen suicides—King Saul and Samson among them. While they weren't commended for the act, I don't see where they were condemned for it. Of course, God isn't *for* people taking their own lives, you know. The Bible says He is the one who numbers our days. And even if He decides that suicide is a sin, it's still not one that His power can't forgive in one of His own. So I'd say that if a person lived for the Lord, then fell into that kind of a serious mental state, I've got to believe God would understand and find a place for them in heaven."

Oliver sighed.

"That make sense?" Barth asked.

"It does. That's what I thought too."

Barth let a moment pass. He wanted to ask Oliver if he really understood, but saw sadness in the younger man's eyes so remained silent. He wanted to put his hand on Oliver's shoulder but didn't, knowing the touch would say as much as a thousand words but invite a lot more questions as well—questions that Oliver may not be ready yet to answer.

"That's good then," Barth said and took the final unsweetened sip from his coffee, now nearly cold.

If Oliver had been surprised or uncomfortable when Samantha showed up that morning, carrying her usual heavy load of coffees and treats, he didn't show an inkling of those reactions. If he had thought that their previous conversation would keep Samantha away from the jobsite, he was mistaken. And if anyone had been particularly observant that morning, they might have seen a flicker of something else in his eyes, as well as in Samantha's—a flicker of acknowledgment, perhaps. Or perhaps something more akin to uncertainty, of the awareness of a quandary that existed between the two of them.

But neither Taller, nor any of the Pratt brothers, nor the pair of Hispanic painters, noticed anything amiss. Everyone was cordial, even if a bit restrained and subdued, this being the first morning of the workweek. People asked about weekend activities, and the Pirates game on Sunday, and whether or not traffic was heavy that day.

As Samantha readied herself to depart, she placed her hand on Oliver's shoulder and gently turned him toward herself. "Cameron Willis will be here this afternoon. I was planning on being here to show her around, but I have a doctor's appointment that I simply cannot change. Some doctors are bigger *prima donnas* than ... well ... carpenters, and Cameron is only in Pittsburgh for this afternoon. Would you be a dear and show her around? I know she already has a lot of footage from before. She won't have a crew or anything with her. Maybe just a still photographer—she didn't say for sure. But whatever—you could be the host, couldn't you?"

Even though Oliver had only met Cameron a few times, he liked her. He felt as if he'd known her for years. He decided that was what made for a good TV host.

"Sure. I'll be here."

"Oh, that's so sweet of you, Oliver. You're an angel."

———

"Mr. Barnett, this is simply a grand transformation. I can hardly believe it's the same place—other than the windows."

"Not Mr. Barnett. Oliver."

"Sorry, Oliver. I knew that."

Cameron Willis held a clipboard to her chest. Her dark hair, now cut short, was tucked behind her ears, as if a backdrop, highlighting her tiny diamond stud earrings. A pair of glasses hung around her neck on a thin gold chain. She wore a simple white blouse and dark slacks. The blouse looked expensive, Oliver thought, and then wondered why he would have noticed.

"I'm sorry Samantha can't be here. But I'll try to answer any questions you have," he offered.

The two of them walked to the back room, formerly the pastor's study and now designated as the private dining area. Robert the Dog padded alongside, his snout rubbing against Cameron's leg every second step or so.

"Robert!" Oliver called out, almost sharply.

"It's okay, Oliver," Cameron replied. "We are now the proud owners of a golden lab puppy. Chance always wanted a dog growing up, and Riley is thrilled as well. So I'm used to dogs. And Robert is very well behaved—compared to Titus, the baby monster we have at home."

"Well, not everyone appreciates a dog who thinks he's part human."

Robert stopped and stared up at Oliver with an aggravated, peeved look.

"The details you've put in the work are so striking," Cameron said. "Like the wonderful molding around that big mirror there. Was that a custom piece of work?"

"Sort of. I mean, it had been. But it was left over from someone else's job. I saw it at a mill shop and knew it would be perfect."

Cameron took a pen, attached to the clipboard. "So this wasn't on the plan? Samantha or the architect didn't specify that particular style?"

The ice grew thin, Oliver thought, and he mentally stammered a bit, trying to answer her question truthfully without appearing pretentious or arrogant or autocratic. "Sort of, I guess. I … we had installed trim there the way it was specified on the plan. But it didn't look right. So I changed it. A sort of upgrade … but I don't plan on charging Samantha for it. Sometimes a builder has to do that. Make it right, not just to plan."

Cameron offered a knowing look. "I understand that completely. My husband is a builder too. He's always trying to make things authentic. Costs him money sometimes. But that's who he is, and it makes him happy. Maybe not happy, but satisfied."

"Exactly. I couldn't have left it the way it was. This way, everyone is happy, even if they don't know why. Even if it costs me something, it's worth it."

"Show me the kitchen and the downstairs, Oliver. If that's okay with you, I mean. I'm just taking notes now so when the film crew comes back, they'll have an idea of what to shoot. You would think after all this time together, they would know—but it's like they are all construction-deaf. They would take pictures of piles of scrap lumber if I left them to their own accord, I bet. More artistic."

In the basement, Cameron's arrival was met with silence and stares. All three Pratt brothers had declared their awe of Cameron Willis during her first visit, and her second, and now, even though it was the third visit, they were no less mute and slack-jawed than the first one.

Cameron, always the consummate professional, greeted each one by name, shaking hands, not even looking to see if they were dirty or clean hands, not caring, and asking each Pratt brother in succession about his role on the job and what they enjoyed most about the project.

She didn't get much information from any of them, just a lot of mumbled words, all expressing the same sentiment, "Whatever Oliver wants us to do, we do. It's all good."

"You trimmed out the basement ceiling with crown molding," Cameron said.

"It needed it," the eldest Pratt replied, then looked away, as if embarrassed that she noticed that small detail. "It only took a few hours or so. And the trim was inexpensive. Figured the waitstaff would be down here a lot."

"But you didn't have to do this," Cameron said, her tone soft and inviting.

The youngest Pratt spoke up. "He's like that, Ms. Willis. He's just a nice guy. Makes sure others have a right, honest place to work."

"And what's the plan for this nice large space?" Cameron asked as she walked into the former Fellowship Hall.

"No plan. It will be used for storage, most likely, for now."

"That's a shame, with all the beautiful windows it has. It would make a great banquet venue."

———

Paula unstrapped Bridget from her carseat and hefted her up, leaning her daughter against her left shoulder. She bent at the knees and grabbed the white plastic bag with a few things she had picked up at the drugstore.

Bridget's getting big, Paula thought. *I don't think I'll be able to lift her like this much longer.*

Inside, Bridget fussed a bit as Paula removed her jacket and shoes.

"Barney is on, Bridget. You want Mommy to watch Barney with you?"

Paula never liked the purple dinosaur, but Bridget seemed to enjoy it. So the two of them sat on the couch, watching, the child clapping occasionally in time to the music and swaying back and forth, giggling and talking back to the TV, using words that Paula could only slightly decipher.

From time to time, Paula looked over to the counter, to the white plastic bag, and told herself that she would have to put the few items away.

"You want dinner?"

Bridget replied with an excited, "Yes!"

"Mac and cheese? Hot dog? Pizza?"

The little girl screwed up her face in fierce concentration. "Macachee," she declared. "Macachee."

Paula went to the cupboard, picked up a box of macaroni and cheese, and glanced at the directions. *Ugh. This is the kind I actually have to cook.*

She placed it back on the shelf. She opened the freezer and rummaged a bit, moving a package of ground beef she had bought on sale and two bags of frozen corn that had been in the freezer for many months. Paula liked corn well enough, but Bridget had developed an intense dislike for it, and Paula never thought of making it just for herself. Behind all that were two boxes of premade, frozen macaroni and cheese.

They were priced two-for-one, right? Paula said to herself, in her own defense.

She bent back a corner of the lid and punched in the numbers on the microwave as the purple dinosaur sang and danced in the background. One of the local television stations played episodes back to back at this hour, probably at the request of thousands of harried parents preparing dinner just like Paula.

When the dish was ready and cooled enough for her daughter to eat, Paula placed Bridget in the highchair and helped her feed herself, slowly, a spoonful at a time. Paula had tasted this brand and thought it was tinny and sharp tasting, but Bridget loved it nonetheless.

After dinner, the two of them watched a cartoon that was aimed above Bridget's age but was colorful and the characters jumped about and moved a lot, keeping her entertained, or at least occupied.

When the streetlights switched on outside, Paula readied her daughter for bed. She thought she might grab the plastic bag but decided she may as well wait until Bridget was asleep.

Twenty minutes later, Paula walked slowly out of her daughter's room, closed the door gently, retrieved the white plastic bag, and walked into the bathroom. She put the toothpaste in the medicine cabinet and the cotton swabs on the top shelf of the bathroom closet. She took the small box out of the bag, threw the bag in the trash, and leaned against the counter to read the directions. Then she read them one more time. The kit was expensive and only contained one test strip; she couldn't go around wasting money. And she didn't want to return to that drugstore to purchase another kit. She had thought the cashier acted odd—condescending, almost—as she rang up her purchases.

There was a snootiness in her eyes. Like she was looking down on me—or judging me. Like she has a right to do that. She's just a cashier at a drugstore, for heaven's sake.

A terrifying thought jumped into Paula's awareness. *What if she knows me? I don't think she does, but what if? And what if she knows Mrs. Mosco? Or Oliver's mother? Oh my goodness.*

Her heart began to beat faster and faster, and her forehead began to sweat. *Maybe people who work at drugstores aren't allowed to say what people bought. Maybe there's a code of ethics or law … like a privacy rule or something.*

She took a deep breath, placed the box on the counter, and followed the directions for the test. The instructions said you had to wait until the results were visible, so she waited, watching the little clock in the digital readout, wondering if the wait would be in hours or minutes. Her tension and anxiety grew with each tick of the clock.

In three minutes, the results were finished. A smiley face popped up in the readout. Paula wasn't sure what a smiley face meant. She grabbed at the instructions, almost frantic, holding them close to the light since the type was tiny and hard to read.

Congratulations! the instructions cheered.

Paula read it twice, just to make sure what *Congratulations* inferred, then one more time. She stared at the test kit, then threw it all in the trash. Slumping to the floor, her back to the vanity, she held her head in her hands and began to weep, silently at first, her shoulders heaving ever so slightly, her body crumpling in on itself with each sob.

CHAPTER NINETEEN

AT MIDDAY, IT was not unusual for everyone to go in different directions. Oliver, not a stickler for exactly a thirty-minute lunch, or even a forty-five- or sixty-minute break, allowed people who worked for him to make their own decisions. And with this current crew, no one had taken advantage of his permissive attitude.

Usually one of the Pratt brothers would announce, sometime around 11:45, that he would be making a run to whatever fast-food restaurant would strike their fancy that day. Within a few blocks they had a choice of the full gamut of American fast-food enterprises, and a number of independent beef stands, pizza places, Chinese-food takeouts, and Jewish delicatessens. If anyone was interested, orders were called out, and by noon, or a little after, lunch would be served. Occasionally the Pratt brothers would bring their lunch from home, but their coolers were usually filled with drinks and snacks, rather than real food.

Today Chinese takeout was the selected food server of choice.

Oliver liked Asian food and ordered a large container of pork fried rice. Since it didn't contain a lot of meat, was not *deep* fried, and had rice with it, Oliver imagined it was a pretty healthy alternative to burgers and fries.

Steven bundled in with a large box filled with white paper containers. "Lunch!" he called out, and the cutting and sawing and hammering stopped, and everyone rushed to grab their orders. Oliver took his and sat on one of the pews destined to be sold or given away, pulling up a pair of sawhorses and a square of plywood to use as a table.

Sometimes when workers dined on the job, they gathered in one spot. Today all three Pratt brothers joined Oliver, asking if it was okay before they sat down.

And I could say no? Oliver thought.

Oliver used chopsticks as he ate. He couldn't remember when he'd begun using chopsticks for all Chinese food, but it must have been a long time prior, because he was adept at eating with them now. The Pratt brothers always appeared just a little amazed at Oliver's dexterity.

The oldest Pratt brother, Henry, often served as spokesman for the three brothers.

"Oliver," Henry started, chewing through one of six egg rolls he had ordered, "we've been thinkin'."

"About?" Oliver asked.

"Well … it's sort of personal."

"Personal to you?"

"No, personal to you. I think. Well, it is. On your side. That's why I'm not sure if this is somethin' you want to talk about. I mean, it bein' personal and all."

"Well, if it's personal to me and I don't know what it is, then how would I know if I mind you asking?" Oliver asked.

Henry stopped chewing, as if considering a very weighty proposal. "That's true. I guess I hadn't thought of that."

After a long moment, and after watching Henry consume another half of an egg roll, Oliver said, "Well?"

Henry snapped up, as if from drifting off. "Okay, sure. Here's the question. I guess it's a question. Sort of."

Oliver waited again. "Well?"

Henry swallowed, then wiped his hands on his jeans. "You know Miss Samantha, right?"

Oliver could tell a preamble when he heard one, and this was a preamble. "Yes, I think I am acquainted with a Miss Samantha Cohen."

Henry's odd grin was admission that it was an odd question. "I knew that. We all did. But we don't know if you've noticed that she is a very, very nice person. She talks to us a lot. In the mornin'. We talk after you go back to work and all that. And it sure looks like you two aren't talkin' as much as you used to. We think that's a bad thing," Henry said as he pointed at Oliver with his last egg roll.

"A bad thing," Steven Pratt repeated, and when Oliver looked over at him, Steven turned his eyes away and lowered his head, as if getting caught doing something improper or illegal.

"None of us know what or why. Miss Samantha hasn't said anything either. But, Oliver, don't you see?"

"See what?" he asked. It was true: He and Samantha had cooled in their interaction. But it wasn't anything he thought anyone would take note of. Apparently he was incorrect in that assumption.

"See that Miss Samantha is perfect. She's a perfect person for you. Really she is."

"Perfect?"

Steven spoke up. "She is, Oliver," he said, not hiding from Oliver's eyes this time. "She's a Jewish person. You knew that, right?"

"I did. I do."

"Well, if it hadn't been for you hirin' us, and for you invitin' Pastor Barth to come here, we might never have been forgiven, or might not have found Jesus. I mean—*really* found Jesus. We all knew who He was before, but there's somethin' about workin' here, with you ... and in this church ... that made Him real. Answered prayers, or somethin'. So if you didn't take a chance on us, we might never have really known Him. Or Pastor Barth."

"Okay ..." Oliver replied slowly.

"So that got us thinkin'. We found Jesus by workin' here. And we were so far from Him and all that. Lost. You know? So that's what's got us worried. If you don't talk to Miss Samantha anymore, then how will she find Jesus? Maybe she doesn't know anyone else who knows Him."

Gene, the middle brother, usually the quietest, spoke up, surprising them all. "She'll see Jesus in you, Oliver. Just like we did. I think that's why we wanted so much to work here—and that was even before we knew. We could see somethin' in you. An honesty we'd never seen before. And I think she can see that too. You can't stop talkin' to her now. It's not right. You need to take a chance."

"Go out on a limb," Henry added.

"Yeah. You do. You have to take a chance," Steven said. "You need to talk to her again. Maybe take her to dinner or somethin'. Could you do that for us? None of us can talk to her like you can. Okay?"

Oliver was almost ready to agree with them, to say that she was a wonderful person, that he missed talking to her, when the front door flew open. Samantha came flowing into the room, like a gentle whirlwind in human form entering the space.

<hr />

The next day, rather than announce the fast-food establishment du jour, Steven Pratt hung up his tool belt, dusted his shirt off, and said in a loud voice, "We're goin' to lunch now. We'll be back in an hour."

And with that, his two brothers followed him out of the door.

The three of them waited in front of Doe's Grill. Samantha, their invited guest, wasn't there yet. She'd originally suggested Cappy's Café, where they could have the delicious egg salad, but the brothers unanimously rejected that place as too fancy, too nice for them, especially with them all wearing their work clothes.

"There she comes," Steven said, standing at the side street, at the corner, pointing down Walnut, relieved she was there. It was obvious he, along with his brothers, thought she might have been just being nice when she agreed to this lunch and might not show.

"Hello, Steven," she said, almost singing, and took his hand, which made him even more anxious, and let him escort her to the entrance of the restaurant.

"Why, this seems very nice," she said as the four of them were seated at a table near a window. "I've been by here a thousand times and have never stopped in. Smells like they have wonderful hamburgers, doesn't it?"

All three brothers sniffed at the air in unison and nodded, murmuring their assent.

And that's what all of them ordered—especially since the waitress said that burgers were the specialty of the house, and that everything else on the menu wasn't nearly as good.

Samantha chatted on while they waited for their food, a task she was well suited for, talking about the job and the remaining details that required a few decisions and the fact that Cameron Willis was going to be there at the end to do a segment on the new restaurant, a revelation that obviously thrilled each of the brothers.

"Will we get to meet her again? Or watch as they take the pictures?"

"I think so. Even if you're done, I'll let you know so you can come back and watch. Maybe you'll get to be on TV. They like taking shots of the people who worked on the project."

With that, the brothers all stopped, midthought, as they tried to grasp the reality of being on an actual television show and not just a face in the crowd at a parade or ball game, which had happened to Henry—twice, actually—and was a story he never tired of telling.

The burgers were delivered; the waitress had been correct.

"This is maybe the best hamburger I've ever had," Samantha said, her mouth nearly full of the juicy meat and bun.

Midway through their lunch, Henry, acting as spokesman again, cleared his throat and put his burger back on the plate. "Miss Samantha, you know Oliver, right?"

Samantha turned her head sideways in a quizzical manner, like a dog at a high-pitched whistle, while she finished chewing. "I'm pretty sure I do, if it's the Oliver we left back at the church with the lost expression—then yes, I do know Oliver."

"Yep. That's the one," Henry said, sealing the identity of the Oliver of which they now spoke. "You think he's a nice fellow, don't you?" Henry asked, almost stumbling on the word *fellow*, having considered *gentleman* and *guy* as alternatives, but neither worked nearly as well.

"I do," Samantha said. "He is a very nice fellow."

"Is there any reason you two aren't talkin' to each other very much now?" Henry asked. Then, seeing the reaction on Samantha's face, he realized the question may have been way too blunt and tried to soften the impact. "I know it's not my business or anything, but we really like Oliver and we really like you, and the three of us think you two are really nice. We thought … well, we thought you two should like each other. You and Oliver. You should, like … *like* each other. And talk to each other more, I guess. We think, anyway."

Samantha's eyes gave away her new profound affection for the oldest Pratt brother and his brave attempt at being an agent of reconciliation, of romantic amplification between two thickheaded, yet not unwilling partners. "Why, Henry, that is so sweet of you to notice. And I do like Oliver. But he … well, he thinks differently about some things than I do."

"I know," Henry added, with enthusiasm. "Like about Jesus and the Bible and all that. If it wasn't for him, none of us would be goin' to church right now. He showed us the way—by just bein' an honest and upright guy … *fellow*. You know what I mean? He's different. He knows what's at the center of things."

Samantha took a deep breath.

"Listen, Miss Samantha, we know this is none of our business. But if we didn't do anything … well, if Oliver had decided it was none of his business to get involved with us, then maybe we wouldn't have a job or be goin' to church now. So it isn't our business, but we want you to be happy. We want Oliver to be happy. We talked to Oliver about this—"

"You did?" Samantha said, surprised in an entirely different direction.

"Sure. You are both people we really care about."

"You do? And what did Oliver say?"

"He sounded like he agreed with everything we said. Like you two are meant to be together—regardless of you bein' a Jewish person right now and him bein' a Christian. Like he agreed that you two are happy when you're together."

"He said that? Really?"

The three brothers nodded in unison. "He did. It's what he wants."

"I'm not sure Oliver knows what he wants," Samantha replied, quiet.

"He does, Miss Samantha. I'm sure he does. Just give him a chance. You have to go out on a limb. Oliver is a good man."

Samantha let her shoulders drop. "I know he is, Henry. But I don't know …"

"Give him a chance. Please. You can do that, can't you?"

Henry saw the shrug of her shoulders, but then it stopped.

Samantha sat up straight. "I can do that, Henry. Yes, I can do that."

Samantha sat at the table, sipping her ginger ale and thinking after the Pratt brothers left.

I can do that ... because Oliver could be the one. He is very, very special indeed. And he does seem to know "what—or who—is at the center of things." He is the only man I know who has the utmost respect for me as a woman, who is with me because of who I am, and not what he can get from me. And he's kind and gentle. He could easily be the one. Really.

Samantha surprised herself.

Really.

As the Pratt brothers walked back to the jobsite, laughing and pushing each other, offering playful punches to each other's shoulders as brothers often do, Oliver burst out of the church with Robert hurrying behind him, tail tucked down. Oliver was rather white—not ghost-white, but pale.

"I have to go. My mother was just taken to the hospital in an ambulance. Lock up. I'll call later." He let Robert in and jumped into his truck.

When he pulled out, the Pratt brothers called out, virtually in unison, "We'll say a prayer for her."

Oliver pulled out onto Aiken, spinning his tires, heading south to Fifth Avenue, hoping beyond hope that traffic would be light.

The call had been from the store manager where his mother worked. He said she had seemed fine all morning but just after lunch, he noticed that her face had appeared ashen, and he'd asked her if she felt all right. Instead of answering him, she had simply collapsed behind the deli counter.

"The ambulance was here in a few minutes," the manager had said, his words tumbling out in an excited exhale. "She was awake, I'm pretty sure, when they got her on the stretcher. Marge—she works up front—was right there and said she was pretty sure Rose was awake."

The ambulance would have headed to Greensburg Memorial Hospital, no more than seven minutes away, Oliver thought. As he navigated through traffic, driving much more aggressively than he had ever driven, he thumbed the hospital's number on his cell phone.

Oliver almost threw the phone out the window when he first

encountered the automated call menu. Swerving around a truck, he decided that selection number 5, patient information, might be his best choice.

The choice proved correct. His mother was in intensive care, the nurse said, but was resting comfortably. She was awake and not in pain.

"We put everyone in ICU who has had a heart attack. It's more of a precaution than a necessity."

"Can she have visitors?"

"Immediate family, and only for a few minutes. Unless she gets transferred out right away. That happens if the doctor says the attack was not severe."

Taller was working with the kitchen contractor, so Oliver tried calling his cell phone and his home phone twice each, getting no response at either number, leaving a message to call him as soon as he received the voice mail. He didn't want to make his brother unduly worried or nervous by telling him what happened in a taped message, then realized the news probably wouldn't upset him. But Oliver decided it wasn't worth calling him back a third time.

Oliver slammed on his brakes after sliding his truck into an empty parking place in the nearest lot to the hospital, almost causing Robert to tumble to the floor mat.

"Good grief. Robert. What was I thinking?"

Robert looked about, happy that the truck had stopped moving, sniffing the air with anticipation. Oliver had never once taken Robert by this hospital, or any hospital for that matter.

It's a mild day. It's not at all hot. I'll just leave the windows open some. I ... I'll lock the doors ... but the windows will be open wide enough to reach in and unlock them.

He stood there, trying to decide what to do; Robert the Dog complicating his thoughts further than he could manage unraveling.

"You'll be okay, Robert," Oliver said as he locked his door. "I'll be back in a few minutes. My mother ... she's sick ..."

He choked back tears and set off for the entrance at a fast jog, hoping Robert would bark furiously at anyone who thought of stealing him or the truck. The information desk was to the right.

"Rose Barnett. In ICU, I think. Do I need a pass, or what? And where is ICU?"

The elderly woman behind the desk appeared flustered. "A pass? No, I don't think so. I … we don't have passes here. ICU is on the fourth floor. You have to see the nurse at the monitoring station."

Oliver heard the last sentence from over his shoulder as he jabbed at the elevator button. There seemed to be no response. The stairway stood next to the bank of elevators. Oliver grabbed at the stairwell door and ran up the first two flights, slowing just a bit on floors three and four. Before he opened the door on the fourth floor, he waited twenty seconds as he gulped in deep breaths, trying not to appear horribly winded and slightly deranged.

"Rose Barnett?"

A scattering of nurses were standing and sitting behind the long, sweeping, curved counter in the middle of the floor, none of them looking the least bit anxious or troubled by the scores of heart-attack patients clinging to life all around them. One of the least-bored-looking nurses stood and pulled out a clipboard.

"Rose Barnett," she repeated as she ran her finger down a computer list of names, then flipped the page once, scanned that list, and flipped back to the first page.

"Oh, yes, here she is. I mean, she's not on this floor anymore. The doctor said she's fine and they moved her to … Room 214. Just for the night, I think."

Again Oliver heard the last sentence over his shoulder as he raced to the stairway door and jogged down two floors, the trek downstairs much easier than the trek up.

At Room 214 he banged open the door, and the sound it made against the wall was much louder and more pronounced than he imagined it could be. He entered the room at a jog.

Rose Barnett was in a hospital gown, sitting up in bed, with a glass of orange juice on the nondescript fake wood nightstand next to the bed, holding a phone to her ear. She waved to Oliver as he entered.

"Yes, Taller," she said, "it was a heart attack. But a small one. I'm in a private room right now. And Oliver just came in."

She waited.

"I know. I understand. If I have to stay another day, then you can come visit me. Okay. Me too."

She hung up the phone as Oliver took the metal chair next to the bed.

"Where were you?" she asked, not harshly but not gently either. "I've been trying to call you for the last thirty minutes."

He grabbed his cell phone. It was dark. "I must have switched it off after I called the hospital, or after I called Taller."

"Oh. I just couldn't get a hold of you," Rose said, almost sounding like it was intentional on Oliver's part that his phone wasn't on.

"So what did the doctor say? A little heart attack?" Oliver asked.

Rose shifted in her bed. "I just told Taller that so he wouldn't worry. No, the doctor said nothing about it being minor. A heart attack, any heart attack, is very serious business, he said. He said I was lucky that I was close to here when it happened. Any longer ... and who knows what would have happened. I guess I could be dead ... just like that."

"But you'll be okay, won't you, Ma? He said you would be okay, right?" Oliver's words were filled with tension and worry.

"Doctors don't like to make predictions like that. He said no one can tell. He'll put me on some medicine—like any of that will really help."

Oliver slid the chair closer. "It *will* help, Ma. Doctors nowadays know what they're doing."

Rose waved her hand and sneered. "They're just mechanics. They poke around and charge you an arm and a leg, but they can only guess what the problem is."

Oliver had heard this all before, hundreds of times, and wasn't about to debate the same argument once more, not now in a hospital, with monitors and wires hooked up to his mother.

"You know what I thought about as they were loading me in the ambulance out there in the parking lot?"

Oliver knew what it was and dreaded hearing it, yet could not stop it. He knew from the slightest inclination in her voice the direction this would go. "What, Ma?" It was the response of a doomed man.

"I was thinking that I don't want to die alone. If I had closed my eyes forever, well, I would be with God, and that would be a good thing, but I would be dying alone. You would be alone. I wouldn't have any grandchildren to watch over from heaven. I would be all by myself up there. All alone."

"Ma …"

"You know your father isn't there. You know that, right, Oliver? You know why he can't be there. And I'll be all alone."

"Ma, please …"

"I don't want to die unhappy, Oliver. You can't let me die unhappy."

"Ma …"

"You know what you should do, Oliver. You know the right thing to do to make me happy. So I can die in peace … if it's my time and all. You know what you can do."

Oliver looked into his mother's eyes, saw her fierce determination, and began to shrink right there in front of her.

"Is that so much to ask? You'll be happy, Oliver, with her. I know you will. You'll make me happy."

"Ma …"

"Just say you'll do it, Oliver. Taller is out of the picture. He'll never make me happy. But you will, Oliver. You will, won't you? You'll make your dying mother happy, won't you?"

"You're not dying, Ma."

"We don't know that. Who knows when the big one might hit, now that I have this heart condition?" Rose took Oliver's hand and squeezed it, stroking the flesh on the back of his hand with her other hand, like you'd stroke a sleeping iguana. "You will, won't you, Oliver?"

Oliver took a deep breath. "Yes, Ma. I'll … I'll make you happy. I promise."

Rose brightened and released his hand. "Oh, Oliver, you have made me one very happy person today. And God will bless you because you are honoring your mother like this, like the Bible says. He will bless you. I'm sure of that."

And then they sat, facing each other, until Rose dozed off, perhaps from the medication, perhaps from satisfaction, as Oliver listened to the steady *beep-beep-beep* of the heart monitor attached to the wall above her head.

CHAPTER TWENTY

FOR THE FIRST TIME in years, Oliver was late for work. He had stayed with his mother until visiting hours were over.

"You could spend the night, Oliver. The nurse said they allow that nowadays. Not like when I had you. Then everyone had to leave. I was alone then, too. But they could bring in a cot," she had said.

Oliver had explained that he couldn't stay. Robert the Dog was still in his truck, and even though he had taken him out several times that afternoon and evening, the dog couldn't spend the night in the cab.

"Sure, go ahead, go home then," Rose had said, resigned. "I'll be fine. I'm sure the nurses will take wonderful care of me. You can see how often they've checked in on me so far."

Oliver had explained to his mother that she was wired up to monitors, and those monitors were displayed at the nurses' station. At the first inkling of a problem, they'd probably come running.

"Probably. But you're not sure, either."

"Ma …," Oliver had replied, his defenses useless.

"Go ahead. Go. Go take your dog out. Go to work. I'll be fine. I'll get a taxi home."

"Call me when you talk to the doctor," Oliver had answered, trying to ignore or overlook her manipulations. And then he'd slipped out, had gone home, had caught a few furtive hours of restless sleep, had overslept, had called to check in with his mother, and was on the job nearly an hour later than normal.

The Pratt brothers knew how to keep busy, but they all stopped to ask somberly how his mother was. "We told Miss Samantha about it. She was here already. She said she would send flowers, but you have to tell her what hospital."

Just what my mother needs. Flowers from the Jewish woman she thinks I'm involved with.

"I'll … I'll call Samantha later. My mother might be discharged this afternoon, so I may have to leave early again."

Henry drew close and placed his arm around Oliver's shoulder. It was an uncharacteristic gesture, an action that made both men a bit uncomfortable, yet showed Oliver that the brothers really cared for him.

"You take all the time you need," Henry said. "We know the schedule and what needs to get done, and the way we figure it, we're just about plumb on target now, timewise, so you can tend to your mother with a clear conscience—okay?"

Oliver puttered about the jobsite, both he and Robert the Dog wandering more than working. Henry was correct: the job was on schedule again. Taller would not be there for three more days since he was still working with the kitchen contractor, helping fit a long series of custom cabinets around the kitchen appliances. He was also crafting cabinetry for the waitstaff area—storage for napkins and glasses and condiments, and the computer screen—all to be done in a sleek, dark stain so as to disappear, rather than stand out.

At 2:00, his mother called, saying she would be released at 4:00 that afternoon and that her sister from Freeport was there and would see her home and spend the night. However, if Oliver could spare the time in his busy day, she would appreciate a few minutes with him.

Oliver knew he'd done no productive work that day.

But I am the boss. So slacking off a little is okay.

He told Henry he'd be back in a few minutes, told Robert the Dog to stay, and slipped outside. He walked with quick, deliberate steps to the one jewelry store, only a block from the church, with a growing sense of purpose and direction to his thoughts.

She might have died.

He looked in the window.

I can do this.

It was the first time in his life that he'd looked at the window display of a jewelry store with the intent and purpose of buying something inside. He had a watch. He didn't wear jewelry, and he'd never bought jewelry for his mother. His relationships with women, other than with Paula, all those years ago, had never progressed to the serious-jewelry-buying level. He might have, he thought, as he peered in the window, purchased something nice for Paula back then, but he wasn't wealthy and always considered jewelry to be a wealthy man's purchase.

He peered through the door. Inside was a series of low glass counters. He thought one of them held rings. He took a deep breath.

It's time ... like she said.

The door opened with a jingle from the bell above the frame. He wondered if he was dressed well enough for the store, then told himself that his money—or his credit card—would be the only important factor. The salesclerk, a very pretty young woman with dark blonde hair and wearing a double strand of pearls around her neck, came over and greeted him. Softly she asked what he was looking for.

"A ring."

"A ring? What sort of ring? For you?"

"No. I'm not much for rings. You can't wear them when you work with your hands."

"What sort of work?"

"I'm a ... carpenter. A building contractor."

She smiled. "My uncle built houses. He never wore a ring either. Not even a wedding band."

"Smart man. Wedding rings can get caught on machinery and stuff."

"Then the ring is for someone else."

"It is."

"What sort of ring?"

"Well ... I ..."

"It's okay," she said, then looked directly into his eyes. "What's your name?"

"Oliver."

"Oliver. I'm not the woman you'll be giving this to, so you can relax. I've done this before. Take your time."

"It's a wedding ring. Or an engagement ring. I haven't asked her … but I'm pretty sure what the answer will be."

"Over here, Oliver." She led him to a back counter and removed four blue velvet trays filled with rings—all with diamonds, some with blue stones added, some with green, all of them intimidating. "I'm going to walk you through this and show you a few styles. Maybe you'll see one that you like. Most women have their own ideas of what a ring should be. So I tell the lucky man that they should think about the woman they love. If that doesn't work, I tell them to pick something they like. If the woman likes it, you've done well. But sometimes the woman doesn't like it."

"Then what?"

"Then you bring it back. You exchange it for something different. Or if she says no, you get a full refund. It's simple, painless—and guaranteed."

Oliver looked gratefully at the salesclerk. "You've made this much easier. Thank you."

In less than five minutes, Oliver picked out a ring—not flashy, but not plain, either. The ring was white-gold, with a center oval diamond surrounded by some small round ones. To Oliver, it looked feminine, classic, and pretty. He pulled out his wallet, handed the young woman a credit card, and stopped thinking—about his mother, heart attacks, Paula, her daughter … everything.

This will make them all happy. This will make them all very, very happy, he thought.

And then he stopped thinking again.

<hr />

Samantha rarely made a habit of traveling through Shadyside during the day, even though she lived two blocks from its downtown.

Too crowded and busy, she told herself, and she found ways around the four square blocks of retail stores and restaurants. That is, until today, a beautiful late spring day. She must not have been paying attention, because somehow she ended up on Walnut, heading home in her sporty red Mercedes, the top down, French music from the soundtrack of the movie *Amelie* playing, hoping that Mally had made something delicious, like *latkes*. Mally usually made the potato pancakes at least once a week.

Samantha thought of stopping by the church, saying hello to Oliver, asking after his mother. She paused at the stop sign on the corner of Bellfonte and Walnut, looked at herself in the rearview mirror while waiting for a delivery van to clear the intersection, and as it did, she saw Oliver leaving a store—the jewelry store. He was carrying a small bag, and he looked ... determined.

What's he doing in the jewelry store?

Samantha waited at the corner until the large SUV behind her beeped and she moved forward. Instead of heading home, she circled the block and found an illegal parking place on Bellfonte. *So maybe I'm unloading something.*

She hurried inside the store.

"Hello, Samantha," the clerk said as she entered.

"Hi, Ilana," Samantha replied. "You're looking wonderful ... as always."

Ilana's father, who owned the store, and Samantha's father, who owned the real estate the store sat on, were old friends from temple. The two women had known each other since childhood.

"You're like your father, Sam. You always say the right thing."

Samantha came closer to Ilana, glancing over her shoulder to make sure she was the only customer in the store. "The cute gentleman that was just in here ..."

"Yes. Oliver ... Barnett. He is *chamud*, isn't he? Too bad he's taken. All the good ones are—at least it seems that way working here."

Samantha blinked several times. "Taken? What do you mean? What did he buy?"

Ilana motioned Samantha closer and whispered in her ear, "I'm never supposed to tell anyone what customers have purchased. My dad thinks it's like a lawyer-client-privilege sort of thing. I don't know why, unless it's some old goat buying baubles for his mistress ... but I don't think Oliver has a mistress."

"What did he buy?"

"He was really nervous. I managed to calm him down enough to pick out an engagement ring. And he bought retail. Didn't even try to negotiate a price."

"An engagement ring?"

"It was nice. Nothing too fancy. Several stones. Not fancy, but elegant. Classic. You would have liked it, Samantha. It was your style."

Samantha leaned back and blinked again.

"Why do you want to know? Do you know him?" Ilana asked.

On autopilot, Samantha managed to reply, "No, he's doing some work on my church project around the corner. He's talked about … a girlfriend. I'm just being a *yenta*. Nosy, I guess."

"Well," Ilana said, in a conspiratorial voice, "please don't let on to Mr. Barnett that I told you anything. If my father found out, he'd probably have another heart attack."

Samantha left while saying, "I won't say a thing. I have to run … I'm parked in a loading zone."

And the little bell above the door chimed as she made her hurried exit.

Really?

A ring? He bought a ring?

That is, well, astonishing … and a little scary. I mean, not that I don't want him to. Not that at all. But no one has ever … I mean, no man has ever wanted … bought me a ring … an engagement ring.

When is he going to ask?

And what am I going to say?

Can I say yes? Can I really and honestly say yes?

After driving around Shadyside for nearly half an hour, lunch forgotten, Samantha decided she couldn't wait demurely in the turret in her house, waiting for her prince to come bearing gifts. She decided she wanted to see him, in the flesh, just to look at his face, to see if she might discern something in his eyes or his demeanor.

He doesn't have to ask me now, but I want to see him … maybe give him a hug … to let him know that it would be okay if he asked me, without actually telling him so.

She pulled to the curb. *I just said it would be okay. That means yes, doesn't it?*

She drove back into traffic and, in a moment, pulled into the driveway of the church. She didn't see Oliver's truck. *Maybe it's parked around the corner.*

She entered amidst the ripping squeal of a circular saw cutting into metal.

"Dagnabbit!" Henry Pratt shouted as a stream of sparks cascaded out below his saw. "Why didn't someone tell me about that electric line?"

His brothers shrugged. Gene spoke up. "We figured you saw the plug just below. I was wonderin' why you were cuttin' there, but … I don't like to interfere."

The two other brothers all hurried over to the trouble spot, offering suggestions as to how to remedy the mistake.

Samantha's entrance had been ignored, overshadowed by the near explosion of saw and electrical current. A slow, furry movement caught her eye.

Barth sat in a pew, facing the work, with Rascal sound asleep at his feet.

She waved to him. "Is Oliver here?"

Barth shook his head. "He left a few minutes ago. His mother was being released this afternoon. I think he felt that he had to be there, even though her sister is coming to stay with her."

Samantha sat down next to Barth, leaned over, and patted Rascal. The dog snorted once, gazed up at her with watery eyes, and let his head loll back against the floor.

She sighed loudly, with drama.

"Problems, Miss Cohen? You seem weary. Or tense. Or confused. At my age, it's getting harder and harder to read a woman's face and expression."

Samantha couldn't stop herself from smiling. She hugged Barth's arm tightly. "I am, Barth."

"Am what?"

"All of those things. Confused. Tense. Weary. Well … maybe not weary. But confused is right up there."

Barth shifted in the pew, turning toward Samantha to fully concentrate on her. "You've been talking to the Pratt boys, haven't you?" Barth said, his words kind. "Or, rather, they've been talking to you. About Oliver."

"They have," she admitted.

"They told me what they did. They think you two should be together. They say that you're perfect for each other. It's their way of being honest and appreciative."

Samantha looked over to the three brothers, now in the midst of a loud, clattering discussion of how to repair the severed electrical line without having to dismantle half the wall. She looked at them with the fondness of a caring sister or aunt.

"Yes, that's what they told me. It was very sweet of them to do so. Like they are really concerned about me. And Oliver."

"Oh, they are, Miss Cohen. Ever since the boys decided to follow Jesus—for real this time—they have changed. I haven't known them all that long, but I see the difference."

"Is that what did it? Jesus? Really?"

Barth shrugged. "Has to be. He has a way of changing people in a way that they can't do on their own, and so that other people notice it."

Samantha stared at her hands for a long moment, then back up at Barth. "You know about these things, don't you? About people who know this Jesus and people who don't? I mean, can people from the two sides be together?"

Barth took her hand in his wrinkled, lined, veined one, almost cold yet strong. "You're Jewish, aren't you, Miss Cohen?"

She nodded.

"I don't know why I asked. I knew you are. Oliver told me for sure. So, as a faith, being Jewish, well, they don't see Jesus as the Messiah, right?"

"Right. I had religious training as a child, but since then I didn't spend a lot of time learning more, or devoting myself to the faith, if you're asking. There's Jewish and then there's *Jewish* Jewish."

Barth nodded. "Just like Christians."

"Really?"

"Not everyone is devout in following Christ. Not everyone has their lives transformed," Barth explained.

"Just like Judaism. Not everyone who follows all the laws is changed inside. Like my mother, for example."

"It's all about the heart," Barth answered and tapped on his chest.

"But what about Oliver? What about me? Can that ... can it work? Or would we be fooling ourselves?"

Barth stood up, flexing his back, and the bones made soft pops. He swiveled his neck, as if preparing for a difficult task. "Miss Cohen," he began softly, tenderly, "Oliver has not asked me about this. But the pastor part of me began pondering on it weeks ago, just in case. Being prepared—that's what a pastor does."

Samantha folded her hands in her lap, like a schoolgirl waiting instruction.

"I'm not the one to make the decision here, Miss Cohen. Pastors sometimes think they are, but we're only guides. We point to the truth. I know you're Jewish. I know Oliver is a follower of Christ. And while the Bible says that believers are not to be yoked with unbelievers—"

"Really? It says that? Sounds harsh, doesn't it?"

"Maybe, Miss Cohen. But as I thought about it, I kept coming back to the story of Ruth in the Old Testament. You remember hearing the story of Ruth?"

"I'm not sure I remember it all."

"Ruth was widowed and left alone, with only her widowed mother-in-law."

"I'm not sure I'm going to like this story, Barth. Mother-in-laws ... I don't think Oliver's mother would necessarily approve of me."

"Maybe not," Barth said, continuing. "Ruth's mother-in-law decided to go back to her homeland. She told Ruth that she should go back to her own homeland as well, because she was a foreigner. But Ruth said no. She said—and this is as direct of a quote as I can remember—'Don't tell me to go back home and leave you. I will go wherever you go and live with you wherever you live. Your people will become my people and your God will be my God.'"

Barth stopped and put his hand to his chin. Samantha could hear the whiskery stubble sound as his palm rubbed against his cheek.

"Ruth chose to forsake her own people. She had to give up what she knew to embrace the people and the God of her mother-in-law, because she wanted to honor her, and she wanted to honor God by being loyal."

Samantha watched the older man's eyes. "Then what happened?"

Barth smiled. "Ruth met a rich man, Boaz, who became her 'kinsman redeemer,' and they got married. The Lord did bless her—and her mother-in-law."

"What's a 'kinsman redeemer'?"

"It comes from an ancient custom. A kinsman—not necessarily a close relative, but a person who is close to someone who was a slave, enslaved sometimes because they were in debt—would buy the enslaved person's freedom. As a result, the redeemer would 'own' the person, but as a close family member or a wife, not as a slave."

"And Ruth and Boaz got together this way?"

"Yes. And with this story, you see, what God is saying to the children of Israel is that He would be their Redeemer and take them as His people, as a man takes a woman as his wife, as Boaz did for Ruth."

Samantha offered a curious smile back. "Ruth. That story is in your Bible?"

"And in yours. The Old Testament. The story is prophetic, and symbolic, too, of how in the New Testament Christ would purchase our redemption with His death on the cross, 'buying' our freedom from the debt of sin that enslaves us. But He did this not just to set us free. Instead, like a husband passionately taking a wife, out of His great love He redeemed us, so that we could have an intimate relationship with Him, be part of His family forever, as Boaz did for Ruth."

"And the Ruth story is supposed to make me feel better?"

Barth sat down next to her again and took her hand again.

"Maybe. But the Bible is full of stories of people who didn't know the whole truth at first, then became aware. Maybe you can be with Oliver. But you'll need to come to that truth at some time first. Maybe sooner, maybe later. It's all in God's time. You'll know when it happens, if you listen. You need to listen closely, Miss Cohen, with an open heart. If you do, God will show you an answer. 'Seek and you will find.'"

"Really?"

"And maybe, like Ruth, you're a woman who can leave her 'home' and follow God's plan, becoming one who is redeemed. Become what is called a 'completed Jew'—one who believes the whole truth, who is set free. Perhaps God wants you to be with Oliver, so that you'll come to know his God—the Triune God—and become His own."

"Triune?"

"Three persons in one: God the Father (Abba, whom you know about), God the Son (Yeshua, Jesus), and God the Holy Spirit, who is with us now."

"Really?"

"Really and for sure. People are praying for you right now."

The words of another old pastor echoed Barth's. *I will pray that you will know the truth, Miss Cohen. I will pray that prayer for you every day.*

Samantha looked over to the Pratt brothers. One of them was on his back, prying at a board, while another held a flashlight into the crevice, the other standing back as if expecting a small explosion any moment.

And at that, Rascal rolled onto his side, snorked loudly, raised his head, then stared at the two of them. Slowly he lowered his head back to the floor and closed his eyes again, snoring softly amidst the clatter of the Pratt brothers.

CHAPTER TWENTY-ONE

"How long until the transformation is finished?" Cameron asked.

"Only a few weeks," Samantha replied, opening the door of the church for her. "Do you want to film after, before, or now?"

Cameron entered the room and immediately, all work ceased. Cameron Dane Willis was not exactly a superstar, but in western Pennsylvania terms, she was certainly a celebrity. Her show, *Three Rivers Restorations*, was still only on cable but was up for national distribution. The show ranked almost as high in viewership as did some network shows, depending on the time and if the network show was a rerun or not.

Cameron did not have an entourage, nor paparazzi and hordes of fans following her, but people did recognize her on the street and in restaurants. What happened inside the church was typical of the jobsites Cameron visited. As soon as the crew recognized her, all work stopped. Carpenters who never cared a whit what they looked like before that moment began to dust themselves off, tucking in shirts, buttoning unbuttoned buttons, primping, in a workman's fashion. Even the Pratt brothers spent a moment slack-jawed, staring at her, and a longer time fixing their appearances—this all despite the fact that Cameron came in with no cameras, no lights, no one other than Samantha Cohen.

After a very elongated silence, Samantha clapped her hands together loudly, echoing in the room. "All right! Show's over," she called out with good nature. "Nothing left to see here. Everybody go back about your business."

It took the Pratt brothers a long time to get back to work.

Oliver came up to them both and extended his hand to Cameron. "So nice to see you again. I was wondering when you would be back. When will the crew be here?"

"A couple of weeks. Just after you're done and before the restaurant opens. That will be easier for everyone. Remember Alice and Frank's restaurant? The grand opening was so hectic we hardly had room to maneuver the cameras. We don't want to get in the way."

"She's looking for the seam between when the project is finished and the cooks start their work, Oliver. I hope you don't mind."

"Not at all," he answered. "I avoided the cameras the first time and I plan on avoiding them this time around as well."

"We'll see about that," the two women almost said in unison.

Henry Pratt came up to the three of them with a pen and a torn scrap of paper from a legal pad in his hand. "My brothers want your autograph," he said to Cameron. "Would you mind? We watch your show all the time, when it's not on opposite somethin' important. I mean ... sorry, like a Steelers game or somethin'."

Cameron couldn't help but laugh. "I'm a die-hard Philadelphia Eagles fan, but I won't hold that against you."

"And I can still get your autograph?"

"Tell you what: I have some eight-by-ten glossy pictures of me that the studio made up. They're out in the car. I'll get one for each of you and sign them. Okay?"

"That would be swell," Henry said and slowly edged away without turning around.

"Let me show you the kitchen," Samantha said, her words bright as a tour guide. "And the private dining room and the bar."

She took Cameron's hand and led her away from Oliver.

———○○○———

As soon as the two women had descended the stairs, Henry came over to Oliver and whispered loudly, "She's pretty. A lot prettier in person than on TV. Do you think she knows that?"

"I guess. Maybe. I don't know if a pretty woman really knows that she's pretty. But ... maybe Mrs. Willis does."

Henry shook his head, as if amazed that a handsome woman wouldn't be supremely aware of just how striking she was.

Ten minutes later, the pair of women ascended the stairs and headed to the private dining room, with Robert the Dog following them, wagging his tail in a most loyal fashion, happy that they both lavished attention on him. Oliver looked on, knowing of Cameron's Christian faith.

I wish Robert could tell me what they are talking about.

"I have someone that I want you to meet, Sam. She's a college sorority sister—Sarah Epstein. You two have a lot in common. She lives in Squirrel Hill and is a top-notch real-estate agent for Chapel and Lawton. You'll like her a lot. She's a completed Jew."

"So she believes that Jesus is the Messiah. Does that mean she's given up all her Jewishness to become a Christian?"

"No. She attends a Messianic synagogue somewhere in Squirrel Hill."

"Oh, I think I've seen it. On Beechwood."

"That's the one. They fully embrace their Jewish heritage and call themselves 'Hebrew Christians.' I know they celebrate the Sabbath and all the Jewish holidays."

"I'd love to meet her. Here's my card. Have her give me a call."

The two women stayed in the private dining area for a long time. Oliver made it his business to walk past and saw they were engaging in what appeared to be a deep conversation, then saw Samantha tilting her head back in laughter, exposing her long, elegant neck. Cameron used her hands more, if that were possible, than Samantha—gesturing, pointing, pantomiming. Robert sat at their feet, staring up at Samantha, as if she were about to give him a treat, which she often did in the morning, but less so in the afternoon.

Eventually, they rose, Oliver noted, and without being obvious, gave each other a hug. Then the two women headed to the door. Cameron hurried out and returned shortly carrying three glossy photographs. She went to each of the Pratt brothers in turn, joking with them, signing their names to the picture, adding hers, with a personal note, and leaving each of them beaming. Samantha and Cameron stood in the vestibule and talked some more.

Oliver kept busy with adjusting windows that did not need adjusting, watching, trying not to eavesdrop and trying just as hard to hear.

Cameron exited again following one more hug between the two women.

I have to talk to her today. I've put it off too long. I have to tell her how I feel. She needs to know. I have to talk to her now, before I let it go on for another day.

Oliver holstered his hammer in his tool belt, then carefully unbuckled it and placed it at the far end of the bar, on top of a sheet of cardboard, careful not to scratch the shiny surface. He took a deep breath. He pushed his fingers through his hair and dusted off his shirt, even though there was no dust on it, and walked toward her.

"Samantha," he said, "do you have a minute to talk?"

He thought he saw her cheeks flush, but maybe it was just the light from the stained-glass window—the scene of Jesus before Pilate, the Roman dictator, who was clad in a bloodred robe, his hand pointing out, his expression scornful.

"Sure, O-not-O. Here? You want to grab a coffee?"

"No," he said, wanting to get the words out before he lost his nerve. He looked at the Pratt brothers, who didn't seem to be paying them any attention, but perhaps they were better at listening in than he was. "But let's go outside," he suggested.

He walked as far as the church driveway, just past the large cornerstone, and stopped at the short decorative wall flanking the port cochere. The afternoon sun was glistening down on the stones, each reflecting myriad beams of light. Oliver leaned against the thick wall.

Samantha stood in front of him, more than an arm's length away, with an unsettled expression.

He swallowed hard, then tried to look in her eyes. "I want to settle things, Samantha. I owe you that much."

It was immediately obvious to Oliver that the conversation had begun on a much different note than Samantha had expected.

"Samantha, this won't work. I mean ... us. *We* won't work. There's too much of a difference in our lives. You have a past. Maybe it shouldn't matter, but I can't let that go. And ... well, you are Jewish. And I'm a Christian. I think we're kidding ourselves if we say that we can overcome all the obstacles. There is just too much. I I—... like you, Samantha, I really, really do, and I wish that it could be different, but I don't think it can be."

As he spoke, Samantha's face grew more and more crestfallen, as if she were watching a beloved pet pass away, right before her eyes.

"But—" Samantha said, her words at the edge of tears, "none of that matters, does it? Me being Jewish. It's okay. It would have been okay."

Oliver stood up and, for a moment, debated taking off at a run, leaving the situation, removing himself from Samantha's increasing disappointment, and now her tears. "No, it wouldn't. I mean ... it couldn't. We're too different in the most important way."

Samantha stepped toward Oliver, and Oliver almost stepped backward. "I could have been like Ruth," she said.

"Ruth?" Oliver replied, confused.

"Like Ruth in the Bible. Barth told me all about her. 'Wherever you go, I will go. Wherever you live, I will live. Your people will be my people.' She followed her mother-in-law into some strange land. And it all worked out. Barth said that God provided for her, led her to her kinsman redeemer, who bought her freedom, and made her his wife. Why couldn't that be us?"

Oliver had expected any number of responses from Samantha—from anger to tears to indifference—but never once imagined that she would use a Bible story, quoting verses. He had no rehearsed response ready.

"Yes, but ... no, Samantha. It wouldn't work. It's not your being a Jewish person that's a problem. I think your culture and traditions are all very interesting. I've always been intrigued by them and would love to know more about them. They're all over the Bible, in fact. But the rest of the Ruth verse says, 'Your God will be my God.' That's the most important part to me. Unless that would happen, we have no future. You have a right to know how I feel, and I know that I should do the right thing and tell you, rather than lead you on."

Samantha's tears turned to something else … closer to anger. Now here was an emotion to which Oliver had prepared a response. Samantha clenched her hands into fists. Oliver would have welcomed it if she had taken a swing at him. That sort of response would be direct and easy to deal with, and over in a few minutes.

But she did not, nor did Oliver expect her to.

"So," she said, after taking a few deep breaths, "you've already decided on all this? Without asking me. Your decision, right?"

"It's the only fair thing to do, Samantha. I want to do the right thing."

She glared at him with that intense, crippling glare reserved for scorned women, then calmly said, "I hope you'll be happy, Oliver. I hope you'll be happy in your narrow little path. I hope you make your mother happy. You two deserve each other."

Her glare did not wane, but something in her expression softened, edging toward civility. More tears fell.

He remained silent.

"It's okay, Oliver, if that's what you want. Fine. But listen. I still want this project finished. You have to stay on the job. Your work is amazing, so let's just pretend that this discussion never happened. We can keep it to ourselves, can't we? Nice and friendly? We're adults here, aren't we?"

Oliver nodded, replying quickly, "Sure, I can do that. Finish the job. We'll be civil to each other. We can be friends."

"Friends." Samantha looked away, as if composing herself again.

"Well, then, good," he answered.

She cleared her throat. "Then I'll see you tomorrow."

And with that she turned and walked away, crossed South Aiken at the corner, and headed down Westminster to her home, away from Oliver, not looking back even once, not even slowing one step.

Samantha walked quickly around her house and entered quietly through the back door, hoping to make it up to her room via the back staircase and not have to see her father or Mally.

She carefully hushed the door closed, and once in the mudroom, turned toward the stairs.

Samuel Cohen stood in the doorway to the kitchen. "I saw you come up the sidewalk," he said. "What's the matter? Is there a problem at the old church?"

"Oh, Daddy," Samantha sobbed, and he opened his arms to his only daughter.

"Come here, *Bubeleh*," he said, and she fell against him, the tears flowing freely now, feeling like a fifteen-year-old with a breaking heart once again.

Oliver was not a man who made snap decisions—not in his work, never in his social life. Decisions were meant to be pondered, evaluated, prayed over. They were not simple choices made by the mental flipping of a coin.

But this decision was. It was quick. It was dramatic. It would solve so many problems. It would make so many people happy: his mother, Paula, her daughter, even Pastor and Mrs. Mosco. It would tie things up in a neat package.

Robert the Dog took his customary nap on the trip back to Jeannette while Oliver's thoughts rested on a single theme.

It's time. I can do this. I should do this. It's the right thing to do. We can grow together—that's the way it used to be. People did not spend years dating. They found a person who was good and pleasant, and they made the best of the situation. I'll be rescuing Paula. I'll give my mother a few more happy years.

He gripped the steering wheel tighter. *It will be enough.*

He pulled into his driveway and let Robert the Dog out. The dog slowly made his circuit around the yard, as if seeing it for the first time. He came immediately when he was called, walked up the steps slowly, and entered the apartment. Finding a place on his dog bed, Robert circled once, then twice, and lay down, settling his head and chin on his paws. He stared at Oliver as his master changed his clothes and sat at the kitchen table, having one more cup of coffee.

Oliver stared at the black velvet box in the center of the table, tied with an elegant silver ribbon. He picked it up and hefted it, as if the box were filled with some uncertain weight. Standing, he slipped the package into his trouser pocket. After saying good-bye to Robert the Dog, he slowly walked down the steps to the sidewalk and toward Paula's house, never varying his stride. Patting the lump in his trouser pocket, he smiled.

Once at the door, he tapped softly at the glass, as if the pane might break into a thousand pieces.

Paula came to the door with a bright expression—*almost too cheerful*, Oliver thought—and embraced Oliver in a long hug. She didn't say anything, didn't express surprise at seeing him, just held him.

"Where's Bridget?" he asked.

"Oh, she's with my mother. They went to McDonald's and then to that Disney movie they've been advertising—the one with the talking squirrels. She's been asking about it for weeks and I just couldn't bring myself to see another cartoon. So my mother said she would take her. She'll sleep through it, probably. Maybe they both will."

Oliver didn't really hear what she said. "So we're alone?"

"For a couple of hours, probably. What did you have in mind? We haven't been alone much, have we?"

"No. But this ... what I need to ask, I mean ... it needs to be between just you and me."

Paula sat on the couch and Oliver joined her, sitting so that he could watch her face. He twisted slightly and reached in for the box, pulling it out as gracefully as he could. The bow was matted down now, and he wished he had just carried it in his hand, but it was too late to change the delivery method.

"Here, this is for you," he said. His words were even, calm ... almost without emotion.

Paula's eyes widened. It was obvious she knew what sort of thing was hidden in velvet boxes of that size. *Everyone knew what those sort of boxes held*, Oliver thought.

"Is that what I think it is?" she asked.

Oliver thought for a moment, trying to come up with a pleasant or romantic or meaningful response, but the proper words failed him. "I ... maybe. I don't know."

She took the box, her hands shaking a little, and untied the bow. She carefully placed it next to her on the couch, on the comforter, bunched up under her leg. Slowly she opened the box. The light from the window caught the stones and the ring sparkled, even before the lid was fully open.

Paula gasped.

"It's time, Paula," Oliver said. "Marrying you is the right thing to do. And I'm ready. I hope you are as well. We've known each other for a long time, and we get along well. And, well … I guess this ring says it all, doesn't it?"

Paula snatched the ring out of the box and held it up to the light. "It's beautiful, Oliver. It's so beautiful." She slipped it on her finger. "And it fits perfectly. How did you do that?"

"I just guessed."

Paula held out her left hand, now with an engagement ring on the third finger, and held it up to see how it looked. She didn't speak for a long time, then lowered her hand and almost threw herself against Oliver, knocking him backward on the couch. Embracing him hard and tight, she wept against his shoulder. He wrapped his arms around her and held her as well. There were no words appropriate for this specific moment.

For what seemed like a very long time, the two of them, Oliver and Paula, simply held on to each other, in silence. Oliver almost enjoyed the feeling of protecting her, of holding her and making everything fine and right with the world.

"Oliver, I am so happy. You don't know how happy this makes me. Like a princess."

"That's good," Oliver replied. "I guess that's what you're supposed to feel like. But I'm not sure, since I've never done this sort of thing before."

She was crying, but she looked happy. She kissed Oliver enthusiastically, her tears making the kiss taste salty and quite different.

"Let's go celebrate, Oliver. Please? Let's go out. I'll leave a note for my mother. We can go out for a little while, can't we?"

"Sure," Oliver replied. "A celebration would be fine."

I can grow to love her. I can. I will.

They wound up at Dino's Restaurant, which was more of a tavern than a restaurant, but Oliver couldn't even think of eating anything at that moment. They sat at the bar, the only two patrons inside, other than a bartender and a bored waitress.

Paula ordered a white wine and Oliver asked for a beer, thinking that a soft drink would be too … too noncelebratory. If they talked much, Oliver couldn't recall any of their conversation. Paula chattered on about setting dates and having a simple, intimate ceremony, and maybe just a dinner somewhere—"only for the immediate family and close friends, of course"—and thinking about where they might live as a family.

"Both of our places aren't big enough," Paula decided. "A contractor would not want to live in my plain old place, and yours doesn't have a second bedroom for Bridget. But we could find a house pretty quickly. There are a lot of homes for sale. Would you want to stay in Jeannette? I think Ligonier would be nicer. Maybe near the quaint downtown. It has a gazebo. There are some nice houses there."

Oliver nodded in agreement. "I'm sure there are."

Paula was on her third glass of wine, while Oliver was still sipping at his first beer.

"Let's go for a drive, Oliver. Just me and you, okay? We can be alone. Maybe we could drive out to Twin Lakes again. That's real private, isn't it?"

Oliver drove as if on autopilot, Paula snuggled up against him, stroking his arm, holding her hand with the ring up for both of them to admire.

Oliver parked the truck at the farthest corner of the deserted lot, just under a canopy of early-budding oaks and maples. When the engine grew silent, Paula pulled his arm around her shoulder.

"This is so nice, Oliver, almost like we're married right now, you know? Just like two married people."

Oliver murmured his approval. Paula's hand roamed over Oliver's chest with a new boldness. She kissed him several times, each more passionate than the previous one.

"Oliver, since we're going to get married, it's different now. A good different … since we're going to be together forever." She drew even closer to him. "I mean, now it would be okay if we … you know … like married people. I know you are old-fashioned and all that. But it would be like sealing our love. Please, Oliver, we could, couldn't we? You want to, don't you?"

Oliver sat up, as if waking from a long dream. "Of course I want to.

But not here. Not now. Not in the truck, of all places. And not until we're actually married. That's what I have always believed. A ring doesn't change what I know to be right. The Bible says we need to wait. And we will wait. It's okay. A few months won't be too hard."

"A few months? But we're engaged, Oliver. It's okay now, isn't it?"

He gently pushed her away. "No. It's not. And I won't cheapen you— or our relationship—for a few minutes of pleasure. I won't."

"But, Oliver," she pleaded, "why not? I don't want to wait for you any longer."

He shook his head. Outside, a chorus of crickets and spring peepers began their evening music.

"I don't want to wait, Paula. But I have to. We have to."

His words were cemented together with such a stern sense of finality that Paula remained silent, almost a pout appearing on her face.

"Okay," she finally whispered. "Okay, Oliver." She slid over to the passenger side of the truck, folded her hands on her lap, and stared straight ahead, into the moonless sky. "Okay."

He waited for a moment, then reached the keys, turned the engine on, placed the truck in gear, and headed back out to Route 30 and toward home.

Oliver held her tenderly at the door and said good-bye in a most gentle manner, placing his hand under her chin, tilting her head up so he could kiss her sweetly on the lips, softly, like a bumblebee on a flower.

"Good night, Paula. Tomorrow we can tell your mother and my mother. When we're not so tired. Or, at least, when I'm not so tired."

Paula felt herself nod in mute agreement.

"Okay, then," Oliver added. "I'll call you early. I can be late to work for one morning."

She closed the door behind him and looked at the ring on her finger one more time.

What do I do now?

She walked to the couch and simply fell into it, like a soldier hit with a sniper's bullet.

What do I do now? Do I tell Taller? Do I tell Oliver? If we wait for a few months to get married ...

She brought her fingers to her temples and massaged them.

We can't wait a few months to get married. By then, everyone will know. Oliver will know. Taller will. Everyone.

She looked over to the pantry. There was a large new amber bottle tucked away on a high shelf.

No. The wine was bad enough. I can't.

She glanced at the clock on the microwave. Her mother and Bridget would be home soon. She wanted to run away. She slipped the ring off, placed it back in the box, grabbed the ribbon, and put them all in the top drawer of her bedroom dresser.

She let herself fall across her unmade bed.

I could get an abortion. I could. There must be somewhere around here, some doctor who could make this all better.

With thoughts of termination in her head, Paula closed her eyes tight and rolled onto her side. She tucked her knees to her chest, her arms wrapped around her legs, trying not to think of anything until sleep would make it all go away.

<hr />

Oliver woke to Robert the Dog growling softly, staring at the front door and sniffing the air.

"What is it?" he asked, and Robert turned his head without moving any of his feet, standing his ground.

A soft tapping.

Oliver squinted at his watch. *5:30.*

In a flash, he jumped out of bed, grabbed his robe, thinking it might be his mother or a paramedic or some emergency personnel standing outside, not wanting to wake the neighborhood with loud knocking or shouts.

He slapped the door open.

Paula stood in the doorway, wearing the same clothes she had on the night before, only now everything was a bit wrinkled, and her hair was tousled and pulled back into a hurried ponytail. "I have to talk to you, Oliver," she said, her words urgent and clipped.

"Come on in, Paula. It's cold. Who's with Bridget?"

She held up the baby monitor. "She never wakes up before seven. If she does, I'm a minute away."

Paula stood in the entryway, as if unsure where her next step might take her.

"Sit down. Please. Do you want coffee? Tea? I think I have teabags."

"No. Nothing. I'm fine …"

And then she started to weep, drawing her hands to her face, drooping, shrinking before his very eyes.

"Paula, what is it? Sit down. Please."

Oliver escorted her to one of the kitchen chairs. Paula slumped down, her arms falling to her side. Oliver caught a glimpse of something black in her left hand. Without looking, she reached up and slapped the ring box on his kitchen table.

"I can't, Oliver. I can't do this."

Oliver sat, stunned, not allowing himself to feel or analyze anything. All he could see was that black box and the top of Paula's head as she stared at the floor. He was glad he'd vacuumed the night before, not being able to sleep either.

"But why?" he finally said, not in the most convincing tone, then added, "What happened?"

Paula looked up, her eyes bloodshot, her nose red, strands of her hair escaping from the ponytail and falling around her face like reeds in a sudden wind. She sniffed loudly and wiped her arm under her nose. "I can't tell you … exactly. But I can't marry you. And you don't need to know more than that. I just can't."

Oliver's heart felt as if it were beating at twice its normal speed. He knew the cause: Paula's sudden, shocking denial of his request for marriage. But there was something else, too. The word *relief* entered his thoughts and he immediately banished it, feeling a tsunami of guilt and deception, dishonesty and duplicity wash over him, crushing whatever nobility and honesty existed inside his heart.

"But … but you can," he said, insisting, wondering if his words felt as hollow and weak as they did in his own ears as he heard himself give them voice. "It will be okay. We'll … we'll be happy together. We will."

Paula shook her head and waved her hand in front of her face, a wordless double negative.

"We would be," Oliver said again, a whisper this time, a delicate, dying whisper.

"No. It would be a lie," Paula said back, her words without any invective or malice but simply the painful truth. "There's something about ... me, Oliver. I can't go through with this. I can't hurt you, Oliver. You're a wonderful man, a sweet and kind and gentle man, honest, and I can't do this to you. I can't."

She stood up. "You can have the ring back."

She turned and ran to the door. Oliver was certain she wanted him to get up and intercept her, to stop her, but he also knew he wouldn't and that she believed that it was what she deserved.

"Good-bye, Oliver. I've always loved you ... in a special way."

And then she slipped out, closed the door behind her, and padded quickly down the stairs.

Oliver sat still in the chair, staring at the closed door for a long time, then at the black box on the kitchen table. That's when Robert slowly walked over to him and nuzzled his hand, not expecting to be petted in return, but simply to say, in his Robert the Dog fashion, that he was there and would wait for Oliver to talk to him when the time was right.

CHAPTER TWENTY-TWO

IT WAS FRIDAY, and Oliver showed up at the jobsite around lunchtime. He stepped inside, called out to Henry Pratt, and explained that he would be gone that day, the following day, and the weekend as well. He and Robert the Dog needed some time to think, he said, in way of explanation, and that they planned to head up to Bald Eagle State Park, and camp out for the weekend, even if it was early in the season.

"It'll be empty, hopefully, and I can get some peace and quiet."

Henry didn't appear nervous or taken aback. "Sure, Oliver, we can handle things here. On schedule. We'll keep things goin' along."

Oliver didn't think much about anything on the drive. The miles clicked past, the towns grew further apart, the scenery became thick with early summer and the scent of new grass and flowers. Summer came later up north, and Oliver felt privileged to step back a few weeks and watch nature bloom all over again.

"So this is what you've spent all the money on," Samuel Cohen declared. "Pretty impressive."

"You think so, Daddy? Do you really think so?" Samantha asked.

Samuel seldom visited his daughter's jobsites until they were completely finished. He didn't have an eye for seeing beyond the mess and the clutter and the chaos of almost-completed projects. He would focus on a pile of debris in the corner, or molding that wasn't finished, and fixate on those imperfections, never able to make the jump from half-done to done.

But since this project was within walking distance of his house, he allowed his daughter to drag him there, to let him see the direction and scope of the work.

"Yeah, I do. This will be one swell place once it's done. The windows are magnificent. That big round one is ... spectacular. Like an eye, isn't it?"

Samantha had decided that she didn't like the thick windows without some illumination after dark, and had the electricians install discrete exterior lighting around each large panel of stained glass. So with the flick of a switch, each window came fully alive at night, the lights carefully angled down and in and hidden by baffles, making them hardly visible from the street but vibrant and alive from the inside.

"Impressive. Really impressive."

She took him by the hand and led him around the nearly completed space. Booths, cleverly constructed out of the old pews, counters, and cabinets, were all installed, and tables had been brought in and placed around the room.

"There's something about this place," Samuel declared, standing in the middle of what used to be the sanctuary. "Makes you feel ... like you want to be a better person. Does that make sense?"

"It does, Daddy. It's a special space. That's what the old Korean pastor said when he stopped in a few months ago. He said the people in his congregation believe that this will always be a place of truth, that it will always be holy. 'Sacred space,' he called it."

"Really."

"He said he prays every day that I will know the truth, that this place will always be its home."

"Every day?"

"I feel it every time I'm inside. Do you feel it too?"

Samuel turned around in a slow circle. "Yeah, I guess I do."

He stopped and his gaze went from the windows to his daughter's face. He looked hard at her, as if trying to discern if anything had changed. "Anything new with you and your *goy* contractor friend?"

Samantha shook her head. "No, Daddy. Apparently Oliver still believes that we're too different. Me being Jewish and him being a *goy*. I don't think it makes a difference, but he does."

Samuel seldom asked about Samantha's social life, and it felt a bit uncomfortable now. "Maybe he's right, *Bubeleh*. But … maybe there is something else. You give it time. Maybe things will change. Maybe he'll convert. He made you happy, didn't he?"

"He did," she said and sat in one of the chairs by a center table. "He is so kind and gentle, an honorable man, but there's no possibility of him converting to Judaism, Dad. He has his strong beliefs. He said there was too much distance between us."

Samuel waved his hand in dismissal. "We'll see. Maybe it's *bashert*— some things are meant to be. You give it time. If it's supposed to work out, it will."

"What about you and Judy?" Samantha asked.

"She's a wonderful woman. I want you to meet her as soon as possible."

"What does that mean, Daddy? Are you two getting serious?" Samantha asked with a coy look.

"It means that maybe it's time for your old man to get a life. Then you won't have to worry about me so much," Samuel answered.

"Oh, Daddy!" Samantha answered as she fell into his arms and began to cry, just like when she was his little girl.

———— ⟨∘⟩⟩ ————

Oliver unpacked the truck at the farthest corner of the campground. As he expected, and as he hoped, there were only two other campers in the entire campground, and they had settled in on campsites near the lake. Oliver took the opposite tack, and selected his site at the top of the ridge, looking down on the lake and valley below, with the forest in new leaf spread out before him.

The tent all but set itself up, and in less than thirty minutes, his sleeping bag lay nestled inside, the Coleman lantern hung on a hook, his camp stove ready for cooking, and a small supply of logs and kindling ready for later in the evening. Oliver liked campfires but didn't like to cook on them;

the soot and ash from the wood made cleaning the pots all but impossible, and the heat was notoriously difficult to regulate.

And then he grinned at his compulsiveness.

How much heat regulation do you need to cook hot dogs and baked beans?

He unfolded the camp chair and sat down and stared out at the scene below.

Why do they call this a camp chair? *It's just like the chair in a bag I got at Home Depot—but this one cost three times as much.*

Robert sniffed in a circle around the campsite, then again, and again, each circle a few yards wider than the one before. Oliver didn't camp all that often, but Robert's routine was inviolate: circle and circle, making sure there were no bears or other wild creatures lurking nearby. He knew Robert would not run off, so he tried to relax.

But relaxation eluded him. His heart seemed to clump in his chest and his thoughts jangled, filled with a tornado of emotions and possible reasons and questions and puzzles and hurts—and relief.

He had stopped at Paula's house that same morning, the morning she had told him no. She could not, or would not, provide Oliver with more concrete reasons for her decision.

"I can't tell you any more, Oliver. I can't. And I will not change my mind."

And then she had closed the door on him, her sobs muffled by the cheap pine hollow-core model that she should replace with a more secure metal door with a deadbolt, at least.

He had decided on camping in a snap.

Staying home might lead to further questions. His mother might find out. Paula's mother might find out. He had no answers for either of them. He had no answer for himself. He had believed he was doing the right thing—why did she change her mind?

———⋙◈⋘———

Oliver dozed, then woke with a start. Darkness crept up the sides of the valley. An unseasonable chill followed the darkness. A stiff breeze, hissing above the tree line, clattered the top bare branches together in a primitive drum beat.

Oliver retrieved a thick fleece pullover from the tent. "Maybe this isn't such a good idea after all, Robert."

Robert stared back impassively, sitting on his haunches a few feet away.

"Are you cold, Robert?"

The dog did not move, nor offer any response.

"It's really not that windy. Maybe I'll start that fire now."

There was a stone circle by the tent, filled with the charcoal of a hundred previous fires and roasted marshmallows and sparks crackling into the chill of a hundred clear Pennsylvania nights. Oliver took two resin-soaked pinecones, lit them, placed them in the center of the stones, and stacked a teepee of wood around the flickering but persistent flame. Soon flames began to encircle the logs, and Oliver felt the warmth on his face and bare hands. It felt good, like a sauna, like a balm, a healing warmth.

"So the pans get dirty," he said to himself out loud. He poured a can of beans into a small pot, tossed in four hot dogs, then thought about it and tossed in the entire half package of six. Robert would eat at least two. Actually, Robert would eat them all if Oliver allowed it, but two, plus his dog food, would be plenty. And without buns, hot dogs weren't exactly a substantial meal.

He placed the lid on the pot, took a sturdy tree branch, and anchored it well, with the pot hung off of it, just above the flames.

"I can wash it when I get home."

The two of them shared a silent meal, Robert enjoying the hot dogs like any dog would do, snapping them up in nanoseconds. Oliver ate from the pot, the steam coming off like a special effect, at least at first. When he was done, he placed the pot back in the cab of the truck, along with the rest of his food. The ranger had said that there had not been a bear sighting at the park in several years, but there were scores of raccoons. And raccoons, while not dangerous per se, could be a horrible nuisance.

Robert sniffed about and walked, with some deliberateness, into the tent. Oliver heard him circle inside and lay down. Oliver knew he'd have to move him later, an act Robert always seemed to think was a personal insult.

"Well … here I am. Away. Giving me space and time to think. That's what I wanted, right?" Oliver said out loud.

He waited in the dark, as the fire slowly ebbed, the warmth eking away as the night grew blacker and thicker and denser.

No deep thoughts came. Oliver didn't exactly expect them to come. He envied the speakers he'd heard at church, talking about going away on spiritual retreats and returning with renewed vigor and deep spiritual insights from the solitude and silence. Oliver hoped that might happen this weekend, but he was also a realist. Epiphanies happened to other people—not plodding, routine-oriented folk like himself. People who worried about dirty pots.

He stared up into the thickness of stars set against the black sky.

He waited, hopeful, anticipating.

Nothing.

No voices, no flash of awareness, no dramatic insight.

Nothing at all.

Oliver felt guilty that he didn't feel more horrible than he did. What Paula had done was a shock, for certain, and if the situation were reversed, he imagined that Paula would be disconsolate, miserable.

But Oliver didn't feel that, not now. Maybe a little when she had told him no, but not at this moment. He felt confused, but that emotion wasn't at all melancholic. He felt even guiltier when sharp pangs of relief popped into his consciousness. He fought them off, not encouraging them by dwelling on them.

He wondered what had happened.

Was I doing that just to please other people?

Of course I was.

He wondered how God fit into this.

Did He do this? I mean, was this part of His plan? Seems like the long way around to do it. Not that I'm questioning it, if it was God's plan. I'm sure there are things I can learn from it. It just seems like I was sure I was doing the right thing—but then it blows up.

He stood up. Off in the distance, a ridge away, he heard the hoot of an owl.

You don't hear that in Jeannette.

He waited, watching the fire die away to a puddle of embers.

But no revelations or insights either.

He climbed into the tent, shoved Robert the Dog ever so gently from the top of the sleeping bag, kicked off his shoes, and slipped inside. As he waited for Robert to reposition himself, he adjusted his pillow, pulled his stocking cap on past his ears, and closed his eyes, knowing sleep was just a dream.

———————————————

Samantha and Sarah Epstein, Cameron's college sorority sister, chose an indoor spot at Coffee Tree Roasters. It was too breezy of an evening to sit outside, so they settled for a table by the window.

Sarah, a petite, pretty woman perhaps a couple of years younger than Samantha, smiled warmly, cradling her coffee in her hands. "So when I arrived, how did you know it was me?"

"Cameron's told me a lot about you," Samantha answered. "And you look very Jewish."

Sarah's laugh was easy. "Takes one to know one, I guess."

"I hear you're a real-estate dynamo with Chapel and Lawton."

"And I hear your father owns half of Shadyside," Sarah replied good-naturedly.

"Well, not quite half. Not yet, at least. But he's working on it."

"Cameron went on and on about your church project. That's quite an undertaking. I've always admired that building. All those marvelous windows."

"It's a beauty, all right," Samantha said. "When it came up for sale, I knew I had to move on it."

"And how's it coming?" Sarah asked, unwrapping a piece of lemon pound cake.

"Great. Really great."

"No builder horror stories to tell?"

"Actually, none. It's all gone really smoothly."

"You're kidding me! That's a new one on me. How do you do it?"

"First, you get a perfect contractor," Samantha answered, smiling.

"Perfect? Really?"

"Perfect. Really," Samantha replied. "It's a first for me, too. Oliver Barnett. He's amazing."

"That's what Cameron says. She's got a lot of respect for him—on and off the job."

The two sipped at their coffee. Samantha looked over at Sarah, who offered her a piece of pound cake. She felt immediately comfortable with this vibrant woman.

"He's ... like no one I've ever met. I'm sure Cameron's told you he's a Christian. And that we've been dating. I've dated other *goys* before, and their religion, or mine, never came up. It was a total nonissue. But Oliver's faith is ... not just what he does on Sundays. It's part of everything he does, and does not do, if you know what I mean."

"So, morally—"

"It's not just that. It's even in the way he approaches his work, like there's something holy or worshipful about it. Hard to explain."

"I get it, Samantha. Was it love at first sight then?"

Samantha laughed. "I used to think that was a joke. But I don't know anymore. I knew he was special from day one."

"And where are things now?"

"He says we have no future because of our differences. I guess that's why I'm here. Cameron tells me you're a completed Jew. I'd love to hear about that."

"Sure," Sarah answered. "Where to start?"

"Start at the beginning. I want to hear everything."

Sarah put down her cup and leaned back. "Okay. I grew up in Philly. Nice Jewish family. My father was a cantor even. Taught bar-mitzvah classes. My mom was chapter president of the JWI—you know, Jewish Women International. Did lots of philanthropy, advocacy, etcetera. After Hebrew school, at twelve years of age, at our temple girls could become *bat mitzvah*—'daughter of the commandments.' Did you have that?"

"No. Just the boys. I guess our synagogue wasn't as progressive as yours."

"It was a huge deal in our family. I stood on the raised platform and read from the old scroll, with its mystical, spidery writing, and felt the warmth of God around me."

"What do you mean by that?" Samantha asked, nibbling at the pound cake.

"Like God's presence was there beside me. But it vanished as quickly as it came.

"Through high school and college, I had one goal—to be a successful businesswoman in my own right, and accumulate all the 'stuff' I thought I needed to live the good life. I worked my *tuches* off, thinking that would bring me happiness. By twenty-five, I'd reached a point where I had hit the wall, felt like I was going nowhere. Oh, I had a great career, friends, all the 'stuff' I'd dreamed about, and I'd done it all myself. My way. But I was still so unhappy. Not just a little, but deeply depressed. I tried to cover it all up with partying, vacations, men, clothes—whatever. Nothing worked."

"I'm with you so far," Samantha said. "Sounds rather familiar."

"You know, Samantha—we Jews always talk about peace. We say '*Shalom, shalom,*' but I had none. Zero. Then I thought maybe if I became more devout, God would be pleased with me, so I ate only kosher foods, stopped going out on Friday nights, and tried to keep all the commandments. Nothing. I wanted that warm feeling again, like the taste of it I'd had when I was twelve. Instead of feeling closer to God, I felt farther and farther away. I thought, *If this is all there is, I don't want to go on living.*"

"So what did you do?" Samantha asked.

"I thought about ending it all, many times. But, thank God, I didn't. I know He protected me. About that time, a new agent, Jordan, joined our real-estate firm, and our manager warned us that she was 'very religious,' maybe thinking that we'd offend her somehow. I was wary at first. But she turned out to be the most kind, loving, honest person I'd ever met. She'd offer her help even when it wasn't convenient or when it meant others advancing instead of herself—who does that? A real servant's heart. We became good friends. Full of unconditional love, she was. Even for me, a Jew. And we'd have these long discussions about God.

"I knew a bit about *Mesach* from my Jewish upbringing. When I started reading about the Messiah in my own Jewish Bible, I became more curious. The picture was sketchy, but I came across verses about *Mesach* in the Old Testament that sounded an awful lot like you-know-who. I tried to explain away the ancient prophecies, like Micah 5:2, which describes an Eternal One who would be born in Bethlehem. Or Daniel 9, that pin-points the time of the Messiah's first coming. And Isaiah 53, which spoke of His life and selfless sacrifice for sin. I found I couldn't explain them away. There are three hundred prophecies about the coming Messiah, forty that are very specific."

"Three hundred? I had no idea."

"And Jesus fulfilled every one, Samantha. My rabbi would say that this is just coincidence, or Christian manipulation, out of context, after the fact. But with the discovery of the Dead Sea Scrolls, we now know with certainty that these Jewish prophecies predated Jesus Christ. So I began to connect the dots."

Samantha leaned closer in, listening intently.

"On my birthday, Jordan bought me a Bible. I started reading the 'other side' of the book, the 'closed side'—Matthew, Mark, Luke, and John. It struck me that they are very Jewish books, written in a way to convince other Jews, and Gentiles as well, that Jesus is the long-awaited Messiah. The more I read it, the more I learned about Jesus, and the more I wanted to know Him. It was like He was irresistible to me. I asked Jordan if I could go to her church with her, and that Sunday the passage of the day was Philippians 3:8 and 9. Here, let me read it to you."

Sarah reached into her purse and pulled out a thin, compact Bible, then began to read. "'What is more, I consider everything a loss compared to the surpassing greatness of knowing Christ Jesus my Lord, for whose sake I have lost all things. I consider them rubbish, that I may gain Christ, and be found in Him, not having a righteousness of my own that comes *from the law*, but that which is through faith in Christ—the righteousness that comes from God and is *by faith*.'"

Sarah put down the Bible. "Keep in mind that those words were writ-ten by Paul, once a wealthy, high-ranking Jew of the first order, who killed Christians, until God transformed him. I heard those words, Samantha, and for me, the earth moved—literally. I knew in that moment that Yeshua was *my* Redeemer, the Messiah, the true Son of God. I began to weep. I can't explain to you how I felt. It was like … like being emptied and filled up at the same time. I was set free. It was so beautiful."

Samantha could see a loving earnestness in Sarah's eyes.

"That's what the truth does, Samantha. For the first time in my life, I knew what *Shalom* really means. The warmth of God was so real. And this time, it wasn't just around me, it was inside. Deep inside. And it has never left me."

Sarah reached over and laid her hand on Samantha's. "That's what it means to be a completed Jew. It's not turning from who we are as Jews, but coming into a fullness of the promise and all God has for us in Jesus. I feel incredibly blessed that God has chosen me to know Him—to really understand what Jesus has done for me. He makes me whole, Samantha. He gives me eternal life. That changes everything. That's what Oliver has. And Jesus wants to do the same for you."

Samantha was still awake. She'd stayed in bed, hearing the clock in the hall chime the quarter hours: *2:30, 2:45, 3:00.* Pieces of her conversation earlier with Sarah swirled in her thoughts.

Shalom. Fulfilled prophecies. The truth. Set free. So beautiful. Whole. Eternal life. Changes everything.

She could almost still feel the caring touch of Sarah's hand.

What would it feel like, what would it change, to really believe that this life isn't all there is?

Samantha heard the clock chime again: *3:15.* She drew the duvet closer around her.

She closed her eyes.

God, I don't know what to say. I want to feel Your warmth inside me. Barth said if I listened closely with an open heart, I would hear You. Jesus, if You are the Messiah, please let me know, like You did Sarah. I want what she, and Oliver, and Cameron have. I want Shalom.

At 4:30 a.m. Oliver awoke to an intermittent drip of water falling on his chest. He looked up and saw a puddle gathered in a fold on the top of the tent, on the outside. Through squinting eyes, he watched a drop of water flow down a seam and stop at a cross member, then drip with a muted splash onto the top of his sleeping bag. He brushed the wetness off, sat up, crawled out of the bag, and leaned to the zippered door. He drew the zipper halfway down. The gray sky seemed to be only yards above the ridge where Oliver had pitched his tent. It wasn't rain, exactly, but more like a thick mist that ebbed and flowed in currents across the rim of the mountains. Oliver could see his breath form in little puffs in the cold air. Robert stirred, then stood, and nosed at the door.

"You won't like it out there, Robert," Oliver warned as he unzipped the door to fully open and let the dog out. The dog took a dozen steps into the cold mist and stopped, turning his head back to Oliver with an obviously unhappy expression. He hurried back inside, shaking his coat twice, leaving a fine splatter all over the tent's interior.

Oliver looked out at the dismal day. He was not a man of snap decisions, but this one was easy. "I'm packing up, Robert. I don't want to sleep in the damp cold, on the hard ground again."

In fifteen minutes, Oliver had disassembled the tent, packed it in its duffel bag, stowed it in a compartment in the truckbed, adding the lantern, the camp stove, and his sleeping bag to the dirty pot already there. He tied the food cooler down to the truckbed and called for Robert, who eagerly jumped into the cab. From the driver's side window, he looked out over the campsite, making sure nothing was left there, then started the truck and drove slowly over the rutted road, avoiding muddy stretches as best he could, driving carefully until he reached the main highway, paved and wet, outside the park.

"We'll drive until we find breakfast, Robert. Maybe there's an IHOP around here somewhere. I have a taste for pancakes. Do you want some pancakes, Robert?"

In fifteen minutes, he came upon a diner, sitting all by itself at a crossroads. No name, just the word *DINER*, unlit, on a big black-and-white sign. Oliver looked at his watch. He walked to the front door and returned.

"They should be open in ten minutes."

The two of them sat in the truck, the engine running, the heater on, and waited. He tried to find a radio station but couldn't.

"Maybe the mountains are in the way."

He took out a vinyl folder from the glove box and slipped out a CD, then slid it into the CD player. The unit whirred and the words started. Oliver had treated himself to a set of CDs last Christmas—the collection containing the entire Bible, read aloud, with occasional music in the background.

When he had purchased the CDs, he had promised himself that he would listen to the entire Bible while he drove back and forth to work. The promise was never fulfilled. He seemed never to be in his truck long enough to actually hear a full chapter. He hadn't even listened to them on the longer drives from Jeannette to Shadyside, keeping the radio tuned to traffic and weather reports instead. But today, he had no real choice in the matter.

The speaker was reading from 1 Corinthians.

"Don't you wives realize that your husbands might be saved because of you? Don't you husbands realize that your wives might be saved because of you?"

Oliver sat up, startled. He punched the *Pause* button, then hit *Back*. The CD whirred. He pressed *Play*. The verse came out again.

"Don't you husbands realize that your wives might be saved because of you?"

Oliver was sure he had heard that particular verse before, and probably heard a sermon or two explaining it. But he had never really paid much attention to it, thinking he would never be yoked with a person who did not believe. And he knew the words didn't give license to marry an unbeliever. At least he was pretty sure they didn't.

But why that verse, and why now? It was a random selection from an entire folder of CDs.

Robert the Dog stirred slightly in the passenger seat.

Oliver reversed the CD and repeated the verse again.

"Don't you husbands realize that your wives might be saved because of you?"

Is this a word from God? Is this why I'm up here in the middle of nowhere with no radio to listen to? Did He want me to hear that verse?

Oliver turned the CD player off.

Do epiphanies happen like this? Is this what I came here to find?

Another truck pulled into the lot, and two men jumped out and headed to the doors of the restaurant. The lights inside flickered on, and the sign by the road lit up, the word *DINER* transformed into a brilliant neon blue. Robert must have sensed it, for he woke up and growled softly in anticipation.

An epiphany from a random selection from a random CD? Is that some sort of sign for me?

Robert clambered over to the driver's side, whining with a greater urgency.

"Okay, Robert. I'll get breakfast."

Robert was partial to pancakes. Oliver knew what to order: two of the "Lumberjack" breakfasts. One for himself, one for Robert.

"Don't you husbands realize that your wives might be saved because of you?"

As he walked toward the front door, with Robert happily bouncing from one side of the cab to the other, a sentence from a sermon simply popped into Oliver's thoughts.

"A Christian husband brings holiness to his marriage."

And then he placed his order for two breakfasts, one with coffee.

He'll probably eat a whole order of sausage too.

Oliver didn't stop in Jeannette. He drove straight to the church in Shadyside and parked in the back. He let Robert out. It had been a long drive through the mountains, filled with thick fog and patches of rain and lightning. Even more fog, dense as cotton, rose from the narrow clefts in the hills as he made his way through Smoke Valley, shrouding the twisting highway in a thickness of gray mist.

He had to navigate slowly, staring hard at the white lines at the side of the road. A trip that should have taken four hours took eight. Robert was tense from sitting in the cab all day as was Oliver, but Oliver was on a mission.

Robert circled the church lot, then came back up the front steps. Oliver waited for him, unlocked the door, let him inside.

"I'll be gone a few minutes, Robert."

Then he thought better of it and hurried downstairs to check if there was adequate food and water for the dog. There was.

Oliver stopped in the just-completed restroom in the basement. He had not showered or shaved. He ran his hand over his chin.

"Could be worse," he said to himself. He pulled off his fleece pullover and put on a sweatshirt, a good bit fresher than the pullover. He patted at his hair.

Locking the door behind him, he walked to the corner and crossed the street.

He didn't hurry. At this moment, he had no idea of what he was going to say, but he knew he had to say something, explain himself one more time, see her face once more—not in a work situation, but in a setting where he could speak freely.

He hesitated only a bit at the bottom of the porch stairs. He took a deep breath, then another, and climbed up the broad staircase, crossed the wide, expansive porch, and pushed at the gold button on the doorpost. Below it, he noticed, was hung a little rectangular box, with Hebrew letters inscribed on the face.

I wonder what the box means. Maybe something to do with Passover.

He heard the chimes from inside, an elegant, muted sound.

More reminders of how very different we are.

He waited. There was a rustling from somewhere inside the sprawling Victorian house. At least he thought he heard a rustling. Panels of frosted glass, etched with an ornate swirling design, surrounded the door. The door opened. He had expected Mally, but another figure stood in the doorway.

"Yes? Can I help you? Just want to know if you're selling something, or carrying a petition, because those are two things I don't do at the door. Ever."

Another day, Oliver might have been rattled by the man's curt greeting. But today he let it wash past him.

"I'm Oliver Barnett, sir. I'm the contractor for the church down the street. I'm working for Samantha. Is she at home?"

The short man with a buttery tanned face peered forward. "You're Oliver? *Oy*. I had pictured someone else altogether."

Oliver waited, not knowing how to respond.

"I'm her father. Samuel Cohen. But you probably knew that. Come on in. I'm watching some boring golf tournament on TV. Sam's not home. No one's home. But if you need something, maybe I can help."

Oliver didn't think the man could but didn't think he could simply walk away either. "Uhh, okay. Did Samantha say when she might return?"

Oliver didn't want to sound like a rude teenager, demanding that a girl's parents provide an estimated time of arrival for their child.

"She didn't. And she didn't take her cell phone. I tried to call her earlier and all I heard was the blasted thing ringing from her case in the kitchen. That's not like her, so I'm assuming she'll be home shortly. Anyhow, come on in. Have a coffee. Or a beer. Or a cocktail. Samantha says that you're not like some of the other *shleppers* she's had working for her. They would take a beer, if it were offered, at nine in the morning."

Samuel headed off into the house, and Oliver felt obligated now to follow him.

"Coffee okay?" he asked, pausing by the kitchen. "Mally made it this morning."

"Sure."

"Come on in. Have a seat." Samuel nodded toward the large table, poured coffee into a mug, then handed it to Oliver. He sat down and turned back to the TV. "You play golf, Mr. Barnett?"

"Oliver ... sir."

"Oliver, do you play golf?"

"I do. Once in a while. I'm not what anyone would call good at it. I like miniature golf, though. But I guess that doesn't count."

Samuel stared at the screen. "I like it when they whisper, those announcers. Like the golfer can actually hear them talking. Or ... maybe they can. Who can tell? But, that, I like. The game itself is ridiculous. I don't really enjoy it, but I've never had the *kishkes* to say no to the boys at the club. Who was it that said, 'Golf is not a game, it's bondage—obviously devised by a man torn with guilt, eager to atone for his sins.'"

The golfer on the screen whaled at a golf ball, and the crowd applauded and cheered in traditional genteel fashion.

"Good," Mr. Cohen said. "No one yelled out, 'In the hole!' I really hate when they do that."

Oliver was silently grateful that he didn't have a chance to respond before Samantha's father spoke again.

"So, Oliver, why are you here? You're not working today, are you? Design decision? Need a check? What?"

"No, sir. I'm not working today. But I needed to talk to Samantha. Sort of on a personal level, I guess."

Samuel swiveled on his seat. His stare was penetrating, and Oliver felt totally exposed. "Ah. Samantha says you two have stopped going out. Very disappointed, she was, Mr. Barnett."

Oliver, who had little experience with dating, had even less experience dealing with the parents of the girls he dated. And Mr. Cohen's comment took him by complete surprise.

"Well, I—" Oliver sputtered, trying to devise a cogent answer, "I guess I was too."

Mr. Cohen's expression remained icy. "She tells me it was your decision. So. How can you be disappointed?"

Mr. Cohen appeared to have a skill at putting people on the defensive, however politely.

"It was my decision, I guess. But I wanted to talk with her about it. That's why I'm here. To talk about it. If she'll talk to me, that is."

At last Mr. Cohen relaxed and took another drink from his martini glass with two olives in it. "She was happy, Mr. Barnett, when you two were dating. She's my *naches,* my pride and joy. I like it when she's happy."

"I can imagine, sir."

Mr. Cohen swirled the clear liquid around in his glass with a stirrer, the ice cubes delicately clinking against the thin glass. "She told me this cockamamie story about the church and how the old pastor there said that the building was a very special place—a place of truth. Apparently he told Sam a secret from his past because of it. I thought it was pretty far out, that story, but hey, now I'm telling you the truth, so maybe there is something to it. You hear about that story, Oliver?"

"I did, sir. Well, Sam told me some of what Mr. Han said. Maybe there is something to it. The building, I mean. I'm trying to be honest now. That's why I need to speak with your daughter."

Mr. Cohen took a long swallow and finished his drink. "Happy she was, Oliver. Very happy."

"Yes, sir."

"It was the happiest I have seen her ... well, since her mother died."

"I'm sorry, sir. Samantha did say that her mother was gone. My sympathies, sir."

Mr. Cohen rose from his chair. Oliver noted the lustrous sheen on his soft leather loafers, the kind with two tassels on each shoe, the kind Oliver would have never purchased for himself.

"She tell you how it happened, Oliver? Speaking about honesty here, and all. She give you the particulars of the story?"

"No, sir. All I know is that Mrs. Cohen is gone and that it seems Samantha misses her a lot."

"Yeah. Well, I guess I'm all for honesty and full disclosure. Samantha's mother committed suicide."

For a long moment, the loudest sound in the room was the almost-muted commentary coming from the countertop television set, still tuned to the golf match.

"I-I didn't know," Oliver stammered.

"Samantha doesn't talk about it much. I tell you, it's a real angry way to die."

"Yes, sir."

"She didn't tell you about the note then, either, did she?"

"No, sir."

"Samantha found her. Upstairs in the bathtub. Blood everywhere. *Oy.* And a note on the counter."

Oliver had no words to reply.

"You know what she said in the note?"

"No, sir."

"She blamed her daughter and her husband for it. Me and Samantha. Blamed us for her death. Not in those exact words. But she said the two of us made her invisible. That we had such big personalities that she started to die inside. That she had been miserable for years. She said that we should have known."

Oliver managed to whisper, "I'm sorry, sir."

Mr. Cohen walked to the window over the sink and stared out at the huge trees in the backyard. "After it all happened, her therapist said that she was bipolar or schizophrenic or manic depressive. I forget which, now—what do I know from mental illnesses?—and had been for a long time. The therapist said it wasn't our fault. She said we shouldn't feel guilty. And yet. We were living with a certifiable *meshugge* in the house and didn't even know it."

Mr. Cohen turned back to Oliver. "You know how hard that is on a young girl, Oliver? Samantha doesn't talk about it. Well, I saw her use alcohol, for a while, and then men ... something to hide from the pain, is what I'm thinking. It's like the *Shiva* that would never end, so long she grieved. *Oy.* But I saw her happy again—really happy, when she was with you. Makes it hard, Oliver. Makes it hard."

Oliver didn't know what to say but wanted to be honest. "Mr. Cohen, are you a religious man?"

Mr. Cohen straightened up, his lower lip pushed up, as if he were carefully considering the question. "Oliver, we have many traditions. Culture and traditions. My wife, she kept all the laws. Wore herself out. I do the best I can, but I am not a man of great faith. There's Jewish and then there's *Jewish* Jewish. Why? Why do you ask?"

Oliver's mind raced. He could say a lot of things—that it's not about keeping the laws, and that's why Jesus came, to set us free. But he wondered what might be appropriate to share in this moment with Samantha's father.

A cell phone's shrill warble broke the solemn air.

Mr. Cohen slapped at his waist. "Samuel here."

The older man listened, then held the phone away from his face, just a few inches, so that the caller would hear everything. He looked at Oliver with that straight, penetrating gaze.

"Seems that my daughter has found a lonely and abandoned dog named Robert inside the old church. She wants to bring him home with her. What should I tell her?"

Oliver was already nearly at the door. "Tell her not to move. Tell her I'll be right there."

And before he closed the door after himself, Oliver called back, "Thanks for the coffee, Mr. Cohen."

CHAPTER TWENTY-THREE

TALLER DIDN'T EXPECT to hear tapping at his door. He had guests, occasionally, but few, if any, of them, ever dropped by unannounced. He switched off the TV, replaced the remote in the antique wooden box where it was stored out of view and uncluttering his coffee table, and walked to the entryway of his apartment. He could tell it was a woman; the shadow through the glass, cast by the streetlamp down the block, indicated his guest's shorter stature.

As a rule, Taller didn't bother to fasten the deadbolt and second chain until he went to bed. He undid just the latch and opened the door.

"Paula?"

A moment passed before she looked up. Her face was drawn, her eyes looked troubled, with a tracing of redness. "I need to talk to you, Taller."

Taller didn't step back, not just yet. "Where's your daughter?"

"With my mom. She's a saint."

Only then did Taller retreat one step and open the door enough for Paula to enter. He looked out onto the street, then closed the door and snapped the lock shut.

Taller stepped around Paula, both of them still in the entryway.

"Can I have … a glass of water, Taller. Please?"

There was a brief pause, then he replied, "Sure. Come on into the kitchen. I have bottled or tap. Or coffee or tea, if you want."

"No. Tap water is fine. Really."

She sat at the table, picking the chair Taller never sat in, like she knew that Taller would never sit at the table right behind the sleek salt and pepper shakers and matching napkin holder. He would have always picked the chair that faced the archway and the window.

He removed a glass from a cabinet, let the water run for a moment, then filled it.

"Ice?"

"No. No thank you. Just water."

Taller placed the glass on the table.

Paula took the glass and took a long sip. "Taller," she said softly. "We need to talk."

Oliver set off for the church at a jog, then slowed down, not wanting to get there all winded and stumbling over getting his words out of his mouth, or arrive sweaty and disheveled. He stood, catching his breath, looking at the church.

At night, when the lights are on inside, the windows look alive.

He stepped inside and Robert the Dog, who had been sitting next to Samantha in one of the center booths, trotted over to Oliver, sniffed at his hand, and deliberately returned to Samantha's side.

"Don't blame him, Oliver. I've been feeding him gourmet dog cookies from Wag, that new dog bakery, or 'barkery,' they call it, on Aiken. I don't know, but I always seem to have a package of something in my purse for Robert. And he looked hungry."

"You can't believe a word he says," Oliver replied as he walked over to them. "He has a full bowl of Kibbles in the basement."

"Kibbles? *Oy.* Just the word is unappetizing. And it's dark down there. Maybe he's afraid of dark places."

Oliver debated if he should sit next to Samantha or facing her. He decided to face her.

"He isn't. He just knows how to play people with a kind heart who fall for his doe-eyed look."

Robert gave Oliver a dog's version of a baleful look, then jumped from the booth and padded off. They could both hear his nails tapping against the stairs as he descended into the basement.

"The carpet will be here on Monday," Oliver said.

"Good. Good," Samantha replied.

Oliver had tested a thousand opening lines during the drive back home. None of them worked. He took a deep breath. "I was talking to your father," he said, one opening line he could truly say that he had never once remotely considered.

"I surmised as much. You being there. Him being there. Me being here."

"He seems like a very nice man."

Samantha moved her purse from one side to the other. *A nervous gesture,* Oliver thought.

"He is. But crafty as well. I mean, he can be. But not always. Or was he? Crafty, I mean. With you."

"No. He was very honest. We talked about golf some."

Samantha couldn't hold her incredulous laugh. "Golf? Really?"

"It was on TV. He asked if I played."

"Do you?"

"Mostly on courses with big windmills."

"Me too."

"Samantha ..."

Samantha looked up, the light from all the tiny new downlights on the rafters catching her eyes and her cheeks and her nose and her hair in just such a fashion as to make her look almost angelic, dreamlike.

"I went camping this weekend."

Her expression grew puzzled.

"It was a cold, wet, miserable time. But I needed to get away. I needed time to think. To sort things out."

"Did you? Sort things out, I mean?" Samantha asked, leaning forward just an inch, reaching up with her left hand to take a curl of her long hair and twist it between her fingers.

"No. Well ... maybe I did. Sort of. But I needed to talk to you."

A horn sounded from somewhere outside.

"And now we're talking, Oliver."

"We are."

Oliver looked down at his hands, calloused and rough, and in need of some tender care. The hands of a carpenter. The result of hard, honest work.

There's that word again. Honest.

"Your father told me about your mother."

He watched her face slowly change, from an expectant look in her eyes, to a sheen of pain, then a noble, wavering disguise. He could see her chest rise and fall, a little more rapidly now, as if her heart had sped up, beating faster as if in flight.

"We never talk about it," she said, her words coming from a very distant place. "We have never really talked about it." Samantha drew in a deep breath, then let it out. "My mother … she said some horrible, horrible things to me, right before she died. I have never been able to get the words out of my head. I can't get away from what she said to me."

Oliver leaned closer to the table. "I'm so sorry, Samantha."

"And finding her like that. It was—"

"I know how you feel," Oliver said, reaching for her hand.

"How can you know how I feel? I can't ever get away from it. Finding your mother like that—"

"I do know. Really. I need to tell you something too, Samantha. Remember when I told you about my father? How he left the family when I was young? How I had to grow up early?"

Samantha nodded, obviously not ready for a speech at that moment.

"He didn't leave. Well—" Oliver said, searching for the proper way to tell the truth, "he left. But … he didn't just go away. He killed himself."

He heard Samantha draw her breath in sharply.

"He hung himself in the basement. I found him there, the rope tied to a bare rafter."

"Oh, Oliver …," Samantha said, clearly distraught, recognizing a shared pain.

"My mother blamed Taller and me. She said he couldn't take the pressure of being a husband and a father of the two of us. He couldn't take it. We were a handful back then. She said he couldn't figure a better way of getting away. It was all our fault."

"Oh, Oliver."

"That's what she said. Taller was too young to understand, but I knew what she meant. It was my fault—and Taller's fault. And the thing is, no one ever found out it was suicide. She made me promise not to tell. My mother knew someone on the police force, and they made it out to be a heart attack. My mother and I alone knew the truth. Taller never found out. And keeping the secret—all these years, carrying it around—it kills me sometimes."

"Oh, Oliver."

"I've spent my whole life trying to make it up to her. Everything was bottled up, and she had nowhere to turn—just like me."

Oliver did not think or debate, but stood up and slid into the booth next to Samantha. He placed his arm around her shoulder and noticed the faint, wonderful smell of her. "I-I know what you feel like inside. How you try to make everything perfect so the pain won't start. How you always try to run fast so the past won't catch up."

Oliver took a deep breath. "I never talked about this with anyone. Not my mother. Not my friends. And Taller doesn't know. Or at least, I don't think he really knows. I talk to God about it, a lot. And that's the only thing that helps. But I can't keep everything in perfect order anymore. I don't want to do this anymore. I just can't … I won't live my life to please my mother."

"I know, Oliver. I know …"

Samantha wrapped her arms around Oliver, under his, and they held each other tight and long and carefully in the dim blue light, inside the big old church, at the center booth.

———◦◦◦———

"Are you sure?" Taller demanded, his words firm and direct but not fully angry … or at least that's what Paula hoped.

"I am. I tested twice. And then I went to the clinic on Route 30—by the mall. I'm pregnant, Taller."

Taller stepped around the table. "And it's mine? You sure of that?"

Paula had expected the question and didn't blame him for asking it. If the situation had been reversed, she would have posed the same question.

And she had debated how to respond—with anger, or disbelief, or damaged innocence.

None of them sounded right.

So she simply sighed and said with a resigned tone, "Yes, Taller, I am sure. Just like you are sure."

Taller pulled the chair out from the table, lifting it slightly, she noticed, so it wouldn't scratch the floor. "What are you—" he began, then stopped. He blinked a few times. "What are we going to do about this?"

A tear began to trail down Paula's cheek, just on the right side of her face. She knew it would be only a matter of time until more followed. She looked down, knowing he was watching the course of the tear, and then another.

He reached over and took her hand. "I don't want you to get an abortion."

Paula looked up, surprised. "You don't?"

Taller took a deep breath. "No. I-I don't know why. I mean, I don't want you to do anything bad. Like an abortion. I've screwed my life up enough already. I don't think I could live with myself anymore if you did that."

She watched his eyes. Behind their normal gray coldness something different was going on, as if he were imagining a highchair in the kitchen, a stack of baby bottles on the empty drainboard, and a scrawled picture or two torn out of a coloring book taped to the refrigerator. She could see all that, in spite of knowing that he'd have to work at acceptance every day. But she could see that he would try.

"Paula, I have to do the right thing—maybe for the first time in my life. We'll work it out. It may not be perfect, but it has to be better than either of us has now. If you want to. I promise to try."

Paula had continued to cry as he spoke. She wiped at her face with her hands and looked up at Taller. "I'll try, too. We can make it work, can't we?"

Taller half-shook his head. "I don't know. But we can try. I can. I will, Paula. Okay?"

"Sure. Okay. We can do that. We can."

Oliver could not tell how long the two of them sat there, entwined in their fierce embrace. Eventually, they both relaxed a degree or two and leaned back. Oliver wanted to see her face again, to memorize the lines and curves and coloring, and the shape of her lips and the structure of her throat and neck. He reached over, then, and touched her hair—gently, tentatively at first, then slowly moving his fingers through its thickness—something he'd wanted to do for a long time.

He bent to kiss her, gently, not assuming anything, not insisting on anything, not asking or demanding, but joining her, feeling the touch of her lips on his, a wordless, soundless, intimate conversation.

They both heard Robert the Dog's nails on the steps again. He circled the room the long way, then sat looking up at both of them, his tail just wagging.

"Oliver, I'm still Jewish, you know."

"I know. But you've read the book of Ruth. And your father said that you had tradition, not real faith in your religion."

She reached over and stroked his arm, her eyes seeking his.

"Teach me, Oliver. Show me the way."

They kissed again, only to be interrupted in a few moments by the cold, insistent nose of Robert, nudging Oliver squarely on the back.

CHAPTER TWENTY-FOUR

"So how did the grand opening go?" Rose asked. "Of your restaurant and, and all that."

If anyone had been observant, they would have seen two things happen almost simultaneously. One, Samantha gripped her glass so tightly that her knuckles went white, just for a moment. And two, her eyes darted about the room, searching for Oliver, searching for someone to parachute in and rescue her.

No one parachuted in.

"Mrs. Barnett, how nice of you to ask," Samantha answered. "It went very well. And *Three Rivers Restorations* was there to film it. That episode should air in a couple of weeks. Lots of good publicity for your son. He was in a lot of it. Isn't that great?"

It was apparent that Rose couldn't keep herself from beaming. The lines in her face softened, her expression warmer than usual. She looked almost sweet at that moment.

"He was? He never said a word about that to me."

"Well, you know how reserved he can be," Samantha confided to the older woman.

"Oh, do I ever," Rose replied. "You practically have to drag things out of him."

Samantha nodded in a knowing manner, not in a too-intimate fashion, she hoped, but familiar.

The two women sat alone at a table near the entrance to the room. It was the smaller dining area off the main ballroom of the local banquet hall in Greensburg, reserved mainly for showers and birthday parties. But Taller and Paula's wedding would not be a large, elaborate affair. Samantha had offered Blue for their wedding celebration, but Taller was certain his mother wouldn't enjoy herself in the former church.

"Oliver tells me that you've already sold the place. Is that true, or he is just fooling his mother again?" Rose asked.

If that had been a veiled comment, Samantha ignored it.

"I have, Mrs. Barnett. The Baptists bought it—just like my father suggested before I started the project. Some large Baptist church received a big donation, and all the donor said was, 'Try something different. Be creative.' They're keeping the restaurant going, but plan on inviting diners to church, Sundays in the downstairs Fellowship Hall. Turns out, the executive chef I hired is a believer, so he's on board. All the restaurant profits will go toward the new ministry. They're hoping to attract students from the university. They want to make it sort of a center for Christian arts as well, a place where artists of all kinds—painters and sculptors and musicians and writers and actors and even dancers—can showcase their work. And they made me a very reasonable offer. I never really intended on running a restaurant indefinitely. I just like the planning and development of the property, really. We met the young pastor who will run the ministry, and I'm sure he will do a wonderful job with it. He's so innovative, so passionate about his vision."

Samantha smiled at Mrs. Barnett, who appeared speechless.

Oliver returned to the table with a bit of a panicked look when he saw that his mother and Samantha were the only ones left sitting there, in total silence.

"Here are the two ginger ales," he said, giving one to Samantha and placing one in front of his place.

He handed the last glass to his mother. "And here's your Seven and Seven, Ma."

She took it, hushing him. "You don't have to announce it to the whole world. Besides, this is a special occasion. Not every day one of your sons gets married. And I'm well on my way to being a grandmother. That calls for a celebration—so don't you start in on me, young man."

Oliver held up his hands in surrender. "I wasn't going to say a word, Ma. It's okay with me. Whatever you want is fine."

She glared back at him, for just a moment, then took her drink and took a prolonged sip from the miniature straw.

The DJ returned from his break and restarted the music. A bevy of Paula's girlfriends stood up and hurried to the dance floor.

"You mind if we take a break, Ma? I need some air."

She waved him off. "I'll be fine, Oliver. Go."

He held out his hand and Samantha took it. He led her through the smoky bar and out onto the sidewalk, where the air was warm, but more refreshing than what was offered inside.

Neither spoke. Oliver was simply content to hold Samantha's hand as they slowly walked down the block.

"It was a nice wedding," Samantha said. "Robert would have loved it."

Oliver smiled. "It was. And yes—Robert would have had a great time."

"He's become quite fond of cake—especially with buttercream icing," Samantha added.

"And he's become quite fond of you, you know." Samantha returned his smile.

"I never expected it to happen. Never expected Taller to do the right thing."

"There's something different about him," Samantha added. "Not that I knew him all that well, but he seems more mature."

"I agree. Something's changed. He seems … like a better man. Maybe the Korean pastor was right about the church. Maybe being inside the place all those weeks did something to my brother. Prayers of Mr. Han's congregation are transforming more than a few people, it seems."

Samantha stopped and pulled Oliver's hand to her, so that he had to turn and face her. She drew her other arm around him and pulled him close, tilting her head, and the two of them kissed within steps of Gaskill Avenue.

"What was that for?" Oliver asked when they were through.

"For being wonderful."

"Well, sure ... but besides that?"

She poked his arm, playfully, and drew him close to herself. "For being a *mensch*. That's Jewish for a good man. For loving me. Teaching me. For giving me a chance ... letting me have time."

He held her close and kissed her back. "That's for being willing," he said. "For understanding me. And loving me."

"Hey, O-not-O, I have been transformed, too. Never in a million years would I have imagined being with such a wonderful man like you—and a Gentile, yet. And learning from the Bible—the whole Bible. Never in a million years."

"Transformed? Really?"

"Don't ask me to leave you and turn back. 'Wherever you go, I will go; wherever you live, I will live. Your people will be my people, and your God will be my God. Wherever you die, I will die, and there I will be buried.'"

Oliver held her hands as she spoke the words from the book of Ruth, watching her eyes, sensing—no, *knowing*—that she was speaking the truth ... that her life had been transformed, that she would be with him and that he would be with her, from this moment, until the rest of time.

EPILOGUE

OLIVER STOOD MORE silent and still than he had in a very long time. He listened to the words of Barth's blessing, knowing they were important, trying to remember each one but also knowing that he would have to rely on the videotape.

"May God the Eternal One keep you in love with each other and with Him, so that the peace of Christ may abide in your home."

Samantha, beautiful in her simple, yet elegant white gown, stood next to Oliver in his tuxedo. He took Samantha's left hand in his, their third fingers each now encircled with a thin white-gold band. After the Seven Blessings and on cue from the rabbi standing next to Barth, Oliver raised his right foot and heard the glass breaking beneath the towel.

He looked at Samantha and knew what he'd always remember would be her face that day, so filled with love and hope—and an absolute belief in second chances.

They kissed, then the two turned to face the congregation and began to walk down the aisle of the Messianic synagogue to shouts of *"Mazel tov!"* and *"Shalom!"*

Robert the Dog, in his black bow tie, jumped from the first pew and followed the beaming couple. The three of them headed out the door on Beechwood Avenue in Squirrel Hill, into the sunshine of a beautiful fall afternoon and into their new life together.

I do not at all understand the mystery of grace—only that it meets us where we are but does not leave us where it found us.
—ANNE LAMOTT

There was once a garret up under the roof, a poor, bare place enough. There was a table in it, and there were some benches, and a water pot; a towel, and a basin in behind the door, but not much else—a bare, unhomelike room. But the Lord Christ entered into it. And, from that moment, it became the holiest of all, where souls innumerable ever since have met the Lord God, in High glory, face to face. And, if you give Him entrance to that very ordinary heart of yours, it too He will transform and sanctify and touch with a splendour of glory.
—A. J. GOSSIP

Be thou comforted, little dog. Thou, too, in resurrection shall have a little golden tail.
—MARTIN LUTHER

ABOUT THE AUTHOR

 After eleven coauthored books with husband, Jim, Terri Kraus has added her award-winning interior designer's eye to her world of fiction. She comes to the Project Restoration series naturally, having survived the remodel, renovation, and restoration of three separate personal residences, along with those of her clients. She makes her home in Wheaton, Illinois, with her husband; son, Elliot; miniature schnauzer, Rufus; and Siberian cat, Petey.

Visit Terri Kraus at her Web site: www.TerriKraus.com.

Other Books by
Jim and Terri Kraus

MacKenzie Street Series
   The Unfolding
   The Choosing
   Scattered Stones

The Circle of Destiny Series
   The Price
   The Treasure
   The Promise
   The Quest

Treasures of the Caribbean Series
   Pirates of the Heart
   Passages of Gold
   Journey to the Crimson Sea

Project Restoration Series
   The Renovation
   The Renewal

His Father Saw Him Coming

The Micah Judgment

The Silence

... a little more ...

When a delightful concert comes to an end,

the orchestra might offer an encore.

When a fine meal comes to an end,

it's always nice to savor a bit of dessert.

When a great story comes to an end,

we think you may want to linger.

And so, we offer ...

AfterWords—just a little something more after you

have finished a David C. Cook novel.

We invite you to stay awhile in the story.

Thanks for reading!

Turn the page for ...

- **A Note from the Author**
- **Discussion Questions**

A Note from the Author

Writing a novel set in the world of the restoration of old buildings has always been a dream of mine. The idea of renovation is in my family's blood. I'm an interior design professional. My brothers are rehabbers. My husband, Jim, and I have survived the renovation of three houses.

I know the upheaval well, the despair of having no control, the agonizing over style decisions, the budget constraints, the disagreements between contractor and owner, and the emotional roller coaster of unexpected problems and unanticipated gifts along the way. Together my clients and I have accepted big disappointments, celebrated tiny successes, and experienced the inexpressible elation at seeing what was once in ruins—old, broken, useless—become, with all its quirks, a beautiful, completely renewed, and usable place for people to share life again. Looking back on all those projects, I can echo the sentiment in the opening line of Dickens' *A Tale of Two Cities*: "It was the best of times, it was the worst of times."

Many of you are probably, like me, HGTV fans who watch the many shows about fixing up old houses. You find yourself glued to the glimpses of contractors and owners engaged in the process. You live vicariously through the rehabbing, renovating, and restoring.

I can relate. I've always been captivated by old buildings. Poring over books about art, architectural styles, and decoration from all over the world has always been one of my favorite pastimes. As I've traveled internationally and visited many of the places I've studied independently and in the course of my education in design, I've become even more passionate about restoration. (I'm the woman you might see sitting on a bench along the wall of the Sistine Chapel, silently weeping as I take in Michelangelo's magnificent masterpiece in the simplicity of that sacred space.) I can talk forever about the importance of preserving buildings that are testaments to the creative impulse, the hours of painstaking effort, the motivation and dedication of artists, designers, craftsmen, and artisans from previous eras. All were, no doubt, imperfect people—but people used as instruments in

God's hands to create perfectly rendered works of art that endure and can stir our hearts so many, many years later.

For me, there's something quite magical about walking into an old place, with all its history, where so much life has been lived, where so many events and significant moments have taken place—the happy ones, the sad ones, and all the everyday moments and hours in between. Imagining who might have inhabited a house, how the family came together, the love they shared, their conversations, the tears and laughter, is irresistible to me. I find inspiration as I imagine how they celebrated and grieved, how they overcame adversity, how they survived tragedy, then moved on to enjoy life within the old walls once again.

One of the joys of my life was visiting the little northern Italian village, nestled among olive groves high up in the Apennine Mountains, where my maternal grandparents were born, grew up, and married before emigrating to America in 1920. A short lane connects their two families' farmhouses. In between them stands a small, now empty house of ancient, mellowed stone where my grandparents lived as newlyweds. How full my heart felt as I walked over that threshold! I pictured them as a young couple in the first blush of matrimony, with all their hopes and dreams … before their brave journey (separately) across a wide ocean to a strange land where all was unknown. Within those aged walls, did they speak of their fears as they prepared to leave their homeland, certain they'd never see their parents and siblings again? What kind of courage did that require? What words did they use to comfort and reassure one another? I wondered. I could see, in my mind's eye, my grandmother stirring a pot of pasta as my grandfather stoked the fire. I could even hear the crackling of the firewood, smell the slight wood smoke.…

A few artifacts remained of their time there, and I was delighted to be able to take them back to America with me. Now I treasure and display them in my own home because they connect me with that place and time and remind me of my rich heritage—all stemming from that small structure, still standing, solidly built so long ago.

I love the metaphor of restoration, which is why I came up with the idea for the Project Restoration series—stories that would follow both the physical restoration of a building and the emotional/spiritual restoration of a character. Perhaps in the Project Restoration series, you'll find a character who mirrors your own life and points you toward the kind of restoration you long for.

After all, God is in the business of restoring lives—reclaiming, repairing, renewing what was broken and bringing beauty from ashes. I know, because I've seen it firsthand. For many years, I've worked in women's ministries. I've seen many women—as well as the men and children they love—deal with scars from their past that shape their todays and tomorrows. They all long for restoration—to live hopefully, joyfully, and productively once again—but that also requires forgiveness. Forgiveness of others (whether they deserve it or not) and, perhaps most importantly, forgiveness of oneself in order to be healthy and available to God. Clinging to past hurts or "unfairness," hostility, anger, grudges, resentment, bitterness, or allowing abuse to alter your self-worth renders your life virtually useless. Unforgiveness shapes your perception of yourself, your outlook on life, the kind of relationships you have, and keeps you in "stuck" mode. It leaves you without hope, in a dark, emotionally paralyzing, spiritually debilitating, physically draining state and causes so much unnecessary pain ... even addiction.

Yet God Himself stands and waits, extending the gift of restoration. The light of His love shines on all those dark places deep within us, exposing what needs His healing touch, renewing hope, providing freedom from bondage. This is the type of restoration I've become passionate about too. For when our souls are gloriously freed through God's renovation, we become whole, useful, and able to extend the forgiveness we have experienced to others. Our hope is renewed. Then individuals, families, churches, and entire communities can be transformed!

What event in your past do you need to let go of? It is my hope and prayer that you, too, will experience the renewal that awaits you through saying yes to God's invitation of heart restoration ... and the life-transforming joy that will follow.

Discussion Questions

1. What was your initial response when Samantha Cohen reveals what she planned to do to the church (convert it into a restaurant/nightclub)? Do you think Oliver should have walked away from the project at the outset? Would you? Why or why not?

2. What struck you about Pastor Han's story? Were you comfortable with him sharing his secrets with Samantha? Explain.

3. How would you describe the relationship between Oliver and Taller, as brothers? In what ways does their perception of each other affect that relationship? Are there ways in which you can relate, with your own siblings?

4. What's the first hint that Oliver has some "issues" with his mother, and her expectations of him? How are these hints confirmed as the story develops?

5. In what ways has Oliver been affected by his father's death when he was a young boy? How was the Barnett family dynamic affected? Look back on your own childhood. What issues have influenced the way your family interacts, even now?

6. In what ways has Samantha been affected by her mother's death—and the manner of her death—when she was a teenager? How was the Cohen family dynamic affected? Looking back on your teen years, do you remember words spoken that you wish had never been spoken? If so, how have those words altered your perspective of that person? Of yourself?

7. How did you feel about Oliver hiring the Pratt brothers as carpenters on the project? If it was your decision, would you have hired them? Is it easy for you to give people "second chances"? Why or why not? What was your reaction when Oliver receives conflicting advice about his decision from Pastor Mosco and Barth? Whose view was closest to your own? Explain.

8. Would you call Paula's faith "authentic"? Why or why not? What clues can you give as proof of your theory? Do you think Oliver believed her faith was authentic? What would make him think so—or wonder? What, to you, are signs of true Christian belief?

9. How is Oliver different from all of the other men with whom Samantha has had relationships? How did the way he refused to compromise his moral beliefs impact their relationship? Have you ever been in a situation where you had to stick to your guns, morally, and it cost you something? What happened as a result?

10. Besides Oliver's influence, what other factors came into play to cause Samantha to think about her relationship to God? How did Sarah—a fellow and "completed Jew," someone more like Samantha than Oliver or Cameron—make a difference in her understanding of Christian belief? In what way(s) can you reach out to those who are similar or different from you in faith and/or background?

11. What's the difference between *law* and *grace*? Explain, using a couple of examples from the book. What do you tend to lean most toward—law or grace? What factors in your background have led you to respond that way?

12. What was your response to Barth's opinion on how God views suicide? In what way(s) do Barth's words influence situations you may have faced with hurting people in the past?

13. Do you think there *was* something special about the church building? The windows? Is there such a thing as "sacred space"? Why or why not?

14. What did you think was going to happen when Paula discovers she's pregnant? Were you surprised by the outcome? Explain.

15. How did God use Oliver to fulfill His plan for "the church," even when he struggled with transforming a church building into something else? How might you use your current circumstances and stresses to help touch others' lives and build "the church"?

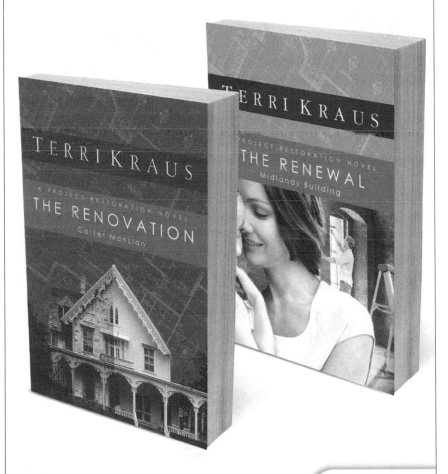

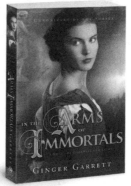